A PATH OF SECRETS AND DREAMS

SILVERBLOOD RAVEN SERIES

NIKKI McCORMACK

*In memory of Jeffrey Cook,
author and friend*

Raven's soft boots found easy purchase on the rooftop of the newly rebuilt blacksmith shop on the northeastern edge of town. It was one of the first structures the Stonebreakers finished rebuilding. The clang of hammer on steel and the heat from the now-operational forge were comforting. Having a functioning smithy in town was one of several things speeding up reconstruction. However, she hadn't come up here to appreciate that or even escape the press of folks working in the streets.

She sank to one knee and watched a harpy circling above the trees at the forest's edge. They hadn't seen harpies this close since they drove them from their nesting grounds several months ago. She leveled an arrow at the creature, ready to try to spook it away with a warning shot. After a few more seconds of observation, she lowered her bow.

The beast dipped clumsily in the air, one side losing power with every few strokes of its great wings. As that side dropped low again, she noticed the rust color of drying blood staining the underside of the tan and ivory plumage. The trail of blood extended from the shoulder to the tip of the last feather on that side. The creature struggled to stay aloft.

She didn't turn when someone came up behind her, recognizing Ehric's solid footsteps. With his height and heavy musculature, it made her uneasy having the dark-skinned Stonebreaker warrior climbing on rooftops. Add to that the weight of the steel and leather armor he wore, and it made sense to her that he should be too heavy to manage such light-footed work. Despite that, she found his presence oddly reassuring. He had been there the night she nearly died – briefly had died in truth – after fighting the Silverblood Brotherhood priest, Father Wayland Mallebron. Ehric had helped Phendaril lift her over the temple gate and get her into the back of the coach. It was irrational, since she had been barely conscious at the time, but she implicitly trusted him now.

His shadow fell over her. "What do you see? Is it a threat?"

"It isn't, but that doesn't mean there isn't a threat." She glanced up at him, smiling faintly at how he shielded his eyes from the light with one hand and peered hard at the distant creature. Without elven or Silverblood eyesight, he would learn little by looking, but that wasn't going to stop him from trying. "It's injured," she said, sparing him the frustration. "The fact that it flew this way instead of back to the nesting ground makes me wonder if it was hurt there."

"Implying there might be a threat out there we should be concerned about."

Raven nodded. The harpies had found new nesting grounds in the northeastern corner of Amberwood territory, far enough away that they posed no threat to the population or livestock of the recovering town. The people of Amberwood were content to let the creatures live in peace, but something else appeared to be causing them grief now.

She stood, watching the beast in the distance as it found a large branch to land on where it could rest the injured wing. "Perhaps we should get a few more scouts together to investigate."

"I already sent word to Phendaril," he answered.

As if on cue, the sound of approaching horses reached her. Disappointment sat heavy in her chest. If they struck out on horseback, that meant they would be going without her. Until a few weeks ago, she had never touched a horse. Even with Phendaril's patient guidance, the experience was far from triumphant. She'd screeched and almost fallen on her ass when the animal lipped her fingers, looking for a treat. Phendaril laughed so hard while trying to soothe the startled horse that she still hadn't entirely forgiven him for it.

Ehric was heading down off the roof of the smithy via a low shed full of coal that groaned under his bulk. Raven took a more direct route, hopping off the front into the street. She wasn't invulnerable, but she was a Silverblood, which meant she had magical enhancements that boosted her physical abilities beyond those of an average individual with equivalent training. Combine that with the instruction her adopted father Jaecar had given her and the better-than-human agility, vision, and hearing provided by her half-elven blood, and she possessed significant advantages. Though the last several months had shown her how little those things mattered in some situations.

Phendaril and Veylin trotted up, stopping their mounts in front of the smithy. Veylin led a third horse behind her for Ehric. Raven glanced up at Phendaril, appreciating how the sun brought out the deep auburn in his long, nearly black hair. She loved his fierce, dark eyes. She even loved the scar that ran down from inside his right eyebrow and along his nose to his lip on that side. What she appreciated most was the pleasure in his eyes and the intimacy of his smile when he looked at her, that dark intensity calming for a second, just for her.

"Ehric said a stray harpy was spotted near the town." He held a hand down to Raven.

She resolutely ignored the offer. "There is. It's in the trees over there. It's injured, but it came here instead of returning to the nest."

Phendaril nodded and shifted the horse so that his hand was again in her line of sight. "Come on. We'll get there faster on horseback."

Raven shook her head, staring at his hand as if it were poison.

Veylin and Ehric, who had mounted the third horse, looked away, trying to hide the amusement she'd already seen in their eyes.

Phendaril chuckled, his patient smile lessening her annoyance. "She's a strong, calm mare, and you'll be riding with me. It'll be fine."

Raven took a step back and shook her head.

"We both know you'd rather come than stay here." He moved his foot around in front of the stirrup so she could use it to climb up.

Raven stared at the mare. The horse twitched her ears and turned her head to look at Raven, soft brown eyes wondering what the holdup was.

"Raven."

His voice – gentle, reasonable, and thick with affection – made her want to please him. Besides, he was right. She would rather go with them than stay here with all these relative strangers. If she climbed up, he would tell her later how impressed he was with her. Then he would love her the way only he could.

She grabbed his hand and put her foot in the stirrup the way she had seen others do. With his pull adding to her own boost, she swung up easily, landing straddled across the animal's back in the saddle behind him. Her heart jumped into her throat when the mare shifted, and she wrapped her arms around Phendaril, squeezing herself against him. He placed one hand on her arm, a gesture meant to comfort, and urged the mare toward the gate out of town.

Raven focused on breathing, on the sensation of lean muscles in Phendaril's back pressed against her chest, and on the progress made in rebuilding this part of Amberwood since the arrival of the Stonebreakers earlier that year. Anything but the volatile, powerful animal she was now sitting on. The other scouts found it amusing that a female who had faced a wyvern and corpse eaters would tremble before a horse. But she would never throw herself on the back of a wyvern, putting herself at its mercy, especially not to hasten a trip into more danger.

They passed through the gate, and Phendaril gave her arm a squeeze. Then he took his hand away, returning it to the reins.

"Hold on."

Raven did precisely that, pinching her eyelids shut and tightening her arms around him when he urged the horse up from a walk to a trot and then to a canter.

"We're going to fall off if you squeeze me so hard I can't breathe."

She caught an edge of laughter in his voice, which told her he could breathe well enough, so she maintained her death grip. The animal's motion beneath her was powerful, yet smoother than she had expected. It was the power that kept her on edge. All that strength in a moderately intelligent beast. Jaecar shared several stories about how horses could kill you without meaning to because they were so big, strong, and prone to panic.

"They're prey animals," he had told her. *"You have to think like one to understand their fear."*

The harpy shrieked at them as they passed near the tree it had perched in. The cry was enough to compel Raven to open her eyes. She peered up at the beast, her shoulder twinging in sympathy for the wound it suffered. Despite her ongoing fear as the horses kept up their canter into the woods, she made herself study the injured creature, catching sight of what she was searching for seconds before another tree blocked her view.

"There's part of an arrow still in its shoulder. Looks like the rest broke off."

She didn't have to see Phendaril's face to know his anger. She felt it in the slight stiffening of his posture and heard it in his voice.

"Wonderful. We're dealing with trespassing hunters, then." He said it loud enough to make sure the other two heard.

Raven squeaked in surprise when he kicked the horse faster.

"Sorry, my love. I just don't want them getting away with this."

Raven said nothing in return. It was hard to be angry with him when he called her his love. She had never been someone's love before. It suited her to be his.

Through the comfort of Phendaril's nearness and the time it took to reach their destination, Raven's fear of horses started to lose some of its power. When they were close to the jagged ravine the harpies had built their new nests in and around, they dropped Raven off inside the tree line. They wouldn't risk anyone seeing what she was and reporting her back to the authorities, given that, as an unsanctioned Silverblood, the Brotherhood would put her to death. Silverblood Brotherhood doctrine also taught that elves, women, and children couldn't survive the magical process of becoming a Silverblood. Literally, everything about her was an affront to the Brotherhood. Her existence broke their laws and exposed the lies they used to maintain control of the Silverblood magic. Still, her need to stay hidden wasn't going to stop her from finding ways to be of use. She simply had to be careful about it.

Raven crept out of the trees, crouching low behind shrubs and a fallen tree, and worked her way to a spot with a view of the activity below. She drew her bow and nocked an arrow, holding it at rest for now. The others continued down the hill out in the open toward where two men were contemplating the collection of harpy corpses they had dragged out into a flat area at the base of the ravine. At a glance, Raven counted eleven of the creatures. An entire flock decimated for no reason.

Her fingers tightened on the bowstring, and she struggled to keep from sending an arrow down to show them how she felt about their slaughter. Then she spotted a third man standing in the shadows with his back to her, not laughing or joking with the other two. When her companions approached, he turned. She sucked back a breath of surprise. Even without the black and silver leather armor, his bright silver eyes would have marked him as a Silverblood.

Phendaril stopped his group at the edge of the line of corpses. "What's going on here?"

A tall man with a liberal dusting of gray in his dark hair stepped forward, one hand coming to rest on his hip next to his sword hilt. "We came to clear out these harpies. Lord Darrenton now owns the land north of here, and they're close enough to be a risk."

Raven's anger exploded, her vision going red at the edges. If the two men were Lord Darrenton's soldiers, then they could have been involved in his brother Jaecar's murder. It took her several months to come to terms with the idea that the quiet, stern warrior who raised her had been a nobleman who chose to abandon his former life. Then again, if she had a brother like Aldrich Darrenton, she might have gone into hiding too. Her fingers itched to draw the arrow and let it fly, but she held still. Even if one or both of these men helped kill Jaecar, ending them wouldn't bring him back.

"The land Darrenton bought is well outside of this flock's range." Phendaril's voice was tight with anger. The scar tugged at his lip, emphasizing his snarl. "I know this because you're well over the border into Amberwood, which is the property of Lady Alayne Valassian. This slaughter was unnecessary." He snapped one hand out to point at the dead beasts. "It's a mistake we'll allow you to make once, recognizing your ignorance. I suggest you get off this land before we change our minds about that."

Veylin and Ehric both rested a hand on their sword hilts now. Some not-so-subtle support for Phendaril's threat.

The Silverblood showed no interest in their exchange. He was a mercenary. It wouldn't matter to him who did what and where as long as he got paid. His gaze moved up the ravine, making her more than a little uneasy, though he didn't appear to have noticed her. She tugged the hood of her cloak further forward, just in case.

"Of course." The younger of Darrenton's two soldiers scratched at the stubble on his chin. The news that this was someone else's land didn't seem to surprise him. He took a step toward the nearest harpy as he was speaking. "We'll get a move on after we collect the feathers and the—"

Raven planted an arrow less than an inch in front of the toe of his boot as it touched down. He jerked back, casting an angry glare in her direction. The Silverblood placed a hand on his crossbow now. He looked at the log she was hiding behind. She shifted closer to the exposed root ball where the shadows were deepest, her heart beating triple-time.

"We made these kills," the young man protested, still glaring up the ravine. "Those feathers are good for fletching."

Phendaril placed a hand on his sword hilt, and Ehric

drew his blades. Veylin changed tactics, pulling out her bow and backing her horse several steps with leg cues as she set an arrow to the string.

"And the breasts and reproductive organs are supposed to make an effective fertility elixir. I'm told they fetch a good price on less reputable markets." Phendaril made no effort to keep his disgust from showing. He urged his mount a step closer to the nearest corpse. "But you need permission to hunt in Amberwood. Unless you have it, you're poaching. We can take it up with the town constable if you'd like to ride back with us."

Raven aimed an arrow at the younger man's throat. She wouldn't give him the chance to hurt those she cared about if it came to a fight. Phendaril was being more generous than they deserved, offering them the option to leave unpunished. If they didn't take it, they would get what they had coming.

One of the men glanced at the Silverblood, but he moved his hands away from his weapons and took a step back. They weren't going to get help from him. He apparently considered this outside the scope of whatever they were paying him for.

The older soldier scowled and then held his hands up in a gesture of surrender. "No reason to make a big deal of an honest mistake. We'll be on our way."

Raven ground her teeth, shifting her aim to target the man who had spoken. This was no *honest mistake*.

Phendaril absently corrected his mount as the animal started to turn away, not taking his eyes off the three men. "Our patrols will be given your descriptions. Should you choose to trespass again, we'll be sure to give you a proper welcome."

The threat that laced Phendaril's words made her want to kiss him. She would have to ask him later if that meant she could shoot them on sight if they came here again.

"Fuck off," the younger man growled under his breath as they turned to walk to their waiting mounts.

Once in the saddle, Darrenton's soldiers kicked their horses to a gallop. The Silverblood held his back, the animal prancing and champing at the bit as it watched its companions depart. He looked up the ravine once more, his silver eyes searching around the end of the log where she was hiding.

"Move on," Phendaril snapped.

The Silverblood glanced over at him, a slight smirk curving his lips before he turned to race after the others.

aven sat cross-legged on their bed with her back to the wall. She rubbed the arrowhead pendant Phendaril had made her out of the remains of her father's bow between the thumb and forefinger of one hand. In the other, she held the adoption papers she had found in Jaecar's belongings, reading the words that declared her his legal daughter. The fact that she was an unauthorized Silverblood nullified the document, but that didn't change the intention, and that made it valuable to her. Jaecar would be happy to see her now. The community he dreamed of where she would be accepted was becoming a reality in Amberwood, the very land he had hoped to build it on. Strange how it worked out that way even without him there.

The scent of a sweet, spicy mead wafted her way as Phendaril entered. The smell reminded her of Eamon. Her first love, or at least the closest she came to such before meeting Phendaril. Eamon might have been more to her if his life hadn't ended so abruptly. His kindness deserved remembering.

She swallowed back against the tightness in her throat, then found a fleeting smile for Phendaril as she accepted the mug he offered. "Every time I watch one of Darrenton's men walk away unpunished, I feel like I'm betraying him." She shifted to one side and straightened her legs as she spoke, making room for him beside her.

"Lord Jaecar?" He asked, moving in to accept her unspoken invitation.

"Just Jaecar, Phen. I didn't even know he had a title until after he died." She ran her fingers down the words on the parchment, stopping below the signature and date with the seal of House Darrenton stamped by his name. "Look at the date on this. I was legally his daughter for eight years before he died. Why didn't he tell me?" She shook her head to silence Phendaril when he started to speak. She didn't want speculation. She wanted answers, and he couldn't give her those. No one could.

He wasn't going to be brushed off that easily, however. He placed his hand over hers and moved it so that her fingers rested below that seal. "Maybe because he was ashamed of this."

His family. A father who destroyed an entire town and its people merely to prove his superiority over another lord. A brother who chose to have Jaecar killed just so he could try to take the land and resources their father had left him. That might not be the correct answer, but it was a reasonable one.

Raven set the parchment aside. She took a drink of the mead before leaning into Phendaril. He slid his arm around her shoulders, resting against the wall behind them and letting her settle her weight on him. How had she lived twenty-two years without once experiencing the quiet pleasure of having someone to lean on?

"Did everything get cleaned up?"

He didn't need to ask what she meant. "The bodies are being handled. My scouts are collecting the feathers. We always need fletching materials."

She nodded, taking another warming drink of the mead. It would have been wasteful not to gather the feathers. Leaving them there wouldn't bring the poor beasts back to life.

"I was proud of you today." He kissed her head.

Raven smiled, resting her hand on his leg. "For riding the horse with you?"

He chuckled. "I never doubted you could handle that. I was proud of you for not shooting Darrenton's men on sight."

She smacked his leg. "I was being serious."

"Easy, Silverblood." Phendaril laughed. "You've got some power in those arms." He continued in a more sober tone after taking a drink of his mead. "So was I."

"They would have deserved it."

He squeezed her arm gently. "I know. I don't think anyone would have held it against you, except possibly you."

There was a steadiness in his voice that told her he meant the words. He wasn't just saying what she wanted to hear. He knew what they had taken from her and hated them for it nearly as much as she did. Knowing her pain was that relevant to him almost made it bearable. The last part she tried to ignore, but he was right about that too. Whether they deserved it or not, she would judge herself harshly for killing them.

"Something else is bothering you." He gave her arm another gentle squeeze. "You can talk to me. Was it the Silverblood?"

She shook her head. "No. I didn't like seeing a Silverblood here again, but I don't believe he saw me. It's these dreams I've been having lately." She took a long drink of the warm mead, trying to chase away the chill that accompanied the new topic.

"About?"

"It doesn't really matter what they're about. They're all different. But in the dreams, someone is always watching me. I can't see them clearly, but I can feel them. They're like a living shadow. Watching. Waiting." She shivered, and he pulled her in closer.

"Waiting for what?"

"For me to do something, I think."

"Do you think they mean you harm?" His muscles tensed.

She loved that he wanted to protect her, even from her dreams. She leaned over and set her mead on a chest at the foot of the bed. He watched, brows pinching in silent curiosity as she took his and placed it there too before moving the adoption papers off. Then she turned around and faced him, straddling his legs. A hint of a smile started to curve his lips when she began to untie the laces of his shirt.

"Do you think, if you wore me out enough, I might not have any dreams at all?"

She leaned in closer, and he came up to meet her kiss. With a light trace of her tongue across his lips, she drew a soft moan from deep in his throat. He pulled her against him, and she could feel him growing hard with wanting.

"I'm willing to try," he breathed.

Raven pulled his shirt off over his head and then leaned back in for a deeper, more demanding kiss. Her hands slid down his lean chest and stomach to the laces of his trousers. Phendaril reached under her shirt, fingers sliding along her skin, igniting a fire in their wake. He took his mouth away and nuzzled in against her neck, the brush of his lips sending shivers of pleasure through her. She leaned her head back, giving into sensation and eagerly losing herself in his touch.

•

Raven woke with a start in the quiet hours before dawn. The shadow figure had been in her dream again. At least, she hoped it was only in her dream. The sensation faded the longer she lay awake with Phendaril's arm strong and reassuring around her. After a time, she slipped free, careful not to wake him, and got up. The candle she had lit before they drifted off to sleep had gone out early. She wrapped herself in a blanket and crept into the front room without re-lighting it. As a half-elven Silverblood, her dark vision was more than sufficient to define her surroundings.

The previous day's heat had faded, though the night was still comfortably warm. The floors, by contrast, were cool and pleasant under her bare feet. The wood was softer than the stone floors of the crumbling keep she had grown up in.

She padded over to the fireplace and gazed into it for a moment, considering whether she should build a fire or not. It wasn't going to get cold today. Perhaps it made more sense to skip it and start the fire in the kitchen instead. Now that numerous homes had usable cooking areas, those with such residences were in charge of their own meals, taking some of the burden off the crew at the tavern. The Stonebreakers also provided for themselves in the remaining camps, which meant the tavern could transition to its normal purpose as a casual gathering place instead of a communal kitchen.

Raven shivered. The dream sense of someone watching her still lingered at the edges of her awareness. She spun, peering into the darkest corners, the doorway into the kitchen, the staircase. The room felt colder. She rubbed her arms under the blanket, trying to reclaim the warmth of sleep that had abandoned her. The hair on the back of her neck stood up. With a sick feeling of dread in her gut, she spun to face the fireplace again.

A shadowy figure loomed behind her, silver eyes gleaming brightly in the darkness. She stepped back, acutely aware that she was naked and unarmed under the blanket. Her foot caught the leg of one of the chairs there. She lost her balance, falling over it, and hit the floor hard, the impact stinging through her elbows when she tried to catch herself.

Raven swept the room with her gaze, searching for the Silverblood, but saw only Phendaril, rushing into the room fully naked with a sword in one hand. She might have savored that sight in a different moment, but she wasn't feeling particularly amorous now.

"Are you all right?" He held a hand down to her.

Raven took it, appreciating that he was still in a ready stance, his eyes scouring the darkness for danger. Something told her they were alone now. Perhaps always had been.

"I'm fine. I saw..." She adjusted the blanket as she glanced around the room again and up the stairs.

Phendaril placed a hand on her arm, and she turned to look up at him. His eyes were black in the dark. Anything other than silver was welcome.

"I felt like someone was watching me. Just like in my dreams, only I was awake. Then I turned and saw eyes in the darkness. Silver eyes." She shuddered again.

He slid his hand to the back of her neck. She moved a step closer, giving to his gentle pressure, and he kissed her forehead. Drawn to the comforting warmth of him, she took another step and pressed herself against him, wrapping her arms and the blanket around him. She turned her head and rested it on his chest, listening to his heartbeat. He put one arm around her, still holding the sword in the other.

"Do you think someone was really here?" he asked softly.

"No. Not in the flesh. Just fear playing tricks on my mind in the darkness."

His arm tightened around her. She wriggled in closer, enjoying the warmth and solidity of his naked body against hers. Then she noticed his arousal as he grew hard against her and breathed a soft laugh, fear fading in his arms.

"Sorry," he murmured. "You did just crush your naked body against mine."

Raven drew back enough to place a light kiss on his lips, then she stepped away, wrapping the blanket around herself again. "I'll start the cook fire."

"You're a cruel woman," he teased, his smile spilling over with fond amusement.

An hour later, after a modest breakfast, they strode together into the town square. Many residents were already hard at work in the early dawn light. A group gathered outside the tavern, most of whom she recognized. The town constable, Karsima, was there, holding hands with her partner Alayne, who owned the Amberwood lands now, thanks to her ties to King Navaran. Ehric and Veylin were there, along with many of Phendaril's other scouts who Raven had gotten to work with over the last several months. All stared up at the tavern where a sign was being fastened into place above the door.

Veylin spotted them coming and bounced in place a few times, a broad grin splitting fine elven features tanned by long hours in the sun. She grabbed Ehric's arm, and he turned, grinning at them, or rather, at Raven, whose steps faltered. Unease moved through her. She knew everyone in the group, but seeing them gathered like this sparked her crowd anxiety. She hadn't spoken to anyone aside from her parents, who died when she was eight, and Jaecar, until earlier this year. Most of them didn't know that. Phendaril, who did know that, took her hand and squeezed it.

"I'm right here with you," he offered in soft voice.

Raven took a deep breath and nodded, forcing herself to continue at a more normal speed. They were almost to the group when the sign above the tavern door shifted fully into place, and tears stung her eyes. It depicted a raven sitting on the head of a prone bear.

The beast had Xs for eyes, its tongue lolling upon the ground. The name *The Bear and Raven* was carved above the image, referring to her now-legendary battle with the dire bear that had been living in the tavern. She had shot the beast in the eye, saving Veylin and helping bring it down. Many a tale of that fight had already been told within those walls, some more exaggerated than others.

Veylin, her brunette ponytail bouncing, trotted over and threw her arms around Raven with a squeal of delight. Phendaril let go of her hand. Raven took a deep, calming breath and made herself return the embrace, releasing a soft sigh of relief when it ended.

"Do you like it?"

The others were watching her now. A powerful part of her wanted to flee from the attention. Another part, closely related to the first, was on the verge of weeping, but out of joy. These people wanted her here. It was strange and unexpected, but they were becoming a family of sorts.

Raven shook her head and managed a smile. "It's a surprise."

"We got a smile out of you," Karsima said. "I'll call that a resounding success. You are expected to attend the celebration of our first named building tonight. No excuses."

Raven wasn't sure how to respond, but she didn't get a chance to figure it out. Karsima's expression darkened, and her hand sank to the dagger she wore. Several of the others reached for their weapons. Ehric went so far as to draw his blades. Raven and Phendaril turned. His bow instantly appeared in his hands, an arrow nocked and ready to fly.

"That's far enough," he snarled.

Silverblood Adept Marek put his hands up, but his silver eyes focused on Raven. "We need to talk."

Raven hadn't seen Marek since the night she fought Father Wayland and escaped the temple with Phendaril's help. Phendaril was an excellent fighter, but she didn't think he could have defeated a fully trained Silverblood adept like Marek, and she had been near death at the time. They wouldn't have gotten out alive if Marek hadn't chosen to let them leave. Still, Marek had betrayed her by taking her to the Silverblood Brotherhood temple in the first place. That wasn't an easy thing to forget, let alone forgive.

"You can talk from there." Phendaril's knuckles were white where he gripped the wood of his bow with the full intensity of his hatred for the other man.

Despite his former betrayal, Raven wasn't inclined to reach for her weapons when she faced Marek. She was willing to give that instinct some credit. Putting one hand on Phendaril's forearm, she applied gentle pressure. He resisted at first. When she didn't let up, he slowly lowered the bow, not taking his eyes off Marek.

"We can talk, but we stay here in the square," she offered.

Marek's gaze moved up to the sign now fixed into place. A crooked smirk touched his lips. "Perhaps we can take a seat at the newly dedicated tavern."

Karsima stepped up beside her, giving an unexpected

nod. "If you try anything, you will not leave this town alive."

Marek merely inclined his head.

A few minutes later, Raven sat across from him at a table in the rear of the tavern. Phendaril leaned against a nearby support post, glaring daggers into Marek's back. Ehric and six other scouts were at the tables to either side of the door. They drank and talked amongst themselves, but all kept bows or blades sitting within easy reach. Even Karsima and Alayne had selected a table between them and the exit. If Marek tried something, he would have a tough time escaping unscathed.

The fresh wood smell of new construction mingled with the aromas of food and drink. Parts of the interior were entirely rebuilt for safety and function. Others had merely been cleaned and rehabilitated as needed. The center of the upper floor was unstable enough that they tore it out, only rebuilding the rooms against the outside walls. The middle they left open to the main floor below with a railed balcony stretching around it. All the exposed wood was polished amberwood, with its striking mix of pale and deep red grains. The interior was beautifully finished for a simple tavern, though Raven rarely came around to appreciate it. As the only business of its kind in town, it got too crowded for her comfort. This early in the day, however, it was relatively quiet.

Marek appeared healthy. His dark blond hair looked like it had the first time she saw him in the woods near Andel, reaching down to the edge of his jaw where a precisely trimmed beard accented his jawline. The hint of a smile and the pleasure that rose in his silver eyes when she sat across from him unsettled her, but she did her best not to let it show.

"Why are you here?" She made her voice stern. Let him see that she was confident now. She had a place to belong. She knew how to be part of a community. More so than before, at least.

"You look good."

"Don't fuck around. Tell me what you want." Her cheeks colored slightly at her own words. Apparently, she had been spending too much time with the scouts and Stonebreaker warriors.

Marek breathed a laugh. It faded quickly, though, his demeanor turning somber. "I honestly wasn't sure you would be here. You had a foot through death's doorway the last time I saw you."

"I did die." A shudder still swept through her whenever she said it. "They managed to bring me back. I wouldn't have gone through all of that if not for you." She made herself look him in the eye, hoping to see guilt there.

"You would have sooner or later, and you might again," he countered as if those words somehow lessened his responsibility. His expression took on a guarded distance that stole the hint of warmth from his eyes. "You're still an unauthorized Silverblood, Raven. Nothing's going to change that. You will always be in danger. That's why I'm here."

His words stoked a fire in her. She glared at him, her tone laced with bitterness. "What? You've come to check up on me out of the kindness of your heart?"

Her anger appeared to set him back. He drew a deep breath and let it out slowly, a hint of sorrow in his eyes. "I'm here because meeting you uncovered the lies the Brotherhood is peddling. You showed me I couldn't trust my own order. Then you trusted me with your truth." He ran a hand through his hair, breaking eye contact. "I repaid you by giving you to them out of jealousy, of all noble motivations."

An undertone of disgust tightened his voice. For a few seconds, he avoided her gaze. When he looked up at her again, she saw something else in his eyes, reflected in the fidgeting of his fingers. Uncertainty. Possibly even fear.

She swallowed her anger. He hadn't come back here, risking being shot on sight by more than a few of the town's citizens, for no reason. "I should hate you. No one has more reason to do so than I do. But I don't believe you're my enemy, Marek. Tell me what's going on."

The swell of gratitude in his eyes made her shift in her seat.

"Father Mallebron survived your fight."

The temperature seemed to drop. For a second, Raven thought she might be sick. Phendaril, who observed attentively, took a step toward them before she held up a hand to stay him. When he settled back again, she gestured for one of the servers. A human youth, affectionately nicknamed Dart by the regulars, rushed over.

"Food or drink, milady?" His regard held admiration, something she noticed was more common among the younger population. Perhaps because they weren't as indoctrinated into the idea that there was anything wrong with what she was.

"Something to drink, please."

"Something strong?" he asked after searching her face for a second.

"Yes. Thank you." She met Marek's eyes.

He nodded. "The same." When the youth hurried away, he continued. "Like you, Father Mallebron briefly succumbed to his injuries. They brought him back, but he was in a strange partial trance. He would eat or drink if we gave him food and care for his basic needs, but he wouldn't communicate or do anything except what was necessary to stay alive. While he was in that state, everyone was content to accept my word that you were dead, especially given the condition we found him in that night and the amount of blood you left behind. About two weeks ago, he snapped back into himself.

"He insists that you're alive. That you took something from him. Whatever it is, he believes he would have it back already if you were really dead, and he desperately wants it back. He started asking some of the newly raised adepts to search for you. I overheard him sending one out by way of Darrenton's new lands just a few days ago."

Raven nodded. "I saw him."

There was a tightening around his eyes. Concern?

"Did he see you?"

She shook her head, but the knots in her gut undermined her confidence. If his purpose had been to find her, had he read anything into the archer hidden up the ravine? Worse, if Wayland had come to a couple of weeks ago, that coincided rather uncomfortably with the onset of her dreams about being watched.

Someone touched her hand. She jerked away with a start. Marek drew his hand back to his side of the table. Behind him, Phendaril reached for his sword hilt, relaxing marginally when the Silverblood picked up his drink. A mug also sat in front of Raven now, though she didn't recall seeing anyone set it there.

Marek's brow furrowed. "Are you all right?"

She met his eyes. "Yes. I think so." Before he could question her uncertainty, she continued. "If Wayland is looking for me, what are you doing? Did you come to find me for him?"

Marek gave a sharp shake of his head. "As I said, you showed me I can't trust the Brotherhood. Nor can I change the fact that I am one of them. If I tried, I would be put to death as quickly as they would put you to death. Father Mallebron. Wayland," he amended with a shrug, abandoning propriety since she had used the priest's first name, "is going to start reexamining what happened after your confrontation. That means he will look more closely at the man who claimed to have killed you."

She remembered his words to Phendaril that night.

"I'll tell them I saw her staggering out and finished her off, then went to check on things inside. When the guard wakes, he'll mention fighting you. They'll assume you took her body. I doubt they'll waste much effort trying to hunt down a dead woman."

"You."

He nodded. "I'm not sure my involvement will stand up to his scrutiny while he's on this obsessive hunt. I decided it might be better to go back to doing mercenary work around the region for a while. I have to ask, though. *Did* you take something from him?"

She considered him for a moment. Had he truly turned his back on the Brotherhood priest? Could she trust him? She'd made that mistake once and paid dearly for it, but he had helped them escape. It was all so confusing. Navigating encounters like this made her miss her isolated life with Jaecar.

"Not intentionally." She hesitated, aware that she hadn't even told Phendaril about this part of that night. Given his elven hearing, he could probably make out most of what they were saying. She hoped her prior secrecy wouldn't upset him. "Wayland was going to kill me. I could feel him gathering his magic so he could use my life to further enhance himself. I guess some part of me recognized the magic because it was already in me. I grabbed onto it and turned it back on him. While he was still reeling, I drove the blade he meant to use to kill me into his chest. That's the simplified version, anyhow."

She paused for a few seconds, memories of pain and despair sending another shudder through her. Marek started to reach out to her again. He hesitated halfway to her, then moved his hand back to his drink. She took a swig of her own. The liquid burned down her throat, starting a coughing fit. When Dart brought out something strong, he didn't mess around. The lad appeared next to her now with a mug of water. Waiting until she took several swallows and nodded her gratitude before disappearing again.

When she had that under control, she looked up at Marek. It bothered her more than a little that his expression held the same fond amusement as that of Phendaril behind him. Staring down into the mug, she continued.

"When I came to later, after they brought me back, I felt... different. I looked different too. My hair, fingernails, and eyes just a hint brighter silver than before. Not enough so that others would notice, but enough to be apparent to the person who had lived with those traits for so long. I'm guessing that's what he's talking about."

Marek shook his head at her. "Remarkable. You used the magic with no prior knowledge or training."

"It felt more like it used me," she countered, pondering whether the comforting heat of the alcohol in her belly was worth the burn of getting it down there.

"You took some of his life, Raven, and yet he still lives. I don't think Silverblood magic is intended to work that way. Maybe that created a connection between you."

"There is no one I would like to be connected to less than him." Raven took another drink, managing not to choke on it now that she expected the burn. She did still chase it down with a swallow of water.

Marek smiled. "That means I'm not at the bottom of the list."

She managed a wry smile. "Well, not now that I know Wayland's alive."

He chuckled.

She lifted her mug and considered him in silence over the brim as she drank. She remembered clearing the corpse eaters out of the mines with him as if it had happened a few days ago. They made a fantastic team, facing down the enraged beasts and looking out for each other. That was when she started to trust him, standing back to back before a swarm of twisted creatures bent on tearing them apart. She wanted to trust him again. Did that make her a fool?

"What do you expect me to do with this information?"

"If I thought you'd consider it, I'd ask you to leave here with me, but I know that won't happen. Regardless, you aren't safe here now, and neither are the people who would protect you."

Phendaril strode over then. "That isn't your concern, Silverblood."

Marek narrowed his eyes, scowling up at the elf. "I'm surprised you still say that with such loathing, given that the woman you love is also one."

"She didn't choose to be," Phendaril countered.

Marek took a swig of his drink and stood. Man and elf stared at one another for several seconds. Raven noticed they were about the same height. Marek lacked Phendaril's deceptive fine-boned elegance, but they were both remarkable fighters in their own rights. The warrior in her was curious which of them would win in a fair fight. The fact that she suspected Marek, with his magic enhancements, would edge past Phendaril despite his elven speed and agility was reason enough not to find out.

Marek finally looked down at her. "I've said what I came to say."

Raven stood. "Thank you. Your warning is appreciated."

He walked around Phendaril and the table, stopping next to her and leaning in close. "I would keep you safe," he said in a low voice.

The sound of a sword being drawn preceded

Phendaril's words. "If you want to leave here alive, I suggest you go now."

Marek held her gaze, not moving or reaching for his own weapons. Was that courage or temerity?

"Perhaps you would," she answered, "but I will figure this out myself. Good luck to you, Silverblood Adept Marek."

He inclined his head. "And to you, Silverblood Raven."

Not once before that moment had anyone allowed her the title of Silverblood. Though she would never admit it, having him do so sent a thrill through her. Keeping her expression neutral, she watched him leave. Everyone else in the building also watched him go. She suspected she was the only one who did so without despising him. Somehow, whether he deserved it or not, she couldn't hate him.

Karsima watched the exchange between Raven and Marek. It bothered her that the distrust in Raven's silver eyes guttered out somewhere along the way. While the two spoke, she saw the gamut of emotions in the young woman's expression. Everything from hatred and fear to determination, resolve, and a flicker of amusement. Even a disturbing glimmer of reluctant affection by the end.

Phendaril was a different story. She couldn't see his expression with his attention turned toward the two Silverbloods, but his rigid posture throughout the conversation suggested anger and unease. When Marek walked out, she gave him a stern glower that was reflected on the faces of almost every other individual in the room. Somehow, even as reserved as Raven was, she had gained the affection and support of most of the original group that had come together to rebuild Amberwood. They were all willing to protect her from Marek and his Brotherhood if it came to that.

She glanced over at Ehric, the muscular Stonebreaker warrior with his long, thick mane of black locs. Raven had gained devotees outside that initial group as well. Ehric went with them to go after her when Marek took her to the Brotherhood. Since then, he had become a regular fixture among Phendaril's scouts, most of whom had taken a liking to Raven. That made sense, given that she had become a valuable member of the team since her arrival and had saved a few of their lives along the way.

Even Ellandra, an elven healer who shared her romantic interest in Phendaril, became an admirer of Raven's after the half-elven female saved her from an enraged wyvern. The healer didn't appear to harbor ill feelings toward Raven over the fact that she had won Phendaril's heart.

Speaking of Phendaril, he had given up glowering after the Silverblood warrior and turned to Raven, who stood gazing out one of the windows, lost in thought. Her hand rose to her chest. Not to the arrowhead pendant Phendaril had made her like usual, but the top of the scar where Wayland had cut a deep gash down her breastbone.

Karsima stood, a spike of pleasure moving through her when Alayne rose with her. Everything was less complicated with Alayne at her side.

Alayne touched her arm. "Should we give them a moment?"

Karsima shook her head. "I suspect whatever Marek told her is relevant to all of us here. When it affects my town, I have to be a leader first and a friend second."

Alayne's smile blossomed with fondness and patience. "Why not both?"

Karsima leaned close and gave Alayne a gentle kiss. "I do love you," she murmured before heading to where Phendaril and Raven stood.

Alayne seized her hand and accompanied her.

"Whatever you're thinking, you know we'll keep you safe here," Phendaril was saying as they approached.

Karsima hesitated. Alayne was right. The two might need a few minutes more.

Raven looked past him, her gaze lighting on Karsima and Alayne. She offered them the same grateful smile that she gave him. A smile that said she appreciated their support but wasn't going to listen to them either.

Karsima leaned close to Alayne's ear and whispered, "See. Phen does need us."

Alayne chuckled softly and squeezed her hand.

"At this point, I'm more concerned with keeping all of you safe," Raven countered.

"If Marek threatened your safety..." Karsima began, trailing off when Raven shook her head.

"He didn't. He came to tell me that Wayland is still alive and believes that I am alive as well. He's started looking for me."

Phendaril gave her a troubled look. Raven responded with another almost imperceptible shake of her head. Whatever information they were choosing to keep between themselves at that moment, Karsima would trust Phendaril to tell her later if she needed to know. The news that the Brotherhood priest was looking for her was upsetting enough. Why did she have to have enemies they stood no chance against? The Brotherhood was powerful, and they, unfortunately, had the support of the surrounding kingdoms, especially to the north in Habarin.

Still, Raven was part of the family now.

"We won't let him have you," Karsima stated firmly. "We'll keep you hidden."

Raven's smile came with the sparkle of unshed tears this time, but she shook her head. "He's not going to be easily dissuaded. It's safer if I leave. It doesn't have to be forever. Just until he gives up."

"And where will you go that this isn't likely to become a problem for you?" Phendaril's voice was tight with frustration.

He was right. Wherever she went, her appearance would mark her as an unsanctioned Silverblood. She couldn't run from that.

Raven's adoring gaze was meant for him alone, though her words encompassed all of them. "Anywhere, Phen. Anywhere that the people around me aren't people I'm afraid to lose."

Phendaril glanced over at Karsima then, his worried look asking for help, but she had no response. Raven was right. Through no fault of her own, her presence put them all in danger. They were willing to put themselves at risk to keep her safe. How could they expect her to feel differently about them? Which meant she was at greater risk of putting herself in Wayland's hands to protect them if she stayed here. The priest knew where she was living before Marek took her to him. That meant Amberwood would be under scrutiny until he gave up. They were all safer if she went somewhere else, Raven included.

Karsima hated the feeling that she was about to betray her best friend, but there was nothing for it. "We'll support you however we can. Just let us know what you need."

Raven nodded, gratitude at war with the pain in her eyes. Phendaril's expression darkened over with fury. He glanced from Raven to Karsima, who couldn't meet his eyes. Then he turned and stormed out of the building. Raven hung her head and closed her eyes, the clenching and unclenching of her jaw making it clear she was fighting back tears.

Alayne, who stood closer to her, placed a hand on her shoulder. Raven flinched at the unexpected contact – even now, she flinched – but she didn't jerk away as she would have not long ago. Alayne looked at Karsima and gestured in the direction Phendaril had gone with her head, releasing Karsima's hand as she did so. Karsima didn't want to intrude in their business, but maybe Alayne was right. She and Phendaril had been friends almost since birth. Perhaps she should be the one to talk to him.

Karsima exited The Bear and Raven and strode across the square. She continued past the medical building and down the street to the left that led out of town toward the river. Phendaril and Raven's house was near the end, close to the freedom of the wilds. She often wondered if he had chosen the location hoping Raven would someday move in with him there. Had he even realized he was falling for the half-elf at that point? Regardless, it appeared to have worked out.

She stepped up to the door and knocked firmly, hoping he had actually gone there.

Phendaril jerked the door open and frowned down at her. "You're one of the last people I want to see right now."

Karsima stepped past him into the house. "Too bad."

He shut the door and followed her with his glare, crossing his arms over his chest. "Thank you for helping me convince her to stay."

His sarcasm cut at her. She faced him, realizing as she did that she loved him more than anyone except Alayne. As much as, perhaps, though it was a different type of love. That didn't mean that she would let him be an ass to her because he was hurting.

"I said what I said because Raven is right. I don't think she's ever had a community like this. I suspect she would do anything to protect it, including give herself to Wayland. We can't fight the Brotherhood, and we're all going to get hurt if we're trying to protect her while she's trying to protect us. But, if she leaves until he gives up, then she can come back, and we can all have what we wanted without having to mourn the people we lost to get it."

He might have a bit of a temper, but he would always consider a well-stated argument and admit when he was wrong. It was one of the traits she admired most about him.

He walked past her and stood staring into their bedroom in silence for a minute or more. Finally, he turned to look at her.

"Where's she supposed to go?"

Karsima swallowed. She dreaded what she was about to say, but it was the truth. "I don't know, but she doesn't have to go alone."

He met her eyes, his gaze searching as if he hoped to dig out her thoughts just by looking. "What do you mean?"

"I mean." She closed her eyes for a second, fighting the selfish inclination to retract the suggestion rather than clarify. "You could offer to go with her."

It was hard not to resent the spark of hope that brightened his features. It hurt to acknowledge that he would be happier if he abandoned everything they had worked for to go with Raven. But what if the situation were reversed? What if Alayne was the one who had to run from Amberwood? Would she hesitate to leave with her?

Then his expression clouded over again. "We agreed to do this together, you and me. I remember how you cried the day our families went their separate ways. We promised to find each other again that day, and we did. I can't just leave."

Karsima smiled fondly, a tear sneaking past her lashes to race down one cheek. "I wasn't the only one who cried, as I recall. But you wouldn't be leaving forever."

"What about my scouts?"

There was a twisting sensation in her chest. His arguments against it were too easy to counter. That meant she would win, and she wasn't sure she wanted to. "Veylin and Jael can manage the scouts between them. You know I'm right, Phen."

Someone knocked softly on the door then, and his jaw tightened.

"We need you here, but I think she needs you more," Karsima offered as a last consideration before she turned and strode to the door. When she opened it, Raven stood there. She gave the half-elf a warm smile, fighting not to let that bit of selfish jealousy show. "You know you live here, right? You don't have to knock."

Raven smiled self-consciously, casting an uneasy glance at Phendaril behind her. "I didn't want to interrupt."

Karsima almost glanced back at Phendaril, but the urge to give him a look of sorrow or longing that would further confuse him might be more than she could bear to resist. Instead, she stepped down to the side, providing Raven room to enter. "I think we're done for now. Take it easy on him. You know how fragile he is."

Raven smiled a little, though the expression faded as she stepped inside. Karsima pulled the door shut behind her. It was up to them now.

●

Raven stepped softly into the dark room. Phendaril had lit one candle in the corner, providing minimal light. He hadn't bothered to open the shutters over the back window. She walked past him to do that. The single candle gave sufficient light with her vision, but she needed an extra moment to gather her thoughts now that they were in the same room alone. He watched her walk past, his gaze following her as she opened the shutters, letting in a bright swath of daylight.

"The silver-eyed shadow started haunting me a couple of weeks ago. What if it's Wayland visiting my dreams?" She stared out the window at the blend of evergreen and deciduous trees along the hillside. Autumn wasn't that far away now. She would regret missing the changing of the leaves here. Next year, perhaps.

He cursed under his breath, recognizing that the timing was too close to be mere coincidence. "Why didn't you tell me?"

She closed her eyes for a second, gathering her courage. Why were these conversations so much more frightening to face than most of the beasts she had fought? She turned around. "About the power I took from Wayland?"

He nodded, his expression unreadable.

"I know how you feel about Silverblood magic. I was afraid knowing I had acquired more by kill—by *almost* killing him would change how you look at me." Her throat tightened. "I love the way you look at me."

He moved toward her so abruptly that she almost backed away. Then he placed his hands on either side of her face, his touch gentle, one thumb brushing across her cheek. He looked her in the eyes. "Nothing is ever going to change the way I look at you. I love you."

She wasn't sure what to say to that, so she tried to take the easy way out by leaning in for a kiss. He shifted back a little, removing his hands. Raven faltered, retreating into a space of uncertainty.

"Where would you go?"

She expected him to argue about the very idea of her leaving. Hence, the question caught her off guard, but she recovered quickly. She'd been thinking about it long before Marek's visit.

"When I was in the Brotherhood temple, Wayland told me some of the history of Silverblood magic. It came from a race of beings, the Acridan, that's now extinct. They were eradicated by something humans unknowingly brought with them. An illness or something. Before the last of them died, they shared their magic with a small group of men so it wouldn't be lost forever. But the Acridan also lived close to a population of elves. Wayland said the magic shows up in the hands of an elf like my mother every now and then. They believe those elves are descended from those that lived near the Acridan. Since that conversation, I've been thinking about trying to find my mother's people."

She saw resistance in his eyes, but he didn't put a voice to it. "How would you find them?"

"Jaecar's adoption papers. My original family name is on them. It would be my father's last name, but I could start with his family. See if they know anything about my mother." Something in his look gave her a charge of excitement, though she couldn't quite place what it was. She reached out and took his hand. "If I could find them, maybe they could help me understand my past and what happened to me when I fought Wayland. Maybe they could even help me break this connection to him, if there truly is one."

He brought her hand up to his lips and kissed it. Then he closed his eyes, holding her fingers against his lips, and took a long deep breath. When he opened his eyes again, they overflowed with a mixture of affection and distress. She could see that he had come to some decision that weighed heavily on him.

"Would you like me to come with you?"

Giddy excitement blossomed in her chest. He couldn't know how terrified she was of going out into the world alone again. Or perhaps he could. She told him a great deal about how she grew up. How her parents, and Jaecar after them, kept her isolated from the rest of the world. He also knew she was at perpetual risk of being called out as an unauthorized Silverblood and put to death by the Brotherhood.

"I would. There is nothing I could think of right now that would make me happier, but this place is your dream. I can't ask you to walk away from it for me."

His jaw tightened for a second, giving her a glimpse

of the emotional battle going on within him. "Would you be willing to come back here in time?"

She breathed a soft laugh. "Oh, yes. This is my home now."

A broad smile curved his lips, the scar pulling up one side of his upper lip a fraction more than the other. He kissed her fingers again, sending little shivers of delight through her. "When Lysanna died, I didn't think I would love again. I didn't think I could. You proved me wrong. I will go anywhere you ask."

Raven moved to kiss him. This time, he met her halfway.

Two mornings later, Raven boarded the *Syra-senne*, Amberwood's river galley. The same ship that first brought her there. The crew was different this time. A mix of humans and elves instead of only elves like before. They wouldn't stop in Manderly. Going south with the current would make for a faster trip, so there was no need for that break. Their last visit involved a violent encounter with the Manderly guards, after which she and Marek helped free the *Syrasenne*'s wrongfully imprisoned crew. Because of that, Captain Narene felt it best to pass the town as quickly as possible with the human portion of the crew above deck to avoid anyone being recognized. They also slopped mud over the galley's name on that side.

Since that unfortunate chain of events, Captain Narene and her crew started picking up supplies to the north in Pellanth. Raw goods were a little more costly there, but the trip was less apt to turn fatal. The altercation in Manderly led to the deaths of Raven's first friend, Eamon, and one of Phendaril's scouts, as well as the galley's former captain and another member of the crew. It also cost Manderly several guards, all because a few of Darrenton's soldiers decided to play a prank on the elven ship by telling the local constable they carried stolen goods. It was a high price to pay for someone's twisted amusement.

They departed early in the morning after an evening spent celebrating something at the tavern. Raven wasn't entirely sure what they were celebrating. It appeared to be a way of saying goodbye without acknowledging the more sorrowful aspects of the process. Their trek to the docks in the early dawn involved only those getting on the ship. After the late night, she envied those who weren't going.

Their group included the crew of the *Syrasenne*, Raven, Phendaril, and Ehric. How Ehric became part of the adventure remained a little unclear. She remembered him offering to accompany them to provide additional protection on their travels. Phendaril declared it unnecessary. Karsima argued with him. She insisted she would sleep better knowing they had one more capable individual traveling with them. Numerous mugs of mead and three tense games of dice between Karsima and Phendaril followed. Karsima won two of those games. Now Ehric was coming with them.

As they pushed away from the dock, Phendaril went to stand at the port side. He watched, hands gripping the railing as they drifted down past the growing town. Raven walked up next to him and set a hand over his. He didn't move or speak. She wasn't sure what to say. Perhaps it was better to say nothing. They stood silent while the ship's crew navigated into the deeper water. They had a larger crew than necessary for heading south, but they would need those extra rowers for the trip back up against the current, primarily since they intended to take advantage of the opportunity to pick up less expensive supplies in Lathwood.

Ehric stepped up on Phendaril's other side. The Stonebreaker seemed to sense the gravity of the moment. He didn't speak until the town disappeared behind them. Then he asked, "Do you think it was a mistake not to bring horses?"

Phendaril shook his head. "We won't need them to get to Andel. Walking there from where they'll drop us off shouldn't take more than a couple of days. After that, it depends on where the trail takes us. We could probably barter pelts for a couple of mounts if we need to, though that will mean stopping in one place for a few days to do the trapping."

Raven pulled off her pack and set it on the deck. She crouched next to it, scrounging out the coin pouch she had found hidden away with Jaecar's documents the night she left the keep. As of yet, she hadn't needed it. Amberwood had provided for her in exchange for the work she had done. It was fortunate since she had no idea how much the coins were worth. She stood and held the pouch out to Phendaril.

"Will this help?"

He cocked his head at her, brows pinching in confusion as he took the pouch and opened it. He peered in and shook it a few times. Then he stuck two fingers in, shifting the coins around for a few seconds in silence. Finally, he met her eyes, looking more confused than before.

"Where did you get this?"

"Jaecar had it hidden in with the deed and the other documents. I don't really know how much it is." Her face flushed warm at the admission. She hated feeling ignorant. It had been happening less lately, but she suspected it would become more common again now that she was venturing out into the world. "Will it help?"

"Are you sure you want to offer this up?"

She nodded and asked again, with an itch of rising irritation. "Will it help?"

"I suppose he was a lord," Phendaril muttered under his breath, gazing back into the pouch. He looked at her thin, a faint smirk curving his lips. "Oh yes, it will help if it doesn't get us murdered in our sleep. Perhaps we should skim a little off the top and split it between the three of us for now. Don't take this pouch out again unless you know it's just us in a secure location, all right?"

She nodded, watching him pull a modest handful of coins out. He resealed the pouch and handed it back to her. She tucked it away before accepting the few coins he offered her. Those she dropped into the smaller sack attached to her belt that she typically used to carry nuts and dried berries on scouting excursions. He gave a few coins to Ehric and kept the remainder for himself.

Raven wandered to the opposite rail to watch the bank whisk by, breathing in the stink of the extensive marshes that dominated that side of the river down to Manderly. At least they didn't have to stop in the dreadful town this time. On the way back, whenever that day came, they might have to, but that wasn't worth worrying about now. She had much more significant concerns with Wayland hunting her.

The last time she had been in a galley on this river, she had been mostly unconscious as Marek's prisoner. The time before that, her first experience on a ship, she had been mourning Eamon as she rode north with a group of strangers, alone and terrified. River travel held no positive memories for her.

Phendaril came up behind her and slid his arms around her. One hand reached out to the railing, taking hold of it, while the other arm curled around her waist, pulling her close to him. Raven pressed into him, appreciating the solidity of his chest against her back. Maybe this would be the happy ship memory that would begin to erase the sorrow and fear that clung to the others.

"I never asked what he was to you."

He didn't need to say who. She supposed it was natural that he should ask now. By tomorrow morning, they would have passed by the place where Eamon died, killed by Manderly guards because he was kind enough to try to help Phendaril and his companions.

"I don't honestly know. He was the first individual I spoke to after Jaecar was murdered. He was generous and accepting of me in a world I expected to be nothing but cruel. A world that has since proven to hold a great deal of the cruelty I expected and much kindness I did not." She placed one hand on his arm at her waist. "I didn't know him long enough to love him. I think I could have, though."

The muscles in Phendaril's arms tensed. A twinge of jealousy he couldn't hide. He kissed her head and held her tighter. "It would be wrong to say I'm glad he's gone, but..."

She turned in his embrace and put a finger over his lips to silence him. A tear slipped down one of her cheeks, and he leaned in to kiss it away.

Phendaril pressed his forehead to hers. "I'm sorry. I didn't mean to make you cry."

"You didn't," she whispered. "I was crying because I mourn the man he was. I was also crying because I feel guilty that I'm glad he wasn't there to stand between us." She shifted back and looked up at him, another tear falling warm down her cheek.

"Do you think he would have? If the two of you had come with us to Amberwood? Do you think you would have chosen him?" The tightness in his voice told her he wasn't sure he wanted to hear the answer.

"I don't think it would have gotten that far. He didn't trust you. I think he meant to put you in Marek's hands and recuse himself of any further involvement." She absently brushed at a dusty spot on his sleeve. "He told me not to follow him that day, but I didn't trust Marek or you not to get him hurt, so I followed anyway." A sad smile stole across her lips. Odd that she had gone to protect Eamon and ended up saving Phendaril.

He cocked his head to one side, curiosity and a hint

of concern in his eyes. "You thought I would hurt him?"

"You, my love, would fight for the people you care about with the last breath in your lungs. Eamon wasn't one of those people." She offered him a fond smile to soften her words.

He nodded. "Not untrue. No matter your reasons, I'm glad you followed him. If you hadn't, the ship's crew and I might also be dead, and you wouldn't be with me now."

She rested her hands on his shoulders and gave him a playful smile to lighten the mood. "I could have never guessed how important those two arrows would be."

Phendaril kissed her, a demanding kiss that she returned with all the conflicting sorrow and adoration that filled her. She opened her mouth to him, tasting her tears on his lips. He pulled her tight against him, every bit of his desire reflected in her, burning through her like a wildfire, never entirely under control.

"Do you two need to borrow my quarters?" Captain Narene called loudly from the quarterdeck.

They parted, both flushed, though Raven had a feeling her cheeks burned much brighter than his. Several chuckles came from some of the other crew members. Raven shook her head and stared accusingly into his eyes.

"How is it that I forget everything else when I'm with you?"

He answered with a wicked grin. "I don't know, but I'd like to explore this phenomenon more."

His scoundrel wink only made her want him more, despite their audience.

The following two nights, they did take over Narene's cabin at her insistence. Though it made her feel somewhat self-conscious, Raven didn't argue. Once they left the ship, opportunities to be alone together would be harder to come by. There was no way to avoid that with Ehric along. Still, she was glad they had him with them. One more pair of eyes to watch for danger. One more blade for protection. One more person to chat with and discuss ideas with as they followed the limited information they had available to find her mother's family.

No, she was happy Ehric had come. Having time alone with Phendaril every day, however, was something she would miss.

The morning after that second night, the three of them disembarked. The place they stopped had no proper dock. They lowered a skiff over the side, and one of the crew rowed them ashore. The crewman left them at the bank with nothing more than a nod before he hurried back to the *Syrasenne*. Raven followed his example, turning away from the river and heading toward the wagon track that would be a few yards to the southwest. She stopped at the edge of it, peering south, the direction they would be traveling. She remembered the route between the keep and the Link River more precisely than she would have expected. Those days spent tailing Jaecar's killers blurred together at the time, but they were crisp in her memory.

Staying on the river as long as they had would shorten the walk. If they kept on this track, they would be in Andel by tomorrow afternoon. If they cut off to the southwest at the right point, they could be at the keep, or whatever remained of it, by that evening. She had absolutely no reason to go there. None at all.

Phendaril placed a hand on her shoulder. "What is it?"

"Would you mind a slight detour?"

Ehric strode into the middle of the track and stood staring south a moment, both of them watching him curiously. Then he looked over at her. "This is your journey, Raven. We'll follow where your heart guides us."

She offered him a grateful smile, uncomfortably aware of the truth in his words. They were only here because she had to leave Amberwood to protect herself and the others from Wayland. They chose to accompany her and assume the risk that being with her represented.

She turned to Phendaril for his input.

The smile that met her flowed over with affection. "I would love to see where you grew up."

She laughed softly, a touch of sorrow subduing the sound. "I'm afraid there won't be much to see."

With their course decided, she started to walk, adjusting her bow and quiver to sit more comfortably with her pack. Her elven sword hung reassuringly on one hip, opposite the matching dagger. Phendaril was equipped much the same. Ehric carried twin swords in two scabbards on his back and a crossbow in a holster at his waist with a strap securing it to his left thigh. As a group, they were very well-armed. If they were lucky, that would discourage opportunists, although Ehric warned that it also might attract those hungering for a fight.

They had to accept that risk. Raven carried or wore everything she owned. That included the armor she'd earned working in Amberwood, the bow Phendaril gave her that had belonged to his aunt, the elven sword and dagger that were Jaecar's final gift to her, and the arrowhead pendant Phendaril carved from a fragment of her father's bow. She owned nothing else of value. Taking all of that with her should have made leaving easier. She hadn't expected to miss the community of Amberwood, but now it felt as if something of even greater value had been left behind. How much worse must that loss be for Phendaril, who walked away from a lifelong friend and their shared dream? Or for Ehric, who left behind the clan he had been a part of his entire life?

She quickened her pace, trying to outrun the unease that came with those thoughts.

Around mid-morning, a wagon overtook them, laden with supplies for the smithy and the baker in Andel. It seemed an odd combination of goods, but Raven supposed the small town didn't merit a lot of separate shipments. They might have offered to pay for a lift if she hadn't decided to detour them to the keep. However, that kind of thing could lead to questions, so it was probably best that they kept to themselves. With her hood forward and her silvery-black hair braided up underneath it, a casual passer wouldn't notice that she was anything unusual.

She turned off the wagon track as the afternoon edged toward evening. Though she had never approached the keep from this direction, she had a sense of something leading her. Perhaps it was simply the call of her old home, drawing her to the places she once felt safe. She started recognizing familiar landmarks within an hour of turning into the woods. An old, moss-covered tree whose branches she had climbed up in for a better view hundreds of times. A pool along one of the regional creeks that she had often visited to clean blood from her hands and dagger after dressing a kill. Before long, they came to the clearing at the bottom edge of the rolling hill where the remains of the keep waited.

As soon as they cleared the tree line, she stopped, staring up at the two partial stone walls that still stood, stretching out from a back corner where the study had been. It was strange to see that bit standing, knowing that the fire originated in that room. The tower's remains were much as they had been the night she dug the chest holding Jaecar's documents out of the rubble in the bottom. The fire hadn't found anything there to devour. The old stable where she used to hide her collection of treasures lost by passers through the woods had burned thoroughly enough that it was hard to tell a structure had ever been there.

On the hillside behind the remains of the keep, silhouetted by the sinking sun, stood the tree that marked her parents' graves. The branches of the vibrant crown were scorched to twisted mockeries of the former grace. The tree was a charred husk of what it had been.

Raven hurried up the hillside, jogging the last several yards. She sank to her knees before the blackened tree, struggling to make sense of the hollow in her chest. It wasn't sorrow, not really. It hurt to see the tree burned, but new growth had already broken through the char on one of the lower branches. It had more to do with a feeling of failure. She promised her parents that she would take revenge against Jaecar's killers. After all, Jaecar had cut down the men who killed her parents. It felt like the right thing to promise when she left. But she hadn't accomplished that. Perhaps it had been wrong to make such a promise in the first place, now that she looked back on it. That didn't change the fact that she had made it.

Two sets of footsteps came up the hill behind her. The heavier set stopped for a few seconds before turning in the direction of the keep. Phendaril's lighter steps continued, bringing him up beside her.

"Your parents?"

She gave a slight nod. "Do you mind if we stay here tonight? I'd like to take a look around in better light."

Phendaril reached down to squeeze her shoulder briefly. "Ehric and I will start a fire. Join us when you're ready."

Raven stayed by the tree until after dark. She joined the other two by their fire inside the crumbled outer wall of the keep courtyard, listening in silence as Ehric and Phendaril compared the good and bad points of the crossbow versus the longbow. It was a conversation that might have interested her at a different time, but it couldn't hold her attention tonight. When they laid down to sleep, she stared at the stars overhead, recognizing the constellations that hung in the sky at this time of year. The Archer. The Twin Serpents. The Banshee, which she still considered an imaginative stretch for that particular cluster of stars. Next to her, Phendaril gazed at the sky and took her hand. It was strange how powerful that simple gesture was, helping her ease off to sleep.

Phendaril shifted some rubble in what had once been the sleeping quarters of the old keep with his boot. The new morning sunlight brought out the red in his hair that Raven was so fond of. Would she ever grow tired of watching him?

He glanced over, and she pretended interest in a piece of stone she had picked up.

"Do you think we'll find anything?"

"No," she answered bluntly.

She didn't see much point in elaborating. There was little reason to be digging through the ruins, but she couldn't bring herself to leave yet. The morning light revealed how thoroughly the fire had destroyed the few sections of the keep that had still been livable when it was her home. She and Jaecar maintained that portion of the keep, letting the rest continue to crumble around it. They didn't need that much to live there. There had only been the two of them.

She stepped over a low stone ridge – all that remained of that wall – into the space that had been Jaecar's study. Ehric was there, digging about where the desk would have been. No trace remained of the wood desk or the numerous shelves full of books. The fire erased them from existence. She picked her way to the opposite side where the outer wall still came up to about waist height and stared out what would have been the window if the rest still stood.

"Aneiris."

Raven whipped around. To have someone use her birth name here, where only Jaecar had used it, and rarely at that, usually when she wasn't paying attention to a lesson, was more than a little jarring. Ehric stood behind her, holding something in the palm of his hand, an unnerving distance in his eyes.

Why had he used her birth name? A few individuals in Amberwood knew it, but none of them ever used it.

Raven began picking her way over to him. "What did you call me?"

He gave himself a shake, then smiled at her. "Raven. What else would I call you?" He took the object in his hands and held it up between two fingers for her to see. "I found this buried in the rubble here."

It was a gleaming metal cloak pin, the three-quarter circle of the body made of elegantly woven strands of silver. At the two ends, the silver was shaped into the profile of a raven's head, each with a fine smoke-colored gemstone for an eye. Despite how delicate the piece looked, it appeared undamaged and strikingly pristine.

She reached out, taking it from him as Phendaril joined them. He came to stand by her shoulder. "That looks elven. Was it your mother's?"

"Perhaps." Something about the object felt familiar, like she had seen it before. It must have belonged to her mother. Why else would Jaecar have an elven cloak pin in his desk, assuming it had been there before the fire? She held it in her palm and ran her thumb over it, marveling at the shine of the metal. How could this have been buried in the runes of a burned-down keep?

"Aneiris," she murmured, contemplating the bird heads at either end of the pin. Her name meant little bird in eleven. Her mother loved birds. That was how she'd gotten her birth name and part of how she had acquired the nickname of Raven. She looked at Ehric, who had resumed his search, shifting around bits of broken stone. "Do you know the elven language?"

He stood and chuckled, raising an eyebrow at her. "No. Not a word. If you're looking for some way to have private conversations with Phen, that would do it, or you could ask me to walk away for a few minutes."

Raven chewed at her lower lip. She *had* heard him call her by her birth name. Or maybe her memories were playing with her in this place.

Phendaril cupped his hand under hers. "It's lovely. You should replace that rusted clasp you're wearing. If this was your mother's, I imagine she would have appreciated you using it."

She turned to him, offering the cloak pin. "Here, hold it for a moment."

Once he took it, she removed the old cloak pin and held the sides of her cloak close together while he fastened the new one in place. He stepped back and nodded approval.

"It looks right on you. Like you were meant to wear it."

Odd as it was, his words held weight. It was almost as if the cloak pin was an object she had been missing, something she couldn't be complete without. She placed a hand over the pin and pressed it closer to her chest.

•

Synderis looked down on the elven village of Eyl'Thelandra from an inner watch platform high in one of the massive evergreens that made up the forest. Since nothing ever got past the outer scout stations, he took a moment to relax against the trunk and close his eyes. A light breeze stirred the back of his long silver-white hair, bringing with it the lush smells of the deep summer forest. Autumn would be upon them soon. The scent of drying leaves would accompany a slight nip in the air. He loved autumn the most for the color it brought to the forest and the welcome cooling after the oppressive heat of summer.

The sound of fast, light footsteps approaching along the suspended walkway drew his attention. He pushed the hair on that side behind his pointed ear and focused to hear the nuances of the newcomer's gait. The barest hint of a smile touched his lips. He opened his eyes, turning to watch Dellaura, one of the council elders, hurrying toward him. Part of her long flaxen hair was woven into a webwork of delicate braids that weighed down the rest to keep it from lifting on the breeze and getting in her way. Her haste was somewhat concerning, though the gleam of excitement in her crystal-blue eyes helped ease his momentary alarm. She held one hand clasped before her while the other lifted the hem of her long blue and silver robes to keep them out from underfoot. Tripping up here could be fatal.

He waited, letting her join him on the platform where they had more space and wooden railings instead of ropes.

"Is everything all right, Dell?" No one called her that who wasn't immediate family. No one except him. He had permission. When anyone questioned it, she told them he was her spiritual grandson, and those who wished to object could take it up with her. She had a feisty side. He appreciated that about her.

"Aneiris is alive." Her eyes shone like stars, a hint of moisture lining the lower lashes as though she were close to tears.

He stood straighter. Had he missed some critical development that might have preceded such a revelation? "Mellaine's daughter? I thought she died when Mellaine tried to make her Krivalen."

"I thought so too. I lost all sense of her when Mellaine died, so I didn't think she survived the magic, but she's alive." Dellaura opened her hand, showing him the talisman she held—a three-quarter circle of finely woven silver, ending on both sides in the head of a bird with a smokey gemstone eye. "She has the matching piece. I felt her through it this morning."

He shook his head. To know that, she had to have been touching the amulet. Had she been wearing it all this time, tucked under her robes, perhaps? "It's been over ten years, Dell. Why was there nothing before now?"

"I don't know, but the talisman only reacts this way to my bloodline. It has to be her."

Dread tightened the muscles in his chest. "I'm happy for you, Dell," he said cautiously, taking a step back from the object she held, "but I don't see how this changes anything."

"I need your help, Syn. I need you to dreamwalk her. Help her if you can. Guide her here." Those bright eyes overflowed with excitement, the set of her jaw warning him of her determination. She had decided what to do with this information, and no one would convince her otherwise.

Still...

He closed his eyes for a second, drew a deep breath, then looked at her. He must be firm. "Any Krivalen in the village could do this." He ground his teeth. That wasn't firm. It was a weak attempt at deflection.

She touched his cheek, warm affection infusing her smile. "You're not any Krivalen. You're like family to me. I would sleep better at night knowing she is in your hands."

His resolve started to waver already. She had a way of doing that to him. "Are you sure you want to do this?

She is a half-breed."

Dellaura's expression hardened. "She is my grand-daughter. I thought I lost Aneiris when I lost Mellaine. I won't lose her a second time."

"She's Krivalen?" He supposed the half-breed female would think of herself as a Silverblood, but that was the human term for it.

Dellaura nodded.

That should at least make it easier to connect with her. The hope in Dellaura's eyes brightened with a spark of confidence. She believed he would give in. The stars help him, but he loved the council elder as much as he did his own mother. Fighting her on this was a losing battle, and they both knew it. He sighed and offered her a weary smile. "I'll try tonight."

"Thank you."

She held up the chain the amulet hung on. He lifted his hair out of the way so she could place it around his neck. Then she stepped back in front of him and kissed him on the cheek.

"Thank you," she said again.

"Go on. You know we aren't supposed to have company at our posts." He waved her away.

Dellaura chuckled. "And you know I'm part of the council. I don't expect anyone's going to report you for my visit. But I will let you be, my heart-child." She touched the talisman, gazing at it for a moment with a strange amalgamation of joy and sorrow that he found too understandable. Then she spun and hurried back out along the suspended walkway.

Synderis turned to look down at the ground, several levels below. The talisman was warm against his skin. He would blame that on how Dellaura had been clutching it in her hand. It was light, almost weightless. So much so that he had forgotten it twenty minutes later, having grown used to the continuing patch of warmth on his chest. It wasn't until that evening, when he stripped down to crawl into his hammock in the little treehouse he called home, that he remembered it again. For a few seconds, he contemplated taking it off, but Dellaura would be eagerly awaiting news from his first dreamwalk with Aneiris. He would leave it on for her, but he suspected it wasn't going to be a restful night.

Settling back on the hammock, he used a little Krivalen magic to anchor himself to the tree, then closed his eyes.

•

Synderis had dreamwalked a great deal since becoming Krivalen. It was a customary practice for communication over distance and for sharing privileged information or, on rare occasions, to help diagnose illness. Whatever he expected coming into the half-elf's dream, it wasn't what he found. This was a scene from a nightmare.

He came into the dream standing among some towering evergreens. Not far away, beyond the edge of the tree line, a man was shooting arrows at an elven female who stood gagged and bound to one post of a lean-to. The female was alive. So far, none of the hits were lethal, though she was bleeding profusely. She struggled and wept, moaning with the pain of her injuries. That alone was almost enough to send him back to the waking world. Then he noticed two more men adding fuel to a fire at the feet of a human man tied to another post. He screamed around the gag in his mouth while fire climbed his body.

Synderis was about to pull himself out of the nightmare when he recognized the bound female. Her name was Mellaine. He met her in the first few dreamwalks he had ever done in which he helped Dellaura visit her under the supervision of his mentor. This was the day

Mellaine was murdered, being lived over again by her daughter in a nightmare.

Then, a broad-shouldered human warrior came charging out of the trees like an enraged boar. Before the man with the bow could react, the warrior cut him down and lunged at the other two. In his wake, a girl emerged from the trees. A half-elven child one moment, the next, a half-elven Krivalen female. She flickered back and forth between child and adult as if unable to tell herself what she was. The child-adult figure rushed to Mellaine and began working to untie the rope that held her, sobbing as she struggled with it.

Then the warrior was at her side, freeing the elven female and easing her down on the bloodstained ground. He knelt to one side of her, the three attackers groaning as they bled out nearby. The man who had been burning, Aneiris's father, lay dying as well, his rasping breaths growing weaker. The half-elven child-adult sank to her knees, sobbing next to Mellaine. While her daughter wept and her lifeblood slipped away, Mellaine began channeling the magic that would draw all this death into Aneiris and make her Krivalen. The child turned into the adult again and seemed to stabilize. Her silver eyes stared at Mellaine, her long, silvery-black hair tucked behind one very elven ear. Tears streamed down her delicate cheeks, her heart breaking as he watched.

Pain twisted in his chest, making it hard to draw a breath. This had happened over ten years ago. How often had Aneiris relived this day in her nightmares? What would it take to stop her suffering?

He started to move, planning to go comfort her in an effort to break this cycle, but then something else caught his eye. A shadowy figure stood watching the scene from the nearest corner of the house. The figure was flickering and inconstant, the same way Synderis would appear in the dream if the connection between the twin talismans weren't so strong. The only feature he could make out for sure was the stranger's silver eyes, but the presence didn't feel elven. The figure moved toward Aneiris, then flickered back several feet, unable to control its presence in her dream. Not only an uninvited dreamwalker but an untrained one. A human Krivalen—a Silverblood—who wasn't here by choice or intention, but something else.

Synderis stepped back, moving out of the clearer frame of her dream into details that mattered less to what was happening. He watched the intruder try several more times to approach her, always flickering uncontrollably to another point in the dreamscape. Then Aneiris screamed, recapturing his attention.

Again, she was a child, fallen next to her mother, her back arched in convulsive agony. It was a wonder she survived the magic at such an early age. The warrior merely watched, perhaps because Aneiris had no memory of what he did at that moment in her past. She screamed again, and Synderis was thrust from the dream as she wrenched herself awake somewhere far away.

•

He lay staring up through the darkness at the living branches that formed the roof of his house. The outlines of leaves were made distinct by his Krivalen vision. He placed one hand over the talisman, his fingers coming into contact with sweat on his chest. No wonder Dellaura had been traumatized after her daughter's death. She had been wearing the talisman, enhancing their familial connection, and felt it all. Every bit of that pain and fear. A tear ran down the side of his face into his hair. He removed the talisman. Tomorrow, he would try again. Aneiris couldn't have that nightmare every night. At least, he hoped, for her sake, that she didn't.

Raven jerked awake. How many times had she woken alone, tears streaming down her cheeks? How many times had she lain alone in bed in the keep and wept until the vivid memories, played back in her nightmares, faded to the background again? The last time she'd had that nightmare, she had been on the boat from Manderly surrounded by strangers, some of whom would become friends. One of whom would become something more than that. When they reached Amberwood, the work there kept her exhausted enough that her nights were peaceful.

After visiting her old home and trying to dig into her parents' past, it wasn't that surprising to find the nightmare waiting for her. She had opened the door for it by coming back here. That didn't mean she was happy to see it.

Phendaril slid an arm around her, pulling her against him. And that was the difference this time. She hadn't woken alone.

"Are you all right?" he murmured in her ear.

"I dreamt of the night my parents were killed."

He slid his other arm under her and wrapped her securely in his embrace, snuggling closer to kiss her cheek. "Can I do anything?"

"You're already doing it." She wriggled her body

into his warmth. Her heartbeat was slowing now. The brief stream of tears had stopped as soon as his arm came around her. Even the hard ground couldn't lessen the comfort of having him there with her. Pressed back into his warmth, she closed her eyes and drifted into a more peaceful slumber.

When she woke again, it was to the sound of Ehric moving around the camp. The Stonebreaker was awake, kneeling on his sleeping roll while he bundled the rest of his things back into his pack. Phendaril stirred then too. She turned herself around in his arms to face him.

"Good morning." She placed a light kiss on his lips.

"Mmm." Desire gave a sultry edge to his drowsy smile as he moved in for a second kiss.

Raven shifted back, putting a finger over his lips. "We've got to get on the road, and poor Ehric doesn't want to watch this."

Ehric chuckled. "I don't?"

Phendaril laughed, and she let him push her over on her back. He lifted himself half on top of her to steal another kiss. His lips were soft. The kiss was lingering and full of longing. So much so that Raven forgot why she had tried to discourage him. She melted before the kiss, opening her mouth to him, and sliding one hand into his hair to hold him there when he started to pull away. When she remembered their audience, she let him go abruptly. He sat back on his knees, devouring her with his gaze.

"Can we get a room somewhere tonight?" he asked, leaning forward to steal another quick kiss before getting up. He offered her a hand up as well. She caught a glimpse of Ehric kneeling with his back to them as he fussed unnecessarily with his pack.

"Sorry, Ehric."

He waved a dismissive hand to one side. "I've seen it all before. Are we eating on the road or settling here for a bit longer?"

They decided to linger there for a light breakfast, then headed toward town. Along the way, Phendaril and Ehric debated whether they should stash some of their weapons outside of town to draw less attention or if staying fully armed was the better choice. For a while, Raven didn't pay much attention. Despite growing up near there for most of her life, she had never set foot in Andel. While they walked, she wandered through memories of her years spent exploring and hunting these woods with Jaecar as her guide and instructor. As they got close to the point that they would need to stash the weapons if they were going to do so, the group slowed to a stop, and she finally joined the discussion.

"Why does it matter so much?"

Ehric looked at her, his brow furrowing as though surprised she would even ask.

Phendaril turned to her. "You really never came to Andel the whole time you lived here?"

The lack of judgment in his regard eased the initial defensiveness that his question triggered. She took a calming breath and shook her head. "I stayed home with my mother whenever my father went to town. The day they died, I became a Silverblood. Jaecar only went without me. It was too dangerous for me to be seen in town."

Phendaril grimaced, lowering his gaze. "I see no one ever told you the truth about this area. You're a half-elf, Raven. It was always too dangerous for you to go to Andel. Humans tore down the statue of the elven founder when they seized control of the town over one hundred years ago. Many of the townsfolk here keep elven slaves. Being a half-elf here is almost a greater offense than being an unsanctioned Silverblood. This isn't a place our kind will find much welcome."

She glanced between them, convinced of the truth

in his words by their solemn expressions. "Why would my parents risk hiding in the woods near such a place?"

"Perhaps someone was looking for them," Ehric offered. "If they were trying to avoid persecution by family or friends for their unconventional relationship, no one would expect them to move closer to a place where their union would be seen as an even greater affront. Sometimes the least expected hiding spot is the best one."

Phendaril's shrug told her he considered it was a reasonable speculation. Had the men who killed her family been from Andel? Were they hunters who had simply stumbled upon their forest home and taken offense at finding a man and elf living together? Or could they have been hunting them intentionally for longer than that? Had they planned the torture they inflicted on her parents over years of searching for them? Was Ehric right, had her mother and father decided to raise her here, in this hostile place, because they believed it would keep people like the ones who murdered them off their trail?

Anger rose in her. A pointless rage that she had no target for. She pulled up the hood of her cloak and stalked toward the town. "We keep our weapons."

The other two followed in silence. They made it about another ten yards when the sound of something crashing through the brush reached her. Raven stopped again and peered into the woods. Phendaril moved up next to her, gazing in the direction she was looking.

"What is it?"

She held up a hand and whispered, "Listen."

The crashing was growing louder fast. Within a few heartbeats, his brow furrowed, and he nodded. "Something big," he said, taking a few steps back and putting a hand on his sword hilt.

Given the direction it was coming from, it would become visible through the dense trees seconds before it was upon them. In that situation, a sword did make more sense than a bow. Raven placed a hand on her hilt as well. She heard steel whisper softly from leather sheaths as Ehric, standing a few feet further back, drew his matching blades.

One of the more terrifying things Raven had ever seen came charging at them through the trees then. A big bay horse plunged through the forest, eyes wide with terror, empty stirrups smacking its sides as it ran, driving it faster. Phendaril took a few steps forward, his hands raised in front of his chest as he moved past her toward the panicked animal. Raven retreated behind Ehric, who put his swords away now. They watched Phendaril open his arms as if he actually expected the charging animal to see him as a barrier.

Raven didn't want him to get hurt. Would he hold it against her if she drew her bow and shot the animal to spare him from being trampled?

"Whoa. Easy." He started repeating the words in a firm but soothing voice.

The animal didn't appear to be slowing, but its attention shifted to Phendaril, its ears swiveling toward him. When its head turned that way, its path veered in his direction too. Raven cringed inwardly, not wanting to watch it run him over but unable to look away. Then, at the last second, its legs locked up, and it skidded to a halt about a foot from him, tossing its head and snorting.

Phendaril's voice softened. He murmured soothing words, slowly taking the reins with one hand. It flinched when his other hand touched its neck, then relaxed as he started to gently stroke the sweaty coat. Raven did her best to swallow her terror, but she kept her distance. One ride on a horse with Phendaril in control wasn't enough to eliminate her fear of the powerful animals. From her more removed vantage point, she noticed deep scores on the saddle, as if a large predator had attacked it. The horse appeared unharmed, though she could understand its panic, given the size and depth of the claw marks in the leather.

The animal stood trembling, its sides heaving and slick with sweat, but it lowered its head and turned to Phendaril, trusting him to protect it. Then she heard the rustle of something else in the trees, comparatively smaller and not moving as fast. A brawny man came storming out of the woods, his mouth twisted in a snarl of rage beneath his heavy beard.

"Stupid fucking animal!"

The horse jumped as if struck. It would have bolted again if not for Phendaril holding the reins. Instead, it spun around him, turning to face what it clearly perceived as an approaching threat. Raven and Ehric had to jump out of the way of its hindquarters, proving Jaecar's warning that horses were dangerous when frightened.

Phendaril narrowed his eyes at the man as he stalked from the trees in his tattered clothes. "This horse yours?"

The man gave him a quick once over, scowling at Phendaril's pointed ears. Raven angled her head down when he looked her way to keep him from seeing into the hood of her cloak. His gaze settled on Ehric, who took a few steps closer.

"The animal's mine. I'll be taking it now." He reached for the reins, and the horse reared.

Phendaril stepped back with the animal as its front hooves touched down again, elegantly placing himself partially between man and horse. "Doesn't look like it wants to go with you."

The man's lip lifted in a feral snarl. "That worthless beast is my property." He moved forward again. The horse backed frantically away, the whites of its eyes showing.

Ehric took another step closer, his hands sinking to the hilts of his swords again. "Animal seems a bit upset right now. Do you live in Andel?"

The man's gaze sank to the blades, noting the blatant threat. Raven deliberately placed a hand on her sword, giving him another reason to consider backing off. It was silly to go to all this trouble to defend a horse. Still, something about this man made her highly uncomfortable. She might have denied him the animal for that reason, even if her companions weren't already trying to protect it.

"I do." He shifted his attention to Ehric, unwilling to speak directly to Phendaril.

"Let me propose a painless solution. We're passing through Andel. We'll walk the horse into town, get it calmed down, and leave it at the stable by the inn for you."

His gaze swept among them again, taking a more thorough inventory of their weapons now. When he lifted his lip in a slight snarl at the horse, Raven saw the flash of a fang. Finally, he backed closer to the edge of the woods. "I suggest you three watch yourselves out here. The forest can be dangerous."

As he turned, she caught a glimpse of yellow in his eyes. She stared after him, noticing the odd loping gait as he jogged back into the trees, her hand tightening on her sword hilt. She moved up alongside the other two, still wary of the horse, though the animal calmed when the man departed.

"He's not human," she stated.

Phendaril nodded to her. "I thought something seemed off about him."

His willingness to trust her assessment gave her a little burst of pleasure.

The horse nudged Phendaril to get his attention and lowered its head to let him scratch between its ears. "Guess we're not giving you back to him, then."

"Do you think the real owner is still alive?" Ehric asked.

Phendaril moved to the horse's side. He held up one stirrup, turning it so they could see the blood spattered across it. "I have some doubts. We'll lead him into town. Maybe someone will recognize the animal."

The edge of town came into sight as they rounded a bend a short time later. The way the horse clung to Phendaril now struck off a twinge of envy in Raven, both for the way he constantly reassured it with soft words and pats and for the affection it offered in return. Maybe horses were more than unpredictable forces of destruction. Or perhaps it was just that she wanted to be one at the moment.

Phendaril glanced back at her and gestured with one hand for her to come up beside him. She did so, watching the horse on his opposite side uneasily. Ehric moved up on the far side of the horse, reaching out to pat the animal's neck.

"Make sure your hood stays up and leave the talking to Ehric," Phendaril advised her. "He may be a Stonebreaker, but he's human. They're more likely to talk to him."

Raven touched his arm and tried for a confident smile, though a surge of nervousness chased the expression away. "Trust me, I have no desire to fight him for the privilege of talking to these people."

Phendaril offered a reassuring smile in return. "I had a feeling."

As they approached the edge of town, five boys playing around a small pond off the side of the road stopped to watch them curiously.

"Children might be worth talking to for basic information," Ehric suggested under his breath, so the boys wouldn't hear. "They don't tend to be as wary as their parents."

Raven had no insight on the subject. The only children she'd been around were the few in Amberwood, and that was at a distance. Like the horse, she would leave the handling of these creatures to her companions.

"Hello," Ehric called out, lifting a hand in greeting.

Three of the five boys dropped what they were doing and bolted for town. Of the remaining other two, the freckled redhead dared to respond with a tentative wave and took two stunted steps closer. His dark-haired companion stayed by the pond, a makeshift fishing rod hanging forgotten in his hand.

"Whatcha want?" the redhead demanded, staring defiantly up at Ehric when he came to a stop about five feet away.

"Is there a tanner in town?"

The boy scowled as if the question disappointed him. She suspected he had been hoping for something more scandalous or otherwise exciting. "'Course there is. Fifth house down on the right. Name's Danby." His eyes narrowed when he turned his attention to Phendaril in a way Raven found unnerving. "If yer lookin' to sell the elf, go to the town hall by the statue."

"We'll sell you if you come any closer," Phendaril remarked caustically.

The boy's eyes widened. He looked to Ehric, his indignant stare demanding that the Stonebreaker do something about his mouthy elf.

Ehric scrutinized the redhead the same way the boy had been eyeing Phendaril a moment ago. "You're a bit skinny, but we could probably get a fair price for you."

The boy glanced from Ehric to Phendaril and back again. Raven had never seen such a sinister smile on Phendaril's lips. She breathed a soft laugh. Ehric continued to stare at the boy as if he were a slab of meat. After a few seconds, finding nothing in their regard to indicate they weren't serious, the boy bolted toward town. Ehric chuckled and tossed a coin to the dark-haired boy by the pond. The child caught it, dropping his fishing rod in the process.

He stared at the coin in his hand, then up at Ehric. "I'm not fer sale, sir."

Phendaril laughed, the sinister expression vanishing. "Glad to hear it. Neither are we."

The boy looked at the coin again. After a few seconds, he grinned and bolted off in the direction his companions had gone.

ndel was small. Not much larger than Manderly, though notably cleaner and without the stink of the river town. The streets weren't crowded in any sense of the word. Most of the tradespeople appeared to work out of shops attached to their homes. Elves and humans wandered through the market street in equal numbers among stalls selling food and other wares. Raven might have thought it an equitable place if not for a few conspicuous disparities. No one in town wore what she would call fine clothes, but the elves, their eyes perpetually downcast around their human neighbors, dressed in garments that were threadbare and torn. None of the shopkeepers suspiciously watching, tracking their progress through town, were elven either. Another glaring sign that things were less balanced than they might initially appear.

Finding the tanner's shop proved easy enough. With only one market street to search, it took little time to spot the modest collection of furs and hides hung up around the perimeter of the booth adjacent to his house. Raven stayed close to Phendaril, following his lead when he stopped several feet away from the shop with the horse.

Ehric closed the remaining distance alone, quickly capturing the attention of the wiry old tanner. No other dark-skinned warriors walked the streets of Andel.

Phendaril stood out less than the Stonebreaker did, although his weapons and leather armor earned him more than a few disgusted scowls from the human passers.

"How can I help you, sir?" the man behind the counter asked, his eyes narrowing a fraction when he glanced past Ehric at Phendaril and Raven.

"Might you be Danby, sir?" Ehric asked, his tone easygoing and polite.

"The only one." The tanner spat a brownish substance to the left of Ehric's feet.

Raven's stomach recoiled when she caught the disconcertingly sweet and earthy scent of whatever he was chewing.

"I've been trying to track down a trapper," Ehric began, giving no indication that he had noticed the spitting. Raven marveled at how dignified he sounded standing there in his hide and steel armor with his impressive mane of long black locs. A magnificent gentleman warrior. "He used to hunt and trade in the area some ten or so years ago. You might not remember him."

"Arek Woodbridge?"

Raven's heart skipped a beat. This man knew her father. She hadn't expected that part to be so easy.

Ehric started to glance back at her and caught himself. "Yes." Surprise raised his voice the tiniest fraction. It was not enough for the tanner to notice it, but enough that Raven could tell he hadn't expected them to get lucky this fast.

"'Course I remember him. He brought me some of the best hides I've ever worked with. Used to come through once a month or so. Always a pleasure to deal with. Then, one day, he simply stopped coming. Always assumed one of the beasts he was hunting got the jump on him. Haven't had hides that nice since."

A smile stole across Raven's lips. It was good to hear that her father had been appreciated.

"Did you recall if he ever mentioned a wife or children?"

Danby's brow furrowed. He spat to the same side again before speaking. Raven realized the red-brown dirt around his shop wasn't damp, as she'd initially assumed, but discolored from his vile spitting. "Nah. Solitary bloke. Shame really. Seemed a good sort. He'd have made some lass a fine husband. If I recall correctly, he said he had some relatives back in Lathwood. Suppose he might have gone back there." He moved a few hides around for better visibility as another man slowed to look.

"Thank you, good sir. Your help is appreciated." Ehric offered a respectful nod.

Danby glanced over at the horse, and his eyes narrowed more. "How did you say you knew Arek?"

"I didn't," Ehric answered without the slightest change in tone. "Is there a stable in town?"

The man ignored the question. "That looks like Marl's gelding. He's been missing for two days now."

Ehric looked back at the animal now. "Could be. We found it on the road coming in."

Danby nodded. "Might as well keep it, then. Old Marl didn't have any next of kin. We've had several people go missing over the last year. Never find more than a few remains. The constable hired a Silverblood a while back to investigate the problem. He brought down a fierce-looking beast. We thought that'd be the end of it, but there must be more out there. Be careful if you wander these woods."

Ehric nodded. "We will be."

"Stable's just down the side street on the left up there. Not a lot of stock if you're looking to buy, but what they do have is usually reliable enough."

"Thank you again, sir." Ehric led them away from the stall. When he fell into step alongside Raven, he glanced over at them. "I assume we'll want at least one more mount if we're going to Lathwood next."

Raven looked to Phendaril. She wasn't sure how far that was, though she recalled that it was somewhere to the east between here and Chadhurst. He took no notice of her questioning glance, glaring death at the air in front of him as he walked, lost deep in his thoughts.

Raven lightly touched his arm. "Are you all right?"

He startled, glancing at her hand before meeting her eyes. "It would have to be Lathwood," he muttered.

"Isn't that where..." She didn't finish. The resignation and old anger in his eyes told her more than his words could. Lathwood was where his mother and his aunt had both died. If she understood the timeline correctly, it was also where his former love had taken her own life after some human men raped her. The men were no longer there – Phendaril had seen to that – but the memories would be. Expecting him to return to a place inundated in such loss was a lot to ask. "Maybe there's another way to find her."

"Let's see what they have in the way of mounts. We can figure the rest out when we're away from here." Next to him, the gelding tossed his head, picking up on Phendaril's darker mood.

At the stable, Phendaril absently handed her the reins for the gelding. She took them, not wanting to make a scene by relenting to her initial urge to refuse. He and Ehric left her alone with the large, unpredictable bundle of muscle, teeth, and steel-shod hooves. A lump of dread rested heavy in her gut. While they haggled with the stable owner over a mount and gear, Raven and the horse stared at one another. The animal snorted, and she jumped, letting out a sharp squeak of surprise. The sudden noise made the horse toss back its head, its eyes popping wide and front hooves splaying out as though preparing to bolt.

Raven froze there, the reins pulled tight between them. It dawned on her that this poor beast probably regarded her as unpredictable and dangerous. The horse relaxed a fraction when she laughed softly, easing the tension on the reins. "You're scared of me, aren't you? You don't even know you're several times stronger than I am." Her soft tone calmed the animal more. It took a step closer, lowering its head. She gave it a warning look. "Don't push it. Willingness to talk it out doesn't make us immediate friends."

The animal advanced again, and she retreated an equal distance, relieved to see Phendaril and Ehric returning, even if they were bringing a second horse. The new horse was a sturdy, rust-colored gelding a little smaller than the bay Raven eagerly handed back to Phendaril. They were sensible enough not to buy her a mount of her own. Taking time to teach her how to ride well wasn't going to get them away from the long judgmental stares of the people of Andel any faster.

Ehric faced them, though she caught his eyes moving as he did a quick sweep of their surroundings, his gaze pausing briefly on several townsfolk in the area. "We should probably continue toward Lathwood today. I have a feeling we're better off taking our chances with the beasts in the woods than finding a room here in town."

Raven and Phendaril nodded in agreement. The looks they received from the humans here made her skin crawl, especially those scowls of angry disapproval when Ehric engaged in respectful conversation with Phendaril. With her hood hiding her features, they appeared uncertain about whether she was elven or human, so they merely judged what they did know. In this case, the apparently unacceptable fact that Ehric treated Phendaril like more than a piece of property.

They made quick work of purchasing extra food to

supplement their stores before heading toward the road leaving town on the eastern side. Ehric mounted the rust-colored horse, and Raven climbed up on the bay behind Phendaril. Being on horseback again was tolerable, as long as it got them away from Andel.

Phendaril kept them at a trot heading out of town. Raven clung to him, trying to make herself comfortable in the shared saddle. It wasn't designed for two, but it was exactly big enough for them to sit in the seat snugly together. When she thought about being pressed against him, this was never how she envisioned it. At some point, if this adventure took them much farther than Lathwood, she might have to relent and learn to ride a horse herself, though the thought made her a little queasy.

The road angled southeast about a half hour out of town, which struck Raven as wrong. Lathwood, if she remembered the maps correctly, was east and a little north of Andel. Still, like rivers, roads were sometimes meandering things, often following the path of least resistance. Phendaril and Ehric knew more about these lands than she did, so she focused on letting her body move with the horse rather than against it to make the ride more comfortable for everyone. That process brought an unexpected sense of connection with the animal, as if they were becoming two parts of the same whole. Despite the barrier of the saddle, she felt every muscle engaging with each stride down to the tiniest alteration in gait when a rock shifted underfoot.

Her focus on the horse's motion was so intense that she noticed instantly when a ripple of tension passed through its body.

"Stop!"

Phendaril pulled the reins back, and Raven leaped off, landing before the animal had come to a complete stop. Ehric drew the new horse up next to them. She held up a hand to discourage either of them from speaking. The horses started to shift in place, their steel-shod hooves grinding noisily on the gritty surface of the hard-packed road. Under that noise, her enhanced hearing caught a low growl. Not a warning growl, but a hunting growl. She'd heard the same deep, throaty growl once before. In the woods the day she first saw Marek.

Phendaril and Ehric dismounted, trusting her lead, and reached for their weapons. As they were doing so, a man stalked out of the trees. The same feral man, with his shaggy beard and tattered clothes that they encountered earlier that day. A toothy grin spread his lips, something wild sparking in his yellow eyes.

"I'll be takin' that horse back now." His words came out garbled, almost more growl than normal speech.

Both horses started to prance about and toss their heads, recognizing the predator before them. Raven moved a safe distance from the nearest animal and drew her sword. The crunching noise of their hooves on the hard-packed road as they danced around made it difficult to pick out other sounds. A potentially deadly problem given that the direction he approached from was not where she had heard the growling. She needed to listen.

The power she felt that night, lying with her neck pinned under Wayland's knee while his dagger sliced down her breastbone, stirred in her again. Her hand went to her chest, reaching for the scar where he had cut her, but touched on the elven cloak pin instead. Something in the pin flashed warm in response as if it contained magic. Swelling power drew in around the delicate pin under her fingertips, providing a focus for the magic and giving her a greater sense of control. She turned toward the horses, willing them to silence, a growl rising low in her throat. Power snaked out from the point of focus, striking at them. Both animals instantly stilled, their fear transformed into lethargic disinterest.

With the horses silenced, she could now hear shifting in the trees on both sides of the road. In her periphery, she caught the uneasy glances Ehric and Phendaril gave her then. A wave of guilt turned her stomach, but they didn't have time for that now.

The man in front of them was grinning, and she noticed with more than a little alarm that his fang teeth appeared to be growing longer and sharper. Another low growl sounded to the left of the road. She glanced at Phendaril, who stood closer to that side, but his attention and Ehric's were, understandably, focused on the man in front of them, whose fingernails were also growing longer, thicker, and sharper.

The creatures in the trees charged the instant Phendaril moved to engage the transforming man-beast in front of them. Raven dropped her sword and grabbed her bow, sending an arrow at the massive canid monster that lunged from the trees alongside Ehric. Like the one she encountered when she first saw Marek, this one was larger than a bear and moved as comfortably upright as on all fours. She hadn't had time to aim, so the arrow caught the creature in one arm, eliciting a yelp followed by a furious snarl. The attack served its purpose, slowing the beast long enough for Ehric to turn his attention to it.

Raven dropped low then, trading her bow for her sword as the beast on her side lunged at her from the trees, one huge paw sweeping over her head as she ducked down. She rolled up behind it, her swing cutting a shallow gash in the back of one leg. If it noticed the injury, it didn't react. Instead, it continued in the direction its momentum carried it, barreling into Phendaril from behind as he swung at the man-beast before him that appeared to be doubling in size as it changed.

A cry of surprise and pain was torn from him when the beast slammed into his back, throwing him down.

He twisted as he fell, landing with his back to the ground and bringing his blade up to block his assailant. The beast didn't have time to pull its attack. Its teeth closed on the sword, and Phendaril shoved forward, slicing into the back of its jaw. Blood gushed from its mouth. It reared up, letting loose an ear-splitting shriek as it lunged away from the threat now.

Ehric was holding his own, his twin blades moving with such speed that the unarmored monster couldn't get an opening without earning another cut through its thick hide. The man-beast in the front still grew taller, arms and legs elongating strangely. Raven dropped to one knee and switched weapons again, bringing the bow up and nocking an arrow. As the monstrosity threw back its head and opened its lengthening jaws to let loose the start of a howl, she fired an arrow into its throat, cutting off the sound. Perhaps it had hoped to call in others of its kind, but the only sound it made then was a liquid gargling as it reached for the arrow in its throat. It staggered to one side.

A few feet to her left, Ehric blocked an attack from the beast he was fighting and swung low with his other blade, splitting open its gut. Intestines spilled out, and the creature started making the same painful shrieking sound the other had made. One more quick slice laid open its throat, ending the noise. The man-beast in the front, its transformation violently interrupted, fell to its knees and wavered there. Phendaril, back on his feet, strode over to the beast that had attacked him where it now lay at the edge of the trees, whimpering. Blood poured from its split face. With a thrust of his blade, he silenced it as well.

In the middle of the road, the man-beast toppled forward.

Phendaril looked at the horses standing placid and unmoving amidst the carnage. Spatters of blood dampened his hair and face. More covered the chest of his armor. He walked over and took hold of the bay's reins, drawing the animal's head down so he could scratch between its ears. The horse let him do so, giving to the pressure on the reins, but it didn't respond to the attention in any meaningful way.

He turned to look at her. "What did you do to them?"

The dark accusation in his eyes caused an uncomfortable twisting in her gut as she reached up to touch the cloak pin. "I don't know."

CHAPTER NINE

It was late afternoon before Dellaura found Synderis. He wasn't trying to avoid her, not necessarily, but not being on duty today did allow him to wander and be a little less available. He spent much of his time considering what he had seen in Aneiris's dream. No matter how he told it, hearing about the experience would be upsetting for Dellaura in multiple ways. The fact that her granddaughter remained haunted by that day to this extent would be a dagger in her heart. Adding the uninvited dreamwalker to the news would be like twisting that dagger.

When she did find him, which he had known she would eventually, he was sitting next to a clear forest pool near where his brother's ten-year-old daughters lay sleeping in the grass. The girls took after their father in enough ways that they could have almost been twins, despite having different mothers. The three had tried to plan their pregnancies so the two could grow up together and had succeeded remarkably well. They were only about two months apart.

Synderis looked after them often on his days off. He had started this afternoon with a diving lesson that devolved into a contest, seeing who could make the biggest splash by jumping off a boulder at one end of the pool. They summarily disqualified him after his first jump because of his significant size advantage.

Another year and the two girls would spend most of this free time outside their regular studies learning a trade or scouting and combat skills depending on their preferences. He hoped at least one of them chose scouting over trade. Then he might still get to spend this time with them, teaching them to fight and read the forest. He had a feeling Merilia would choose that path, though Aurelia showed an inclination toward herbology and healing.

He leaned over the edge of the pool, examining his reflection to see if the braids he had worked into the sides of his hair were neat enough for scouting duty early tomorrow morning. The two braids on each side were part of the uniform of the Krivalen scouts. Two slightly different configurations marked those currently on or off duty. In addition to keeping their hair out of the way on the elevated walkways, where a misstep could be lethal, the braids made it easier for others to recognize the scouts from a distance in an emergency. Krivalen scouts were the primary defenders of Eyl'Thelandra. Life within the village was safe and comfortable because no one knew they existed. The Krivalen scouts were vital to maintaining that isolation, so they patrolled those borders constantly.

His attention caught for a moment on his silver eyes, the irises gleaming like steel, and the faint shine of silver in his white hair. It was his choice, though he sometimes wondered what it would have been like to have children, like his brother. Becoming Krivalen required certain sacrifices. The ability to have children was a big one in the obvious lack of offspring and because the magic-induced sterility discouraged many prospective partners. Births among their people were too rare, something that made his brother's two girls rather exceptional. A few non-Krivalen elves might consider a Krivalen partner as lover or secondary life-bond, but not often as primary or exclusive life-bond. That was why the Krivalen frequently sought companionship amongst their own kind when their duties allowed time for it.

Soft footsteps in the moss caught his attention. He stood and turned in one fluid motion. A flicker of unease tightened his chest when he saw who approached. Dellaura glanced at the sleeping girls and smiled fondly. He met her eyes when she turned his way and moved further from the children so they could talk without disturbing the two.

"We're you admiring your reflection?" Dellaura asked, her teasing smile easing some of his tension. "You know you're devastatingly handsome."

"Devastatingly bad life-bond material, you mean?"

Dellaura's smile was full of adoration and patience. Talking to her did feel like conversing with his mother sometimes, although Dellaura had significant authority within the village through her place on the council. Something he tried not to lose sight of.

"Ilanya is considering the Krivalen..."

He shook his head. "Don't try to match-make, Dell. I'll figure that out for myself. Besides, I know you came to ask about your granddaughter."

Her hands clenched, and hope sparked in her eyes. "Were you able to reach her?"

He glanced over to confirm that the girls were still asleep before gesturing to a sun-bleached log strategically positioned near the pool. "Sit." Her brows pinched with sudden worry, but she did as directed. He sat next to her and took her hand. "I did dreamwalk her last night. She was having a nightmare." He stopped. Perhaps he should leave it at that, but she had a right to know. "About the day her parents died."

Tears sprang to Dellaura's eyes even faster than he expected. "Oh no. The poor dear." Her voice cracked. "I can't imagine..."

"I'm sorry. I didn't want to remind you of that day. It was even more awful than I expected."

"I don't want details. What I felt through the talisman was bad enough." She wrapped her other hand over his, her pleading gaze making him wish he had lied. "Tell me you stopped it."

He shook his head. "I couldn't. There was another dreamwalker there. From what I saw, someone who's connected to her somehow, but not intentionally. Whoever they are, they were only there in shadow and didn't appear to have control over their experience."

Her eyes widened, one hand rising to her chest. "Not one of us, then."

He shook his head. Compounding guilt at causing her such distress made him feel like a monster for telling the truth, as odd as that was. However, it was better for her to know the whole situation, no matter how much it upset her. "It has to be someone from the Silverblood Brotherhood. There's no one else it could be."

She stood, pulling her hand free of his. "This is terrible. If the Brotherhood knows about her, if they're after her..." She turned her piercing gaze on him, brusquely waving away a butterfly that flitted next to her face, drawn by the flowers woven into her hair. It was unlike her to be annoyed by such a thing. "Is there anyone helping her outside of her dreams?"

"I don't know. I can't risk talking to her with the other there."

"You have to, Syn. You have to help her."

He saw the half-elven female in his mind, Aneiris, flickering between her adult and child self as she knelt beside her dying mother. It made his chest ache to think of what he'd seen. He did want to help her, but not at the expense of their people. She was a half-breed. He narrowed his eyes a fraction, hating that the situation forced him to be cruel, but Dell wasn't thinking this through. "Doing so would put all of our people at risk, Dell. If you think that's what we should do, they should have a say. We should take this before the council."

"They'll refuse," she snapped. "They'll let her die."

He took a deep breath and shook his head, turning away from her. For a few seconds, he rubbed at his temples, fighting a growing headache. This was a beautiful, peaceful spot, but he couldn't appreciate that serenity knowing the young female whose nightmare he had visited last night was in danger and how much it would hurt Dellaura if she died. Still, he would feel better about trying to help her if he believed they had the support of the village elders. "You didn't talk to the council about this before you came to me, did you?"

The silence behind him was answer enough.

"Dell." He faced her. "You're on the council. You can't go sneaking around behind their backs. Tell me you at least ran it by the Delegate first."

She wouldn't meet his eyes.

"You knew they would refuse because she's a half-breed." Sympathy threatened to weaken his resolve, but this was not the way to handle a situation this delicate. "We have no choice now. If I try to interact with her with the other dreamwalker there, it could threaten our existence. I can't continue without their approval." He waited for the change in her expression, that return of sanity in her eyes.

It didn't take long. She shook her head, looking toward the village built on the forest floor as well as on multiple levels in the massive trees. "You're right. I can't put our people at risk for one individual, no matter who they are." She exhaled heavily, sorrow dragging down her features, making her look older.

Synderis placed a hand on her shoulder. "I'll keep checking, Dell. If I get a chance to approach her without the other there, I'll do what I can to help her, but you have to promise me that you'll at least talk to the Delegate about what's going on."

She nodded and placed a kiss on his cheek. When she drew back, she managed a fleeting smile, though it didn't come close to reaching her eyes. "Thank you."

After returning the girls to their parents that evening, Synderis sat for a long time on the edge of the platform outside his home in the high branches, feet dangling over the considerable drop. He'd been ten when Mellaine left the village to search for elves from other regions willing to relocate to the safe haven of Eyl'Thelandra. The council sent volunteers out about every five years to do so, ensuring their survival through the introduction of new bloodlines. Dellaura hadn't wanted Mellaine to go, but she was a restless soul. She made her choice. But she never returned because, instead of finding elves to bring back with her, she fell in love with a human man and chose to stay with him. A human would never be welcome here. Even bringing her half-breed child here would be frowned upon, regardless of her family relations.

It wasn't hard to see that it still broke Dellaura's heart when she spoke of her daughter. After Mellaine died, those close to Dellaura expected she would mourn and move on. He could imagine her sitting on her bed alone, holding that talisman while mourning her daughter and granddaughter. How often had she handled the talisman? Every day? Only occasionally, when the memories stirred in her?

He touched the silver pendant hanging around his neck.

Why had Aneiris come into possession of the talisman's mate now, more than twenty years after her mother's death?

The only way to answer that question would be to ask Aneiris herself, which meant catching her in the dream without the intruder there. It was late enough that she would probably be asleep wherever she was.

He stood and sauntered into the house. He had kicked off his soft boots when he got home, so he simply pulled off his shirt and lay down on the hammock. With one hand touching the talisman, he anchored himself with the magic and closed his eyes to sleep.

•

He was standing in the shadows of a narrow walk between two houses, looking out on a bustling town square. It was evening, and the town's occupants had gathered around numerous fires in the square outside a tavern. It was an odd arrangement, though what he found more peculiar was that humans of all colors – including a fair number of dark-skinned Stonebreakers – and elves intermingled around those fires like equals.

It took him a moment to realize that the female standing a few feet away was Aneiris. Flickering firelight glinted in her silver eyes no matter which way she looked. There was a softness to her beauty that he rarely saw in elven females, but then, she was half human. She shifted her feet and tightened her trembling hands into fists as she stared out at the square.

He scanned the area, searching for any sign of the strange dreamwalker. Once he was confident the other wasn't there, he carefully walked around behind her, sneaking close enough to hear her talking to herself.

"Too many. There are too many," she muttered under her breath, her hands clenching and unclenching.

People? Was it the crowd that upset her?

She started gathering Krivalen magic to her. He could feel her focusing it through the cloak pin talisman she wore. He took a step back, wary of his power getting pulled into whatever she was doing. The Acridan never taught humans how to use the magic like this, and no Krivalen elves ever left the sanctuary of Eyl'Thelandra. How had she learned to draw upon it this way? She had to be untrained. They had a bigger problem if she had figured this out alone.

She brought her fists up near her face, then slammed them down by her sides again, shouting, "Too many!"

Power burst out from her violently enough that even he staggered.

An eerie silence fell around them. Synderis glanced around the square. Everyone stood still and silent now. Those who had been drinking or eating lowered their hands, food hanging forgotten, the drink spilling from mugs that hung limp in their fingers. Aneiris stood staring at them for a few seconds. With a slight shake of her head, she walked out among them. At first, she just looked at them, sometimes trying to speak to them. Then she started to grab their shoulders, shaking them to get them to respond to her in any way. None of them did.

"No." Her voice waivered with a hint of rising panic. "Please. Not again."

Synderis snagged the cloak off one of her dream folk and pulled the hood up. He followed silently after her. It was only a dream, but dreams were fed by waking life. If she was using the magic this way in her dream, it was most likely a reflection of something that had occurred when she was awake.

A disembodied male voice spoke, sounding all around them then. "What did you do to them?" the speaker demanded.

"Phen," Aneiris called out, an edge of distress making her voice crack. She spun in a quick circle to look around her.

Synderis froze, glancing away at the last possible second so she wouldn't see his face and recognize that he didn't belong.

"Phendaril," she shouted, desperation raising her voice.

"What did you do to them?" Harsh judgment gave a sharp edge to every word.

"I don't know!" Moisture welled in her silver eyes when she glanced past him again.

Synderis drew on the magic, borrowing some from what she had put into the dream to spare himself effort and give it a familiarity that would be less likely to alarm her. When he pulled it in, the magic bore a tang of her unique energy that swept through him like a static shock, startling him with its vibrancy. As soon as she turned away again, he stepped up behind her and placed his hands on her arms, using power to pass a sense of comfort and safety through that contact. She froze beneath his touch.

He leaned close to her ear, catching the salty tang of horses overlying another scent that reminded him of the violet orchids growing near one of the pools in the deeper forest of his home. Though the association surprised him, he adhered to his purpose. She needed his discipline and focus. "You put the magic in them, Aneiris. You just have to take it back."

"Take it back," she murmured.

"Yes."

"No one calls me Aneiris," she said softly.

A shiver moved through the dreamscape. The other dreamwalker had arrived. With the cloak hiding what he was, it was unlikely the dreamwalker would suspect him of being anything other than one more part of her dream. Still, it was a bad idea to risk it. It was time for him to leave, and yet, he had to ask.

"What do they call you?" He leaned a little closer, whispering the question. That unexpected scent of the orchids baffled his senses, confusing his waking world and the dream.

"Raven."

Raven. He smiled. There was something endearing about the name. A nickname? Perhaps given by her mother, whom Dellaura said had a love of birds. It wasn't elven, but neither was she, at least not entirely. "The magic is yours, Raven. It's as much a part of you as your flesh and blood. You have the power to take it back."

"Of course." A hint of revelation and relief were apparent in her tone.

When she gave a slight nod, he pulled himself out of the dream. It was past time to go.

Raven snapped awake. It was still dark, a blanket of stars shining bright overhead. She had woken because of the watcher. Or at least, partly because of the watcher. The nightmare might have continued to run wild as it typically did if there hadn't been another presence there tonight. Male, judging by his voice. Though she never saw him in the dream, when he rested his hands on her arms and spoke to her, the fear dispersed like dandelion seeds before a stiff breeze. When had physical contact from a stranger ever helped calm her?

The newcomer also knew her birth name, which she supposed should have alarmed her, but it hadn't. He had felt safe and had told her how to fix what she had done. The only thing about the encounter that left her feeling ill at ease was his departure within minutes of the arrival of Wayland. Even the Silverblood priest's shadowy presence hadn't bothered her while the other was still there. In his absence, she sensed Wayland creeping closer. A flood of awful memories connected to him jolted her wake.

She sat up.

The stranger in her dream told her how to fix what she had done.

Raven got up from her sleeping roll. It was easier

tonight. Phendaril seemed less inclined to snuggle up to her after what she had done to the horses. In fact, he hadn't touched her at all since then, which was unusual for him. He usually couldn't get enough of being close to her. The sudden behavior change was jarring. It left her feeling hollow and alone, though that too had gone away for a moment with the stranger's gentle contact in her dream.

She walked over to where the animals stood staring ahead. They didn't react to her approach. Nor had they eaten or drunk since the earlier incident. They would move if directed, but that was about it. If something didn't change, it appeared they would let themselves die. Phendaril had chosen to lead them here, not wanting to risk exerting them as long as they were apparently incapable of tending to their own needs.

She remembered the voice from her dream, confident and kind.

"The magic is yours, Raven. It's as much a part of you as your flesh and blood. You have the power to take it back."

Closing her eyes, she touched the cloak pin. Whether or not she truly needed to use it to connect to the magic in her, focusing on it helped her do so. The power in her responded, waking slowly, like a cold serpent. As it uncoiled, it gradually extended beyond the boundaries of her body, reaching out to the part of itself that remained behind in the horses. A faint shocking sensation danced across her fingertips when the two portions connected. She drew back a little at a time, still focusing on the pin as a reference point. The magic returned to her, pulling into her chest.

The horses both startled in the same instant, tossing their heads back against their ties. The bay stomped his front hoof, and she reached out to him.

"Hush. I know." She did her best to mimic the soothing

tone Phendaril had used when they first encountered the animal. It responded, calming and letting her place a hand on its forehead as he had done. The other gelding followed the bay's example, relaxing its head forward. She placed her free hand on its neck, marveling at the strength of their reaction to physical contact. As big and powerful as they were, they had a surprising gentleness and an almost childlike need for reassurance. "I think I owe you both an apology. There's a creek nearby. The grass down there is some of the best I've seen."

She exhaled a laugh at the fact that she had noticed the quality of the grass. A byproduct of her guilt over what she had done to them undoubtedly.

"Just don't do anything unexpected." She started untying the ropes. "I've had enough excitement for one day."

"I can lead one."

Raven nearly jumped out of her skin. She couldn't remember the last time someone had snuck up on her that completely. Her attention was so wholly invested in the horses she hadn't heard him approach. Phendaril stepped out of the shadows, his expression unreadable. He held out a hand, and she gave him the lead to the rust-colored gelding.

He said nothing as he turned and led the animal to the creek. Raven placed a hand on the bay gelding's shoulder as she walked beside it, appreciating how his warm presence filled in a little of the lack of such from Phendaril. At least horses didn't appear to hold grudges, though she doubted they understood what had happened to them.

Both animals drank deeply from the creek before turning their enthusiastic efforts to the grass along its bank. Their ravenous eating did nothing to help alleviate the weight of guilt sitting heavy on her shoulders.

"You figured out how to reverse it?"

It had only been a dream, but she felt those hands on her arms as vividly as if they still rested there. Though the presence exuded a sense of safety, easing her panic and fear, those hands stopped her from turning around. Why? Who was the stranger that she responded to him that way? Or had he controlled her reaction somehow? She should probably tell Phendaril about it. As positive as the interaction seemed at the time, there could be something more sinister behind it.

She looked at him. In the moonlight, with her vision, she could see the lingering icy distance in his regard. A shield closed protectively around her heart. She glanced away from him, placing a hand on the gelding's warm shoulder again.

"I did," she stated simply.

"Good."

The sharpness in his tone drew her gaze back to him. "Why are you so upset with me?"

That anger blazed to life in his dark eyes, scalding in its intensity. "You took their will away, Raven. Any inclination to keep themselves alive disappeared. You effectively convinced them to let themselves die."

She flinched away from the horror of the truth in his words. "I didn't mean to."

"You realize that almost makes it worse. I'm glad you're not that cruel, but if you don't know what you did or how, what's to stop you from unintentionally doing it to one of us?" He gestured roughly to himself, then toward the camp where they had left Ehric. "What if you can't reverse it next time?"

Raven stepped back from him. Her chest felt as if it was collapsing. She couldn't get a full breath. Everything was closing in – the horses, Phendaril, the sky, and the ground under her feet – all contracting around her. She dropped the bay's rope and spun back toward the trees, only to slam into Ehric walking up behind her.

He caught her arms, keeping her from falling. "Are you all right?"

Why hadn't she heard him? Was it the power of her heartbeat pounding in her ears?

She twisted away. He wasn't strong enough to hold her if she didn't want to be held. Neither of them was. She bolted for the trees, ignoring the calls of her companions. At least one of them would have to stay behind to handle the horses. That increased her chances of putting distance between herself and them. She had to get away. Find a place where she could breathe and think.

She did what she had always done. The same behavior that led her parents to start calling her their "Little Raven" as a child. She climbed a tree and found a perch on one of the bigger branches, relaxing against the trunk. As a child, she was drawn to the trees. They became her place of sanctuary, a place to hide away and figure things out in peace.

Her thoughts wandered back to the dream. The stranger had known how to help her. He had recognized what was happening and knew how to fix it. He hadn't sounded afraid of the magic or angry with her for how she used it. Then again, it was possible she had simply made him up. In that moment, she had believed he was real, another individual who found his way into her dream like Wayland. That didn't make sense, though. No one else had a connection to her the way the Silverblood priest did. Besides, the solution to her problem struck her as simple now. It was an answer her unconscious mind might have come to on its own, using the stranger in her dream as a means for presenting the information.

She caught the sound of Phendaril's light footsteps approaching.

"Raven," he called softly.

She looked down at him. It irked her that he had gotten almost to the foot of the tree before she noticed him. He was elven and grew up scouting in the forests, but she wasn't usually this easy to sneak up on. She was distracted and tired. Her senses weren't focused.

She kept quiet, hoping he hadn't seen her yet and might pass by. He stopped below the tree, his elven vision picking her out of the shadows, then jumped up into the low branches and worked his way to a spot near her. He crouched on the branch, his intense gaze riveted on her. The way his head cocked slightly to one side made him appear a little more animal than elf.

"I've never heard of someone doing what you did to the horses. Was that some kind of Silverblood magic?"

Her jaw tightened convulsively. She didn't want to talk about it, but she got the feeling he wasn't going to let it go.

"Yes." At least, all evidence suggested it was.

"Can all Silverbloods do that?"

She considered Marek and the men she had met at the Brotherhood temple and shook her head. "I don't believe so. I think they would use it more if they had that power." She twisted around and dropped from the branch, catching hold of it with her hands. From there, she made a hasty descent to the ground.

Phendaril landed next to her a few seconds later. He eyed her thoughtfully. "Maybe that's why women and elves aren't made Silverblood. Maybe it gives them different kinds of power."

She gave a curt shake of her head. "No. I don't think that's it. Wayland would have told me if that were the case."

Phendaril's eyes narrowed. "Why? Because you two were such good friends, he would tell you all their secrets?"

Red exploded across her vision. "Don't mock me! You have no idea how terrified I was. Nothing has ever scared me like he does, but I was willing to die at his hands to keep you safe."

His expression changed in a second, and he reached for her. She took a few abrupt steps back from him. Her throat constricted with the memory of Wayland holding her up against the bookcase, his hand tightening around her neck while her feet dangled a foot above the floor. The Silverblood Priest had been so fast and so strong. Her fingers moved up to touch her neck, remembering the pain. Tears spilled down her cheeks. She hated those tears, but the anger scared her now more than ever. What if she did do what she had done to the horses to Phendaril? That, or something worse.

"Wait." He held a hand up in a staying gesture. "Raven, what do you mean you were *willing to die?*"

She shook her head at him. "Did you honestly believe I thought I could defeat him? I attacked him that night to force his hand. He was going to kill me regardless. I tried to get him to do it sooner before you could get killed trying to rescue me. I never expected to live through it."

Phendaril stepped closer to her and wrapped his arms around her, pulling her against his lean, warm chest. He held her tight – so tight – and she found a sweet sense of security in that embrace. "I'm sorry. I didn't know."

She closed her eyes, breathing in the scent of him. The red faded away. "Of course you didn't. I never told you."

He was trembling now. Something wet dripped on her head. Was he crying?

"I failed you."

The pain in his voice tore through her. She should never have told him that truth. The female he had intended to life-bond with years ago killed herself after being raped. What Raven had done had also been an attempt to kill herself. More than an attempt, really, since she had died briefly. She did it because she didn't believe she could escape the Brotherhood alive and didn't want Phendaril to die for a hopeless cause. To him, however, was there any difference between what she had done and what his former love had done? The way he clung to her now told her there wasn't.

"You didn't fail me." She wriggled her way free and looked him in the eyes, placing a hand on the side of his face. The dampness of tears under her fingers made her chest ache. "You didn't fail me, Phen."

"I left you in town with Marek that day because I was a jealous fool." His voice cracked, the power of a long-held shame breaking through.

"Marek knew what he was doing. He played us both into his plan. It wasn't your fault."

He brushed his fingers across her cheek in a light caress. "I wish I could make myself believe that."

Raven shook her head and made herself smile up at him, though sorrow stole through her. Would he trust her again after what had happened today? Would he ever forget what she had done? "I love you."

He kissed her. She wasn't sure if it was his tears or her own that she tasted on his lips.

"Heleath le'athana," he murmured.

Raven flashed back to her mother for an instant. The words were elven. The sentiment expressed a connection of love blessed by nature. She hadn't heard it since the morning she left to go hunting with her father when she was eight years old, right after her mother wished them a good hunt. She had leaned down, taken Raven's hands in hers, and spoken those words before placing a kiss on her head. The memory was so vivid she could feel her mother's lips on her brow.

Unprepared to face Ehric or even the horses, she slipped back into Phendaril's embrace and clung to him. He held her for a long time until he eventually eased himself away and led her back to the campsite. Ehric had returned and tied the horses loosely so they could continue grazing. Phendaril moved his sleeping roll up next to hers, and they drifted off in each other's arms.

Not long after she fell asleep, her watcher returned. The shadowy form of the Silverblood priest lurking around the edges of every dreaming moment, his silver eyes tormenting her rest. She woke to lay staring at the stars, wishing each sound – each movement of a leaf on the breeze or a bat flitting past – didn't strike panic through her.

When morning came, exhaustion dragged at her, but she made herself ready to move on. One way or another, she was going to find her mother's family, hopefully before Wayland figured out how to find her.

CHAPTER ELEVEN

Synderis approached the temple, drawing on the calm of the surrounding forest for guidance and serenity within that sacred space. The temple itself wasn't a building. It was a natural clearing enclosed in a ring of towering evergreens, their draping fronds creating the soaring heights of the temple walls. A shimmering white stone path led between the two trees that framed the entrance. Inside, it continued over a small bridge made of a single slab of white stone set across a crystalline stream. The same stream fed into the pool he had been at with the twins the day before. Beyond the stream, the path led to an ornate arch of woven white branches.

Beneath that arch stood the Delegate. She turned to watch him approach, her face a mask of patience and tranquility. She wore pale white robes with a silver shine, almost the exact color of her light skin, which also had a faint silvery sheen. Her hair and eyes – even her fingernails – were like liquid silver, glinting in the noon sun that shone down through the trees. Her delicate lips, curved with the barest hint of a smile, had a silvery gloss to them.

She was at least two hundred years old – though none of that age showed in her features – and sacred to their people. To the Krivalen in particular, she was a spiritual leader. Being in her presence was enough to take his breath away.

"Synderis," she greeted him, her voice clear and resonant.

"Delegate." He inclined his head.

"Dellaura told me her granddaughter lives. She said that she asked you to dreamwalk her. I sense there is much more to this than what she disclosed to me. Something about this situation casts a shadow over your heart."

Relief swept through him, knowing he didn't have to expose Dellaura's secret. She had spoken to the Delegate as she promised.

The Delegate held a hand out to him, palm up, and he placed his hand in hers, allowing her to guide him away from the archway toward a pedestal near the creek. A shallow, white stone basin rested on top. An ivory bird with wings tipped in the brightest blue was dipping its beak in the water that filled the bowl as they approached.

The Delegate released his hand as she held her other hand out to the delicate creature. It hopped up onto her finger and began preening its wings. She smiled at the little bird before facing Synderis.

"Tell me what worries you." Her gaze moved through him, drawing out the emotions accompanying his thoughts. He had no secrets the Delegate couldn't know if she wished to. Every Krivalen in Eyl'Thelandra was connected to her by the magic that made them.

He always struggled with an impulse to kneel when speaking with her. How could he face her as an equal? She carried a part of many of their ancestors within her. Yet she often stated that she didn't require such deference. Even so, he kept his head inclined slightly, offering her that respect.

"I've dreamwalked her granddaughter twice now. Both times, there was someone else there. A human

Silverblood who's connected to her somehow, though his presence in her dreams doesn't appear intentional. Whoever he is, he can't control his appearance or movement in the dreams."

The Delegate nodded, her gaze returning to the bird. The gentlest of smiles touched her lips as the creature stopped preening and tilted its head to look up at her.

When she didn't speak, Synderis continued. "Last night, when I dreamwalked her, she appeared to be struggling with the Krivalen magic, as if she had used it without meaning to in the waking world and wanted to undo whatever she had done."

The Delegate's perfect eyebrows rose a fraction at this. "Used it how?"

"In the dream, she seemed overwhelmed by the people around her. She used the magic to strip their free will from them."

The Delegate's lips pressed together for a moment. She lowered the bird back to the edge of the bowl, waiting until it left her finger to turn to him. "This young half-elf poses a much greater threat than Dellaura realizes."

He nodded with reluctance. Guilt created an uncomfortable twisting sensation in his chest, not because of what this would mean for Dellaura, though. It had more to do with what it might mean for Aneiris. Raven, he supposed, since she seemed to prefer that name.

"I haven't mentioned this to Dellaura yet."

"I know." She started walking back toward the arch.

Synderis followed. "It's much too dangerous to talk to her with the Silverblood there," he prompted.

"And yet we can't allow her to go unchecked if she's learning how to use the Krivalen power on her own. She has elven blood in her. The magic must be responding to that, but it would have taken something traumatic to awaken it like this." She stopped before the arch, gazing up at the towering trees. "She already has the attention of the Brotherhood. Her other dreamwalker tells us that much. If they learn what she can do, they will stop at nothing to attain that knowledge for themselves. We must not allow them to get it." She faced him.

Fear for Raven brought a metallic taste to his mouth. He met the Delegate's eyes, and her calm, confident regard battered it back. Relief rose in him with the certainty that she would know what to do. She would find a solution to this dilemma.

She reached out and took hold of the talisman hanging around his neck, her fingers cold against his skin, leaving a chill in their wake. Her brow furrowed as she gazed down at the benign-looking object. She closed her fingers around it and closed her eyes. Synderis waited, unease digging its claws deeper into him the longer she stood that way. When her eyes opened, she carefully set the talisman back to rest against his skin, that chill following her touch again.

"We should be able to break the connection to the Silverblood, but only if she comes here, and she *must* come here. She is a danger to all of us if she starts using other Krivalen magic out in the world."

"But how do I bring her here while the stranger stalks her dreams?"

She touched his cheek, her fingers like ice against that sensitive skin. "He won't always be there. He can't be asleep every moment that she is. Someone will have to dreamwalk her. Every night, perhaps several times a night, at least until they get the chance to approach her without the other present. Is this a task you are willing to take on? You do not have to, Synderis. I can easily pass it to another."

He tried to hide his disappointment. He had been sure she would have a quick and easy solution, but she only told him what he had already figured out on his own. Now, if he continued, any mistake could put all of Eyl'Thelandra in danger, and it would be on his head. They would all know it was his fault. But Dellaura trusted him with her granddaughter. More importantly, the Delegate was willing to trust him with this important task. That trust wasn't something to turn away lightly.

Besides, the thought of someone else dreamwalking Raven made him uncomfortable in a way he didn't quite understand. She had been through a great deal. His two experiences with her barely scratched the surface of her pain. He had managed one brief but successful connection with her. When haste was called for, it didn't make sense to ask someone else to start the process over, did it? He was a skilled dreamwalker. One of the best among the Krivalen. Besides, to leave her in someone else's hands and walk away seemed cruel when he had already planted the seeds of curiosity and trust between them.

The Delegate was smiling at him when he emerged from his thoughts. "Thank you, Synderis. Keep us informed of your progress and any problems you encounter. You are not alone in this."

He inclined his head. "I will. Thank you for your time, Delegate."

"You are always welcome."

He turned and strode away, taking hold of the talisman that hung around his neck. It was still cold from her touch. He would do whatever it took to show the Delegate and Dellaura that they had made the right choice. He would rescue Raven from the danger that haunted her dreams and bring her to Eyl'Thelandra.

•

Karsima stalked toward their house. Alayne stood outside, two younger-looking Silverbloods next to her. Acolytes, perhaps. The men waited perfectly still, watching the activity in the square with their eerie silver eyes. Alayne, a step in front of them, rolled her eyes dramatically.

Karsima struggled not to smile. Silverbloods were no laughing matter. Since Marek, she preferred to keep them out of Amberwood altogether, excepting Raven, of course. Although, technically, she did have to give Marek credit for warning them about the Brotherhood priest's survival and renewed interest in Raven. If not for him, they wouldn't have known to expect the Silverbloods poking around again, and Raven might still be here where they were far more likely to find her.

"Gentlemen." She gave them each a nod. "I'm Karsima, the constable here in Amberwood. I understand you wanted to speak to me."

The darker-haired of the two stepped forward. "Silverblood Acolyte Olwen."

The other, his hair a dirty blond, stepped forward in turn. "Silverblood Acolyte Damen."

She gave another nod and gestured to the door. "Come inside."

Alayne entered ahead of them, leading the way to the office that had become as much of a shared space for them as the bedroom, though its uses were less fun... most of the time.

She grinned to herself, trying not to think too deeply of those more delightful moments that had occurred in their office, and followed the two acolytes in. Jenner had snuck in a second chair on the other side of her desk. She would have to thank him later, even though the two men opted to stay standing behind the chairs. She wasn't about to let them determine the mood for the encounter, so she walked around the desk and sat. Alayne leaned against the wall a little to her left, one hand casually rested on the hilt of her sword.

"How can I assist the Brotherhood?" Karsima asked after a few seconds spent moving a few roughly sketched maps off her desk and into one of the drawers. It pleased her to see how many tagged threats they had crossed out on those maps. Her favorite map she left out. That one showed the state of the town itself. How many shops were up and running. How many homes were restored enough to be lived in, and how many residents had moved into.

"We're looking for Aneiris Darrenton. We know she was living in Amberwood."

Karsima offered a tight smile. "Was," she emphasized. "As far as I know, she died when they took her to the Brotherhood several months ago. Thank you for bringing it up, though. I hadn't yet had a reason to be sad and pissed off today."

Acolyte Olwen smirked at her. "None of the lies your people spin are going to stand up to our investigation. If she's here, we will find her."

"Amberwood is in protected neutral territory. You don't have jurisdiction here, but even if you did, you wouldn't find her. Raven isn't here."

Olwen narrowed his eyes at her. "Where did she go?"

Karsima glared back at him. "You have your answer."

Olwen smirked at her again, then his features turned cold.

Damen, who had worn that same unreadable expression a moment ago, looked down at her. "What about the elf? The one who took her from the courtyard. Phendaril, I believe."

Karsima cursed Marek in her head. He had to be the reason they knew Phendaril's name. "He's not here. He went with one of our ships to barter for supplies in Chadhurst."

"Is she with him?"

"If this pointless interrogation is the only reason you're here, you can see yourselves out now."

Damen and Olwen smiled then, and the expression made her highly uncomfortable.

"This is neutral territory, as you pointed out." Damen held that falsely pleasant smile as he spoke. His gaze flickered to Alayne with a hint of open disdain. "King Navaran may have granted his niece ownership of it for now, but would he hesitate to issue a new deed if the Brotherhood expressed an interest in these lands? Amberwood is only yours so long as Father Mallebron doesn't see a need to take it from you."

She managed to muster up a smug look as she sat back in her chair and crossed her arms. "I find it amusing how convinced you all are that this half-elven female survived a fight with the head priest of your temple."

Anger cast a dark shadow over Damen's features. He spun on the ball of one foot and stormed toward the door.

Olwen smiled and inclined his head in a slight nod. "A pleasant day to you, Lady Karsima." With that, he followed his companion from the room.

Karsima stood abruptly, grabbing the dagger she kept hidden under her desk as she rose.

Alayne caught her shoulder and muttered under her breath, "Don't. We can't win this with blood."

Karsima looked into her eyes, hoping to find reassurance there, but the look of dread that met her made her stomach turn.

"They didn't get anything useful this time. Let's not antagonize them further."

"Do you think the kings would give them Amberwood?" Karsima's throat was tight as she asked it.

Alayne peered out the window. Karsima followed her gaze, watching the two men striding across the square toward the edge of town.

"I believe King Saldin would. As for my uncle, I'd like to think family ties would hold up against the wealth and influence of the Brotherhood, but I'm not sure they would."

A soft knock drew her attention back to the open doorway. Jenner stood there, hat in his hands and brown hair in disarray. Veylin and Jael stood behind him. Both wore leather scout armor, and their long hair braided back.

"Milady..."

Karsima nodded wearily, and Jenner moved to the side to let the two scouts in. She gave a nod of greeting to each of them, wishing either of them was Phendaril. She hadn't expected to miss having him around this much, especially with Alayne there, but everything seemed more difficult without him.

"What's going on?" she asked, trying to convey strength and confidence in her voice that she didn't feel.

"It's Darrenton's men again," Jael stated.

Alayne lifted her lip in a sneer. "Are they hunting on our land again?"

"Not exactly." He glanced at Veylin.

She stepped forward. "We've seen them inside our borders several times lately, but they don't seem to be hunting. Well, not game anyway. So we decided to conduct a little experiment. I went out on a solo patrol near the border."

"And I followed secretly, keeping out of sight," Jael added.

"What we found is that it is us that they seem to be hunting. They're following our routes and watching us."

Veylin's words sent a chill through Karsima. She didn't have a sound reason to forbid outsiders from entering Amberwood, as long as they weren't hunting or causing problems. And yet she could come up with no benign motive for them to be tracking her scouts, though the act of doing so wasn't openly hostile. If they retaliated against Darrenton's men simply for that, it would create a more antagonistic relationship with their new neighbor. She didn't like it, though. What reason did Darrenton even have for purchasing that land? It might be developed into decent cropland, but nothing there was worth much otherwise.

"I don't think we should do anything aggressive at this point. Keep an eye on them. Send all patrols out in pairs. If you see one of his men even draw a weapon while on our land, you have my permission to bring them in for questioning."

Both scouts nodded and began to turn away.

"Also…" She waited until she had their full attention again. "Please be careful. I don't trust Darrenton."

Jael smirked. "Neither do we. Don't worry, we'll watch each other's backs and yours."

Karsima watched them leave. Alayne put an arm around her shoulders. "Phen will come back as soon as he can. In the meantime, maybe I can find a way to ease your mind."

Karsima turned and slid her hands around Alayne's waist. "I bet you can," she murmured. She pulled her into a deep kiss, her worries fading before the unending joy of having the woman she loved by her side.

Phendaril held the bay's reins and gave Raven a nod. She looked up at the saddle. The seat appeared higher up without Phendaril sitting in it. Or maybe that was a lack of sleep playing with her mind.

After two long days on the road, they were finally within a day's leisurely ride out from Lathwood according to Phendaril. The last two nights, she hadn't slept much. Every time she slipped into a dreaming state, the shadowy watcher with his silver eyes, the one she was now certain was Wayland, was there trying to reach her. Worse, he was becoming a little more solid every night and managed to get closer to her than ever before last night before flickering to another location in her dreamscape. The stranger who helped her with the magic hadn't appeared to her again, though he wasn't getting much chance. She couldn't stay asleep with Wayland's shadow form there. Convincing herself to fall asleep at all was becoming an increasing challenge.

She eyed the horse standing quietly there, unlike Ehric's gelding, who stomped impatiently and pranced in place.

"He should have a name."

Phendaril's eyes sparkled with the laughter he was holding back. He'd been more affectionate toward her since their talk about the night she faced Wayland. Almost to the point of being too attentive. "He should. You can discuss that with him once we're moving. We did want to make Lathwood by dark, didn't we?"

She rolled her eyes at him and reached up to grab the front of the saddle. Putting her foot in the stirrup, she swung up and over, settling in the seat as lightly as possible. She wanted it to be a positive experience for the animal in the hope that he would return the favor.

"Gracefully done," Phendaril praised, holding the reins up to her.

Raven stared at them and shook her head. "I thought you were going to lead him."

His smile was patient while he kept the reins extended to her. "You are the same woman who threw herself in front of a wyvern to save an elven healer she barely knew, right?"

"An elven healer who was flirting with you," she added acerbically.

His brows rose, a pleased smile tugging at the corners of his mouth. "You were jealous? Even back then?"

Raven's face grew hot. She grabbed the reins and considered kicking the gelding to flee her embarrassment, but a jolt of fear shot through her chest, and she stopped before making contact. Ehric chuckled, and she cast a withering glance his way. He hastily altered the chuckle, turning it into a cough into his hand, then stared ahead.

Looking a little too pleased, Phendaril faced forward and began strolling down the road. Ehric urged his mount to follow. The bay joined them without any input from her.

They continued that way for most of the morning. Raven slowly settled into the gelding's movement the way she had when riding behind Phendaril. It was different, being alone up there, but she knew the basics of how to control him. Phendaril had been schooling her on it over the last two days. In reality, she had to do very little as long as Ehric guided his mount alongside her. The bay was more than happy to stick close to the other horse.

After a noon rest, Phendaril traded places with her. She handed him the reins and informed him that the horse's name was now Dusk. They were trying to give the gelding a break from carrying both of them, so she walked for a time. After they intersected with the main road leading into Lathwood, she swung up behind Ehric on his gelding and pulled her cloak hood forward. She had named his horse Autumn for the rust-red color of his coat.

The forest gave way to open grasslands and more frequent farms. Traffic increased significantly with people traveling alone or in groups on foot and horseback or sometimes in wagons. A few waved or offered polite nods in passing. Others offered nothing, focusing on their own business. They did receive several longer looks. An elf, a Stonebreaker, and a female hidden in her cloak. Though elves were more common here than in Andel and more societally accepted, they still struggled to find work outside servant-class jobs and represented the minority in all but the poorest sections of town. Being mounted and well-armed marked Phendaril as an outsider here.

Stonebreakers weren't overly common in Lathwood, though some clans lived in the grasslands to the south of the city. Ehric was still human. Fortunately for him, being a Stonebreaker was far less offensive than having pointed ears, faster reflexes, and superior low-light vision. The longer lifespan of elves was a problem too. Humans resented it. Of all the ways to offend humans, being born an elf was one of the worst, second only to being born a half-breed, which was equally offensive to the elves in some circles.

When the town came into view as evening started to lay its blanket over the landscape, she switched horses, climbing up behind Phendaril. Lathwood was larger than Andel, though Phendaril told her Amberwood had been of comparable size before its destruction. When they finished rebuilding, it might be this big again. She tried to convince herself this was an excellent opportunity to adjust to that idea.

She tugged her hood farther forward when they entered the town proper, riding into the mucky outer streets. People on foot were well-positioned to look up into the shadows of her hood, so she kept her head down and closed her eyes if they passed too close to anyone, despite how unnerving it was to be robbed of her sight for seconds at a time. They continued into the nicer parts of town, where the streets grew wider but somehow more crowded. She shifted closer to Phendaril, using his back and the edges of her hood to create a barrier that blocked her from the view of strangers as much as it blocked them from hers. The many voices blended into a loud cacophony around her, overpowered only by the pounding of her own blood in her ears. Anxiety was spiking, making her breath come in quick, panicked gasps. She squeezed her arms tighter around Phendaril. He placed a comforting hand on her arm. That simple touch slowed her heartbeat and made it possible for her to breathe again.

It felt like an eternity before they stopped next to a tavern. Attentive to Raven's emotional state, Ehric came to help her down between the two horses, hiding her from view. They had discussed securing a room in town to facilitate asking around about her father's family in the morning. Now it didn't seem like such a clever idea.

Once Phendaril dismounted and came to stand with her, Ehric disappeared inside to check for a room. Phendaril slipped his hand into hers and gave it a squeeze.

"Are you all right?"

She tried to keep her voice steady. "I'm just not used to so many people. It's so much bigger than Amberwood."

He smiled wistfully. "You should have seen Amberwood when I was a child. It was at least as big as Lathwood and so much more beautiful. There wasn't all this separation between humans and elves either. It will be that way again." His smile faded after a few seconds.

Now Raven squeezed his hand. "You will get back there. I promise."

He smiled again, though it didn't quite reach his eyes this time. Ehric walked out then, giving them a nod. Raven stuck to the shadows while they got the horses settled into the stable now that they were officially guests. It irked her that Ehric and Phendaril had to do all the communicating with strangers to keep her Silverblood nature from being discovered. That irritation in itself was confusing, given that she didn't actually *want* to talk to strangers. What she wanted was to be a valuable part of the group.

The tavern was larger than The Bear and Raven, although the main room full of tables and patrons gave the illusion of being smaller without the center open to the upper floor. A band of minstrels played on a stage in the back while people ate, drank, talked, and gambled at the many tables. There wasn't much time to take in the scene. Ehric escorted them hastily across the common area and up a set of stairs, stopping at the third door on the left. Once she was in the room, Phendaril and Ehric headed down to find them something to eat.

The room was clean, and the beds were as nice as the one they had in their house in Amberwood. It was an outer room, which meant it had a window. Whether Ehric had asked for that, or they had simply gotten lucky, Raven appreciated it. Being able to see outside made her feel a little less trapped. She stripped off her leather armor and then took advantage of the moment of privacy to wipe away sweat and dirt at a basin on the vanity set against one wall.

When they returned, she was standing by the window gazing down at the people in the street, her cloak back on and the hood pulled up. Even from here, someone might catch the glint of the silver in her hair or eyes, so she tried to be careful. A fair number of folks wandered in and out of the tavern or gathered out front in the light that spilled into the street after dark fell.

They dined on a stew that probably wasn't as delicious as it tasted after days of travel rations and unseasoned meat. Once they had eaten and taken a few minutes to digest, Ehric stood up and collected their plates.

"I'm going downstairs to watch the musicians and have a drink." He met her eyes, then Phendaril's, and offered an encouraging smile. "I'll probably be gone a couple of hours."

Phendaril breathed a laugh. Raven gave a shake of her head that she hoped didn't negate the appreciation in her return smile. The instant the door shut behind him, Phendaril gave her a relaxed, amorous grin that made her skin prickle with anticipation. He sauntered over to where she was sitting at the head of one of the beds.

Despite the unconcealed desire in his regard, he simply sat on the edge of the bed next to her and brushed a strand of hair from her face with gentle fingers. "How are you holding up, my love?"

"I'm afraid," she blurted. She hadn't meant to use this rare moment alone to bring that up, but something in his expression told her that was why he asked.

He took her hands in his. "Afraid of what?"

"Afraid of the presence in my dreams. Afraid we won't be able to find my mother's family. Afraid that

I'm putting you in danger. Afraid, more than anything else, that you'll resent me for taking you away from everyone and everything you love." Tears stung her eyes when she finished, and she glanced away.

"Raven. Please look at me." The weight in his tone pulled her attention back. "I love you. The other things and people I love don't need me like you do now. They'll be fine while you and I figure this out together." A fierce determination shone in his dark eyes that contradicted the extraordinary gentleness with which his hands held hers.

"Even though you had to come back here—"

He leaned in and cut her off with a kiss. It was amazing to her that he could light her on fire with a simple kiss when he wanted to. When he started to draw back from the kiss, she moved with him, flicking her tongue teasingly across his lips. The desire that burned through her blazed to life in his eyes, and he corrected his course, kissing her more deeply this time. Raven opened her mouth to him and sank back on the bed, drawing him down with her. Tonight, for a little while, she was determined to forget everything else and be with him.

•

Raven stood on the third-floor balcony overlooking the entrance hall of the Silverblood Brotherhood temple. It was empty below now, but she suspected it wouldn't be long before Wayland appeared. The previous time she was here, in the waking world, Alayne and Lord Darrenton had been below, making a plea for her life before Father Wayland Mallebron. Phendaril and Ehric were also there then, acting as Alayne's guards. On that day, Marek brought her to this room. He had stood behind her with a hand on her shoulder while she watched her companions from the shadows. This time, she was alone.

A hand came to rest on her shoulder. Raven startled, spinning and retreating a step out of habit to give herself room to fight. Her hand reflexively dropped to where her sword would be. Then her breath caught in her throat.

The man behind her this time was a Silverblood, but that was where the similarities between him and Marek ended. He was tall and lean. His long white hair had the faintest silvery shine, a braided lock hanging in front of his elegantly tapered elven ears on either side. The lines of his face were bold, with that distinct elven angularity, his skin smooth. His features possessed a touch of beauty, though not in a particularly feminine way. She didn't have to ask to know he was the one who had helped her with the magic. That same sense of safety and comfort emanated from him.

There was a distinct sound of relief in the soft exhalation that preceded his smile. "Finally," he murmured.

"You're a Silverblood elf?" She couldn't stop staring at those silver eyes, their bright color complimented by thick, dark lashes.

His distracted nod suggested that his being a Silverblood was nothing significant to him. He glanced around them, a few fine lines creasing his brow. "What is this place?"

"Who are you?"

His silver eyes focused on her again. "Yes. That first. I'm Synderis. I've been trying to dreamwalk you for a while, but there's always someone else here."

"Dreamwalk?" Raven gave herself a shake. An elven Silverblood was talking to her in a dream about things that made no sense. This couldn't be real.

His expression turned apologetic. "Explanations will have to wait. Do you know who the one invading your dreams is? Other than myself, of course," he added.

His warm, encouraging smile made her feel like she

could tell him anything. "I do."

"We can help you sever that connection, but you need to come to us first." He glanced around again, a troubled frown pulling at his lips.

Perhaps he sensed the same disruption in her dreamscape she did. "Who is we? Where do I find you?"

He cursed under his breath at the same instant that unwelcome presence fully entered her dream. His movements took on the speed of urgency as he dug under his shirt and lifted out a chain. On it hung a pendant that was the twin to the cloak pin she wore.

"Keep yours close." Frustration showed in the tightness of his jaw and around his eyes as he disappeared.

Below her, on the dais at the back of the room, the shadowy figure with silver eyes had appeared. She pushed herself against the wall, memories of Wayland and the terrifying power he wielded sweeping in around her. Placing her hand over the cloak pin, she snapped awake.

●

Ehric was asleep, snoring contentedly in the next bed. Phendaril's naked warmth pressed against her back, his breathing slow and even. On the floor beside the bed lay her cloak. She reached down and pulled it up on the bed. Grasping the cloak pin in one hand, she pressed it to her chest and stared into the darkness.

Could Synderis be real?

She needed him to be real and not merely a figment of a desperate mind. On the off chance he was, she would do as he said and keep the cloak pin close until he came back.

ynderis finished stringing his bow. He didn't expect trouble, but wasn't that when it was most likely to appear?

His brother, Kelwyn, reclined against a tree, chewing at a piece of grass as he watched him. The eldest and the tallest, though only by a small margin, Kelwyn, with his lanky figure, always managed to appear relaxed.

"You look a little tired, brother." Kelwyn spit out the grass and pushed away from the tree to join Synderis as he started his patrol circuit.

Technically, scouts weren't supposed to have company on patrol unless another scout was assigned to be there. In this case, Synderis suspected the distraction of someone to talk to might be a boon, helping to keep his sleepy mind from drifting off. Besides, Kelwyn wasn't hopeless with a blade. It could be argued that he was at least a skilled companion.

"I am," he answered a little more curtly than he had intended. Trying to communicate with Raven was becoming an exhausting task. Every time he ended up abandoning the dream because of the other presence. Last night at least, he had managed to talk to her for a few minutes on his first attempt. Not nearly long enough. She had seemed amazed by the fact that he was Krivalen. The hopeful look and the awe in her voice were so candid and poignantly endearing.

"What are you smiling about, then?" Kelwyn smirked at him, his eyes narrowing with friendly suspicion.

Synderis allowed himself to feel his weariness, letting that sober his expression. "Nothing. I managed to speak with her last night, but the Silverblood appeared before I could accomplish much."

"It hasn't been that long." Kelwyn gave him a firm pat on the shoulder. "You'll get another chance soon."

"She seems bright and willing to listen. I think she would catch on to things quickly if I just had a few minutes more." That instant of intense frustration when he had to leave the dream swept back through him. He yearned for something to take it out on. Anything.

A trio of autumn leaves dropped from one of the trees up ahead. He raised his bow and fired off three arrows in quick succession, pinning all three leaves to the tree's trunk in a close line.

Kelwyn chuckled. "You do seem a little tense. Perhaps you should take a night off for the sake of innocent foliage everywhere."

Synderis gave a tired laugh, eyeing the line of executed leaves. "I might consider that."

They walked to the tree, and Kelwyn helped him pull the arrows. They were embedded deep in the wood, so it took some effort to work them out, attesting to the power behind the shots. Without the added Krivalen strength, it took Kelwyn longer. He handed the one arrow he had pulled to Synderis to return to his quiver with the other two.

"Impeccable archery, though. You might be the fastest draw out of all the Krivalen."

Synderis shook his head and started walking again, guiding them back on route. "Telandora has me beat."

Kelwyn grinned at him. "I hear her sister Ilanya is thinking of becoming Krivalen too."

Synderis gave him a warning look. "Don't start. I'm not looking for a relationship right now. It isn't like you'll get any nieces or nephews out of the deal anyhow. Besides, Ilanya will face an uphill battle in convincing her parents and the council to go along with it. They already have one Krivalen in the family."

They continued in silence for a time, the robust scent of evergreens filling the forest. Kelwyn started singing an elven folk song. Synderis smiled, breathing in the fresh air and enjoying the sounds of the forest that moved through and around Kelwyn's song. He did have a soothing voice. His daughters shared his penchant for music. Their young, vibrant voices made them a great accompaniment in his songs. Synderis loved teasing a song out of the three of them whenever he visited their home near the central part of the village. All he had to do was weave a piece of a song lyric into something he said. One of them was sure to pick it up within seconds, and they would be off and singing.

Kelwyn stopped singing as he ducked under a low-hanging branch and glanced over at him. "Maybe if you were life-bonded, you would spend less time alone out here."

"I'm a scout. This is my job. Besides, I like spending time alone out here. I get the feeling my time alone bothers you far more than it does me, brother." He smirked at Kelwyn's scowl.

The sound of something shifting in the brush caught his attention. There was a difference between the normal noises animals made traveling through the forest and the sound a predator made creeping through the undergrowth when stalking prey. Kelwyn opened his mouth to speak, and Synderis brought a finger to his lips, gesturing him to silence. With another quick gesture, he signaled him to stay where he was. Then he slipped into the bushes and up into a tree for a better vantage.

It took a moment to spot the creature, even with his enhanced vision. A movement in the brush to the right of where Kelwyn waited caught his eye. With a coat of leaf-shaped green feathers instead of fur, the lalyx cat was nearly invisible in the undergrowth. As he'd hoped, it decided to stalk Kelwyn after he left. It lifted its black nose, sniffing for danger, but Synderis had deliberately placed himself downwind.

"Syn, this isn't amusing." Kelwyn was turning in a slow circle, peering into the trees.

The cat charged. Synderis dropped from his perch. It bunched, ready to lunge at Kelwyn, who jumped back in surprise. When Synderis landed, the big cat twisted around, snarling at him. He drew on his magic and thrust it into the animal, willing it to silence and calm. The animal stilled, the threat vanishing from its posture. Its long, feathered tail drooped to the ground.

Kelwyn narrowed his eyes at Synderis. "Did you just use me as bait?"

Synderis did his best to stifle a grin. "You wanted to help with my patrol." He strolled up to the cat, admiring that magnificent coat that acted as camouflage in the dense foliage of the forest. The animal was easily as tall as his hip at the shoulder, with tufted ears and a long tail for balance. The broad paws had longer toes than other species of wild cats, designed for gripping branches. One of those remarkable paws had an open wound on it.

He knelt next to the cat. It remained docile, held in the thrall of Krivalen magic. It was tempting to stroke that fantastic coat, but the power to do what he had done wasn't a thing to be abused. Less contact was always better for the animal. In this rare case, however, he might be able to do something beneficial for it.

He lifted the injured paw and took a closer look. One of the toes grew at a strange angle as if it had broken at some point and healed wrong. The claw appeared unable to retract. As a result, it had grown around into the paw itself, creating a perpetually open wound.

"You poor thing," he murmured.

Kelwyn sat heavily on a stump. "Poor thing was going to eat your brother."

Synderis chuckled. "I wasn't going to let it eat you. Can I have that little boot dagger you always carry?"

He dug the dagger out of his boot and offered the hilt to Synderis. "Of course. Since your daggers are all too thick and sexy for such work."

Synderis laughed and rolled his eyes at his brother. "Are you done?"

"Oh, hardly. I think this deserves some extended suffering on your part."

Turning his attention to the cat, he eased the dagger's point under the claw and cut through it as close to the quick as he dared. Then he drew the tip out of the paw. With that done, he wiped a dab of salve over the wound and sat back on his heels to consider the animal. The claw was going to grow out again. It would continue to plague the poor creature and could eventually lead to its death, especially if it infected.

Normally, he would move away now and pull the magic back out of the animal, encouraging it to flee as he did so. He only took most of the magic out this time, leaving a trace behind to identify himself as a friend in the creature's mind. If he could convince it that he was safe to approach in times of need, he might be able to continue helping it.

The cat shook itself suddenly, feathers flaring over its back and shoulders before settling down again. It met his gaze, its brilliant blue-green eyes soft as it considered him. Then it turned and, upon seeing Kelwyn there, hissed and bolted into the trees.

"Oh, nice." Kelwyn gestured after the cat. "You get

the warm, new-best-friend look, and I get the 'I'll eat you later' hiss."

"Well," Synderis said as he stood, "I helped it by fixing its paw. You failed it by refusing to become dinner."

"And I would do so again," he said, accepting the dagger Synderis handed back to him.

Synderis only smiled and resumed his patrol, Kelwyn falling into step beside him again.

"What's she like?"

He hoped his brother didn't catch the slight misstep that question caused. "Dellaura's granddaughter?"

"Who else? She's a half-breed, right? Is she more elven or human?"

Synderis fought to tone down his smile. "She appears to take after her mother. I'd say she looks almost all elven, except for a hint of softness to her cheekbones and jaw that betrays her human blood. She wears it quite well, though."

"She's Krivalen?"

"Yes." He could still see those bright silver eyes staring at him as if she meant to drag out all his secrets with only a look. Given more time, she might do just that. "There were five who died when she was made. From the looks of her, I would guess the magic absorbed three, maybe four of their lives."

"And the problem is that she has a friend in the dreamscape getting in the way?"

He shook his head firmly at Kelwyn, a little surprised at the ire that rose in him at the thought of Raven's dream stalker. "Definitely not a friend."

Kelwyn gave him a long, thoughtful look. "You need a break, Syn. Come into town. Share a drink with me tonight. Have a relaxing evening and give yourself the night off. She'll be there tomorrow night, ready to frustrate you all over again. I think even the Delegate would prefer that to you burning yourself out."

Synderis turned away from Kelwyn, pretending interest in a rabbit that darted between two trees so the other male wouldn't see him bring his hand up to touch the talisman through his shirt. Would she be all right? Would it matter if he took one night to relax and get some real rest? If it concerned him this much, maybe that was a sign that he needed to step back.

He moved his hand away from the talisman.

"Maybe you're right, Kel. Maybe I should take a break."

Kelwyn clapped him on the back. "I'm always right. I'm the eldest." He strolled past. "Let's finish your patrols so we can get to the carousing and relaxing part of the day."

Synderis laughed and followed after him. "You didn't say anything about carousing."

Phendaril left the room early, saying he wanted to check if a particular shop was still open. While he was gone, Raven convinced Ehric to take her through some of the Stonebreaker's dual-wielding sword forms. They slid the beds to the sides to make space for practice. He was muscular and tall but moved with an elegance that struck her as almost elven. It was rare that she felt clumsy around anyone. Trying to mimic the forms he showed her after watching him do them certainly didn't make her feel graceful.

When Phendaril returned, Ehric had his arms around her, his hands on hers to help guide her through one of the motions. They both froze and looked at Phendaril, whose brows pinched together, though a hint of amusement lit his eyes.

"I've barely been gone an hour, and you're already making moves on my Stonebreaker?"

Raven laughed, and Ehric let out a chuckle as he stepped away, taking his swords back. All humor disappeared when she caught the scent of what Phendaril was carrying. Sweet and savory aromas wafted through the room, leaving her salivating. She hurried over to him, Ehric fast on her heels. In the package he held an array of pastries, the likes of which Raven had never seen. She leaned in closer, breathing in a smell so rich it evoked flavors on her tongue.

"Don't drool on them," Phendaril teased, moving past them to set the package on a dresser. He lifted one of the pastries and held it up to her lips. "Try it."

She met his eyes and opened her mouth, taking a bite. It practically melted on her tongue, the soft flakes of pastry crumbling around a savory meat-paste filling.

"Mmm." She looked over her shoulder at Ehric and pointed at the pastry. "This is amazing."

He reached for one, dark eyes alight with anticipation. "You don't have to tell me twice."

Silence fell over the room as they devoured every morsel of what he had returned with. Raven licked her fingers when they finished and gave Phendaril a hopeful look.

"Do we get to do that again tomorrow?"

He smiled. "We'll see how today goes." He rose from where he sat cross-legged on one of the displaced beds. "Come on. The town's awake enough now. It's probably reasonable to start making inquiries about your father's family."

"We're looking for the Woodbridge family?" Ehric asked.

Raven caught something in his tone that said he had information if the answer was yes. She gave him her full attention. "That's right."

"I asked a few servers downstairs last night if they knew of the family. One said they had seen the name on a house in the eastern quarter. She gave me directions."

Raven smiled appreciation at him, trying to ignore the way the thought of approaching her father's family made her stomach turn. "Thank you, Ehric. You're the best."

He answered with a rakish grin. "Considering I did it all while I was giving you two time to, uh... talk, I would have to agree."

Raven flushed and turned to collect her cloak and weapons. They might need the room in town again if they couldn't find any helpful information today. However, there was also a chance they would have to leave in a hurry if anything went wrong. They agreed it was better to take their belongings with them and risk having to find a new room than to pay for another night and not end up using it. Raven had a fair sum of coin, but they had no way of predicting at this point how long they might need to rely on it.

Ehric's lead brought them to a wealthier part of town. There were several downsides to that. The trio of riders, bristling with weapons, stood out dramatically among the well-dressed gentry in that quarter. The elves there wore simple clothes and bustled about with their heads down on various errands. Phendaril explained that working for the wealthy was the best employment most elves in Lathwood could hope for unless they were fortunate, like his late aunt, to have skills the city guard found attractive. His mother had been employed by a wealthy human family when they lived there, doing work that was little better than slave labor.

Phendaril received furtive glances from the elves they passed. The wealthier human population cast them looks of suspicion and disdain. Raven kept her hood forward and rode quietly behind Ehric to encourage the assumption that she was human. What self-respecting human woman would ride double with an elf, after all?

"Did you know your father came from a wealthy family?" Ehric asked.

"No. I was only eight when they died. I didn't have an interest yet in the family history. Neither of my parents spoke of their past much that I can recall." Talking was a welcome distraction from her nerves and the awkwardness of having her arms around him, so she attempted to keep it going. "What of your family? Do the Stonebreakers always stay within their birth clan?"

"Most do." He steered Autumn around a trio of women chatting in the street in their elegant gowns. An older man standing near the group watched them warily as they rode by. "On occasion, individuals will leave their clan to experience other parts of the world or join another clan."

"And other clans will take them in?"

A girl of seven or eight and her mother passed close to Autumn. The girl looked up at them. Raven turned hastily away, hating that she couldn't watch around her as Ehric and Phendaril could. It put her at a disadvantage if anything unexpected happened. She couldn't plan escape routes or keep watch for danger. She had to trust them to do it for her. It wasn't a comfortable situation to be in.

"There is competition between the clans, but it tends to be good-natured. A little movement between clans encourages the mixing of bloodlines. It's good for all of us."

"Woodbridge," Phendaril alerted them, directing Dusk to the side of the street before a three-story manor house.

Raven glanced over, spotting the family name above the door. A mix of excitement and apprehension made her skin prickle, and her palms grow sweaty. This was it. This was her father's family.

They dismounted and approached the door. Ehric stayed with the horses this time while Phendaril strolled up as if he had every right to be there and knocked, Raven lurking a little back to one side. After a few minutes, the door opened. A tall man stood there. His fine clothes were tidy and clean, but he didn't quite look the part of a wealthy gentleman.

Phendaril offered a slight nod of greeting.

The man's eyes narrowed as he looked them over,

taking visual note of Ehric with the horses. "How can I help you?"

"We're looking for the family of Arek Woodbridge."

An older elven female stepped up behind the man, peeking around him to see who was calling. Raven made sure to keep her head turned to the side and down enough to hide her features.

The man's eyes narrowed more, and he lifted his chin, looking down his narrow nose at Phendaril. "I'm afraid Arek was renounced by his parents many years ago. You'll find nothing here."

The elven female turned and disappeared into the house as he started to shut the door.

Phendaril stepped forward, settling one foot over the threshold. "Please. It's important. Perhaps we could speak to the head of the household for a moment."

"The man who was his father passed away several years ago. Bringing up Arek to the woman who was his mother with her failing health could upset her enough to kill her. There is no one here who can help you. I'm sorry." He swung the door shut hard, barely giving Phendaril time to jerk his foot out of the way.

Phendaril pressed his lips together, anger drawing them into a grimace. He reached for the door to knock again, and Raven grabbed his arm. He looked down at her.

"Don't bother, Phen. There's no point. Their son ran away with an elf they probably saw as little more than a slave. I doubt they know anything about my mother or her family." Sour disappointment curdled in her gut.

His brows pinched together, and he shook his head firmly. "We have no other leads. We can't just give up."

Raven dredged up a soft smile for him, loving that he so earnestly wanted to help her. She brought her hand up, touching the cloak pin. "There may be another way to find her, but let's not talk about it here."

He searched her eyes for a moment before nodding. They rejoined Ehric and Phendaril took Dusk's reins, though he didn't mount yet.

"Are we leaving town or going back to the room?" Ehric asked. "It is still ours for a few more hours."

"The room might be a good place to talk," Raven suggested. It was time she told them about Synderis. After their last dream encounter, she believed he was real. She was reasonably confident that he was connected to her mother, or at least her mother's family, in some way. She only wished that the lingering doubts didn't nag at her so. How was she supposed to tell them she was conversing with a strange Silverblood elf in her dreams and not sound like she had lost her mind?

A female voice called out behind them. "Hey! You! War elf, or whatever you are."

Raven snorted a laugh as she turned with the others to see the older elven female from the Woodbridge house, hurrying toward them down a narrow walkway alongside the residence. She was waving a hand to get their attention.

Phendaril gave Raven a sideways glance. "Thank you. I'll remember how you snorted at that the next time you need someone to watch your back." His smirk told her he, too, was struggling not to laugh.

The female slowed as she got closer to them, suddenly wary. Her gaze drifted over Ehric, with his dual blades, and Phendaril with his bow, sword, and several daggers. However, when her gaze shifted to Raven, it went straight to the cloak pin, ignoring the weapons she also carried.

"What's your name, dear?"

Raven hesitated a moment. The elven female wasn't asking that just to be friendly. The quiver of excitement in her voice suggested something deeper behind the question.

"Aneiris," Raven answered.

The female smiled and wiped hastily at a tear that slipped down one cheek. "That's what she said she would call the baby if it were a girl. I recognized her cloak pin when you came to the door."

Raven's eyes started to sting with the threat of tears. She took a step closer, trying to remember to keep her face turned away enough to hide her eyes. "You knew my mother, Mellaine?"

The woman's wistful smile broadened. She reached out to take one of Raven's hands. "I did. She wasn't like the rest of us. She came here from someplace special. Someplace she meant to go back to. She said she was gonna take some of us with her, and I believe she meant it. No one hated the humans here more than she did. That was, until she started to fall for your father. We all thought the world had gone wrong side out."

"How did they meet?" Raven felt like her heart might burst. If her parents had ever told her about their courtship, it was when she was too young to remember.

The female leaned closer still. Raven ducked her head more, keeping her eyes in shadow. "Oh, you should have seen them when they first met. Your mother came to work for the Woodbridges for a time. Arek was their son, obviously. She was so determined to despise him. He was human, after all. And she was an elf. Not just an elf, but an elf from a people so pure and secretive they're a myth among most of us here." She cast another glance at Phendaril, her gaze sticking on his scar, and edged closer to Raven.

"But Arek was sweet and charming. A good young man, unlike his parents. Mellaine would let her guard down every once in a while, and you could see by her smile that she was enchanted by him. Still, it was quite a surprise to the rest of us when they started sneaking off together in the evenings. Then she came to me crying one day. She was pregnant. She wanted to keep the child – you, I suppose – but she knew she could never go back to where she was from with a human man, and his family would kick him out if they knew he was fornicating with an elf. I didn't know what to tell her. There was nothing I could do. I guess they made their own decision because, a few days later, the two of them up and ran away together."

A few slow tears crept down Raven's cheeks. "What's your name?"

"Devina."

"Thank you, Devina. I'm sorry to tell you that my parents both died when I was eight." More tears raced down the woman's cheeks, and she brushed them roughly away. Raven pressed ahead, struggling not to let her own emotions control her. "I'm trying to find my mother's family. Do you know where they are?"

"I'm so sorry, dear." She shook her head, squeezing Raven's hand. "Mellaine told stories of how beautiful it was, but all I know is that she came from an elven village in the deep forest somewhere. Farther east and to the south, if I recall correctly, but I'm not even sure of that. She was meticulous about not giving too much away."

Nothing, really. A vague location that might not even be right. Raven forced a smile, lifting her head enough for Devina to see it, and squeezed her hand in return. "Thank you. I appreciate you telling me all of that. I really don't know that much about them."

"Will you be in town later? I could meet you somewhere. Tell you a few stories that might do your heart some good."

Phendaril placed a hand on Raven's shoulder, and she fought back a flare of resentment. It wasn't his fault. The longer she talked to this female, the greater the risk that she would slip up and let her see what she was. They all knew it. She desperately wanted to hear more about her parents, but it couldn't be.

Raven extracted her hand. "I'm afraid we're leaving shortly."

Phendaril gave her shoulder a gentle squeeze before taking his hand away.

"Well, if you find her family, don't forget about me, all right?"

Raven managed another tremulous smile. "I won't."

When she turned around, Phendaril was mounting Dusk. He held a hand down to her. She supposed it didn't matter who made what assumptions about them now. They weren't going to be in town much longer. Placing a foot in the stirrup, she took his hand and swung up behind him. They left the wealthy district at a trot and hurried back to the tavern.

When they entered the common room, it was about as busy as the day before. Phendaril took Raven's hand and headed for the stairs, but they didn't get far. Someone grabbed Raven's arm and yanked her away from him. Her hip hit one of the tables, shoving it noisily aside and drawing the attention of all the patrons. The culprit was an elven female with shoulder-length red hair and bright green eyes. She would have been attractive without the sneer twisting her delicate features.

"It *is* you," she hissed, glaring at Phendaril, one hand still gripping part of Raven's cloak. A slight waver in her stance suggested she had been drinking. "How dare you show your face around here with some little tramp in tow."

"Let go of her, Jayla." A dark shadow fell across his face. The threat in his tone even gave Raven a chill.

One of the male elves who had been sitting with Jayla stood now. His eyes carried a warning that Phendaril disregarded with a slight shake of his head.

It had occurred to her that they might run into someone who had known him from before. She just hadn't expected it to be such a confrontational experience. His past in Lathwood appeared to have been even more troubled than he let on.

Raven jerked her cloak free. "Let it go, Phen. She's not worth it."

Jayla's glare moved to her now. "Fine one you are to talk of a person's worth, secretive little slut."

Phendaril's hand balled into a fist. Raven grabbed his wrist, shaking her head. She could see his anger in the tightening of muscles in his jaw, but he relaxed the hand.

Another yank on her cloak pulled her hood off. Fury blossomed, and Raven spun, catching Jayla with a fist to her jaw that sent her sprawling back over the table. The female's eyes popped wide in surprise, though not as wide as those of her companion, who stared open-mouthed at Raven now.

"You're a Silverblood," he gasped. "A female elven Silverblood. How's that possible?"

Raven yanked up her hood, but it was too late. Whispers of "Silverblood female" and "Silverblood elf" spread around them.

"We need to leave."

They hurried for the door and out to the stable. It took several minutes to get the horses ready again. As he was saddling Dusk, Phendaril glanced over at her.

"Why didn't you let me hit her? Once in a while, you could let me come to your aid."

She shook her head, checking that the packs were secure on Autumn while Ehric was cinching the gelding's saddle. "No. If you had struck a female, it might affect how I look at you."

"You aren't worried about it affecting how I look at you?"

She peered over the horse's rump at him. "Did it?"

He grinned and gave her a suggestive wink. "I have to say, it did."

"Are you two ready? I've seen more than a few off-duty guards in there. We shouldn't linger." Ehric's words and tone brought a metallic taste to Raven's mouth.

Phendaril's expression sobered, and they led the horses out. They had gone a few feet from the front of the stable when she spotted a man she had seen in the tavern outside now. He pointed their direction while looking back over his shoulder.

"There she is," he shouted. "Elven Silverblood!"

Raven glanced in the direction he was looking. Three guards were jogging their way, but what made her gut twist was the Silverblood adept coming up behind them.

Phendaril leapt up on Dusk. She took his hand, swinging up and finding her seat as he kicked the horse. At least the guards and the adept were on foot for now. They urged the horses up to a gallop, and she held on tight as they wove through the streets at speed.

CHAPTER FIFTEEN

Raven rested her head against Phendaril's back. "Who was that woman? Jayla, I believe you called her?"

They had slowed their pace after a wild sprint from the city. The horses needed the break. Their coats were slick with sweat and their sides still heaving. With no direction planned, they had struck out east on a road that veered slightly southward.

"I told you about Lysanna, the woman I was supposed to be life-bonded with."

Hearing the edge of pain in his voice, she squeezed her arms tighter around him. "Yes."

"That was her sister. The night Lysanna was raped, I was supposed to be with her, but I ran late, helping my aunt with a difficult hunt. Jayla blamed me for what happened to her sister. To be honest, I blamed myself too, but while she was still alive, Lysanna insisted to both of us perhaps a thousand times that it wasn't my fault. I try to believe that. After she killed herself, Jayla turned on me with a renewed desire for vengeance. She needed someone to blame, a place to channel her sorrow and anger into, and I'd already killed the men responsible. She's one of too many reasons I decided to leave Lathwood."

"I'm sorry."

He placed a hand on her arm, guiding Dusk with the other.

The sound of distant hoofbeats reached her ears. She perked up, scanning around and behind them.

"What is it?" Ehric asked, turning in the saddle to follow the direction of her gaze.

The sound grew louder quickly. She spotted four riders farther back on the road, coming their way at speed. The pounding beat of more fast-moving horses off to their left drew her attention to a trio of riders angling toward them across the rolling field.

"They apparently aren't willing to let us go that easily."

Phendaril patted Dusk's neck. "Sorry, boy." Then he kicked him back up to a gallop.

Raven held on tight again, feeling the heaviness in the gelding's strides. They were both reliable mounts, but they weren't conditioned for this level of exertion, and Dusk was carrying two. She didn't like the way their odds were looking. Maybe it was better to stop now and surrender. Phendaril and Ehric were less apt to get hurt that way. Weren't they? She didn't know much about the men chasing them other than they appeared to be guards from Lathwood. That meant they wouldn't needlessly kill anyone, didn't it? There were laws and procedures to follow.

An arrow whistled past, sinking into Dusk's side near the girth with a meaty thwack. The gelding let out an agonizing cry as his front legs gave out under him, sending all three of them tumbling toward the hard-packed roadway. Raven flew several feet through the air, landing solidly on her back. Pain blazed through her ribs as the air burst from her lungs. She wheezed, desperately struggling to recover her breath and move.

She managed to roll up on one arm, the activity around her disjointed and hard to focus on while she fought for air.

A few feet away, Phendaril lay sprawled, one leg trapped under the unmoving gelding. To their right, she spotted Autumn limping with two arrows protruding from his left hip. Ehric was on the ground, still standing, though he had an arrow in one thigh. As she watched, another planted deep in his shoulder.

The Stonebreaker snarled and started to lift one sword with his remaining functional arm as both groups of riders galloped into the midst of them. Two of them had their bows trained on him.

"Don't try to interfere," one of the archers warned Ehric.

Why was Phendaril not moving?

She managed to suck in enough air to call out. "Ehric, do as they say."

They all looked around at her. The defeat on Ehric's face as he lowered his sword hurt her heart. The Silverblood she'd seen in town rode up alongside her. He hopped off his mount.

Still sitting in the dirt, she nodded toward Phendaril. "Let me check on him. Then I'll go with you." She held her hands up in a gesture of surrender.

He smiled down at her, an expression that didn't come close to reaching his eyes. Then he grabbed her wrist in a crushing grip. "Yes. You will come with us."

His eyes flared brightly. A chill of terror raced along her skin seconds before blackness consumed her.

•

Cold stone and bars surrounded Raven when she woke. The stenches of fear, waste, and unwashed bodies filled the air. There was a window. A single tiny window placed high up in the wall, but it was enough to differentiate this this cell from the one beneath the Brotherhood temple in Pellanth. It was hard to make such a small thing a comfort, but she needed something. Phendaril lying motionless in the roadway haunted her, leaving a hollow of despair in her chest. Was he alive? Ehric had been severely injured. With those wounds, how much help could he be to himself or Phendaril?

Other cells lined the wall to either side of hers, mirrored by more along the opposite side of the hall. Each had a similar tiny window near the top of the outer stone wall, letting in minimal light. It was better than nothing. That light told her that it was evening now. Nausea and a headache from the magic the Silverblood had used on her were already fading. When Marek had used that magic on her, he had done it several times consecutively, keeping her unconscious until he got her to Pellanth. The side effects appeared to be cumulative, making her reaction before much more severe. She also had that to be dubiously grateful for.

They had left her clothes and her cloak with her. All of her weapons lay piled haphazardly on a table at the end of the hall with other objects she assumed must belong to occupants of the other cells. Those things didn't matter to her. She wasn't sure what did matter. Did it matter that she was alive for now? Did it matter that she could breathe again, even if it was somewhat painful?

Phendaril.

Tears threatened, but she fought them back. She refused to cry as if she had lost him. She wasn't about to give up on him that easily.

A guard entered the hallway and swaggered down to stop in front of her cell. Hope sparked in her. She stood and moved close to the bars, grimacing at the many aches from the violent impact with the road. They had killed Dusk. They had seriously injured Ehric and Autumn. Phendaril was alive, though. He had to be.

"My companions. Are they all right?"

The guard shrugged. "We got what we were after.

We didn't stick around to find out." He cocked his head, peering at her for a few seconds, his eyes narrowing as he stared into hers. After several seconds, his gaze flickered to her ears. "You really are a pointy Silverblood." He gave her a quick once over. "And a girl." He shook his head, a bemused smirk flitting across his lips.

"Please. Can you find out?"

"Not my problem. Once they figure out if we're sending you to Pellanth or Chadhurst, you won't be my problem either." He started to walk away. Apparently, he had only stopped to gawk.

She grabbed one of the cold bars. It was so dreadfully solid. So unyielding. "What do you mean?"

He stopped. "We got word from Pellanth that Father Wayland was looking for you just yesterday. However, this area falls under the jurisdiction of Father Markon in Chadhurst, so there's a little gray area around who gets to deal with you. I suggested sending half to each, but apparently, they weren't satisfied with that." He chuckled, amused with himself, and started walking again.

Raven stepped back from the bars, watching as he disappeared through the doorway at the end. Candlelight flickered dimly in the hallway beyond. When he had gone, she sank onto a bench tucked against the wall and rested her head on the stone. She focused on breathing and feeling the pain in her ribs for a time, trying to determine if anything was broken from the fall. If there were any breaks, it didn't feel like there was any displacement of the bones. It still hurt. Though not as much as the hollow aching in her chest.

"Let them be all right," she murmured.

Darkness fell outside. Someone a few cells down broke into a violent coughing fit, then silence filled the space. Raven lay back on the hard bench, one hand pressed to the cloak pin. She thought of Synderis as she drifted into a restless slumber, yearning for that sense of comfort he carried with him.

•

"Well done."

Raven opened her eyes. So much joy and relief filled her at seeing Synderis standing in the cell that she might have gotten up and hugged him, except that part of her that was still wary of strangers quickly stifled the inclination. Instead, she sat up on the bench and gazed quietly up at him, unsure what to say. What exactly had she done well? Getting caught by the Lathwood guard didn't strike her as much of an accomplishment.

"You managed to reach out to me through the talisman. I felt it growing hot against my skin and knew you must need help." He looked around them. His pleased smile faded, a flicker of sorrow casting a shadow over his features. "Is this where you are in the waking world too?"

"Yes. I've been arrested for being an unsanctioned Silverblood." She tilted her head, noticing an unexpected bloom of grass and flowers that had sprung up in one corner of the cell. "Though that's new."

He followed her gaze, and a more subdued version of that pleased smile curved his lips. "Sorry. I believe that's my fault."

A weary smile danced briefly across her lips. A little greenery was not much cause for celebration, though she had to admit that it improved the place. "If there's anything you shouldn't apologize for, it's making this cell any less horrible."

He crouched in front of her, a sudden intensity in his regard. "If I can alter your dream environment unintentionally, then you're trusting me more."

Raven bristled. "I don't know you."

Synderis chuckled, a hint of good-natured humor stealing the cold edge from the silver of his eyes. "You're going to need that spirit. The more you trust me, the more I can help you. Let's start with this. If both of us want badly enough to keep him away, we should be able to block your unwanted dreamwalker out for a brief time."

"I very much want him to stay gone."

He nodded, his pale hair and silver eyes gleaming in the moonlight that now crept through the little window, making him appear almost more spirit than flesh. "Good. Keep that in the back of your mind. Now, who are your captors?"

She met his eyes. His expression overflowed with kindness, patience, and, most importantly, confidence. That look found a guttering spark of hope deep inside her and ignited it. He believed he could help her. Maybe, with his assistance, she could still do something for her companions. "Mostly the local guards in Lathwood, though there is a Silverblood here."

"All right." He moved to sit on the bench next to her, and she turned to face him. "The humans will be easy. The Silverblood is harder, but we can manage him if we have to. From your appearance, I'm going to guess that you're at least a life stronger than I am, probably more. That means the magic will be stronger when you use it. You have to trust in it. It will respond to your need."

"Like the time I stole the will from the horses?"

His brow furrowed delicately. "Is that what happened?"

She nodded, feeling a flush of shame rise on her face.

"Were you able to undo it?"

"Yes. Thank you," she added, realizing she owed him that.

"Rest assured, you can't do that to an entire village

of people like you did in your dream. The more sentient the creature, the more resistant they are to that kind of magic." Around the cell, the steel bars were transforming into saplings, sprouting branches and leaf buds. Grass grew across the entire floor now. "You should be able to influence a few guards, though. Try to catch one coming through alone. All you need to do is believe that you need out of this cell and that the guard should leave it unlocked. Focus the magic on them through the filter of that need the way you did on the horses."

"If that works and I get out, what do I do if I run into the Silverblood?"

"It will work." His confident grin made her want to trust in him. "As I said, the Silverblood's a little harder. Krivalen magic—"

"What kind of magic?" she interrupted.

"Krivalen. It's the Acridan name for what humans call Silverblood. The *proper* name. We can talk about that more when you get here." Again, that inspiring certainty. "Krivalen magic will try to protect itself, so this Silverblood's magic will defend him from your attempts to manipulate him. However, there is a trick to getting around that. Even the Silverbloods seem to know it."

"The way they put me to sleep."

A brief scowl cut through the warmth in his regard, then the reassuring smile returned. He nodded. "I assumed they must have used some unfair tactics to bring you down. How else would they have taken you?"

She tried to smile, but it faltered. Twice, she had been taken down by a Silverblood using that magic. It made her feel a lot more vulnerable than she liked.

He leaned forward a little, the pendant that matched her cloak pin slipping free of his loosely laced shirt. "It's not a simple trick. You must essentially lie to yourself. You have to convince your magic, and theirs through it, that you want to put them to sleep for their own benefit.

The Brotherhood has its warriors so fully indoctrinated in their teachings that convincing themselves controlling you is as much for your good as theirs is probably easy. For you, it may not be as straightforward. I suggest you do your best to avoid the Silverblood. If things go wrong, have a backup plan. Come up with something you can use to try to mislead the magic. I can't offer you any help with that. You're less likely to believe a reason I put in your mind."

She nodded, already running through possibilities in her head. Her stomach turned at the thought of trying to break out of this prison. She yearned to feel his certainty. "Are you always so confident?"

He brought one hand up as if he might touch her and her chest tightened with what she tried to tell herself was apprehension, though it was much closer to anticipation. Then he brought the hand back to his side. The warmth of his regard caught her off guard. For a few seconds, she wanted nothing more than to curl into his arms and be held by him. Why did she feel so safe with him?

"You can do this, Raven."

"How do you know?"

His smile broadened. "Because if you don't, you'll never get answers to the questions I see burning behind your eyes. I can't imagine you settling for that."

That familiar sinister sensation swept through the dream then, and the grass near the far corner of the cell began to wither. Synderis glanced at it and his teeth clenched for a second, the strong muscles in his jaw jumping with aggravation.

His look carried an unspoken apology. "He's coming. I've got to go."

"Wait. Why do you have to leave when he appears?"

Urgency was apparent in the tightening around his eyes when he cast another glance at the withering grass, but he hesitated. "The Brotherhood doesn't know my people exist. I jeopardize that if I let him see me. I'm sorry." He stood. "You can do this," he repeated firmly and disappeared.

CHAPTER SIXTEEN

Synderis stared through the trees, not seeing the treehouses, walkways, and platforms that made up the elevated part of their forest village. All he could see was the joy in Raven's eyes when she saw him in the dream and the glimmer of hope that he had managed to restore to her. If only he could have chanced gathering more information about her circumstances, but he'd known they wouldn't be able to keep the other out for long. He had to focus on the immediate problem of helping her escape as quickly as possible.

He needed more time with her. She still didn't know where to go next, if she even managed to escape, which he had doubts about. She was in a dire situation and had no formal training with the magic, but he had at least succeeded in putting up a confident front. He hoped that confidence would be enough to help her with the unpleasant task ahead of her, assuming it didn't get her killed.

"What are you making?"

He glanced up at Kelwyn, then, noting the faint amusement in his brother's expression, he looked down at the bit of wood he had been whittling. Initially, he had been carving a feathered lalyx cub, part of a matched set inspired by the encounter in the woods. He intended them as a gift to Kelwyn's daughters. This one, however, he had shaved down into a tiny blob of nothing.

"Shit." He tossed it back through the door of his home.

Kelwyn sat next to him, dangling his feet over the edge of the elevated path. "You left rather abruptly last night. Is everything all right?"

Synderis set the dagger behind him and rested his arms on the railing. "Dellaura's granddaughter's been arrested for being an unauthorized Silverblood."

"Ah." Kelwyn picked at a sliver of wood peeling off the railing. "Have you told Dellaura or the Delegate?"

"No. Not yet. I tried to explain to her how to use Krivalen magic to escape, but a few minutes of description in a dream won't compensate for a lifetime of missed training."

"They'll put her to death."

Synderis ran a hand roughly through his hair, clenching his jaw against the agonizing sorrow that thought brought him.

Kelwyn was silent for several seconds, then he cleared his throat softly. "Have you considered that it might be better for everyone if—"

Synderis silenced him with a glare. "Don't say it. She doesn't deserve to die just because it would be easier for us." He stood up and stalked into the house, aware that his brother followed him. "Where are the girls?" He picked up a pack that was on the floor under his hammock.

"I asked someone else to watch them today."

Of course. He couldn't have his sleep-deprived brother watching them. "Then why aren't you training with the alchemists or shadowing one of the council members?"

"Because I wanted to talk to my little brother."

Synderis pulled a few changes of clothes together and shoved them into the pack. "About what?"

A hint of tension showed around Kelwyn's eyes, and he cleared his throat twice before speaking. "I think you should ask the Delegate to give this task to someone else. There are plenty of other Krivalen who can dreamwalk."

"Why?" He shoved a chunk of wood and his carving dagger into the pack. It seemed likely that he would find time to carve the second lalyx cub where he was going.

"Because I think you care too much. I think she's gotten under your skin. What's it going to do to you when the moment comes that you have to choose between saving her life and risking our people? Because I'm certain that moment will come eventually the way things are going."

Synderis spun to face him. "I'd never risk our people!" But he had felt such enormous guilt over leaving her alone in that cold cell when the other appeared in her dream last night. It had been so hard to go.

He turned back to stare at his pack and took a deep breath. He didn't get angry quickly. The fact that he was doing so now was arguably evidence supporting his brother's point.

He glanced at Kelwyn. "Perhaps you would like to explain to Dellaura how someone who cares less should be in charge of her granddaughter's life."

Kelwyn winced and gave a slight shake of his head. "I feel for Dell. I do. But Syn, how much life are you putting into this?"

He didn't want to see the worry in his brother's eyes, so he resumed packing. "Those lives were never mine to begin with. I see nothing wrong with putting them toward saving someone else's." He stepped around his brother, going to gather his bow and other weapons from the far corner.

"What are you doing?"

"I'm going to volunteer for an outer patrol." When

he turned around, Kelwyn was standing between him and the door.

"Absolutely not. If you insist on continuing this, you need to be here where you can get help if you need it."

He stepped up to Kelwyn, stopping when they were almost nose to nose. It helped that they were close to the same height. If anything, he was only an inch or two shorter than his older brother. Drawing on the Krivalen magic, he infused his presence with a sense of threat. It didn't make him feel good, manipulating his brother that way, but it was better than getting in a full-on brawl with him. They hadn't behaved that badly together in years.

"Do you really want to try to stop me? You're not Krivalen, and you're not combat trained. You know I'll win."

Kelwyn shifted, the slightest hint of uncertainty in his eyes. It was a statement to his determination that he stood his ground. "You won't hurt me."

"Nothing you won't recover from." Guilt battered Synderis as he moved a little more magic into play. This was far better than physically hurting his brother, but he hated doing it.

After a few tense seconds, Kelwyn broke eye contact and stepped back out of the way. "This is a bad idea, Syn."

He grabbed the pack off his hammock and slung it over one shoulder. On the way past, he gave his brother a stern look. "I'm an adult, Kel. I'm allowed to make stupid decisions on my own."

It surprised him a little when Kelwyn didn't follow him. Perhaps he'd put too much magic into the threat. Fortunately, since it wasn't necessary to clear this decision with the council or the Delegate, he would be far away by the time the effect completely wore off. Patrol assignments were up to the scoutmaster, who never turned down scouts willing to take an outer post. Those duties tended to be long and lonely, requiring the scout to be away from the main village, sometimes for weeks at a time. Because of that, they were typically only sought after by a few, like Telandora, who jumped at any opportunity to escape the drama between her sister and their parents.

Two hours later, after persuading the scoutmaster to let him take the northwest corner post for a few weeks, he was well on his way. That was the direction Raven would be coming from if she survived her current predicament. The scout posted there could return to the village for a break or move between the outer posts to add an extra set of eyes on the patrols.

The longer Synderis walked, keeping a swift pace, the more his anger and frustration faded. Worry for Raven slipped into the newly vacated space. Would she try to do what he had advised? Could she? She had no training but had managed to use the magic that way at least once by accident. Still, a horse was much different from a human, and using it accidentally wasn't the same as intentionally directing it. She had succeeded in undoing the magic, which showed promise. Would it be enough?

He became aware that something was following him. Tuning his senses to his stalker, he caught the sound of an animal breathing, four paws moving through the brush, and a slight hitch in the steps. He spotted a fallen log and diverged a few degrees off his path to sit on it. Pulling out a dagger and some hard cheese, he cut off a slice and began to eat it, deliberately ignoring the approaching creature.

After a few minutes, the lalyx crept into his peripheral vision, ears swiveling to listen for threats as it watched him.

"Care for a bite?" He held out a slice of the cheese to it.

The lalyx froze, perfectly still and poised to run, its ears turned toward him now. It sniffed at the air, trying to catch the scent of the cheese he offered. It flinched when he tossed the morsel over but didn't run. After a few seconds, it moved warily to sniff at the cheese. It nudged it once with its nose, then took the morsel, swallowing it without hardly chewing. He didn't want to make the animal too comfortable with elves. However, this particular creature would have to get used to someone, and he'd already put the idea in its head that he was trustworthy.

He tossed it another bite, waiting for it to finish eating before standing. The lalyx flinched away, poising to run again when he rose. It relaxed a little, watching him with keen interest as he started to walk away.

"I've got to go, I'm afraid."

The big cat started following him again.

Synderis stopped and looked back at it. "I'm going to be walking for a while. Are you sure you want to follow me?"

The animal watched him, both ears swiveled toward him and one paw lifted in preparation for its next step.

Synderis shrugged and resumed his walk. The lalyx followed.

•

Raven woke after the shadow appeared in the dream and stayed awake, waiting. Not just waiting but preparing. She reached into herself, remembering how it felt to take the magic back from the horses. The magic stirred, and she kept practicing, trying to make that reaction faster. Silverblood. Krivalen. It didn't matter who called it what at the moment. What mattered was whether she could do what needed to be done with it. Synderis believed she could. She was going to prove him right.

An elven servant slipped through in the early morning, leaving a dubious-looking bowl of food behind. She didn't try to use the magic on him. The last thing she wanted to do was get an innocent killed trying to steal the key while under her influence. Instead, she choked down the dreadful meal, aware that she hadn't eaten since the prior morning. It was hard not to dwell on that. Only yesterday, she had been dining on delicious pastries with her companions. Today she was forcing down awful gruel in a dirty, foul-smelling jail cell, not knowing if those companions were even alive.

It was mid-morning before a guard came through, carrying a torch to compensate for the poor lighting and peering into each occupied cell as he passed. Raven got up from the bench and went to the bars.

"How long will I be here?"

He sneered at her. "Not enjoying our hospitality?"

Raven swallowed the myriad angry retorts that tried to burst forth and held her silence.

Her lack of reaction deflated him. He frowned. "It'll be a couple of days. We're waiting for a response from the Brotherhood in Chadhurst."

"Thank you."

He spat at her feet and strode away.

That was good. It gave her a little time to regain her strength. She wanted to break free now to start searching for Phendaril and Ehric, but trying it during the day, when she could hear a constant drone of voices coming from the adjacent halls, was suicidal. If they weren't transferring her on right away, it would be better to wait for dark to fall and make her move when fewer guards were in the building.

It was hard to wait, though. She could barely sit still. Her body needed the rest, and she wanted to conserve what energy she got from the meager meals they offered, but her nerves twitched with impatience. If what

Synderis told her to do worked, it would only be the start of solving her current problems. She yearned to get things moving and end the torturous suspense.

She passed a little time testing the magic, though there wasn't much to do without a target to practice it on. She managed to sleep a little, a restless and broken slumber. It was at least marginally restful since Wayland made no appearances. Unfortunately, the fear of sleeping too long kept her snapping awake every time she started to sink into a deeper sleep.

Eventually, dark fell outside the tiny windows, and she waited. Magic coiled inside her, ready to strike the moment a guard came through. It seemed like an eternity before the light of a torch bobbed into the cell block, and a guard turned in from the adjacent hallway. She stood and walked to the edge of the bars again.

"Please," she started as he reached her cell, "I need water." What she needed was freedom. What she needed – desperately, truly needed – was for him to unlock her cell and walk away. She focused on that and on the magic that uncoiled within her. Unlock the cell. Unlock the cell and walk away.

"You'll get some in the morning," he replied curtly, continuing past.

No. He needed to unlock the cell.

"Please. Just a sip." She moved down along the bars to keep up with him. "Is that too much to ask?"

He stopped and turned, bringing his torch close enough to the bars that she had to step back. "You're that half-elf Silverblood monstrosity."

Raven retreated another two steps, hatred rising in her. Her eyes narrowed. He needed to unlock the cell.

The guard glanced down at the lock. "I don't think you'll be around long enough to worry about it." He stared at the lock for a few seconds more, then continued on his way.

With a soft sob of despair, she coiled the magic back into herself and returned to the bench. There was no point waiting. It would be a few hours before another guard came through. She rested her head against the wall and stared at the stone ceiling. A few quiet tears crept down her cheeks, turning cold as they slipped over her skin. It was chilly in the stone cell. The nights were growing colder with the coming of Autumn.

Footsteps sounded down the hall. The same guard came into view. He wasn't holding the torch now. Raven held her breath as he walked to her cell. He fumbled with a set of keys for a few tense heartbeats before unlocking the door, then wandered back the way he had come as if nothing unusual had occurred.

She sat up, one hand going to the cloak pin. It was too soon to be offering thanks to Synderis. This might well prove to be the easiest part.

The hallway was quiet again. She started to open the cell door, cringing at the squeak of the hinges. In the relative silence, it was painfully loud. Once the opening was wide enough for her to slip through, she snuck out into the hall and crept hurriedly to the table where her weapons lay in a disorganized heap. She strapped on her elven sword and dagger set, then swung the quiver onto her back.

Footsteps drew her attention to the other end of the hall. She spun, nocking an arrow and moving closer to the cell so he would have to enter the room to see her. When he came through the doorway, she let the arrow fly, hitting him in the throat the way she had the man-beast outside Andel. He made a gargling noise and fell to his knees before slumping to one side.

"Gabe? Everything all right in there?"

The voice came from beyond the entrance closest to her. Raven slung her bow over her shoulder and grabbed her boot dagger off the table. She pressed back against the wall in the darkness near the doorway. A guard strode past her, holding a torch before him as he peered into the poorly lit hall between the cells. The flickering light of the flame cast wild shadows around the cellblock.

"Gabe?" The guard held the torch out farther in front of him, looking at the prone figure at the other end. His other hand fell to his sword.

Raven stepped up behind him. In one quick motion, she brought the blade around his neck and cut deep across his throat. He stumbled around to face her, and she threw up one hand to knock the torch from his grip. He wobbled there for a second before falling into her. Raven caught him with both hands against his chest, her stomach turning as blood spilled hot over her skin. She shoved, and he fell over, landing with his face in a pool of moonlight, his eyes staring blankly at the ceiling. There was a glimmer of comfort in the fact that she recognized him as one of the guards who had left Phendaril lying in the road.

"Let me out," a faint voice called from one of the closer cells.

The torch lay on the floor, casting eerie shadows on the two bodies. Raven crouched and wiped her blade clean on the guard's trousers before sheathing it. She did her best to rub the blood off her hands, but there wasn't time to be thorough about it. She had no idea how extensive the jail was, how many guards might be on duty, or even what direction would take her to the exit.

Moving swiftly, she snuck out the doorway the second guard had entered through. It was closer, which made it as reasonable an option as any. She had only gone a few strides down the hall when she heard banging on the bars of one of the cells and someone shouting for the guards. Voices came from somewhere behind her, at least one yelling for the prisoner to shut up. If they went to the cell block, the nature of the shouting would change fast.

Raven hurried, keeping her steps light and speedy as she listened for sounds ahead. The hall she followed was long and dark, with the rare torch placed at intervals along it. About a third of the way down, she came to a set of stairs leading up. Louder, more urgent shouts rang out from the cellblock behind her. She had no time to vacillate about directions now.

Sprinting to the top of the steps, she peeked through a grated window into the room beyond. It was large, with four tables and benches set out in a configuration that suggested it might be used for eating. One guard sat at a table, flipping playing cards and humming to himself. Raven was comfortable confronting one guard instead of the several she heard back the way she had come. She pushed to open the door and met the resistance of a bolt. The shouting behind her grew louder. Two or three guards raced down the hall now. The guard in the room heard the noise and jumped to his feet, scattering the cards and knocking the bench back.

Raven pressed against the wall, but he didn't bother checking through the window before unbolting the door and throwing it open. He took one step, and she put her leg out in his path, sending him tumbling down the stairs. She didn't stop to see how he fared. Instead, she stepped through the door, shut it behind her, and threw the bolt home. Rather than waste time hunting for a conventional exit from the building, Raven sprinted for a window at the far end of the room. She leaped through the glass, leading with her shoulder and tucking her head to minimize injury.

Rolling her landing didn't save her from the surge of fresh pain in her injured ribs as she hit the ground. A cry burst from her, agony exploding with a flash of white behind her vision. Forcing herself to keep moving, she completed the roll to her feet and sprinted for the fence that surrounded what appeared to be a training yard.

"Stop!"

She ignored whoever was yelling at her. The instant she reached the fence, she leaped, catching hold of the top, and hauled herself up and over. On the other side, the fall was farther than she had expected, landing her in a shallow creek. Another blast of pain stunned her for a second, and she sank to a crouch, balancing her hands in the cool water while she tried to catch her breath.

She couldn't stop now. One more time, she made herself start moving. She splashed down the creek bed for a ways behind the fence that separated the jail and part of the town from the creek until she found an old maple hanging over it. Fighting pain and exhaustion, Raven leaped up into the branches and climbed across. Two barely dressed women stood in the back doorway of the building below, having a hushed conversation about the endowments of their customers. When they wandered inside, Raven dropped down in the narrow alley that paralleled the main street behind the brothel and other businesses along the way.

She managed a complicated route through that part of the town for a time, slinking along the dark alleys with her hood up. Twice, she had to climb to the roof-tops to avoid guards searching those darker pathways. As she had predicted, they weren't searching that aggressively in town after seeing her leap the fence. When the path was confusing enough to throw off most trackers and their dogs, she made her way to another point far away from the jail and crossed back over the fence. From there, she followed along the creek bed, letting it mask her scent as it led her out of town on a search for someplace she could rest and reach out to Synderis.

CHAPTER SEVENTEEN

Mere seconds after Raven entered the dream version of Amberwood, Wayland appeared, his flickering shadow form standing near the well in the square. The pain and exhaustion that forced her to risk stealing a few moments of sleep now blossomed into potent rage, strong enough to blur the buildings around them into a red haze. She'd had enough of the Silverbloods trying to execute her and endangering those she cared about.

The shadow with its bright silver eyes was more solid than before, as if he were starting to figure out how to control his presence there. Long silver hair shifted into focus as the rest of the shape began to take on a recognizable human outline. It moved toward her, occasionally flickering back a few feet, but making more consistent progress than any time before.

"Where are you?" A broken voice hissed across the abandoned square, the tone and volume fluctuating with each syllable.

She'd had enough of being frightened in her own dreams. The elven sword she used the night she fought Wayland in his collection room appeared in her hands as she stormed toward the shadow.

"Get out!" She lunged across the last few feet, swinging at the figure. Wayland flashed out and in as he stumbled back, retreating before her furious onslaught. "Leave me alone!"

She kept at it, slashing repeatedly, hatred and frustration driving her rage until the shadow flickered out one last time and didn't reappear. Raven staggered another step. The sword vanished, and she sank to her knees, gasping for air. After a few seconds, she curled over, sobs tearing through her. Someone's arms moved around her shoulders, drawing her into a warm embrace. Someone safe. She sagged against him.

"I've got you, Raven," Synderis whispered. "He's gone."

She wasn't sure how long they stayed that way, but eventually, she calmed and disentangled herself from him. He took her hand and helped her to her feet. She turned away, self-consciously wiping the lingering moisture from her cheeks, her gaze wandering to where Wayland's shadow self had been.

"Do you think he'll come back?"

Synderis chuckled. "I certainly wouldn't after that." His tone turned serious. "I wouldn't expect him to give up for long, though. Not so long as he remains connected to you. Who is he?"

She turned to face him, unable to stop a fleeting smile at the foliage that had sprung up around his feet. "Father Wayland Mallebron of the Silverblood Brotherhood in Pellanth."

He sucked in a deep breath and blew it out. "You couldn't have started with some less powerful enemies?"

She glanced away. Maybe her mother simply hadn't thought it through when she did this to her. That didn't make it all right, but it made it a little less troubling. "I feel as if I was made to attract powerful enemies."

He placed a hand on her shoulder. "You were, through no fault of your own." His smile was gentle and supportive when she met his eyes. "I'll need to know more about how you became connected to him if we're going to break that connection, but that will have to wait until you're here. Did you get away from the jail?"

Raven nodded. "I did as you said. It worked." She wiped brusquely at another tear. "I killed two of the guards, though."

His jaw tightened for a few seconds, a shadow falling over his face. It disappeared as quickly as it came, and he beamed at her like a proud parent. Undergrowth sprang up next to them, and a towering tree shot up where the well had been. "You did well. Are you safe where you are in the waking world?"

"Safer." She glanced around, watching as more trees popped up, going from sprouts to soaring giants in seconds. A stream took the place of one of the streets. She heard it gurgling over the rocks and smelled the crisp scent of clean water.

"It takes about three to four days to get from Lathwood to where I'll be waiting. Less if you can get your hands on a horse. Follow the road going southeast until you reach a fork. One road goes east to Branwill. The other heads south to Millerscreek. Keep heading southeast between the two roads, and you'll come to an old stone monument. If you can get to that monument, I'll find you there."

Raven listened intently, trying not to be distracted by the forest filling in on all sides of them. "Is this where you are?"

He glanced around at the altered dreamscape. "It is."

"Does that mean you've taken control of my dream?" The idea made her a little uneasy. He told her she was probably "a life stronger" than him, but he obviously knew how to control the magic far better than she did.

"I'm only able to do this because you trust me more now, and because you're exhausted. I can feel that much through the link the talismans create. I suspect my taking control might make it slightly harder for your Brotherhood priest to return. Though we already know it won't block him completely. I also hoped you would find this environment soothing."

She smiled wearily. Both were reasons she could appreciate. "I do." So far, she had no sense of Wayland returning, so she took a few seconds to regard him thoughtfully. "Why are you helping me? *How* are you helping me?"

"The cloak pin is a talisman. I'm guessing it only recently came into your possession?"

She nodded.

"It and its twin," he said, pulling the matching pendant out from under his shirt, "were created so your grandmother, Dellaura, could stay in contact with your mother when she was away from home. She only found out you were alive when you took possession of it and immediately asked me to help you find your way home."

Home? What a strange idea. That someone she had never even met wanted her to come home to them. "Why hasn't she dreamwalked me?"

"You have to be Krivalen to dreamwalk, and she's not. It is possible for a Krivalen to guide someone else into a dream. That's how she was able to visit Mellaine. But this situation is riskier with the uninvited walker in your dreams."

How casually he said her mother's name, as if he'd known her, or at least knew enough of her to be comfortable with it. It was a lot to wrap her head around, but it made sense in a peculiar way. She had endless questions she wanted to ask. Still, she found herself gazing distractedly at the magnificent forest that had wiped away all traces of Amberwood.

He took a step closer to her, his strength and the warmth that flowed off him comforting. "That sword you brought into the dream to fight the priest. I've seen drawings of it before, or one nearly identical. It's an elven relic, isn't it?"

She smiled at the unabashed curiosity in his voice. "It's part of the story of how I became connected to a Silverblood priest. I'll tell you about it when I find you. Now I should wake. I said I was *safer*, but I'm far from safe yet."

His brow furrowed. "You're also exhausted. Is there no way you can get a little more rest?"

Raven looked into his silver eyes, at the genuine concern in them, and felt a flutter in her chest. Could he care that much for someone who was little more than a stranger? She wanted to reassure him. More than that, she yearned to curl up in his arms again and bask in that sense of security. That was reason enough to leave, even if her companions weren't out there somewhere, likely in need themselves. Besides, she really wasn't safe in the waking world.

"It was almost sunrise when I closed my eyes. Once the sun is up, I'm at greater risk of being found. I can't afford to stay asleep." She placed a hand on his arm, a thrilling shiver racing through her for daring to initiate contact with someone so unfamiliar to her. "I'll get to the monument as quickly as I can."

He nodded. "Be careful."

•

Raven woke to the sound of hooves clopping along on the nearby road. She rolled out of the pile of leaves and sticks she'd half-buried herself in and climbed the tree next to her to get a better view. Pulling herself up into the branches drew a hiss of pain from her. Everything ached, far more than it had the day before. There was little she could do for it. The one thing that hadn't been on that prison table was her pack, so she had nothing but her clothing and weapons to work with.

A trio of riders passed by on the road. Their cloaks up and heads down, shoulders hunched against the early chill. A little morning traffic was of no concern as long as they weren't guards or Silverbloods, though she was still careful not to let them see her. Once they passed, she climbed down and started walking, keeping the road in sight, but staying off it. Small stands of trees were scattered here and there, but much of the area was grassland. The tall gold grass was high enough to duck down in when she was between stands of trees.

When she reached the place they had fallen, she found Dusk's body lying several yards off the road where someone dragged him and left him for scavengers. Something had been feeding on the unfortunate thing. It brought an aching to her chest to see the gelding lying there. She had been growing fond of him, which had done much ease her fear of horses. The packs and the saddle were missing, which she hoped meant her companions had them, or at least the packs. The saddle had come with the horse and, while possibly worth a little coin, wasn't much use without him.

She crossed to the other side of the road and found a spot to sit in the tall grass not far from a grove of trees and upwind from Dusk's corpse. From there, she watched quietly, waiting. Hunger nagged at her, so she chewed at bits of grass to give her stomach something to do. She observed several passers going by in wagons or on horseback, none of them aware of their audience. A few hours had passed when one wagon rolled to a stop almost directly in front of her. It carried a heavy load of straw, a few barrels near the front, and Ehric perched on the back edge.

Excitement burned through the meditative haze that had come over her during her vigil. She watched him climb gingerly down, fighting the desperate urge to help him. He limped to the front, passed a few coins to the driver, then moved off to the side, waving at the man as he drove away. Raven held her position. Ehric peered both directions along the road and then started scanning down along the far side. She waited until the wagon was out of sight before getting up.

"Ehric."

The dark-skinned Stonebreaker turned, relief banishing some of the tightness from his posture and smoothing the lines from his brow. He started limping toward her. Raven hurried over, trying to save him the pain, though her ribs protested the movement. When she reached him, he moved to embrace her with his good arm. She put a hand out to hold him back.

"Easy. As much as I might appreciate a hug from you, my ribs can't take it. Is Phendaril ali... is he all right?" She stopped herself from asking if he was alive. That opened the door for the alternative to be true.

Moisture rose in Ehric's eyes as he stared at her with a weary smile. "He is, and when he sees you..."

A gasp of relief escaped her, and she wiped at the cascade of tears that spilled down her cheeks.

Ehric's tight smile was full of sympathy. "He's hurt bad. One leg is broken, and he's got several cracked ribs. I knew you'd be worried after what happened, so I went to the jail to ask the guards to let me talk to you three times yesterday, but they refused. When I went back to try again this morning, they told me you had run. I told Phendaril that, and he said you would come here. I guess he knows you fairly well. I waited until I was sure no one was watching me, then I caught a ride out of town." A hint of that smile returned. "I can't tell you how relieved I am to see you."

Her chest tightened. Phendaril was alive, that was something, but it sounded like he needed more attention than he would receive in Lathwood. They undoubtedly had decent healers in town, but they weren't going to give a mere elf access to the best ones. "He'd get better care from the healers in Amberwood than he will here."

Ehric nodded. He peered up and down the road before continuing. "The guards have orders to kill you on sight now. Phendaril said he and I could book passage on a ship to drop us back at Amberwood. If you can make your way west and toward the river, keeping out of sight, there's a small fishing village called Turlep. We could bring you on board there."

Raven shook her head, a sickening hollow opening inside her. "It's not safe for me to go back to Amberwood. I'd venture it's more dangerous now than ever for me to be there. You'll have to take him home." She held up a finger to silence his protest. "I know how to find my mother's people now. They can help me break my connection to Wayland. Then maybe he'll stop looking for me."

Ehric's brow furrowed. "How do you know this?"

She touched the cloak pin. "This. You found it in the keep ruins. It was my mother's. It's a magic talisman. My grandmother used its twin to talk to my mother in her dreams when she left home. Now, one of her people has the other talisman and has reached out to me in my dreams. It..." She looked down at the pin then. They would have to go separate ways, but she might be able to still reach out to Phendaril. She started to remove the pin. "Take this. Give it to Phendaril and tell him what I told you. Tell him to keep it close. Once I reach my mother's family, I'll use its twin to reach out to him in his dreams." She let her cloak fall from her shoulders and held the pin out to Ehric.

He lifted one hand partway to the pin, then hesitated. "If you do that, how will your mother's family reach you?"

Raven grabbed his hand and pressed the talisman

into his palm. "I told you. I already know how to get there. They'll just have to be patient."

She heard the creak of wagon wheels in the distance. "Go. There's a wagon coming, heading toward town. If you start limping along now, you can probably guilt them into giving you a ride by the time they catch up."

"Raven—"

She put her finger to his lips. "Tell Phen I love him."

Ehric heaved a sigh and nodded. "I will. Be careful."

She gave him a smile she hoped was reassuring. "You too." Fighting the swelling panic at the prospect of striking out alone without even her dream guide to help her, she snatched up her cloak and ducked back into the grasses.

He stood a moment longer, staring at the cloak pin. Then he tucked it in a pouch and started limping down the road. As she told him, the wagon picked him up when it caught up with him. Raven waited until it was out of sight to get up and resume walking. She had only just entered the comfort of the grove when she heard something larger moving through the brush to her left.

She turned toward the sound and spotted a figure coming through the trees toward her. As much as she wanted to be wrong, she recognized that black and silver cloak and armor. There was a sinking sensation in her chest, but she couldn't run now. He was too close for that. Raven faced the approaching Silverblood.

CHAPTER EIGHTEEN

I had a feeling you'd come back this way. You were desperate to check on your elven companion before we took you. Not your smartest move." He sneered the words, making his tone mocking, though she refused to see her concern for Phendaril as the weakness he appeared to think it was.

Raven lowered her hand closer to her sword, paying careful attention to where his hands were. He carried a sword and dagger like she did, so there might be similarities in their fighting styles. She moved around a narrow tree, forcing some distance between them without losing sight of him. His hand sank to the hilt of his sword.

"Your precious Brotherhood lied to you about elves and women becoming Silverbloods. Aren't you worried what else they might have lied about?" That knowledge had made Marek's loyalty falter. It was worth a try here.

He grinned. "You get albino creatures in nature now and then. That doesn't make them normal."

It sounded like something Wayland might have said. That tactic wasn't going to work with him, not that she had honestly expected it to. Raven stopped and dropped her cloak. She kept her eyes on him as she took off her bow and quiver and tossed them on top of it. He didn't move, confident enough to allow her a minute to prepare.

He had his blond hair pulled back in a band at the nape of his neck, a style that would keep it out of his way in a combat situation.

Raven took a few sidesteps away from her cloak and drew her sword. His grin broadened as he followed suit. She focused on her breathing, letting go of everything else. Smooth, even breaths, shallow enough not to cause distracting pain in her ribs. This was single combat. One of the few situations Jaecar had thoroughly prepared her for.

"I appreciate my work most of the time." He shifted into a fighting stance and spun his sword with a flourish. "It's moments like this that I truly love it."

He lunged toward Raven. She feinted a block, darting to the side at the last second to throw off his balance. He twisted and leaped back, managing to avoid her counterstrike. He spun his blade again as he faced her once more. He took part in her capture. He would know she was tired and hurting. There was little reason for him, as a Brotherhood adept, to doubt the outcome of this fight. But he had no elven advantage, and the Silverblood priests made their warriors with only a single life. Hopefully, those two facts would level the field, if not give her an edge. He'd come out here alone, assuming he could defeat her. Not the most brilliant move.

She smiled. It wasn't that she felt like smiling, but she recognized now that it was a useful intimidation tactic. The slight tightening around his eyes and adjustment of his grip on his sword confirmed that she had at least made him a little uneasy.

"Not as much fun as you'd hoped?" she taunted.

He narrowed his eyes, the slight tightening of his hand on the hilt warning her before he lunged. Raven blocked with the blunt side of her blade and spun fast, coming around to slam into his shoulder with her own. The move threw him off balance long enough for her to spin so she was now on his flank, facing the same direction. She rammed her knee into the back of his hamstring right above his knee. He let out a grunt of surprise and pain as the leg buckled. He managed to twist as he dropped, lashing out with the dagger in his other hand. It was an awkward slash, but it found flesh, cutting in above her belt and into her side. She twisted around, pivoting against his back, away from the blade and the pain. As she came to his other side, she kicked the elbow of the arm he had put down to catch himself. There was a loud crack. He cried out as the arm bent the wrong way and lost hold of his sword.

Raven caught hold of the back of his neck before he fell and seized the Krivalen magic. The talisman was gone, but she didn't need it. This magic was part of her. After speaking with Synderis, she was confident it had reacted to protect her when Wayland tried to kill her. It wasn't going to fail her now. The Silverblood needed to sleep, or he would die. That was very much to his own benefit.

He collapsed unconscious at her feet.

"Weren't expecting that, were you?" Raven half smiled before pain twisted her mouth into a grimace.

She stared at him for several seconds, one hand pressed to the wound in her side, the other holding her blade poised to drive through his neck. He would remain a threat if she let him live.

Blood ran warm between her fingers, drawing her attention away from him. She sank to one knee and cut two long strips from his lovely Silverblood cloak. Sheathing her sword, she folded one strip and pressed it against the wound. The other she used to create a tight wrap around her waist, tying it snugly in place over the folded cloth.

It was hard to think past the pain, but she could do nothing more for the wound now. The fight had also aggravated her injured ribs, but that discomfort was a mere itch by comparison. She got to her feet and searched the area until she found broken grass and disturbed dirt to indicate the direction he had come from. She followed his trail, quickly spotting a dappled grey horse tied among the trees. When she reached the animal, she noticed the familiar brown cloak draped over the back of the saddle. He had been one of the three riders who passed by earlier, slipping past unnoticed under her nose.

After removing the cloak pin to use on her own cloak, she tied the extra one behind the saddle. The saddlebags had a few provisions in them, though not much. Enough that he might have been planning to be away from town for a day or two. She didn't need a lot. Now that she had a fit horse that, given his owner, was conditioned for long hours of travel, she intended to make the three- to four-day journey to Synderis in no more than two.

She patted the stallion's neck, then pulled a bit of grass and fed it to him. Not that he couldn't reach it himself, but horses seemed to appreciate such offerings even when they could easily obtain them on their own. There was no point starting off on the wrong foot, given her limited experience with the big animals. The nagging concern that its owner might wake up and come after her before she escaped forced her to limit their introduction. After a few more bites of grass and some neck scratches that the horse appeared to enjoy – pressing hard into her fingernails – she untied him and swung up.

The blazing agony that rewarded that effort left her curled over the saddle, groaning. With no one offering guidance, the horse turned and started toward town. Raven clenched her teeth and guided him in the other direction. It took more than a bit of courage to urge him up to a trot when a few steps at a walk amplified her pain. The only thing that helped was knowing that this would get her where she needed to go faster. Clinging to the front of the saddle with one hand, she urged the horse to a gallop.

•

Aldrich Darrenton had been perfectly content at his new property, checking in on the construction of his new manor and doing a little hunting with some of his men. Then a Brotherhood acolyte arrived to tell him his presence was required at the Silverblood temple in Pellanth. It was a tedious nuisance, riding all the way back into town. To make matters worse, a rather unexpected rain began to fall along the way. The sun shone bright and cheerful that morning, so he hadn't bothered with a carriage or protective attire. As they trotted into the temple courtyard in the closing dark, his hair and clothes plastered to his body, he was in even less of a mood to bandy words with the Silverblood priest. He had met Father Mallebron the one time. As he recalled, the man was haughty, insufferable, and more than a little intimidating.

"If you'll follow me," the acolyte stated, somehow managing to look undisturbed by the short black hair dripping water down his face and the weight of his wet cloak.

Aldrich took note of the lack of a milord or any other respectful address. He didn't care for Silverbloods. That he could never safely express how intensely he disliked them without the risk of creating a dangerous enemy for himself made him like them that much less.

He swung off the horse and followed the other man, making a futile attempt to wring some of the damp out of his cloak as he walked. He signaled his two men that had accompanied them to wait with the horses. He would rather leave them there than risk them seeing him cowed by the priest.

A barrage of wild rumors had gone around the day after his prior visit suggesting that a portion of the temple was destroyed in some internal conflict. A few even dared to imply that the Brotherhood priest suffered a dire injury in the incident. Those rumors were disregarded by the Silverbloods, who claimed they were merely renovating a portion of the aged structure. Aldrich didn't notice anything different on his way up to the towering double doors at the entrance. The building was still constructed of the same unwelcoming black stone with angry spires reaching to the sky. The one unusual element, the room with the half glass walls and ceiling through which part of a stuffed wyvern could be seen, looked exactly as it had upon his prior visit. Although, now that he really looked, it did appear that the metal framing between the glass panels was newer than the rest.

The acolyte standing outside the door opened it to let them both in. When they were inside, his escort glanced back at him.

"Wait." He made a stopping gesture with one hand before striding to the rear corner and disappearing through a doorway.

Aldrich wandered into the massive entrance hall. Chandeliers hung high above, their light unable to penetrate the darkest depths of the arched ceiling. Torches put out flickering light along the two levels of the balcony running around the perimeter of the room. More torches lined the walls at the ground level, and a few candelabra stood situated in the center. Despite those dancing flames, most of the impressive chamber with its soaring arched ceiling remained lost in shadow.

The floor caught his attention. He hadn't noticed it before, but patterns in the grey and white marble looked vaguely like screaming faces. It made his skin prickle until he wished he could climb up on a chair to get his feet off it.

Oppressive power preceded Father Wayland Mallebron into the room. He appeared unchanged from the last visit, his unnatural liquid silver hair cascading down over his shoulders along with the cloak of magic that flowed out from him. He was tall. Aldrich remembered that about him, and it struck him as distinctly unfair that a man with that kind of power should also have such a physical presence. Aldrich noticed one difference as he started to sink to a knee when the priest approached the end of the raised dais. Notable shadows darkened the skin around Wayland's eyes as if he hadn't been sleeping well.

Aldrich finished kneeling and bowed his head. "Father Mallebron. It is an honor."

"Don't fuck with me, Darrenton. I know you don't want to be here. I can see it in your false smile."

Aldrich's chest seized. Had he done something to earn the wrath of the priest? When a Silverblood warrior insisted on joining his soldiers on their hunt a short while back, encouraging them to cross into Amberwood, they had obliged. Today, when another one came to summon him, he had come without hesitation, despite how he wished to refuse. Perhaps another of his men done something to offend?

"Don't panic. It's unbecoming." Wayland sneered. "Stand up."

Aldrich did as ordered, forcing his hands to remain still at his sides. He wasn't a confrontational man, not the way his father had been. He liked things to go his way without hassle. And he hated being reminded that he was really not that powerful. This man made his bowels quiver with fear.

"You purchased the land next to Amberwood."

"I did."

"Do you still want Amberwood?"

Was this a trick? "I do."

"The current leaders of that town have... offended me. The Brotherhood would generously pad your coffers if you would consider taking it from its current owners by force."

So much for avoiding conflict. Aldrich shifted his feet, unable to keep still before those bright silver eyes. "But, Father, an attack would be quite costly and take time to prepare. I'm sure the Brotherhood could easily persuade the king to draw up a new deed and nullify the current claim if you want the land."

"I don't. I want something its residents have, and I want them to regret not giving it to me."

Aldrich swallowed. How fortunate that he wasn't the object of the loathing in the priest's eyes. "If that's what you wish," he answered, his voice sounding weak in his own ears.

"It is. Start preparations. I expect you to make your move by the turn of the season. Hit them as winter is falling, when it will hurt them more."

The priest was gazing over his head now, a wild look in his gleaming eyes made more ominous by those dark shadows beneath them.

He cleared his throat. "Is that everything, milord?"

"Yes." Father Mallebron turned away. The priest spun around again just as Aldrich started to retreat, startling him back to his knees. "No. I want you to bring me one of their scouts."

"I'm not sure..." He trailed off when Mallebron stepped closer. The air in the room grew thick and heavy, making it hard to breathe. It took a conscious effort not to pull at the collar of his shirt. Mallebron glared at him. Why was he being argumentative? It wasn't that much to ask. He bowed his head. "Of course, milord."

Synderis woke to the feeling of something heavy and warm pressed along his right side. Since he was in the woods not far from the perimeter scouting post, supposedly alone, alarm swept through him. Wary, he kept still and opened his eyes a slit. The lalyx lay beside him, its hindquarters resting against his arm and its head turned to the side, pillowed on his shin. Morning light danced upon the tiny little feather tips that rose above its ears, trimmed in almost translucent pink.

He gazed up at the treetops high overhead, watching the leaves wave down at him on a light breeze while he considered the strangeness of his circumstances. After a few seconds, he chuckled to himself. The big predator sprang up like it had been stung, bounding away from him. It stopped with its back arched and its hackles up, the leaf-shaped feathers lifted in a brilliant emerald display.

He sat up. "Don't look at me like that. You decided to sleep next to me, not the other way around."

After a few seconds, the cat calmed and sat, then proceeded to groom one paw as if nothing had happened. He watched it for a few minutes while digging some fruit and nuts out of his pack. The lalyx paused its grooming to sniff his direction. Upon deciding he wasn't eating anything of interest, it stood and loped off into the trees.

"Farewell, friend."

A few seconds after the lalyx departed, thoughts of Raven swept into the vacant space. He had never seen anyone take to manipulating the dreamscape as fast as she had. She summoned a weapon from the waking world and used it to drive out her unwanted dreamwalker with the ability of someone far more experienced. He should have left when he realized the other was there, but there had been such grace and skill in her furious attack that he couldn't bring himself to turn away. Then she broke down. He had gone to her, unable to bear the idea of her having to cope with that exhaustion and overload alone.

How she had clung to him. It had only been a dreamwalk, but it felt more genuine than many emotional encounters in his daily life. What would it be like to have her there in the waking world? A magnificent fire raged in her that he ached to be closer to, even at the risk of being burned.

He could do nothing more to help her, no matter how he longed to. She knew how to find the monument. It was up to her now. All he could do was be there in her dreams to encourage her along the way. He hoped that would be enough.

He finished the light meal and then wandered to the stream, splashing cool water in his face to drive away the lingering grogginess of the night. Dreamwalking was never as replenishing as regular sleep. A restful night's sleep would be another benefit of having her there in the flesh.

He crouched next to the water for a few seconds, running back over their encounter in his mind. Pain and exhaustion had poured through the dream link. Not just physical pain and fatigue, but emotional. Almost more of the latter. It had been no more difficult than breathing to take control of the dreamscape and turn it into a reflection of his waking world. Even if she trusted him implicitly, it shouldn't have been that easy.

He cupped his hands to drink from the stream. Then, pushing his concern for her to the back of his mind, he began walking. He would reach the scouting post before long.

Within an hour, he found himself with a companion again. The lalyx loped out of the underbrush, hurrying to catch up. It slowed to walk along a few yards from him. Synderis nodded a greeting to the big cat. Perhaps he should try to take back more of the magic if it drew the animal to him this intensely, but he appreciated the company. Alone, his mind wandered to Raven too often. The cat supplied a welcome, if unconventional, distraction.

It was approaching noon when a rustling ahead caught his attention. He slowed, and the lalyx stopped. Its ears perked in the direction of the sound. After a few seconds, poised there like a statue, the cat growled low in its throat. Synderis continued forward cautiously. The lalyx followed, staying a few feet behind him now.

A familiar elven female stepped out from the shadows of a tree ahead of them. The cat bolted, climbing up the nearest tree with several powerful lunges. It prowled out on a branch overlooking Synderis and crouched there.

"Syn!" Telandora strode out. She was lean and tall, her skin tanned because she tended to request posts that would put her out in the sun, away from the deeper forest. Her silver eyes took inventory of their surroundings out of habit. She stopped a few yards back, her attention shifting up to consider the lalyx crouched on the branch behind him. "Where did you get your follower?"

Synderis followed her gaze up to the cat. "It's got an injury that will require ongoing care. I put myself in its head as someone safe, so I could manage the problem."

She laughed lightly. "I'd say it worked." In one swift motion, she brought her bow into her hand and knocked an arrow, aiming at Synderis. The lalyx snarled fiercely and shifted its weight, poising to leap. Telandora lowered the weapon and exhaled another small laugh. "Looks like you've got yourself a guardian. Now all the kids are going to want to be Krivalen."

Synderis chuckled and walked over to join her. They exchanged a brief embrace, and he could feel the wiry muscles under her clothes.

"Have you been eating out here?" he asked, stepping back to take a longer look at her. She had always been lean, but her cheeks were a bit hollower, and her clothing and scout armor hung more loosely on her frame than he remembered.

She rolled her eyes. "By the stars. Please don't start sounding like my parents." She turned in the direction of the post, motioning for him to follow. "Come on. We can talk at the hut."

Synderis strolled along with her. Behind them, he heard the lalyx jump down from the tree. It moved to shadow them several yards to his left, opposite Telandora.

She glanced over and shook her head, chuckling softly.

Synderis shrugged.

She gave him a somber look now. "You should know the Delegate dreamwalked me last night. She said you were coming and told me about Dellaura's half-breed granddaughter."

"Raven," he corrected, a little more sharply than intended.

Telandora's lips pressed together, and she gave an almost imperceptible nod. Then her expression eased. "I thought it was Aneiris?"

"She goes by Raven." He tried to maintain a more casual tone this time. "What else did she say?"

"Why Raven?"

"I haven't had a chance to ask," he answered with feigned disinterest. "What else did the Delegate say?"

She offered him a sideways glance that told him she was debating her answer.

"Tel?"

She reached back to pull the band out of her long brunette hair and began combing through it with her fingers. She would do that for several seconds, putting the band in place again when she finished. It was a nervous tick. He'd seen her do it as often as once every five minutes when agitated. Sometimes he wondered how she managed not to pull all her hair out.

"She's confident in your ability to guide the female here. She also expressed concern about the toll this is taking on you and that you may be becoming too attached to your subject." Her gaze flickered over to him again and away before he could read her expression. "She asked me to stay out here so you're free to bring her back to the village as soon as she arrives without leaving the post empty. That in itself is quite the vote of confidence."

Fair enough. He had not planned that far ahead. Perhaps it was good the Delegate had.

She gave him a longer look this time. "Are you?"

He glanced at her. "Am I what?"

"Becoming attached to the half-breed?"

"Raven," he corrected again.

"So that's a yes."

"Probably."

"You know my sister's fond..." She trailed off. "Your expression tells me you've had this conversation recently. What have you got against Ilanya?"

"The same thing I've got against you. You two are like sisters to me. Our parents pretty much raised us as siblings. Besides, she's got a lot to work out before she'll be ready for a real relationship. She'll be lucky to convince your parents and the council to let her become Krivalen when you already are. What will she do if they refuse?"

Telandora lowered her gaze as she finished replacing the band in her hair. A hint of sorrow tugged down the corners of her mouth.

Ahead, Synderis spotted the hut nestled at the base of three towering evergreens that had grown together in a semicircle. A few pieces from the trunk of a fallen tree were cut into seats around the fire pit out front. When threats entered the area, such as roving bandits or mercenary bands, they assigned more than one scout at the outer watches. Or, on occasion, an off-duty Krivalen would wander out to the perimeter to visit with one of their own. Although they were a welcome and necessary part of the society here, they were different, and they tended to gravitate to each other for company.

What the post lacked, however, was an extra hammock inside, but he was willing to sleep on the ground. He had his own living heat source now, after all.

"Do you know why she wants to do it?" He pulled off his pack as they approached and set it down against the side of the hut along with his bow and quiver. Then he slipped off his sword belt and placed it there too.

Telandora discarded her weapons by the building and ducked inside. She came back out carrying a water skin. After taking a sip, she offered it to him. He sniffed at it, earning a mock offended look from her. The sweet, light aroma told him it was one of their dessert wines.

He cocked an eyebrow at her. "You have a skin full of lamel wine?"

She grinned and sat on a stump, putting her feet on another piece of wood set there as a table. "You need something out here to remind you of the little luxuries now and then."

He sat, took a sip, and handed it back to her. The lalyx crept closer to him before lying down to watch Telandora warily.

"I think Ilanya's scared. Our family has a history of difficult childbirth, and it's only gotten worse with each generation. Succession and inheritance follow the female line, so I can see why my parents aren't pleased with the idea of only my brother having children. Still, it's her body. I don't know." She gave herself a slight shake. "I just know I'm staying out of it."

"Why not go back and support her?"

He cringed as she took a swig of the wine and wiped her mouth.

"You know that's meant to be sipped, right?"

"Conformist." She rolled her eyes briefly skyward, though a smirk pulled at her lips. "My parents are upset with me for the rather unpopular opinion I offered last time I was home that our line should be allowed to die out. The childbirth problem gets worse with every generation. My mother almost died with two of her three pregnancies. Ilanya might not fare as well. If she gets through it, any daughter she had would probably suffer the same problem, only worse. There's no reason to put anyone through that."

Synderis reached out for the wine, and she passed it over. He took a long drink this time, grimacing at the overwhelming sweetness in quantity.

Telandora laughed at him and accepted the nearly empty skin when he offered it. She gestured to the lalyx with it. The cat flattened its ears back, tensing. "You going to name it?"

"I suspect that would be frowned upon."

"Nonsense. As you pointed out, the animal has a special need. It wouldn't be the first time such a thing has happened. There are a few companions in the village now that started through similar circumstances."

"But none of them are predators. You don't think it's wrong to tame such a creature?"

He watched the lalyx. It gazed back at him, blue-green eyes blinking slowly. He mimicked the gesture in return. After a few seconds, the cat got up and strode over to him, its long legs consuming the distance in a few loping strides. It growled a warning at Telandora, then curled on the ground next to him.

"Looks like it has already made its decision." She lifted the skin as if to offer a cheer, then took a long drink.

He shook his head at her. Even as he did so, however, he allowed his other hand to dip down and touch the animal's head. The strange feathered coat was silky under his fingertips, and the cat didn't move away from the contact.

"Well." Telandora removed her feet from the table as if preparing to stand. She handed the wineskin back to him. "When are you expecting your dream lover?"

He exhaled heavily, hiding how much her attempted tease pleased him. "Raven won't make it here before tomorrow night if she has a horse and keeps up a relentless pace. If she's on foot, it'll be several days."

"Good. Lindyl is at the next post east of here. I thought I might check on him tonight." She stood, and the lalyx tensed, watching her suspiciously as she went to collect her gear.

Everyone knew she and Lindyl were an item. He arched an eyebrow. "You're going *check* on him?"

"Shut up. You've got your own lalyx to cuddle with while you *guide* this Raven through her dreams. I don't want to stay here and listen to you moaning in your sleep." Amusement sparkled in her eyes.

Synderis threw the cap from the skin at her, catching her in the shoulder with it. "Get out of here."

"See you tomorrow, dream lover." Her light laughter

lifted into the treetops as she trotted away from the post.

He took another sip of the wine and gazed out at the forest. A meadow lay beyond a few more ranks of trees. If he followed the creek that flowed along the lower edge of the meadow back into the trees, it eventually came to a clearing, in the middle of which stood the monument he had sent Raven to.

Dream lover.

It wasn't like that. He was only helping her, and, by doing so, he was supporting Dellaura and keeping the secrets of Eyl'Thelandra safe. It wasn't as if he had any intentions beyond that. Nor as if he longed to hold her in his arms again.

"Lying to yourself never works," he murmured as he scratched between the lalyx's ears. The deadly predator pressed its head up into his hand, the deep rumble of purr rising from its chest. "How about Koshika? It means spirit in Acridan. You can be my guardian spirit."

The cat settled its full weight against his seat, shifting it a few inches, and continued to purr.

Raven kept the horse moving through the day, alternating between brief walks and long stretches of trotting. She gave him breaks as often as necessary to eat, drink, and rest. Then she would drive him on again. With her cloak pulled over her head, she hurried them past other travelers at speed, hoping no one would take an interest or notice the trail of red slowly soaking its way down her leg. The few travelers they saw didn't appear inclined to investigate anything outside their individual purposes.

When they took breaks, she stayed mounted. The pain in her side was so intense that she wasn't sure she would be able to climb back into the saddle if she dismounted. The effort might also make the bleeding worse again. It had abated to a slow trickle of blood now. She needed to avoid aggravating it and stay functional long enough to reach Synderis. The more blood she lost, the less likely that became.

As evening drew near, she let the stallion stop to graze, daring to slide off to relieve herself and change the wrap around her waist. The pieces of the cloak had soaked through with blood. She dropped them, leaving them where they fell. Animals would tear apart the blood-drenched fabric before anyone found it. The fading light made it difficult to get a good look at the injury, so she poured water over it, hissing at the pain, then untied the other cloak from behind the saddle. She sliced new strips from it, the cuts more jagged this time. Pain and continued bleeding left her weak and uncoordinated. After too much struggling, she managed to cover the still oozing wound.

When she finished, she took hold of the saddle, put her foot in the stirrup, and sucked in a bracing breath. She swung up. A flash of pain as the cut pulled open and the accompanying dizziness blacked out her vision for several seconds. She sat in the saddle and ground her teeth against the blazing agony, fresh blood flowing warm beneath the new bandage. When she could breathe again, she urged the horse on, giving his neck a pat with one trembling hand.

"Sorry about this," she rasped, alarmed at how strained her voice sounded.

The animal was fit and impeccably well-trained. Neither of which was surprising. Silverblood warriors were constantly on the road. Their mounts needed to be prepared for long hours under saddle and the danger they often rode into.

It was decent of them to have helped her out like this.

She let out a small laugh that turned quickly to a pained groan.

By morning, she struggled not to drift off in the saddle. Even with the constant throbbing and frequent piercing pains from her side, exhaustion dragged at her. The wrap was soaking through again. Before long, she would have to cut up more of the cloak and replace it if she had the strength left to do so. She would have to try changing the bandages while mounted. She wasn't foolish enough to believe she could climb back up another time.

She found dried meat in the saddlebags and chewed

on that for a mile or two, letting the stallion walk. After managing to finish a few pieces of the meat, she urged the animal on faster again, clenching her jaw against the pain. It was an ongoing balancing act between reaching her destination as quickly as possible while trying to keep their energy up to do so.

Late afternoon found them still moving, though Raven had to snap her heavy eyelids back open every few seconds and struggled to stay upright in the saddle. The stallion's steps were dragging, though he forged onward. The fields had given way to sparse forest. In the distance, she saw a green blanket of heavier trees leading up to a mountain range. That had to be where she was heading. Somewhere in that dense forest, her mother's family waited.

She urged the stallion even faster.

Dark was creeping in when they came to the fork in the road. She could no longer sit upright in the saddle. Pain and fatigue had her leaning over the stallion's neck, her hands gripping the pommel to keep from falling off. Tears of relief sprang to her eyes at the sight of the words on the worn wooden signs, one pointing south to Millerscreek and the other east to Branwill.

"Good job," she whispered, resting one hand on the horse's neck.

The animal had turned to grazing. She barely had the strength to pull his head up this time. When she urged him on with a weak nudge of her heels, pointing him off the road between the forks, he didn't move.

"Please. We're almost there." She tried to shift her legs to give him a firmer kick but ended up groaning in agony as the movement caused another burst of pain.

There was another way to make the animal move. The thought of what she had done to Autumn and Dusk when they were fighting the wolf-beasts outside Andel made her hesitate. Then her vision spun, everything lurching nauseatingly around her, and she held on, desperate not to fall. If ever there was a right moment to use her magic on a horse, this was it.

Drawing on the magic, she pressed her need upon the stallion. They had to reach Synderis. If they didn't, she wasn't going to survive this. No one was here to bring her back from death a second time.

The stallion started moving again. Before long, the roads were no longer visible beyond the trees. Raven clenched the front of the saddle, trying to focus on her breathing. She had dropped the reins at some point, leaving them resting on the horse's neck. It was too hard to keep track of them, and she no longer needed them to direct the stallion. Every step made her pain worse. The terrain rolled like a ship on rough waters, making it impossible to look ahead without feeling like she might throw up. Instead, she stared at the horse's mane and the ground beyond, her vision going dark every now and then when her eyes slipped shut.

Sudden impact drew a cry from her. She opened her eyes, looking up at the stallion who had stopped moving and now stood over her, staring ahead into the darkness. The dirt was cool against her back. When she turned her head, she could see stone structures. Old, worn stone. The monument.

"Synderis," she sobbed softly, unable to stop her eyes from drifting shut.

Would he come fast enough? She recalled the feel of his arms holding her in the dream and the sense of safety that poured off him. She needed him.

"Synderis, please."

•

Synderis was restlessly pacing the camp when Telandora arrived after dark the following evening. Koshika lay nearby grooming. Occasionally, the lalyx cat would stop mid-lick to watch him, its head tilted to one side, tongue hanging partway out in a manner he might have found humorous at a different time.

"She no longer has the talisman."

Telandora picked up the wineskin sitting on the table and uncorked it. She shook it and peered inside with a frown of disappointment. "Who has it?"

He had tried to dreamwalk Raven several times the previous night. He got nothing from the talisman link but a barrage of confusing sensations and emotions. "I'm not sure. Whoever it is, they're in pain, and their dreams are broken. More like fever dreams. I can't get in, but it doesn't feel like her."

She tossed the empty skin over by the front of the building. "Do you think whoever has it did something to her?"

Panic caused a spasm in his gut, though he held his voice steady. "Perhaps. I don't know."

Telandora stepped into his path, forcing him to stop. She put her hands on his shoulders and looked into his eyes, her silver ones glinting in the moonlight as he imagined his own did.

"Relax a minute. You said you told her to come to the monument?"

He nodded. "I've gone out there a few times this evening, though she would have had to have kept up a hard pace or ridden all night to make this fast."

"Do you think that's likely, given what little you know of her?"

He thought about the half-elven female. She had an intensity and determination he found inspiring. If she wanted to reach him this fast, she would find a way to make it happen. "Yes. Especially if she's traveling alone."

"Then consider this. You're both Krivalen, and you've dreamwalked her several times. The magic may have initiated something of a link between you by now, just based on the frequent interactions. If you're developing feelings for her," she added with an arched eyebrow of shrewd accusation, "that's even more probable. If she is close, you may be able to feel her. Calm down and focus."

He relented to a smile. "When did you get so practical?"

"When I stopped spending so much time around you and your brother," she teased, releasing his shoulders.

Before he could turn his attention to trying to focus on Raven, a strange sensation swept through him. Almost like a warm breeze circling around and into him, compressing to a ball of heat at the center of his chest. Then something tugged at that center point, pulling toward the monument. He gasped in surprise.

"Syn?" Telandora's brows pinched together. "Are you all right?"

He peered into the darkness as if he might see her. "She's here."

"How do you know?"

"She reached out to me." Ignoring Telandora's look of surprise, he turned and broke into a jog toward the monument.

Koshika was up, loping along beside him in seconds. He could hear Telandora's footsteps as she followed after them.

"You named the cat. I like it."

He smiled tightly. A war waged inside him between excitement that she was finally here and the nagging certainty that something was wrong. What happened to the talisman? Was she alone? A hint of desperation in that tugging sensation put him ill at ease.

The towering stone columns of the monument stood aligned in four rows of varying lengths alongside a sunken stone basin. They barely entered the remains of the old structure before he spotted the horse. The animal waited, staring into the darkness, still as the monument itself except for the heaving of its sides from recent exertion. He recognized that distinct lack of interest in its surroundings. She had used Krivalen magic on the beast. But where was she?

He slowed, holding one hand back to signal Telandora to caution while placing the other on his sword hilt. As he moved cautiously between two pillars, he spotted a figure lying in the grass alongside the horse. Telandora noticed it too, judging by her muttered swear before she broke into a jog. Synderis sprinted ahead of her, ducking under the horse's head and sinking to his knees by Raven's shoulder. He placed two fingers against her neck, feeling the faint pulsing beneath her cold skin. She didn't react to his touch. Her eyes had dark shadows under them, and her skin was deathly pale.

"She's alive?" Telandora asked.

He nodded, moving into position to slide his arms under her and lift her. "Bring the horse. We may need him. And see if you can undo whatever she did to him so he can eat and drink."

"I'm already working on it."

Telandora brought the horse along, keeping the two of them between it and Koshika. Even with the buffer, the stallion startled and nearly pulled free when she broke the hold Raven's magic had on it and it spotted the lalyx. A few seconds later, it walked calmly, reaching down to snatch bites of grass. Now under a less rigid influence put in place by Telandora.

Something warm and damp began soaking through Synderis's shirt, and he smelled the copper tang of blood. Raven was hurt. That much was obvious, but how badly?

When they made it back to the post with her, Telandora grabbed a blanket out of the building and spread it near the fire. He laid Raven down on it carefully, wary of worsening any injuries. Before he could do much else, Telandora was kneeling next to him with her dagger out, cutting away a blood-soaked bandage wrapped around the half-elf's waist.

Stealing one second, he brushed the hair out of Raven's face. This was not how he had hoped to get her into his arms again. She looked as though she had been through quite the ordeal. Her face and hands were smeared with dirt and blood, which didn't bode well for the wound's cleanliness. Still, he couldn't imagine anything that would make her less than extraordinary in his eyes now that she was finally here.

"If you're done admiring, perhaps you could help me with her armor."

Without a word, he turned to unfastening and removing the chest piece of her leather armor. The wound was slightly below the edge of the armor, making it hard to get a clear look with it there. With the armor gone, they could see the slice in her shirt painted red with blood. They carefully peeled it away from the wound. Telandora dampened a cloth and began to gently clean off some of the blood.

Raven woke with a cry and started to rise. Synderis caught her shoulder, holding her down so she wouldn't hurt herself more. She gazed at him, the moonlight reflecting in her bright silver eyes. Relief eased the fear from her face when she recognized him. It made his chest ache to see the trust in her eyes. He took her hand, and she clasped his in return, her grip weak and shaking.

"You are real," she breathed.

He smiled at her, hoping she would find encouragement in the expression. "And you're safe."

A pained smile played at the edges of her lips. "I know."

"Syn." Telandora's voice dragged him back to their situation.

They needed to deal with her injury. It would be

less unpleasant for her if she were unconscious during the process. He eased his magic into her, not surprised when her own stirred in response, ready to defend her. However, this really was for her own good, to save her a great deal of pain. It took mere seconds to convince her magic of that.

"Rest."

Her eyelids fluttered shut, and her hand went limp in his grasp. He nodded to Telandora, and she began to clean the wound again. He watched, one hand resting on Raven's shoulder, feeling the slight movement of her breathing. Koshika lurked in the shadows behind them, pacing the way he had been a short time ago.

The cut was long and deep, though not something they couldn't manage with proper care. Unfortunately for her, instead of getting stitches and rest, the wound got inadequately cleaned and dressed, and the stress of riding kept it bleeding.

Telandora sat back on her heels and pondered the injury. "She needs proper care. We have to get her back to the village. As weak as she is, her body may not be able to recover from too much more blood loss."

He glanced up at the horse. "It looks like she still needs your services, my friend."

Telandora followed his gaze and nodded.

They covered the wound and pulled the saddle off the horse. After he got her to the healers, he would send someone back out for his and Raven's gear. Telandora helped him situate Raven in front of him on the animal's bare back. As much as he hated to make her suffer, he had to wake her. With her able to help manage her own balance, they could ride faster through the woods.

Once they were moving, she leaned her head back against his shoulder, her eyes closed, and little groans of pain escaped her lips anytime the horse stumbled in the dark. Synderis focused on their route, using his Krivalen enhanced elven vision to guide the horse, not with the reins, but with magic. That left his hands free to stabilize Raven when she drifted or when weakness put her balance off.

"It won't be long now," he murmured in her ear.

She said nothing. Instead, she placed her hands over his, and he opened his fingers, letting her twine hers into his so she would have something to hold onto. Then he held her tight and focused on getting them back to the village.

The jail was cold and miserable. Every part of Raven hurt as she lay on the bench, waiting for a guard to wander past. The barest hint of morning light crept in through high, narrow windows.

But hadn't she escaped the jail? Had that been a dream? Was this the dream?

She felt for the cloak pin. It was missing. She recalled giving it to Ehric to pass along to Phendaril, hoping she could reach out to him once she found the matching talisman. They were returning to Amberwood to get Phendaril proper medical care. They would go without her because she was still a danger to anyone around her.

An aching hollow spread through her chest, and she squeezed her eyes shut, fighting against tears.

But she had given the talisman to Ehric after escaping this place, hadn't she?

"Where are you?"

Her eyelids snapped open. She sat up to face the front of the cell. Wayland stood outside the bars, staring at her with his liquid silver eyes. His form flickered in and out of focus. Sometimes all of him solidified into his human shape. Other times nothing more than an arm or part of a leg would shift from shadow to solid and back again.

Raven tried to stand, but her legs gave out, and her

knees hit the stone floor. She thought of the sword, trying to summon it to her the way she had before. Nothing happened. Pain thwarted her efforts, creating an impenetrable fog in her mind. She was too weak and exhausted. She couldn't face him like this.

Where was Synderis? He would keep her from harm. He had to.

Wayland faded into shadow and stepped through the bars.

Her fingers moved again to where the cloak pin should be. Phendaril had it now. Without it, Synderis wouldn't be able to come to her aid. He might not have appeared anyhow. Not with the Brotherhood priest there.

Wayland stalked toward her. He flickered back a few times, rage tightening his features whenever it happened. Then he flashed forward to stand over her, triumph widening his smile as he stared down at her.

"Where are you?"

"Why would I tell you?" she snapped between gritted teeth.

Around them, the cell faded into darkness. A different room started to form in its place. The massive entrance hall of the Brotherhood temple, with its ceiling soaring up into shadows. Wayland's shape solidified, seeming to draw strength from the familiar environment. He clasped a hand around her throat, lifting her up to eye level, her toes dangling at least a foot above the ground.

He shoved her back into the wall, leaning in close enough that she could only stare into his eyes. "I will find you."

She couldn't breathe. Fear closed in, scattering her thoughts as panic made her heart race. Then she felt a familiar presence tugging at her, not physically, but through her magic. She grabbed hold of that sensation and pulled herself toward it.

"Not today," she choked out.

•

Raven woke gasping for air, the weight of deep sleep still making her eyelids heavy. She started to sit up, but firm hands pressed on her shoulders, holding her down.

"I told you not to leave her out too long."

The familiar voice sent relief flooding through her. She relaxed back, no longer trying to fight the hands that held her down. One of them moved away and took hold of her hand.

"Raven?"

With some struggle, she managed to open her eyes. Synderis leaned over her, worry in his silver eyes, his long white hair hanging loose around his face, tinted with just a hint of Krivalen silver.

She exhaled softly, a weary smile curving her lips. "You found me," she murmured.

The adoration in his answering smile promised her safety, kindness, and more if she would allow it. Given everything she had experienced in the many months since she left the keep, those were significant things to be offered so openly.

"I believe you found me, but I'll take the credit if you like." A hint of light humor eased the concern in his tone.

She became aware then that they weren't alone. She lay on a bed in a relatively large building, given what she could see of the domed ceiling, though a set of ornate room dividers blocked this section off from the rest. A Krivalen elven female stood at the foot of the bed, distinct silver eyes watching Raven impassively. Another elf sat next to the bed. This one wasn't Krivalen. She was wiping blood from her hands with a damp cloth, her lips pressed together in a tight line of disapproval.

"I was barely finished putting her back together, Syn. It would have been kinder to keep her out."

Synderis glanced over at the female, his expression hardening. "I told you, she has an uninvited dream-walker. She—"

Raven quieted him with a hand on his arm. "It's all right. You woke me in time." Despite her words, a tremor shook her when she recalled the feeling of suffocation as Wayland held her pinned against the wall.

Synderis looked at her, taking note of her shudder with a slight raising of his brows, but he made no further arguments.

"Aneiris?"

The soft voice drew all of their gazes. The healer and the other Krivalen retreated hastily, moving out of the sectioned-off area to make room for the newcomer. The female stopped at the opening between the dividers. Her flaxen hair and crystal blue eyes sent Raven back to her childhood. The female's coloring and the structure of her face evoked memories of her mother, Mellaine. The resemblance was unmistakable, and tears welled in Raven's eyes. She struggled against pain and weakness, trying to shift upright. For a second, Synderis looked like he might stop her, then he shook his head slightly and helped her sit up. The process hurt, but she couldn't just lay there at such a moment.

"Grandmother?"

The elven female smiled and advanced, quiet tears spilling from her eyes. She came to sit on the edge of the bed. "I can see my daughter in your features and your expressions. When she died, I thought you died too. I thought the magic killed you." She placed a hand on Raven's cheek. "I'm so glad you're alive. I feel like you brought some piece of her back with you." With that, the tears came faster. She leaned in, wrapping Raven in a careful but firm embrace. "Welcome home, Aneiris."

It was strange being held that way by someone she had never met. At the same time, this female was so obviously related to her mother that she almost felt as though she truly had come home. She embraced Raven so tenderly, yet with a hint of desperation as if she feared Raven would disappear when she let go. Raven hesitated for a few seconds, finally mustering the courage to return the embrace. She closed her eyes and breathed in the sweet forest scent that clung to the other elf, tears spilling silently down her own cheeks.

"Dell," Synderis said gently. After a few seconds, he tried again. "Dellaura." He placed a hand on the female's shoulder. Raven was quietly grateful that he spared her having to awkwardly ask her own grandmother's name. "She needs to rest if she's going to heal."

Dellaura drew back and wiped her cheeks with a soft cloth she pulled from one wide sleeve. Raven studied her more closely now, noting the ornate webwork of delicate braids woven in her hair and the exceptional quality of the ivory robes she wore. She didn't look much older than Mellaine had when Raven was eight, but she was elven. Age was hard to discern with them.

Dellaura looked at Synderis, flashing him a smile that could have lit the darkest night. "And you." She stood, wrapping him in a vigorous embrace. "Thank you for bringing her here. I knew you could do it." She kissed him on the cheek and took hold of his hand before sinking back down on the bed.

She smiled at Raven again. "I recall Mellaine telling me your father had darker hair."

Raven nodded.

That overwhelmingly bright smile flashed again, and moisture welled in her eyes once more. "Isn't she beautiful, Syn?"

Raven looked up at him to see him turning away, the muscles in his cheeks working as he fought to hold back a smile.

"I..." He hesitated, glancing down at her then.

The fondness in his eyes both excited Raven and subsequently alarmed her. The elf she loved was somewhere dealing with terrible injuries while she was here getting flutters in her chest for someone else. Were all hearts that fickle, or just hers?

Another feminine voice spoke into the moment of silence. "She could almost pass for a full elf."

The dignified, melodic voice demanded Raven's attention. The elven female now gliding gracefully between the dividers had liquid silver hair and eyes that immediately reminded her of Wayland. Even her lips and skin had a silvery sheen, enhanced by the flowing pearlescent ivory robes she wore. She was as magnificent as she was terrifying. Raven's breath caught in her throat, her lungs seizing so she couldn't draw another. How many lives did it take to make such a creature?

"Leave us." The woman's gaze remained on Raven as she waved a hand toward Dellaura and Synderis.

Dellaura gave Raven's shoulder a squeeze. "The Delegate is here to help, Aneiris. Don't be afraid. We'll talk again very soon." With that, she hurried out, pausing in the opening to glance back one more time before she disappeared.

Synderis moved to follow Dellaura, and Raven reached out to him in desperation. Not physically or with her voice. She had frozen in place, her throat too constricted for her to make a sound. Instead, she tried to capture his attention with her magic, and he hesitated.

The Delegate arched one delicate eyebrow as if she somehow noticed the interaction. She placed a hand on Synderis's shoulder. "On second thought, why don't you stay. Your connection may be helpful for this."

When she sat on the bed, Raven shifted away, wincing at the pain the movement caused. This close, she could see that even the Delegate's black pupils had a silver shine. Her stomach flipped at the thought.

How many lives?

Synderis pulled up the chair the healer had been sitting in and sat next to the head of the bed. It helped some that he was staying, though she was more aware than ever that she didn't really know him. He had become a beacon of safety in her dreams, but how did that translate into the waking world? Why did she matter to him at all?

The Delegate was regarding her now, her fine-boned hands clasped before her. "Aneiris is your birth name, but that isn't the name you've chosen."

"Raven," Synderis offered.

Those silvery lips curved slightly up. "Of course." The hint of a smile faded then. "Raven, this uninvited dreamwalker you bring with you is a danger to us all here. I must sever that connection quickly, and I need your help to do it."

Wayland? If this female could break free her dreams from him, maybe it was worth trusting her, at least in this. Perhaps only in this. She glanced at Synderis, realizing as she did so that she was looking to him for guidance the way she had Phendaril when she arrived in Amberwood. He gave a slight nod.

Raven forced herself to meet the Delegate's eyes. Eyes that reminded her unpleasantly of Wayland. "What do I need to do?"

"First, tell me who this dreamwalker is and how you became connected."

"Father Wayland Mallebron of Pellanth," she offered, watching with a disconnected sense of fascination as the Delegate's eyes narrowed a little more with every word. "He tried to kill me and use Silver... Krivalen magic to take my life."

"Fool." She scowled.

One icy hand came to rest against Raven's cheek,

and she fought the urge to pull away, focusing on her breathing instead. The Delegate leaned closer, gazing intently into her eyes as if they held answers that she alone could extract.

"You cannot forcefully take the life of another Krivalen. It must be given willingly or—"

"The magic will protect its host," Raven interrupted.

The Delegate offered an approving nod to Raven and another to Synderis, rightfully assuming he was the source of her knowledge. "Precisely. What happened when he tried?"

"He almost succeeded, but the magic in me reacted, and I managed to turn it back on him. We nearly killed each other."

"Neither of you died, but if you turned his magic back on him, I'm going to guess that you ended up taking some of it. You must have taken him remarkably close to death to do so."

Raven nodded.

"What about you? How close to death were you?"

There was an edge of demand in her tone, and something in her expression told Raven she already knew the answer, but she wanted to see what Raven would say.

"I did die shortly after I escaped him." The smallest inhale beside her marked Synderis's surprise, but he said nothing. "The elven healers were able to revive me."

The Delegate took her hand away and sat back, nodding in satisfaction. "I thought so. There is something darker to the magic in you. Not in a bad way, necessarily, but it was changed by what happened. It's a little more hostile to outside influences. I'm surprised Synderis didn't have more trouble dreamwalking you. I'm not sure whether that is a tribute more to his skill or his charm, but either way, it is worthy of admiration."

A hint of flush rose in Synderis's face, and Raven found herself reluctantly starting to fear the strange female a little less. Still, it was hard not to think of the lives it must have taken to make her the way she was. Had she traded the Brotherhood for something just as corrupt? At least they didn't seem to want to kill her here. That was a substantial improvement.

"Now what?"

The Delegate's gaze drifted to the edge of the bed, her focus turning inward. She sat that way, silent and thoughtful, for at least a minute. "Imperfect," she murmured, "but it will have to do." She met Raven's eyes again. "I need to dreamwalk you while he is there if I'm going to break the emotional connection between you. It's morning now, however, so I don't imagine he'll be making an appearance for a while. If you will allow it, I would like to induce a dreamless sleep in you, just as a precaution. It won't be as restorative as normal sleep, but it will get you some rest and help you heal. Tonight, you and I can dreamwalk together and resolve this problem more permanently."

Raven found herself looking to Synderis again. Perhaps it made sense, given that he would know far more about this female than she did, but why did she trust him so implicitly?

The Delegate also turned to him then. "Actually, Synderis, I would rather save my energy for later. If you would be so kind as to help Raven get some rest, I would greatly appreciate it."

Synderis inclined his head, the gesture weighted with deep respect and deference. "Of course, Delegate."

She touched Raven's hand with her cold fingertips. "We shall speak more later."

Raven nodded, not sure what to say.

When the Delegate got up and left them, Raven turned to Synderis, wishing she knew him well enough to guess what thoughts ran behind his silver eyes as he watched the Delegate make her exit.

Synderis waited for the Delegate to leave them. He knew what she was doing. She had noticed the connection between him and Raven and was taking advantage of it to help put Raven at ease. He got the impression Raven had figured that out as well. Knowing the connection was there and how it was being used didn't necessarily mean it wouldn't work, but it would require Raven to be a more willing participant now.

She was watching him when he turned back. He met her eyes, and she flushed a little, glancing away.

"This must all be somewhat overwhelming."

"You have no idea." She breathed a soft laugh, but the slight tremble in her hands told him how unsettled she was.

"Raven." She looked up, and the weight of worry on his chest eased as it did every time she met his eyes. "I'm glad you're here. I'll help you get through this part too."

Her answering smile was full of gratitude, though her expression turned serious when she glanced after the Delegate. "Doesn't she have a normal name?"

"I assume so."

She gave him a shrewd look. "You don't know what it is?"

"I don't know that anyone knows what it is at this

point. She is the Delegate. She has been Delegate for the Krivalen among our people for a very long time. Like everyone else, she respects the will of the council, but her influence is considerable. You can trust her."

Raven looked down at her hands then, sorrow casting a pall over her features. "The way Dellaura held me." She closed her eyes, and a tear slid down her cheek. "It felt so wonderful. It actually felt like home." She opened her eyes and gave him a pleading look full of heartfelt desperation. "Synderis, I don't even know her."

His heart broke for her then. She had been so young when her mother and father died. Who had raised her? Did she have anyone at all that she could call family?

He moved over to sit on the bed next to her. "Dellaura has been mourning your mother and you for a long time, Raven. You're a dream come true for her. You're her family. You are home here as far as she is concerned. But this is all new to you. It's natural that you should need some time to adjust to that idea."

She shook her head as if to deny his words. Then she looked at him. Not only at his face this time, but more at all of him, as if considering what he was to her. "I barely know you, yet I find myself wanting to curl in your arms again like I did in the dream. Is that wrong?"

It was only wrong if his longing desperately to hold her that way was wrong. Many here might say it was, mostly because she was a half-breed. Even he might have thought that once, but she had changed his mind so quickly. He no longer believed that her blood made her less than them.

He shook his head, then pulled off his boots and slid one leg behind her, moving into place so she could lean against his chest. When she rested her weight against him, he wrapped his arms around her and held her there.

They sat in silence that way for a while. When he

sensed that she was starting to drift off, he shook her arm gently to rouse her. "Do you trust me to help you sleep?"

Her answer was so soft he couldn't make it out, but she put up no resistance when he moved the magic into her. As gently as he could, he eased her to sleep and extracted himself, lying her back on the bed. He gazed down at her for a moment, finding it hard to walk away. He could only marvel at the courage and strength it must have required for her to make it this far. Having her there felt more like a dream than his dreamwalks had. With everything she had been through, she deserved every ounce of protection they could give her now. Once they freed her of her connection to the Brotherhood priest, no one would ever find her here.

He didn't want to leave, but he still had her blood on his clothes and needed to rest himself. First, he would send someone out to collect his and Raven's things, and he wanted to talk to the Delegate. The horse Raven had arrived on was grazing peacefully in a meadow nearby, receiving a well-earned break. Koshika had slipped off into the forest when they got close to the village. As tired as he was, he couldn't fight the feeling that he should take time to locate the big cat or at least warn the patrols that it might be lurking around.

"Synderis?"

He glanced over to see one of the healers standing there, a bundle of cloth in her hands that she offered him.

"I wasn't sure how long you meant to stay, but we keep extra clothing on hand in case someone needs it. This shirt ought to fit you. You can bring it back later."

He nodded and accepted the bundle, finding it difficult to smile. That struck him as strange. He was more than happy that Raven made it here. But she had nearly died in the process. Now that she was safe, how would she feel if she knew they weren't going to want her to leave again? None of the Krivalen ever ventured out into the wider world. Their existence was a secret, and keeping it that way required that they remain hidden. Raven may not have been born in Eyl'Thelandra, but she knew enough now to put them in danger. The council would insist that she stay, regardless of her impure blood. How far would they go to protect their people if she didn't want to?

Those were things he had no answers to yet. Maybe she wouldn't mind the idea of living here. In this place, no one would throw her in jail or put her to death for being Krivalen. She had true blood family here in Dellaura, and she knew him at least a little. With some encouragement, perhaps she would see that staying was the better option.

He took off his shirt and balled it up, using a clean spot to rub away the blood that had soaked through onto his skin. Then he pulled on the fresh shirt. It fit surprisingly well. More than adequate to see him through a few tasks before he retreated to his home to sleep.

Reaching down, he brushed a strand of hair out of Raven's face, aware that it was just an excuse to touch her. He couldn't wait for her to recover enough that he could show her around the village. She would love it. How could she not?

When he entered the evergreen temple a short time later, the Delegate was standing near the basin, her hands resting on the sides as she gazed into its depths. He was almost beside her before she looked up to acknowledge his presence. She let go of the basin and took a few steps to close the remaining distance, stripping away his secrets with a quick glance.

"You are quite fond of her."

It wasn't a question, but her expectant gaze made him feel some kind of answer was necessary. It was uncomfortable to consider admitting it to her, even if she had already figured it out. Would she try to discourage him? Would she suggest that he stay away from Raven?

"I suppose…" He trailed off when she held up a hand.

"Some things require more certainty, Synderis. Affection can't be a muddled thing if it is to have any power. Fortunately for you, I am certain you're fond of her." She turned and walked toward the arch, gesturing for him to accompany her. "What is it you wished to ask me?"

"Raven seemed… afraid of you. Especially when she first saw you."

Her lips pressed tightly together, and he wondered if he should have kept his curiosity to himself. Then she considered him for a few solemn seconds. A sorrowful hint of a smile gave the slightest curve to her mouth. The softness of affection in that expression put him more at ease.

"You are kind, Synderis. I knew you had the empathy required to help Aneiris. It isn't over yet, however, especially for her." He waited patiently as she plucked out a twig that had fallen into the archway. She would continue at her pace. Experience taught him that trying to rush her would only lengthen the pause. "The man who haunts her, Wayland Mallebron, was one of the men who first encountered the Acridan and took the Krivalen magic as their own. A founder of the Silverblood Brotherhood."

His chest tightened. "That would make him a few hundred years old."

She nodded calmly. "It would. Think of how many lives would have to be taken to make a human live that long. Consider how that would make him look. His hair. His eyes."

A dizzying blast of realization hit him, bringing with it an even greater sympathy for Raven. "Like you."

"Yes. She doesn't know our ways. She doesn't understand the differences that make Wayland a monster while I am a revered member of our village. This is where the power of your affection comes in. Tonight, I want you to be the one who sends the two of us into the dream. I want you to hold her asleep until after I have woken and left. What I must do in the dreamwalk may leave her unsettled. After we have rid her of Wayland, it should be safe to begin her induction into our culture. I trust that, through your affection and patience, you can help her see how we are not like the Silverbloods she is more familiar with."

This wasn't spoken as a question either, but he could tell from her expectant look that she intended for him to answer. If she wanted him to commit to spending time with Raven and helping her understand their ways, she didn't need to ask. She must know that. Perhaps she merely wanted him to say it.

He inclined his head. "Of course, Delegate. If you wish it."

She breathed a laugh. "You would have found some other excuse to be around her had I not given you this one. Do be careful, though." The humor disappeared. "She is young, and the world has not been gentle with her. There may be wounds in her heart that you can do nothing about."

He nodded. He could still try.

"Get some rest. We have work to do tonight."

"I will. Thank you, Delegate." He bowed before exiting the temple.

From there, he completed the remainder of his tasks and returned to his home in the trees. When he slept, it was a deeper, sounder sleep than he'd had in a while. He woke nine hours later, in the early evening, with a borderline panicked need to see that Raven was alive and safe. He made himself clean up first and dress in some of his own clean clothes. Then he hurried back to the healer's building on the ground level near the center of the village.

When he rushed to the sectioned-off area, trying not to walk like dragonlings nipped at his heels, he found Raven sitting up in the bed, picking at a selection of fruit and grains with one hand. She held up the side of the shirt they had given her with the other. A healer sat beside the bed, placing clean bandages over the wound.

Raven's color had improved. Rest and proper care stimulated her Krivalen healing. Her shy smile made him hesitate in the opening between the dividers. After everything they had been through together, the new shyness struck him as both out of place and somehow inevitable. Did she regret that she had let him hold her here, in the waking world? It couldn't matter. They had no time for awkwardness.

He forced himself to enter. "How are you feeling?"

"Better. The rest helped, and your healers are quite skilled." She let the side of her shirt down as the healer sat back.

The healer smiled. "That should do for now." She glanced up at him apologetically, and he sensed that he had gained stature in the elven female's eyes. She must have noticed him working closely with the Delegate. He had seen her around before, though he didn't know her well. "The Delegate sent word that we should see to the injury and get her some food before tonight to help bring her strength up."

He nodded. "Has Dellaura been back?"

"She came by, but the Delegate said not to let anyone visit until the dreamwalker is dealt with." The healer stood and stepped away from the bed. "You can have the chair," she offered. "I'll be back later."

Raven watched her depart before arching an eyebrow at him, her amused smirk easing some of his new uncertainty. "Does that mean you're not anyone or that you're too important for her to send away?"

He chuckled. "If they were willing to send away Dellaura, then I'm definitely not too important. I guess that makes me not anyone."

"You're someone important to me." She stole a piece of his heart with a few casual words, then turned her attention to the platter. "I don't even know what some of this is. I'd be happy to share if you'll educate me."

CHAPTER TWENTY THREE

Raven watched Synderis sink into the chair, avoiding her gaze. She couldn't stop thinking of how it felt to be in his arms. So secure and warm, yet he was still unknown to her in most ways. Was that why he wouldn't meet her eyes now? Did those same realizations nag at him?

She nudged the food tray closer to him and pointed to a juicy purple wedge of something. "What's that?"

He grinned, a little of his hesitancy disappearing, and took one of the pieces. "This is the best thing on the platter. It's called lamel." He held it up in front of her. "Try it."

Raven's fingers brushed his as she accepted it from him. She paused there, hungry for touch as much as she was for the food. His gaze moved to her face, the searching look acknowledging that extra moment of contact. She forced herself to continue through the motion, taking ownership of the wedge and biting into it. A hint of delicate floral scent rose from the fruit. The flavor that broke across her tongue was lightly sweet. It was refreshing rather than overwhelming like some other items on the platter. A cool stream on a hot day.

She smiled in appreciation as she ate the rest.

"What did I tell you?" he said, taking another for himself.

"Does Dellaura hold rank here? Your earlier comment seemed to imply so."

He nodded. "She's a member of the council. They make most of the decisions around the health and safety of the community, among other things. Even the Delegate is guided by their decisions."

They both reached for the same wedge of lamel. He withdrew his hand, his grin infectious, and gestured for her to take it.

"What do you mean by *guided*?" she asked, then bit into the slice, awaiting his answer.

He took his time enjoying another piece of fruit before responding. "The Delegate is responsible for overseeing the Krivalen. She guides us. She advises the council on how we should be utilized and managed. She also has the final say on whether someone will be allowed to become Krivalen."

He spoke as if becoming Krivalen were a common occurrence. Did they care no more about taking a life than the Brotherhood? Didn't it bother them that those who chose to become that way could die in the process or that other lives were consumed in the making?

Raven shifted away from him, fighting a sense of panic. She worked so hard and suffered a great deal to come here. To find her mother's family. Had she made the wrong choice? But where else was she supposed to go? Those she cared about were in danger as long as she stayed with them. Recent events made that clearer than ever. Phendaril and Ehric could have died when the guards overtook them. Her brief conversation with Ehric made it apparent that Phendaril hadn't escaped death by much. She couldn't be the reason the ones she loved died. Nor could she sit here and pretend she saw nothing wrong with the methods required to make someone Silverblood... or Krivalen. Whichever word they chose to use for it.

"Raven? Is something wrong?"

He was watching her intently now, concern furrowing his brow. His silver eyes were bright and brimming with the kindness she repeatedly sensed in him. The sheen of silver in his white hair told her that more than one life ended to make him. She didn't choose to become this way. He had. He had made a choice.

The familiar melodic voice of the Delegate alerted them to her arrival. "There will be time to discuss these things later."

Her appearance turned Raven's blood to ice. Sorrow constricted her throat as she looked away from Synderis. If this was who they were, she couldn't stay here, but her journey would not be a complete waste if they could sever the connection to Wayland.

She made herself meet the Delegate's eyes, so like Wayland's. "It's time?"

The Delegate nodded. "It's late enough now. The Silverblood priest seems intent upon finding you. I doubt he'll waste any time getting back to his search."

Synderis held up the platter next to Raven. The hint of unease undermining his smile doing nothing to soothe her nerves. "Any last selections before we do this?"

Raven shook her head. Her appetite had disappeared. A hint of worry lingered in his regard as he moved the fruit away, but he didn't press. He wouldn't, she suspected, with the Delegate there.

"What do we have to do?"

The Delegate sat on the edge of the bed, her gentle expression at odds with the cruelty suggested by the liquid silver hair and the silver gloss of her lips. Those things made her a murderer in Raven's mind. It was hard to trust her, but she forced herself to stay calm, remembering the breathing exercises Jaecar had taught her.

"Synderis will put you asleep. That will be easier than trying to fall asleep naturally when you're already anxious. Since he has dreamwalked you so many times, he will guide me into your dream. Then he will back out and wait for us." Her gaze flickered to Synderis, who gave a slight nod. Her gaze shifted to Raven. "This is particularly important, Raven. Once we're in the dream, I need you to let Wayland think he has the upper hand. If this is to work, you must not try to cast him out. You must not try to leave the dream yourself either. No matter what happens. We only get one chance at this."

Raven's familiar anxiety began rising. They were strangers, and the Delegate frightened her. How was she supposed to trust her? How could she stop herself from trying to cast the Krivalen female or Wayland out of her dream? After the last encounter with Wayland, how could she stand there and face him without trying to get away?

"The last time I faced him in my dream..." She trailed off when the Delegate placed one cold finger on her lips.

"None of that matters. This dream is the only thing that matters. Do you want to be free of him?"

"Absolutely. Yes."

The Delegate nodded. "Focus on that certainty. Make that your only thought. This will free you from your connection to him if you have the courage to follow through with it."

Raven set her jaw. She had walked into a mine infested with corpse eaters in the company of a Silverblood. Of course she had the courage.

"I thought so." The Delegate stood, gesturing to Synderis. "Help me move these dividers and slide another bed over. It is time to break Father Mallebron's connection to her."

Within a few minutes, Raven was lying back on the

bed, her stomach doing flips. Synderis gave her his encouraging smile full of confidence.

"Are you ready?"

She wasn't, but she made herself nod.

●

Raven stood outside her childhood home in the forest. The gate to the little goat paddock hung open. The lean-to the men had tied her parents to stood there. A simple, harmless-looking structure. It had no memory of the way it was used to torture them. She did, though. Their screams echoed in her head still, muffled by the tight gags those men had put in their mouths.

She shook herself, trying to clear away the memories as she walked into the paddock. There. That was where her father died. And over here... She sank to her knees in the same spot she had knelt that day, next to where her mother had bled out.

"Why did you do it, Mom?"

That unwelcome tremor moved through the dream then. Her heart beat triple-time as she got to her feet and turned to face him. Wayland stood at the paddock entrance. He was solid this time. No flickering. No struggle to control his movement within her dreamscape. He looked around the paddock, his lips curving slowly up.

"This is where you were made?"

Raven tried to swallow the lump of terror in her throat. She was stronger now. She could call the sword back and drive him out like she had before. But she hesitated. For some reason, she wasn't supposed to. She was supposed to face him but let him believe he was winning. Why?

Fear clouded her thoughts.

"You don't need to answer me, little Raven. I can feel it."

"Don't call me that," she hissed.

"Why? Did your mother call you that? Or maybe it's the name your elven lover calls you?"

He advanced a few feet in a blink. She sucked in on a scream and stepped back, but her heel hit something. She felt behind her with one hand. She had run into one of the lean-to posts, the same one her mother had been tied to when the man used her as an archery target. She swallowed panic and started to move away, but her hand was bound. Reaching back, she felt the rope that held her and began trying to untie it, but she couldn't. Her other hand was also tied to the post.

Terror surged through her. She tried to jerk away, but her wrists were tied high above her now, stretching her so that her feet barely touched the ground. Wayland grinned, a wild, hungry light in his silver eyes. He appeared in front of her and caressed his fingertips down the line of her neck.

"Ensnared by your own nightmare. How poetic." His hand closed around her throat, squeezing like a vice. "Where are you, little Raven?"

She fought a wave of panic. This wasn't going to happen. No matter what she was *supposed* to do, she wasn't going to let him do this to her. Both hands were suddenly free. She wrapped her fingers around the sword hilt. With one hand, she grabbed the wrist of the hand at her throat. With the other, she slammed the blade home under his breastbone as she had done before in the waking world.

His mouth dropped open in surprise.

"I should have killed you the first time," she snarled.

He started to try to pull away. The scar down Raven's breastbone split open with pain equal to the original injury. Blood-slicked silver vines burst from the reopened wound. They wrapped around her sword arm and climbed up the weapon, plunging into his chest. Something moved under the skin of his forearm, then similar vines, wet with silvery blood, ripped out, crawling up his arm to wrap around her neck. Agony blazed through her as the vines from his arm burrowed into the flesh of her neck.

Wayland howled with pain, thrashing to break away, his eyes wide now with horror.

Raven wanted to thrash and howl with him, but her body no longer responded to her wishes. Her weight shifted forward, pushing on the blade, driving it deeper into him while the vines from his arm tore through her skin, writhing beneath her flesh.

"We're connected, you and I." Her lips moved. The voice was her own, but she didn't speak the words.

Raven started fighting against whatever had taken control of her, until she saw the terror mirrored in his eyes—the complete desperation as he struggled to free himself. Her thoughts cleared. She remembered the Delegate's words. This was intentional. Though every fiber of her being wanted to fight, she made herself stop resisting, giving in to the suffering and the strange force that had taken over.

"We'll always be connected," her voice snarled.

The vines writhed under his skin, putting him through the same agonizing torture she suffered. The visible portions of the vines sprouted sharp, curved thorns then. Nausea assailed her as those thorns grew from the vines inside her flesh as well, protruding through the skin in places. The same thing happened to him, wicked thorns tearing out of his flesh.

"Noooooo!" Wayland grabbed a handful of the vines sinking into his chest as his scream reverberated through the dreamscape. With one violent effort, he ripped the vines out of his flesh, spraying silvery blood over both of them. He fell on his back, blood streaming from torn skin over his arm and chest. For a second, he seemed frozen, staring up at her in horror, then he disappeared.

The vines in Raven's body vanished, along with the pain and the presence that had taken control. She sank to her knees, shaking violently, and threw up on ground painted silvery-red with their blood.

•

Synderis struggled to wait for the Delegate to awaken. Raven's terror poured through their fledgling connection. Sweat broke out over her face while she twitched and moaned in her sleep. Meanwhile, the Delegate lay silent and still, her breathing even. Finally, when the temptation to wake Raven had almost overcome him, the Delegate's eyes opened. She calmly sat up, glancing over at Raven before rising to her feet.

"Considering she has only a fraction of the lives in her that I do, she's remarkably strong. She nearly forced me out." The Delegate looked at him. "The moment I am gone, wake her. She will need comforting."

With no further explanation, she strode away. Synderis waited until she was barely out of sight before waking Raven. Her eyes snapped open. She gasped and sat up so fast that he didn't have time to stop her. A grimace twisted her lips as one hand pressed against her injured side. She was trembling.

Synderis reached out to her, and she jerked away from him, wincing at another apparent jolt of pain from her side.

"Don't touch me!"

"Raven." He moved a little closer, and she threw a hand between them.

"Don't. Touch. Me." Her gaze shifted to something past him. "None of you touch me."

He glanced over his shoulder to see one of the healers standing there. He sent her away with a slight shake of his head, then turned back to Raven. Drawing on his magic, he pushed a sense of safety toward her.

"Please, Raven. Let me help you."

"No." Her voice cracked.

He saw the break sweeping over her and moved onto the bed as she crumpled, drawing her into his arms. She fell against him, one hand gripping his arm and the other draped over his shoulder as she wept against his chest. He wrapped his other arm around her shoulders, folding her in the warmth of his embrace.

"You're safe now," he murmured, kissing her head. It was hard not to hate himself for playing a part in this. He didn't even know for sure if it had worked. The Delegate hadn't said, though he suspected she would have looked much less satisfied if it hadn't. He hoped it was worth whatever she had put Raven through to do it.

CHAPTER TWENTY FOUR

Rapid knocking on the bedroom door dragged Karsima up from sleep. Alayne stirred next to her, beginning to extract herself from their tangle of limbs. She was on the outside, so she got to her feet first, throwing a blanket around her naked torso as she strode to the door. For a few seconds, Karsima stopped trying to get up and let herself admire the line of Alayne's muscular shoulders above the blanket and the curve of her toned calves sticking out beneath it.

Alayne pulled the door partway open, and Jenner peered in, his brows pinched with concern. "Milady, Phendaril's back. Synal's tending to him now."

Karsima was on her feet and pulling on her clothes before he finished speaking, no longer caring if he saw her naked. "He's injured?"

"Yes." He turned to stare out into the hallway. "I'm not sure of the details. I came to get you straight away."

"Thank you." She was still pulling on one boot as she half hopped to the door. When she glanced around for the other, Alayne held it out to her. Karsima nodded her gratitude, finding it impossible to smile. Dread chilled her to the core.

"Go. I'll be right behind you." Alayne made a shooing motion.

Karsima tugged the other boot on and rushed out,

fear coiling inside her stomach like some fast-growing serpent. Jenner hurried along beside her as she strode downstairs and out the front door into the square. It was early yet. The sun had barely begun to lighten the sky on the horizon, and the air was brisk.

"What about Ehric and Raven?"

"Ehric is with him. Looked to be limping, but not too bad. No sign of Raven." Jenner shook his head, his expression apologetic as if he had any control over the news he carried.

The entrance to the medical building was standing open. An ox-drawn cart from down near the docks waited out front. Karsima broke into a jog, rushing through the door. Inside, Synal, Talis, and Ellandra gathered around the bed on which Phendaril lay. Sweat beaded on his forehead, his dark auburn hair slicked back with it, and he looked unnaturally pale, but his eyes were closed and his breathing even. The three healers turned when she entered. Synal nodded to the other two and walked over to intercept Karsima.

Ehric got up from where he had been sitting on one of the other beds. He limped over to join them.

"How is he?" Karsima demanded.

"He'll be all right." Synal spoke in the professional, calming tone she used for worried loved ones. "He's got some broken ribs and a broken leg, but his biggest problem right now is his hand. The bone broke through the skin in the back of his hand and wasn't set properly. The wound was infected under the bandages. He's got a high fever. We put him to sleep to clean the wound and see if it's necessary to make any additional repairs while he's under."

Karsima leaned to one side to see her old friend where he lay still on the bed. Too still for her liking. She wanted to help, but there was nothing she could do here that the healers couldn't do much better. "Do what you need to do for him? I can wait."

Synal nodded and returned to the bed.

Alayne came up behind Karsima, sliding her arms around her waist. Karsima leaned back into the comfort of those arms, turning her attention to Ehric. The dark-skinned warrior had bandages wrapping his shoulder and one leg.

"What happened?"

"Lysanna's sister found out Phendaril was in town and caused a scene in Lathwood. Raven was exposed in the encounter. We left town right away, but some of the guards and a Silverblood came after us on the road. They shot the horse out from under Raven and Phendaril. He was injured and knocked unconscious in the fall. They shot me in the leg and the shoulder. We were beaten before we even had a chance to fight. Raven knew that, so she offered herself up to them to protect us. They took her and left us there. I managed to get him back to town." He nodded toward Phendaril, his grimace recounting some of that ordeal for him. "Unfortunately, the healers in the elven ward had little training and inadequate supplies. They did their best, but I knew he'd get better care here."

"You did the right thing." Her gut twisted at the thought of Phendaril having to leave Raven behind, not that he would have been in any shape to argue the decision. "And Raven. Is she still . . ."

She trailed off when Ehric exhaled softly and shook his head, admiration in his tone when he spoke again.

"She's a wonder, that one. Somehow, she managed to escape the jail. With the Brotherhood still hunting her, she didn't feel like she could come back here without putting everyone else in danger. She told me she knew how to find her mother's family. So she decided to continue on alone."

"She's got a bigger heart than her body can afford,"

Alayne said softly over Karsima's shoulder.

Maybe she did. That meant that Raven was on her own again unless she had managed to find her mother's family. "Do you think she was telling the truth about knowing how to find them?"

Ehric was watching the healers work on Phendaril. His brow furrowed. "She seemed confident when she said it. It wasn't easy convincing him to leave without her, though. If he could have gone after her himself, I think he would have. I'm almost surprised he didn't try crawling after her."

"It wouldn't have surprised me, either." A wry smirk turned Karsima's lips. Phendaril hadn't had the best luck when it came to relationships. That was why she tried to warn him against falling for Raven. The young half-elf was guaranteed to find herself in trouble.

A few hours later, Synal nudged Karsima awake where she had dozed off on one of the empty beds. Alayne and Ehric were both asleep in chairs next to the bed. Synal gestured for Karsima to follow, so she got up and snuck after the healer, careful not to make enough noise to wake her companions.

The healers had managed to move Phendaril into one of the private rooms without waking any of them. He rested propped up on some pillows, his hair and skin dry of sweat now. That meant the fever had broken. A good sign. Clean bandages wrapped his hand, and the broken leg was properly braced. A shallow cut along the right side of his jaw was cleaned and healing. They had taken off his shirt, and, with the blanket not pulled up all the way, she could see dark bruising along his rib cage.

He watched her walk in, his dark eyes full of anguish that no amount of healing would ease. His uninjured hand held something that hung from a string around his neck, though she couldn't see what it was. Synal left, shutting the door behind her as Karsima went to sit in a chair next to him.

"How do you feel?"

His smirk was bitter. "Like a horse fell on me."

Karsima touched his arm. "I'm just glad you're alive."

"I couldn't keep her safe." His jaw clenched. He rested his head back, closing his eyes against the pain.

"She made the right choice, Phen. She's a capable woman. She'll be all right."

"She's not invincible. She's walking around out there with a perpetual target on her." He opened his eyes. A tear slipped free, though the anger in those eyes was quickly overtaking the sorrow. "She shouldn't have to do this alone."

He was right. Raven would always be in danger out there. Perhaps, if she found her mother's family, they could keep her safe better than Amberwood managed to. "You're not invincible either. This time, she's doing what she needs to do to protect you. Let her. When you're healed, you can reconsider your options."

He opened his hand and gazed at the item hanging from the string. It was three-quarters of a circle of woven silver ending in two raven heads. It looked like a cloak pin.

"What is that?"

"We found it at the keep where Raven grew up. She thought it was her mother's. When she last spoke to Ehric, she told him that she would use its twin to reach out to me in my dreams once she found her mother's family."

Karsima stared at the object, almost hoping it would do something to prove that those odd words could be true. She had a feeling Phendaril was waiting for the same thing. After a few seconds, he let it fall back against his chest and closed his eyes again, his hand sinking to his side.

"Do you think there's anything to it?" she asked.

"I don't know. I thought I felt something from it the first night, but my sleep was plagued by pain and fever. I might have imagined it. Since then, with my condition worsening, I'm not sure I've slept soundly enough that I would know if she tried to reach out to me."

Karsima nodded. She contemplated the cloak pin for a long time. How strange would it be if Raven could reach out to him through such an ordinary object? It seemed unlikely, but it at least gave him something of hers to hold close.

She glanced up at him. His eyes were still closed, but his features had relaxed, and his breathing evened out. She desperately wanted to talk to him about the soldiers his scouts had spotted gathering on Darrenton's property, but that would have to wait. It would be cruel to wake him again now.

Whatever Darrenton was up to, Alayne was sure it didn't bode well for them. She had the Stonebreakers running extra patrols around the perimeter of town now while Phendaril's scouts continued patrolling the outer borders of their land. They had begun rebuilding the town walls on the northeastern edge, working night and day. Even with their numbers, there wasn't much chance of finishing a wall around the entire town faster than Darrenton could gather troops. If he meant to attack, which she suspected he did, they wouldn't be ready.

Alayne sent a missive to her uncle, King Navaran. It was debatable if that would do them any good. If the king even considered sending troops, they wouldn't arrive anytime soon. It would take several days for the missive to reach Chadhurst and even longer for him to decide how to respond and organize a force if he chose to do so. Then that force had to reach Amberwood by coming up the river or overland and around to the east. Perhaps the smart thing to do would be to try bargaining with Darrenton. Or would it make more sense to attack him before he managed to gather more soldiers to his side?

To add to their problems, Veylin hadn't returned from her last patrol. Karsima feared Darrenton's men might be involved in the young scout's disappearance. Whatever they were going to do to deal with this threat, they needed to devise a plan soon.

Alayne was outside the door when Karsima left Phendaril's room. The other woman met her eyes. "Want to go work on the wall with me?"

A smile tugged at the corners of her mouth. Driving herself to exhaustion moving stone and wood to build their wall sounded cathartic. "Yes, my love. I do."

CHAPTER TWENTY FIVE

Raven spent the next two days in the care of the healers. They kept everyone away, insisting that she rest and recover. They assured her that someone would show her around the village as soon as her side was sufficiently healed, She considered fighting for an early release, but the two Krivalen alternating guard duty outside the partitions looked more than capable of meeting that challenge. The day after her nightmare dreamwalk with the Delegate, they brought Raven's sword, dagger, bow, and quiver to her, laying them next to the bed. The gesture of trust earned her cooperation for a time.

By the afternoon of the second day, however, she had made three attempts to sneak out. Somehow, the Krivalen guards managed to stay a step ahead of her. Perhaps simply because her injury slowed her down so much. They did allow her a bath. Since she couldn't submerge the wound yet, one of the healers helped her clean off with a sponge while she stood in the tub. The process reminded her a little too much of her time in the Brotherhood temple being prepared to meet Wayland. When they finished, she was nauseous and struggling to hide the shake in her hands.

That evening, she sat scowling at the healer over the supper they had brought her.

"How are you sleeping?" the healer asked, impervious to her glower.

Raven stopped with a bite halfway to her mouth. After the Delegate's intervention, she had slept more soundly than she had any time since Wayland started appearing in her dreams. Her dreams were her own. There hadn't been even a whisper of his presence in them. As much as she hated to admit it, she owed them something for that.

The healer gave her a pointed look and nodded. "I thought so." She stood up and turned to walk away.

"Wait."

The healer paused.

"What's your name?"

The female's expression oozed with annoyance, but she kept her tone civil. "Sillara."

"Thank you, Sillara."

The healer gave a curt nod and left.

The following morning, Raven was awake and dressed early, hoping that she might convince them to let her leave. She was sitting on her bed cleaning her weapons when Synderis came in around mid-morning. A tiny amused smirk touched his lips as he watched her, though she refused to offer anything resembling a smile in return.

"I begin to see why the healers were concerned about whether they would be able to keep you here any longer."

She swept a cloth along the edge of the sword blade resting across her crossed legs. "Do they intend to do so?"

He grabbed the chair and spun it around, straddling it and resting his arms on the back. "That's beautiful." He gestured to the arrowhead pendant that hung out of her shirt.

She let him dodge the question for the moment

while she touched the wooden arrowhead, an ache spreading through her chest. Was Phendaril all right? "It's made from a piece of my father's bow."

His searching look offered her no insight into what he hoped to find. He tapped the back of the chair with two fingers and considered her for a second before speaking again. "You are something of a difficult patient, you know. The healers don't feel that their efforts have been appreciated."

Raven took a deep breath and set aside the blade. "I do appreciate the healing and the assistance with my dream stalker." She shuddered at that memory, and a hint of sympathy flickered across his features in response, melting away a little of the defensive shield she was trying to put up between them. Were her emotional barriers that flimsy, or was it just him? "It's only that . . . how many Krivalen are there here?"

He looked genuinely puzzled for a few seconds before a light sparked in his silver eyes, and he smiled. She hated that handsome, infectious smile. Or she at least tried to hate it.

"I think I see the problem." He stood and slid the chair out of the way, then offered her a hand. "Are you up for a walk?"

"Yes, please." She accepted his hand, letting him take some of her weight to avoid straining her side as she stood.

She found herself standing close enough that she felt the warmth of his body next to her. The smell of him brought a sense of comfort, likely inspired by the many times he had held her when she was in distress. She knew too well how strong his arms were and how gentle his embrace was. Her legs bumped the bed when she shifted back from him, hastily extracting her hand from his. As he turned away, she caught a glimpse of the chain he wore that held the talisman. The object that would let her reach out to Phendaril. Somehow, she had to convince him to give it to her.

Instead of leading her toward the front, he took her around a corner and up a set of stairs. Climbing steps pulled on the stitches in her side far more than level walking did, but she managed it without complaint. At the top, he opened a door, and they emerged onto a platform on the roof. Raven scanned their surroundings and her breath caught in her throat.

His smile broadened, and he spread his arms wide. "Welcome to Eyl'Thelandra, Raven."

A forest of massive trees stretched as far as she could see on all sides, their tops lost in a canopy of green high above. Woven through them at different levels were elevated walkways and structures of varying sizes built around the trunks and into the branches, all designed to blend with the pallet and shape of the forest. Myriad more buildings sprouted up on the ground with white pebble pathways winding between them amidst lush gardens. The houses below reminded her of her early childhood home, with living vines and plants growing upon them in aesthetically pleasing arrangements. Her mother's natural decorative flair was all around her here. This place was where it originated.

Raven brushed away a tear, aware of Synderis standing quietly next to her, allowing her the space to experience her emotions. The other thing she noticed as she stood there was how many elves wandered the paths below and the elevated walkways above. Only elves. They all wore comfortable or functional attire, moving about their morning with an ease that came from knowing they were safe. It was almost like being in Amberwood, only this was all theirs, and they looked as if they belonged here.

"Eyl'Thelandra," she murmured. Her gaze shifted to steps leading up from their position to a higher platform against the tree next to them. She started up them, moving slowly. After the first set of stairs to get up on the roof, she had an insistent ache in her side.

Synderis stepped up beside her. "If you would allow it." He offered out his arms.

Raven looked up at the tree's trunk, then at him, and nodded. He slid one hand around her back and the other under her knees, lifting her with gentle care. With no apparent effort, he carried her up the remaining steps. She did her best to ignore how acutely she missed the contact when he put her down at the top.

She approached the tree, placing her palms against the massive trunk, feeling the rough bark of that ancient living giant under her skin. Then she leaned in, resting her cheek against it, and closed her eyes as she breathed in the delicious fragrance of evergreen.

Behind her, Synderis chuckled.

Keeping her eyes closed, a smile moving across her lips, she asked, "What's so funny?"

"Well, I'd say there is no doubt that you are your mother's child."

She opened her eyes and turned, leaning back against the trunk. "Did you know her?"

He shook his head. "I only met Mellaine a few times. I guided some of the dreamwalks Dellaura went on to meet with her after she left here. Dell loves to talk about her, though, so I feel a little like I did know her."

"Tell me about her."

To her surprise, he shook his head. "I'll leave that to Dell. I think she would be quite cross with me if I took away her chance to share that with you." He glanced at an elevated walk where a Krivalen male was striding past. The other elf gave him a nod that he returned. His gaze moved back to her. "You and I have other things to discuss, and I have many things to show you."

Raven hesitated. She wanted to see everything, yet

the desire to learn more about her mother was insistent. "When will I get to speak with Dellaura again?"

"If you're patient, I believe she is planning to invite you to stay with her now that the healers and the Delegate are willing to let you venture out. Don't worry. I'll make sure you run into her today." He took a step toward the stairs down and offered her his hand for support. "Unless you'd rather I carry you again."

His grin told her he wouldn't mind doing so. Her cheeks warmed in response, making her wish she could refuse entirely, but she accepted his hand. Descending would be a little easier. Still, having his support to take some stress off would reduce the chance of worsening her injury. When they were back below, he led her out through the front.

On the ground level, amongst the elves, their presence became far more intimidating. She was among strangers again. Worse, these were all pure-blooded elves. She might take after her mother in appearance, but she recalled how easily Phendaril noticed her mixed blood the first time they met. The inclination to sink back behind Synderis slowed her steps.

He stopped and faced her, a mix of curiosity and concern in the tightening around his eyes. "Are you all right?"

She nodded, trying hard to keep her breathing steady, though her hands trembled. After a few seconds, she shook her head. "I don't..."

"Belong?"

His gentle tone and fond smile eased some of her rising anxiety, but she still found it difficult to put her fears into words. He didn't know her past like Phendaril did. He had no idea how hard this was for her, and she wasn't sure she wanted him to know. As much as she longed for someone to understand her current dread, there was freedom in the fact that he knew nothing of how broken she had been. Perhaps still was.

"Do you trust me, Raven?"

"No," she answered abruptly.

Synderis chuckled. "Are you sure of that?"

She shifted her feet and blew out a heavy exhale. "No."

"Follow me."

He led her down a series of paths, visibly shortening his strides to match her pace and avoid causing her pain. When others greeted him, his responses were friendly enough, but she caught the occasional slight shake of his head to discourage extended interactions. Raven did her best not to hide behind him. She might not be a pure-blooded elf, but she was the granddaughter of one of their council members. That must be worth something. She did get several lingering glances, especially from other Krivalen, though their looks were always the hardest to read. Did her Krivalen nature make her more or less acceptable to them? Did she want their acceptance?

Within five minutes, they were outside the more densely populated part of the village. He led her through the trees to the edge of a swift-moving creek. It cascaded over several levels on a gradual slope, the crisp scent of the clean water cutting through the aroma of the underbrush and trees. He sank down to sit cross-legged in some soft moss near the bank, gesturing for her to join him. She sat carefully, making a point of not sitting too close to him. Her emotions were confused enough already. She held her silence, running her fingertips over the moss to feel the tickle of it against her skin.

He twirled a twig between two fingers as he spoke. "When I mentioned the Acridan in one of our dream-walks, you didn't question it, so I assume someone told you something about them."

She adjusted her seat to mask a shiver. "Wayland told me a little."

"Hm." His eyebrows lifted slightly at that revelation, and he tossed the twig aside. "The Brotherhood priest. What did he tell you?"

"Not much. He said the Acridan were the originators of the Silverblood – Krivalen – magic. They all died because of something humans brought with them. Some disease or something they were resistant to that proved deadly to the Acridan. He also mentioned a group of elves that lived close to them as the probable source for occasional elves, like my mother, who know the magic. I'm going to guess those elves are your ancestors."

"Our ancestors," he corrected. She couldn't stop a smile in response to that inclusion. "The truth is that those elves lived much more closely with the Acridan than the human visitors ever knew. We were practically a single culture when the men arrived. Because the history between men and elves was already tumultuous, the Acridan encouraged our ancestors to keep their distance while the humans were there. As a result, the men assumed we were only distantly acquainted.

"The Acridan were a generous race, to a fault. Krivalen magic was part of their everyday life. It was core to their culture, so they started sharing it with the humans as they successfully had with us. As soon as they discovered how often the magic was lethal to humans, they stopped teaching it to them. Then they realized that their own kind were dying because of something the humans brought with them. They began recording the history and use of Krivalen magic in a book they meant to give to the elves."

Raven remembered the tome in Wayland's collection room. How he touched those pages with their strange words. "I've seen that book. In the temple in Pellanth."

He sat forward. "Really?"

She took more than a little pleasure from the awe and admiration in his tone. "Yes, though I didn't know enough to appreciate it at the time."

"A trio of men, who would become the founders of the Silverblood Brotherhood, stole the book. Fortunately, they don't know how to read Acridan. Our people pretended ignorance at the time. After the last of the Acridan died off, our ancestors disappeared into the forests so that those men couldn't try to use them to learn more about the Acridan. Eventually, they ended up here."

He shifted position, moving so he could look at her more directly. "We continue to honor the values and many of the traditions the Acridan shared with our ancestors. You see, the Acridan believed that to die without your spirit being Accepted by another was to become stranded between worlds. Every Acridan became Krivalen by their seventh year. That way, if one of them died, anyone could prevent their spirit from being lost by Accepting it into themselves. It is the greatest of honors to be the vessel for another life.

"They taught our people everything about the magic. Not only how to become Krivalen, but all the ways to use it afterward. Unlike humans, and in direct opposition to the lies the Brotherhood tells about it, elves rarely die in the transformation as long as we are healthy and strong at the time of our making. Like the Acridan, we consider it an honor to serve as a vessel for our people when they die. And, unlike the Brotherhood, we never deliberately kill anyone to make ourselves Krivalen. If someone is near death, then the option arises for a new Krivalen to be made."

He was watching her intently. Her cheeks grew hot with the realization that her assumptions had been wrong. He and the other Krivalen here hadn't killed anyone to gain power. They had chosen to be vessels for the spirits of those who were dying.

"I didn't know," she murmured, barely loud enough

to be heard over the burbling of the creek.

His smile was forgiving. "That's why I brought you here. It was obvious that what you believed you knew of the Krivalen magic was eating away at you. I thought you might be able to appreciate Eyl'Thelandra and its people more if you understood."

"Thank you." His kind regard reminded her of Eamon for a moment. Had she known all of this then, would she have tried to take Eamon's spirit into her? She gave herself a mental shake to push him out of her thoughts. "Then the Delegate—"

"Is nothing at all like Wayland Mallebron."

She buried her face in her hands and closed her eyes. An almost giddy relief swept through her, making her want to laugh and weep simultaneously. She drew a deep breath, trying to maintain her composure. When she opened her eyes, a large cat with emerald feathers was staring intently at her from a rock a few feet behind Synderis. She reached for her sword, remembering that she hadn't brought it as her hand closed on air.

ynderis caught the sudden change in her demeanor and the reach for her absent blade. He glanced over his shoulder. The lalyx cat's ears pressed against its skull, but it swiveled one forward when it looked back at him. He held up a hand to Raven.

"Don't worry. This one's a friend." He held his other hand out to the cat. It crept closer, watching Raven so intently he was impressed that it didn't slip off the rocks and fall into the creek. The lalyx finally pressed its head into his palm, never taking its eyes off Raven.

"What is it?" Raven asked, her tone soft now to avoid startling the cat.

"A lalyx. They're common in the forest." He glanced around to see Raven up on her knees now, her eyes bright with delight as she watched the big cat. "They aren't usually this friendly. I'm afraid I influenced this one to help care for a chronic injury. I call it Koshika. It means spirit in Acridan."

Her gaze flickered to him for a second. "You kept their language alive too?"

He nodded, enjoying the new admiration and acceptance in her regard. She no longer saw him as a killer like the Silverbloods. She understood now that the Krivalen were different from their human counterparts. That changed everything, and he liked what it did to the way she looked at him.

Raven held out a hand, and he opened his mouth, intending to discourage her, but Koshika moved past him. The cat's feathered coat fluffed up with tension, making it look even larger than it was. It stopped a few strides past him and leaned forward, sniffing at her outstretched fingers. Fully aware of how little Raven would appreciate losing her hand because he startled the cat, he moved very slowly up alongside the animal, bringing himself closer to Raven. Then he placed a hand lightly on the feathered shoulders.

"You can trust her, Koshika," he murmured, keeping his tone soothing.

"Don't use your magic," Raven said softly.

The cat took another wary step, putting itself within Raven's reach.

"I'm not." Surprisingly, he was telling the truth. Using the magic in this situation would reduce the risk, but the cat appeared receptive to her offered contact.

He watched in awe and with a hint of jealousy as Raven brought her fingers forward, and the cat rubbed against them. Raven's joyous smile banished the jealousy, making him suddenly more envious of Koshika. The cat settled alongside them within a few minutes, purring while they stroked the silky, feathered coat. Raven sat to one side, relaxing next to him. He followed her example.

"The feathers are so much softer than I would have expected." She gazed at the lalyx, letting those feathers slide between her fingers. He caught a slight edge of sorrow in her voice when she spoke again. "I'm ashamed to admit I would have gone to my sword first. Perhaps it's good that I can't wear it right now."

"I wouldn't have let you." His fingers brushed hers as they both reached to stroke the cat's head again. He swallowed, trying hard not to think about how close they were sitting now. Whatever they shared in the dreamwalks didn't preclude a need to know her better in the waking world. "You're Krivalen, Raven. You can use that magic to avoid harming creatures like this one. Just remember to take back what you put into them. Under most circumstances, it's preferable to leave them wild."

She nodded. Her gaze caught on the talisman that had slipped out from under his shirt. "I meant to ask you. When the Delegate dreamwalked me, there was no talisman. Is that because you were there?"

He met her eyes. Somehow, through the process of petting Koshika, they had ended even closer than he realized. The slightest lean, and...

He looked down at the cat. "Only a Krivalen can initiate a dreamwalk. It typically requires either two connected talismans or physical contact. However, someone who isn't Krivalen can be guided into a dreamwalk the way your grandmother was with your mother. In the case of the Delegate and you, she could have initiated through physical contact, but she felt it would be better if I did it since we already had some rapport built up."

"Except I no longer have the other talisman."

He leaned back, coming to rest with his hands behind him, holding him upright. It gave him room to think. "If both parties are Krivalen, it is possible for a connection to form that precludes the need for talismans or physical contact."

"Merely through repetition?"

He cleared his throat and stood slowly, careful not to startle Koshika. "Something like that." He held out his hands to help Raven up.

She narrowed her eyes at him, though she accepted his offer, letting him lift her to her feet. "You're being deliberately evasive now."

He met her eyes for a second, then turned away. Was he supposed to tell her that repetition had nothing to do with it? It had more to do with developing an intimate emotional connection but saying that felt manipulative. It would put in her head the thought that there was a bond between them. Although it wouldn't be a lie. For him to dreamwalk her the way he had or feel her need the night she had reached the monument, there had to be something there for both of them.

"Come. I promised the Delegate I would bring you by the temple." He started walking but stopped when he realized she wasn't following. He glanced back to find her looking back at Koshika, who was standing staring after him.

"Can she come with us?"

He chuckled. "You're certain it's a female?"

She glanced up at him. "Isn't she?"

"Given its build, probably. I was respecting its privacy."

"That's reasonable. Are you going to answer that question or leave me hanging again?"

A trace of demand hardened her features. He found it unexpectedly attractive.

"Koshika will follow as far as *she* is comfortable."

To his surprise, Koshika followed them back to the edge of the village. She stuck close at his side as they skirted the perimeter and entered the temple of trees. The whole way, Raven peered around them with an expression of wonder, taking in the forest and the village. Having lived here his entire life, he rarely considered how it would look to someone else. Seeing this home they had created within the oldest forest on the continent through her eyes made it new and more magnificent.

The Delegate was waiting for them by the archway within the temple. Koshika hung back short of crossing the creek and settled there to watch them.

They stopped before the Delegate, and Synderis inclined his head respectfully. After a moment's hesitation, Raven did the same. In the brief time her gaze was cast down, the Delegate gave him a pleased smile.

"Welcome." The Delegate nodded to each of them before looking past them to offer a third nod to the lalyx. "It has been a while since I last had a companion in my temple. She is yours, Synderis?"

Raven cast him a smug look. He fought back a grin. Yes, the cat was female.

"I believe she is hers, Delegate," he answered, inclining his head again.

"Indeed, she is. I merely wanted to be sure you understood the relationship between you." The Delegate turned her attention to Raven. "Your connection to the Silverblood is gone?"

Raven nodded, though a hint of anger clouded her expression. "Was everything in the dream your doing?"

"Your memories chose the location. I only intervened after you were bound."

Tears welled in Raven's eyes, but she swallowed them back. He had a feeling he knew where they had ended up. The night of her parents' deaths would always be the first thing her memories turned to in times of uncertainty. No wonder she was shaken when he let her wake up.

"Why didn't you tell me what you were going to do?"

To his surprise, the Delegate averted her gaze for a few seconds, silvery tears welling in her eyes as well. She drew a deep breath and met Raven's eyes again. "To break the connection, I had to make him want it broken as badly as you did. I needed him to be afraid and in pain. I also needed him to doubt himself. You sowed the seeds for that when you escaped him in Pellanth. I made you both feel the pain and fear so that he would see his suffering mirrored in you. Then, when you appeared to overcome it, he would remember that you defeated him once before. It made him doubt himself and fear you. It made him willing to escape at any cost, even if it meant breaking his link to you."

Raven cast her gaze down again, a flush of shame

creeping up her cheeks. "But I didn't overcome it. That was also you."

Synderis itched to comfort her. But this moment was between Raven and the Delegate. He had no place interfering. However, that haunted look in her eyes made it hard to hold himself back.

The Delegate reached out, sliding her fingers under Raven's chin and forcing her to lift her gaze. "I know no one who could have overcome what I did to you. I had to be sure Wayland would break the link. He is far too dangerous an enemy to let wander within our borders, even if only through your dreams. Dreams can be powerful. I'm sorry I had to hurt you." She drew back her hand.

Raven nodded once, though the hard swallow and the lingering pain in her eyes told him she hadn't fully reconciled with what had happened. Some things took time. Some things took a lot more than that.

"There is more we could discuss, but I think today is not the day. You've been through a great deal, and I know Dellaura is eager to see you. I'm sure Synderis would be willing to help gather your things and show you where your mother grew up."

Raven and the Delegate both turned to him. He made a point of meeting the Delegate's eyes before he inclined his head. "I would be honored to do so."

Koshika left them outside the temple when they started back into the village. Synderis escorted Raven back to the healer's building. Together, they gathered her weapons, cloak, and the armor and clothes she had been wearing when she arrived. She was quiet through the process, lost in her own thoughts. When they approached Dellaura's home, she stopped and gazed at the building for several minutes.

It was a beautiful structure, stretching in a three-quarter circle, like the raven-headed talisman. Meticulously cultivated plants and vines grew upon the roof and sides of the house, turning it into a living structure that seemed like a part of the forest itself.

It wasn't visible from their current vantage, but at the back, where the two ends didn't quite meet, was a flower garden, ideally situated to catch bright sunlight that shone through a break in the forest canopy. That one spot never grew over, as if Dellaura had an agreement with the forest itself. The butterflies and bees were regular visitors in spring. Raven would love it most then. At least, Dellaura said that was when Mellaine had most loved to sit out there, and he got the impression Raven took after her mother in several ways.

"My mother used to grow plants on our little house like this." Raven's voice was soft, caught somewhere between sweet memory and sorrow.

"Dell told me they used to spend hours working with the plants together. She said Mellaine had a true natural talent for making things grow."

Raven shifted her weapons to one hand and wiped roughly at her cheek. Then she walked up to the door and lifted a hand to knock. She seemed to freeze there. This was her grandmother, but she didn't know her yet. She didn't know anyone here. Not really. How alone must she feel?

"Go on. Dellaura can't wait to see you."

Her shoulders lifted as she took a deep breath, then Raven knocked.

The door opened a few seconds later. Dellaura stood there, tears falling upon her cheeks as she urged them inside. "Come in. Put those things anywhere."

An hour later, they all sat in the back garden drinking tea while Dellaura entertained Raven with stories about Mellaine. Raven looked more at ease now. She sipped at the tea and alternated between watching Dellaura and gazing around the array of colorful plant life with an expression of almost childlike wonder. When a break came in the stories, Synderis stood. This was their moment. He had intruded upon it long enough.

"I'll leave you two to catch up."

"Nonsense, Syn," Dellaura countered. "Without your help, Raven wouldn't be here now. Stay and dine with us. This reunion belongs to you as well."

He glanced at Raven, needing her approval more than he did Dellaura's.

She regarded him thoughtfully for a second, unaware she held his heart in her hands. Then she nodded. "I would like it if you stayed."

He drew a breath, realizing he had been holding it while awaiting her judgment. Then he turned to Dellaura and reached under the collar of his shirt, removing the chain with the raven-headed talisman. "I appreciate the welcome. Let me give this back to you before all this wonderful company drives me to forget again."

Dellaura smiled at the talisman but waved it away. "Set it on the table in the front room. I already have the best gift it could give me."

He started for the door, catching the intense look Raven gave the talisman as he walked past. It appeared that his earlier assumption was wrong. She hadn't lost the pendant's twin or had it taken from her. She had given it to someone. Someone she intended to reach out to using this one. He would have to make sure she didn't get herself into trouble in the process.

When he returned from putting the talisman on the front room table, Raven was asking, "Why did my mother leave here?"

Dellaura leaned back in her chair, a wistful smile dancing across her lips. "It is sometimes important to bring in new blood to keep our people healthy and strong. About once every ten years, we send a small number of elves out to find other elves possessing the right disposition and a desire to get away from the outside world. Then they bring them back if they want to come. Your mother had a hunger for adventure from an early age. She volunteered for one of these scouting missions. But things often don't go as we expect them to. She knew she couldn't come back here when she fell in love with your father."

Raven's jaw tightened. "Because he was human."

Dellaura's brows pinched together at Raven's tone. "Yes, I'm afraid so."

Raven looked from Dellaura to him, then back to her grandmother. "Why am I allowed?"

Dellaura drew a deep breath and exhaled slowly. "I convinced the council that it was a greater risk for you to be out in the world."

"Because I'm a half-elven Silverblood?" The hardness in her voice gained a sharp edge now.

"Krivalen," Synderis corrected, earning a scathing glare from her.

"They don't want me here, do they?" She set her tea on a side table with vines climbing up the legs before glancing down at her silvery fingernails. "Not even here," she murmured.

"I'll go make some dinner," Dellaura murmured, getting up to flee from a truth she didn't know how to soften. She gave him a pleading look on the way past, perhaps hoping he would know how to make it better.

Synderis started toward Raven, yearning to comfort her, but she held up a hand to stop him. "I want a few minutes alone."

He inclined his head in a show of respect for her wishes and turned to go inside. "I'll be helping Dell if you need me."

They ate a delicious meal and drank sweet wine well into the evening. Raven eventually pushed past her melancholy and encouraged Dellaura to talk about Mellaine's childhood. It kept them from other, more upsetting subjects, and taught her things about her mother that she never thought she would learn. This included the fact that her mother's love of birds had led her to be an avid tree climber, like Raven, at a young age. It was comforting to know they had something so simple in common.

When they finally succumbed to exhaustion, Dellaura offered her the modest yet elegantly appointed room that had been her mother's. Synderis also stayed over, slipping off to a room he had apparently used several times in the past. Throughout the evening, she noticed Dellaura treating him much like family. The two had the relaxed and affectionate relationship she longed for, but those relationships took time to grow.

Once the house was quiet, she tiptoed out and grabbed the talisman from the front table. With it firmly in hand, she slipped back into the room and lay on the bed. She wasn't sure of the process for initiating a dreamwalk, but she had some ideas about how it might work. With the talisman resting over the scar on her chest, she eased her magic through it and into herself to put herself to sleep. The magic in her had no reason to defend her from itself, so sleep claimed her instantly.

•

Raven appeared in the middle of the road outside Lathwood. A dark red sunset cast a bloody tint upon the fields around her. She was in the place where Dusk had fallen to the arrows of the town guards. It was also close to where she fought the Silverblood. A creeping unease drove her to scan the stand of trees, looking for him, though she knew he couldn't be there. This wasn't the waking world. But would Phendaril be there?

"Raven?"

She spun at his voice behind her. A wild surge of relief made her dizzy when she spotted him standing on the road, long, dark-auburn hair framing angular features she had desperately missed. Her heart leaped into her throat, choking off her response. Giving up on words, she simply ran to him, letting his body stop her momentum. He swept her into a powerful embrace, lifting her off her feet.

"You're alive." She breathed him in as he set her down. Perhaps her memories made him smell the way she expected, but it was comforting regardless.

He drew back enough to claim her mouth in an ardent kiss. Raven pressed against him, running her hands into his hair, fighting that part of her mind that tried to imagine it was someone else's hair, long and silvery-white, slipping through her fingers.

He broke away from the kiss and wrapped her in his arms, holding her in a tight embrace. "Is this real?"

She drew back from him, smiling. "It is. I'm really here. Did you and Ehric make it back to Amberwood? How are your injuries?"

He tucked a strand of silver-black hair behind her

ear, a look of almost boyish wonder in his eyes. "We did, but it isn't the same here without you." The happiness in his eyes faded some then. "Synal and the other healers have done what they can for my injuries. My hand is the worst. It should heal, but Synal said I will never shoot a bow again without pain."

Concern caused a twisting pain in her chest. "Your hand? Ehric only told me about the leg and ribs."

"Perhaps he didn't want you to worry too much. I know I don't." He leaned in and gave her another brief, soft kiss. "Are you safe? Did you find your mother's family?"

"I did find them. I'm probably safer here than I've ever been," she answered honestly. "I wish you could see it. This place is beautiful."

He slid his arms around her waist and drew her close again, kissing her with enough passion that it sent her head spinning. She braced herself with her hands on his arms when he set her free and grinned at him.

"Missed me, did you?"

"More than you can imagine." He placed another light kiss on her lips, seeming unable to resist them. "What about your nightmares?"

That was news he would be happy to hear. "They broke my connection to Wayland. There's a woman here—"

"That's enough," a familiar voice stated firmly behind her.

Phendaril's expression darkened as he looked over her shoulder. She spun to face Synderis, trying to ignore the sinking in her gut. How had she not known he was there? Had she become so accustomed to his presence that she missed it? More importantly, how *long* had he been there?

The dark red cast to the sky reflecting off silver in his hair and eyes made him look fiercer than she would have thought possible, given the kindness he had shown her so far. He stalked over to them, and Phendaril reached for the sword that had appeared at his waist. She stayed him with a hand on his arm.

"This is Synderis. He's the one who guided me to them. Synderis, this is... Phendaril." At that moment, she wasn't sure how to introduce him. Her companion? Her lover? The leader of the scouts in Amberwood? Just Phendaril was going to have to be sufficient. "What are you doing here, Syn?"

Synderis offered a solemn though respectful nod to Phendaril before turning a challenging gaze on her. "Do you have any idea how many of us have died to keep our home, and everyone here, a secret? Would you waste all of their sacrifices in the course of one dream?"

"We can trust Phendaril," she countered, the sting of guilt bringing out defensiveness in her tone.

"Maybe you can, Raven, but who are we to him? Nothing more than the strangers who have you. What reason does he have to protect our secrets?" He glanced at Phendaril, and she wondered if he caught the same spark of jealousy in the scarred elf's eyes that she did, jealousy she was surprised to see mirrored on his face.

"You knew I would do this." She narrowed her eyes at Synderis. How had he figured her out so quickly?

"I had my suspicions."

Anger surged in her, though she kept her hand on Phendaril's arm, discouraging him from acting in her defense. "You followed me to spy on me?"

"I followed you to protect my people." She flinched slightly at the fact that he had now switched from *our* people to *my* people. His tone softened a fraction when he continued, though. "I also followed you to ensure you could get out again."

A jolt of uncertainty flared in her chest. She let her hand fall away from Phendaril's arm, and he took a step back, almost as though deferring to Synderis. She searched the bright silver eyes watching her now. "I just have to wake up."

"Do you? This isn't your dream, Raven. You're the dreamwalker now. If you didn't anchor yourself to something in the waking world, you won't be able to wake up from it after he's gone. Not ever. Did you do that?" No humor lit his eyes. Only hurt and concern dwelt there, in the company of faltering anger.

Fear sent a chill through her. "I didn't know."

The hurt pushed to the fore then, and he started to reach for her. Then he stopped, his gaze jumping briefly to Phendaril as he returned his hand to his side. "All you had to do was ask. I would have told you. I would have helped you."

She didn't know what to say. She was in the wrong, and they all knew it. Even Phendaril, who had averted his gaze. "How do I—"

"I'm anchored. I can bring you out with me."

She gave a nod, unable to meet his eyes. She turned to Phendaril. "I didn't mean for it to go like this. I'll reach out to you again soon. I promise."

"And I'll make sure she can do so safely," Synderis added, his voice tight.

"Thank you." Phendaril inclined his head to Synderis before stepping closer to her. "Be careful, Raven."

He placed a light kiss on her lips, and she hated how acutely aware she was of Synderis watching. When they parted, the Krivalen elf held a hand out to her. She made herself look up at him as she started to reach for his hand.

"Syn, I'm so—"

He took hold of her hand, and suddenly she was gasping awake alone in her mother's bed. Feeling sick, she curled onto her uninjured side and hugged her arms around herself, staring into the darkness at the shapes of all these things that had never been hers.

•

In the morning, Raven woke to Dellaura baking something that smelled sweet and light. What she imagined happiness would smell like if it had a scent. It was enough to counter a little of the lingering sorrow from her nocturnal blunder. Only a little.

When she entered the open kitchen area, Dellaura's smile lit the room. She strode over, holding a fluffy wedge of pastry to Raven's lips. She took a cautious bite. It melted across her tongue with a delicate sweetness that even the pastries in Lathwood couldn't compare to. Instead of a savory meat paste, there was a lightly spiced cream and chopped nuts inside.

"This is remarkable," she said, eagerly accepting the rest of the delectable treat from Dellaura. "Is Syn up yet?" She tried to maintain a light tone as she asked, but a hint of anxiety crept in despite her efforts.

Dellaura gave her a long look as if searching for something in her expression before she turned back to her cooking. "He left early this morning to meet his brother at one of the springs. Ilanya is stopping by soon. She can show you the way if you need to speak with him."

Raven nodded. She would have to be patient. "Can I help you?"

Dellaura grinned and handed her a spoon. "Stir this."

Raven did as directed while Dellaura began combining other ingredients at the table. "From what I've seen, you don't eat meat here."

"We choose not to." Dellaura tossed more chopped nuts into the mixture.

Raven inhaled deeply of the magnificent aromas, trying to keep her mind off Phendaril and what he must have thought of their dream encounter. Right now, she could do nothing about that. Synderis was another matter. "Synderis said that two Krivalen could form a dreamwalk connection without needing physical contact or talismans. How does that work?"

The silence behind her drew out long enough that she turned to look and met Dellaura's eyes. The woman glanced away, though not before Raven caught the hint of a pleased smile curving her lips.

"The connection forms naturally if there is a blood relation between the two Krivalen. Otherwise, it requires a strong intimate connection."

Raven paused her stirring. "Physical intimacy or emotional?"

Dellaura lifted her brows and wiggled a finger in the direction of the bowl. "Keep stirring." When Raven resumed, she said, "Emotional intimacy creates a stronger connection. Something like love or even a powerful friendship. Romantic love and physical intimacy combined create the most unbreakable connections."

"Does it work if only one of them feels that way?" She knew the answer before she asked it. The connection between her and Wayland could only be broken if they both wanted it to be, which told her enough.

"Does a rope create a connection between two trees if it is only tied to one of them?"

"No." Raven let out a heavy exhale. If only she could convince herself it was simply a powerful friendship that allowed Synderis to follow her into Phendaril's dream. She knew better, though. The fondness she felt for him ventured beyond friendship. Why did everything always have to be so complicated?

"You don't need to stir it that aggressively." Dellaura walked up next to her and placed a hand on her shoulder. "Are you all right, Aneiris? Can I do something to put you more at ease?"

"I'll be fine. All of this is so new to me right now." She slowed her stirring, watching the cream as it rippled around the edge of the spoon.

A knock on the open door to the garden drew Raven's attention to a young elven woman with shocking red hair. She sized Raven up with a quick once-over as she entered, her blue-green eyes narrowing. A broad, warm smile appeared by the time Dellaura turned to her. She was a few inches taller than Raven and remarkably slender to the point that it looked like a strong breeze would whisk her away. She possessed an ethereal beauty that left Raven struggling not to stare.

"Good morning, Dell. That smells fantastic."

Dellaura hurried over and handed her one of the pastries. "Ilanya, I'd like you to meet my granddaughter, Aneiris."

Ilanya made a show of closing her eyes and smiling as she ate the pastry. When she opened them again, she looked Raven over once more. A falsely sweet welcome smile curved her lips. "It's nice to meet you, Aneiris."

"And you," Raven answered, not convinced she agreed with the sentiment.

"Ilanya, before we head to the council hall, would you be willing to show Aneiris to the Everlight Spring?"

"Of course." She offered another false smile to Raven. "We can go now if you're ready?"

Raven accepted two more pastries Dellaura pressed on her before nodding. "Lead the way."

She thanked Dellaura and then popped one of the delectable morsels in her mouth, hoping eating would allow her to avoid conversation for at least a minute or two.

Ilanya led her out along one of the paths cutting through town. Raven tried to ignore the glances she got. They judged her the way Ilanya had and seemed to find her lacking. Pureblooded elves might be uncannily beautiful on the outside, but they weren't all so lovely on the inside.

"What's happening at the council hall?"

Ilanya glanced over at her, not trying to hide her distaste this time. She turned them down a path heading away from the central part of the village. "Among other things, I am presenting my case for them to grant my request to become Krivalen."

One more reason for the elven female to dislike her. Not only was she a lowly half-elf, she already had something Ilanya apparently wanted. "Why wouldn't they grant it?"

"My sister is already Krivalen, and my parents would like grandchildren from me."

They stopped at the edge of a clearing. Several yards beyond the tree line, a natural spring bubbled up at the base of a rocky outcrop, feeding a sizeable stone-lined pool. Two young elven girls, similar enough in age and appearance to be sisters, laughed and splashed in the pool, vastly out-powered by the two elven males, one of whom was Synderis, splashing back from the other side. Synderis disappeared under the water only to burst up a few seconds later next to one of the girls, who squealed with surprise as he tossed her in the air. The other elven male caught her, though Raven paid little attention to him. She watched intently as Synderis brushed back his wet hair, water streaming down the lean musculature of his bare chest.

She made herself look away only to find Ilanya staring at him, lips slightly parted, her eyes warmed with desire. This might be another reason the other female regarded her with such ire. After all, Raven had taken up a considerable amount of his time lately.

"Dad! You and Uncle Syn are cheating." One girl laughed as she made the accusation, her voice light and joyful.

"How are we cheating?" the girl's father asked as he returned her to the water.

"You're too big," she answered, giggling and splashing him again.

Raven gave herself a mental shake, pulling her thoughts back to what they had been discussing. "Why should wanting grandchildren be an issue?"

Ilanya glanced at her, the slight flush rising in her cheeks suggesting she had forgotten that Raven was there. The candid moment vanished quickly, and she arched one brow at Raven. "You don't know, do you?"

A stone of dread in her gut answered the question. "Know what?"

"The magic takes that away. Once you become Krivalen, you can no longer bear children. I suppose that's a relief for you, though."

The revelation was like a punch to the gut. Black anger seeped in at the edges of her vision. "What do you mean?"

"Well, if you had children, they would be mixed like you. You'd have to be cruel to intentionally bring such a creature into the world."

The words were a vile insult to Raven and her mother, who had knowingly chosen to have a child with a human. Raven yearned to punch Ilanya the way she had the female in Lathwood. She forced her hands to her sides to hide the shake of rage in them.

"I think I'm going to explore on my own for a bit."

Ilanya shrugged, the hint of a smile tugging at her lips. "Suit yourself."

Raven turned and headed in whatever direction seemed most likely to get her away from others the fastest. She had only taken a few steps when she heard someone climbing out of the pool. She took a few more strides and moved behind a tree, leaning against the supportive solidity of the trunk to try to compose herself. After a few seconds, she heard Synderis speaking, a low growl in his voice.

"Ilanya, I'm surprised that you, of all elves, would forget that Krivalen have enhanced hearing? That was unkind. I would have expected better from you."

His footsteps continued toward her hiding spot then. Raven considered bolting, but he knew these woods far better than she did.

"Syn," Ilanya called after him, her tone pleading now. "Wait. I'm sorry."

He stopped next to Raven, where she still leaned against the tree. His gaze settled on her, then he glanced over his shoulder at Ilanya. "I'm not the one you should be apologizing to."

Ilanya spun and ran back the way they had come. Synderis tracked her departure with his gaze, his eyes cold and unforgiving.

Raven looked up at him, guilt twisting in her chest. "You *are* the one *I* should be apologizing to."

He stared down at her, a flash of anger slowly fading from his eyes. Raven tried not to notice how his long hair dripped water over his still bare chest. Her pulse quickened. Seconds crept past in silence. He ran his hands over his hair again, pressing out some of the water, then turned away.

"I'm sorry. I should have talked to you before I tried the dreamwalk. I made a mistake."

He exhaled softly as he set a hand on her shoulder and leaned in to place a kiss on her forehead. "You're not the first to do so," he murmured. "Come meet my brother and his daughters."

"Wait." She caught his hand as he started to move away. "Is what she said true?"

He nodded, his gaze soft with sympathy. "The magic puts us through many physical changes. It wasn't so for the Acridan, but for us... yes."

Raven released his hand. Drawing a deep, shaking breath, she followed him into the clearing.

ynderis walked back into the clearing and grabbed a towel off one of the rocks. Kelwyn had climbed out of the pool and was drying off. He glanced up as they approached. The girls were still bouncing around in the pool until they spotted Raven. Then they swam for the shore, their eyes alight with curiosity.

"Raven, this is my brother Kelwyn."

Kelwyn moved the towel to his left hand and offered her the other. "Just Kel is fine. It's a pleasure to meet you, Raven."

Kelwyn's disarming smile eased some of the tension in her, though an edge of unspoken sorrow lingered in her expression that Synderis intended to ask her more about later. It wasn't really his business, though. Even less so now that he knew she carried someone else in her heart. If she and the one she loved had grown up here, that might not matter, but the outside world was different.

The image of her kissing Phendaril snapped to the front of his mind. He turned away, watching the girls splashing one another as they tried to climb out of the pool, dissolving into fits of giggling. The elf from the dreamwalk was a fighter. That much was apparent in his bearing and how he called a sword so naturally into his dream. He also was, like Raven, no stranger to hardship.

The scar on his face was adequate to prove that, but it was in his eyes, too. An unyielding, dark edge that whispered of suffering and sorrow. Perhaps that was the kind of partner she needed, someone who understood what it was like to struggle.

"A pleasure to meet you as well," Raven was saying.

He finished drying off enough to pull his shirt and pants back on. The girls had finally extracted themselves from the pool and came sprinting over. Kelwyn grinned down at them, and Raven managed a more sincere smile that reached her eyes this time.

"These are my monsters, Merilia and Aurelia. They're ten this year."

Raven turned and offered a hand to Aurelia, who shook it tentatively. When she presented the hand to Merilia, the girl took it confidently and met Raven's eyes.

"I'm going to be Krivalen like you when I'm older."

The comment made Raven's jaw tighten. A hint of moisture rose in her eyes, but she kept a light tone. "Are you?"

"Yes," Merilia answered definitively. "I'm going to train with Uncle Syn." She grinned up at him.

He arched an eyebrow at Kelwyn in question and got a shrug in response. Then he reached down and mussed her hair. "Don't think I'm going to go easy on you just because you're family."

Merilia stuck her tongue out at him.

"Raven, come swim with us." Aurelia took Raven's hand, her wide eyes sweetly pleading.

She let Aurelia pull her forward a step, but she shook her head. "I'm sorry, I can't."

"Raven was injured when she got here and still has stitches in her side," Synderis explained.

"Oh." Merilia's eyes widened. "Can we see?"

Raven glanced at Kelwyn.

He shrugged again. "Up to you."

Aurelia released her hand. Raven lifted the side of her shirt, showing the long, stitched cut. The wound's edges were healing together now, though it was still dramatic enough to earn exclamations from the girls. Even after several days of good food and rest, she was too thin, but she looked far better than she had when she arrived.

Synderis caught himself focusing a little too much on the curve of her waist and the pale skin he longed to touch. Being a friend and guide to her was a tremendous privilege. If that was all she needed him to be, he would accept that.

"Did it hurt?" Merilia asked.

"Of course it did," Raven answered with a small laugh. "I strongly advise against getting one of your own."

The girls grinned.

Synderis caught Kelwyn's eye and made a tiny gesture toward Raven with his head.

Kelwyn answered with a subtle nod, reliably quick to catch on. "Dry off, girls. I told your mothers we'd come by so they could show you how they fletch the arrows."

The girls squealed with delight and ran to grab towels, Merilia perhaps a little more enthusiastically than her sister. Raven smiled after them, though the sorrow returned, weighing heavy in her gaze.

"It was nice meeting you, Raven." Kelwyn inclined his head to her. "Perhaps you two could join the family for dinner some evening."

"I would love to. Thank you."

Synderis touched her arm, and she took the cue to follow him.

They had barely left the more populous pathways in the village before Koshika appeared. The big cat padded silently up between them. They both reached to scratch her head. Their fingers touched, and Raven drew back, clasping her hands in front of her.

"Is there anything else I should know about being made Krivalen? Any other changes I should be aware of?"

He heard the pain in her voice and an underlying edge of resentment. Was she upset with her mother for doing this to her? Given how hard her life must have been, he supposed she had a right to be.

"You should know that the magic is finite. When you become Krivalen, some of the power of the spirit you Accept is used to remake you physically. The rest increases your lifespan. With every spirit you Accept after that, the same happens again, enhancing your physical attributes to a lesser degree and adding to the extension of your life. But when you use the magic, you take away from that accumulated pool of life. Sometimes you can reclaim some of the magic after using it, as with temporarily controlling an animal. Any magic you can't reclaim is a portion of your gathered life that's gone forever."

She glanced up, watching a red-chested warbler flitting between the branches of the trees. Her steps were confident even when her eyes were off the path, attesting to her comfort in the forest environment. Being half human didn't change the fact that she belonged in a place like this.

"Can you use up all of the spirits you've... Accepted?" Her gaze flickered to him for an instant, seeking confirmation of her word choice.

He gave a quick nod of affirmation. "You can. If that happens, it doesn't stop you from using the magic – you're still Krivalen – but it will continue to draw upon your life. It is possible to start cutting days, months, or even years off your life if you use it too much. I doubt you have much to worry about at this point, though."

They continued in silence for a time, Raven's gaze taking in the forest around them while he took her in. The way she moved captivated him – a little like a predator even when she was at ease. The occasional flicker of sunlight between the trees glinted off the silver in her long black hair. She stopped next to a bush with late summer blooms clinging to it and leaned over to sniff them. A lock of hair slipped forward into her eyes, and she absently brushed it back behind one ear. He delighted in her company, no matter what their relationship was to be. But he couldn't pretend there was no attraction.

"Is the inability to have children why you aren't with anyone?" she asked when she resumed walking.

"I suppose it's part of it. If we desire a monogamous relationship, we're discouraged from selecting life partners that aren't Krivalen because of it, given that our population is limited by a low birth rate already. My brother was always more into the idea of family than I was, so it made sense for me to choose this path. Besides, I never felt like I needed to have a relationship to be happy." He caught a low branch and lifted it, holding it up while she stepped under. He followed her through and took the lead again. "Did you want children?"

"I don't know. I never thought about it much before. I just assumed I would never have the option because I would always be hidden from the world. After my adopted father was murdered, everything changed. I risked being discovered trying to go after his killers. I never expected to find a home in Amberwood where people would accept me. I certainly never thought I would find someone to love who would love me back."

"Phendaril." He was proud that he managed to keep the anger and jealousy from his tone, though the other man's name tasted like regret on his tongue. Why? For years he hadn't minded being single. He had his romances now and then, but never anything serious. Why did he want this to be different?

She stared down at her hands, her nod almost imperceptible. "Why didn't you try to stop me before I dreamwalked him?"

It was a good question, and the answer was unlikely to make her feel better about the situation. It certainly didn't make him feel better about it. "Because I hoped you would wait and ask me about it first. I wanted to see if I could trust you."

The muscles in her jaw tightened. She swallowed hard and nodded. Then she met his eyes, which he hadn't expected. He fought the urge to look away, wary that she might see the whispers of his heart in his eyes.

"How did you know you would be able to follow me into someone else's dream? Were you so certain it would work, or were you willing to take the chance that I would never wake up?"

He searched her eyes. How much did she understand about the connection between them? Had she asked someone else? Or had she perhaps guessed at the meaning? "I knew what you were going to do, and I was prepared to protect you. I was never going to let you be trapped there."

"You never doubted that our connection would be strong enough?"

"Let it go, Raven. It doesn't matter now."

"Doesn't it?"

He stopped and turned to face her, frustration flaring. Koshika moved a few feet away and sat to watch them. The anger that threatened in response to her stubborn persistence melted like sugar in water before her tormented gaze. He wanted desperately to hold her, kiss her softly, and tell her everything would work out, but that wasn't his place in her life. She had someone else to do those things for her. Although that someone was a long way away from here.

He clenched his jaw, at a loss for what to say. She closed the distance until no more than a foot separated them. He defied the urge to move in to meet her, retreating instead, but only by a half-step.

"It's not just you." Her hand came up as if she meant to touch his face, then stopped short, hanging in the space between them.

A wild, reckless longing surged in him, and he took her hand, pulling it against his chest, drawing her closer still. Then he kissed her. She responded, pressing her lips to his and moving close enough that he could feel the warmth of her nearness. More than that, he could sense the connection between them, like a lifeline growing stronger.

She opened her mouth to him, deepening the kiss. Her other hand slid around the back of his neck. He slid his free hand carefully around her waist, intending to pull her closer. Then he tasted the salt of tears on her lips and pulled away instead.

She drew her hand away and retreated a few steps, tears sliding down her cheeks. Her gaze darted to one side and then the other, searching for a direction to flee.

"I'm so sorry," she blurted.

"Raven." He would have asked her not to run, but she didn't give him a chance.

She spun and bolted.

Koshika popped up, glancing from Raven to him. She leaned forward on her paws, her muscles tense as if she might give chase, but her ears swiveled to him, waiting for his decision. Like the cat, Synderis wanted to pursue her, but it was the wrong thing to do. Kissing her in the first place had been the wrong thing to do. His desire had hurt her. It didn't matter if she shared his feelings. She was with someone else. That meant they had three hearts to break if they weren't careful.

He ground his teeth, watching as she disappeared into the trees. If he couldn't trust himself to be responsible around her, maybe it was time to put some distance between them.

Within the hour, he had secured permission to return to the outer post. He packed up a few things and sent someone to tell Dellaura where he was heading and give her a carefully edited version of what was happening. When he finished that, he dropped by the healer's building and asked Sillara to explain anchoring to Raven. If she tried to dreamwalk Phendaril again, he wanted to be sure she did so safely but had no interest in being part of that process. With all that taken care of, he left the village and headed for the outer post, Koshika loping along beside him.

Aldrich cantered out around the fields of his new second estate. The manor here was coming together quickly. Not a significant surprise since it was perhaps half the size of his manor in Pellanth. More importantly, his new army was coming together twice as fast. Father Mallebron had kept faithful to his end of their agreement, providing a generous sum with which to purchase weapons and pay mercenary wages. To honor his part of their agreement, just over a day ago, Aldrich watched two of his personal guard ride off with an enclosed wagon heading for Pellanth. Inside was an elven scout from Amberwood, gagged and glaring death at anyone bold enough to meet her eyes. He didn't care. The Brotherhood was lining his coffers. He was happy to follow through with his end of the deal.

Several hundred men camped on the property now, making a mess of his fields. Mostly mercenary bands drawn by the lure of gold and conflict. The private guards he brought with him from the city had their quarters in the unfinished south wing of the manor for now. There were no Silverbloods. They were too expensive, and Wayland refused to offer any up as part of the bargain.

He still needed more mercenaries. They were going up against a couple hundred Stonebreakers. The dark-skinned people trained their children to fight from the moment they were old enough to carry weapons, though not all were full warriors. They also had to consider the Amberwood human and elven scouts. All skilled archers and many trained with a blade as well. The rest were craftsmen and villagers, though certainly some among them could fight too. While they were less of a threat, he wouldn't ignore them. Desperate folk protecting their homes could be innovative and dangerous.

Amberwood had no Silverbloods anymore. His brother's adopted daughter was either dead or had left the area. It was hard to get a clear answer from anyone on that. Most he spoke to, when he so much as suggested a female Silverblood existed, simply shook their heads and looked at him like he was too deep in his cups. Even the elven scout had responded that way, although something in her eyes made him confident that she was deliberately lying to him.

His father had commanded a siege for Amberwood and won, though he utterly destroyed the town in the process. Back then, the land hadn't been of much value. The war for its ownership stemmed from a desire to show up another lord who tried to claim the territory. If only he had known that the value of the resources would rise dramatically many years later. Then he might have bestowed the lands on Aldrich instead of Jaecar, who left them to waste away while he shirked his noble duties off playing father to a half-breed Silverblood freak.

The grounds around the camps smelled of mud with an underlying stench of refuse and waste that would worsen the longer they stayed here. A little autumn rain combined with hundreds of men and horses made for a mess. If not for the stink, he wouldn't care much. He bought the land because it was adjacent to Amberwood. Not out of a sudden interest in farming, though he might put some people to work on it once this campaign was over. No point in letting it go to waste as his late brother would have.

"Milord! Riders approaching!"

He turned his mount. A group of five riders was indeed trotting up the road toward him. Some of his guards wandered over as they drew near, bringing a few of the mercenaries along with them. By the time the riders reached them—three Stonebreakers and another human following a black-haired male elf—he had about twenty men gathered around him.

"Look," someone in his group shouted, "they're following a pointy."

A few chuckles followed that, though Aldrich gestured for them to quiet down. For a wonder, they did so.

The five eased to a stop, getting only close enough to be heard if they spoke loudly.

"Lord Aldrich." The elf inclined his head.

Aldrich declined to return the respectful gesture.

After a few seconds, the elf narrowed his eyes and spoke again. "I'm Jael—"

"Was that a request? Lock him up, boys." Aldrich got a round of laughter from his men for that.

The elf had the nerve to sneer at him. "Original. I come from Amberwood to—"

"Given those ears, you obviously didn't come from here," one of his men jeered.

More laughter kept the elf from trying to talk for several seconds. The four behind the elf placed their hands on their weapons.

Aldrich gestured for his men to quiet down again. "Let him speak, boys. We don't want to be bad neighbors."

Jael smirked and cast a glance around at the camps. "Is that why you're gathering soldiers? To show us what good neighbors you are?"

"These men are just workers, no different than the

camp full of Stonebreakers you had outside your town. If you have concerns, however, please tell your constable or Lady Valassian they are welcome to come discuss these things."

"I'll let them know." The civility had gone out in the elf's eyes like a candle being snuffed. "In the meantime, one of our scouts went missing near your border—"

"I can assure you, we're keeping none of your scouts here. There are plenty of dangers in the woods. She's probably just gotten turned around or eaten by a dire bear."

Hatred cast a dark cloud over the elf's features. "And I can assure you, Lord Aldrich, our scouts don't get turned around. I'll share your answer with the constable." He started to turn his horse, then stopped it and met Aldrich's eyes. "I would like to note that I didn't tell you the missing scout was female." With that, he and his three companions spun their mounts and departed at a gallop.

Aldrich scowled after them.

"We letting them go?" one of the mercenaries asked.

"Yes. We're not ready to make our move yet. Nothing will come of this." He turned his mount and resumed his circuit of the camps, leaving the small gathering of men to disperse on their own. Nothing would make him happier than to see the diverse community in Amberwood go up in flames.

•

Synal cast Karsima an exasperated look when she strode into the healer's building. "I'm glad you're here. You can try keeping him on his ass for a while. With that hand and his ribs, he can't use a crutch, but he's still trying to find ways to get up and move around."

"This is Phendaril. Are you surprised?"

Synal cracked a fond smile. "No, and to be honest, I'm happy to have him back even if it does mean dealing with his obstinance. He is a terrible patient, though."

Karsima gave her a conspiratorial wink. "I'll see if I can keep him occupied for a little while."

"Thank you." Synal gestured toward his room, then wandered off, snatching up a rag that someone had left lying on one of the beds along the way.

Karsima entered to find Phendaril propped up against the wall, reading through one of the books Raven and Marek had found when they first started cleaning up the upper residential area of town. He set the book down when she entered. The way his brows lifted slightly when he saw it was her told her he had something he wanted to talk about. She did too, but it seemed right to let him speak first, given his relative captivity.

"Something's on your mind?" She sat in a chair next to the head of his bed.

"It works." He tapped the cloak pin hanging against his chest.

She had started leaning back to put her feet up, but his words caught her attention. She sat forward. "She was able to come to you in your dreams?"

A slight scowl curved his lips down. The muscles in his jaw twitched, suggesting the experience wasn't as pleasant as he might have hoped. "I'm fairly certain it has something to do with her being a Silverblood, but I didn't get a chance to ask."

Her brows pinched. This was not the manner of a male who'd had a joyous reunion with the one he loved. "You don't look that happy about it. What happened?"

"I'm ecstatic that she's alive and safe with her mother's people, but someone else followed her into the dream. A Silverblood elf. He's apparently the one who helped her find her way to her mother's people."

"There are more elven Silverbloods?"

He nodded. "And I got the impression that this one has feelings for her."

That made every bit of his melancholy clear in an instant. "You don't think she feels the same, do you?"

He shook his head at first, then stopped and lifted his shoulders in a slight shrug. "I honestly don't know. I can say he was an impressive figure. I'm not so self-absorbed I can't recognize attractiveness in another male, and I'm confident this one doesn't have any trouble getting attention."

"But looks aren't everything," Karsima countered. She yearned to chase away the sorrow in his expression, but the situation was admittedly a difficult one. "Besides, you're the best-looking elven male I've ever seen."

"Thank you." He smirked. "That's the thing, though. It wasn't just his looks. He treated me with respect, considering the circumstances. I hate that he struck me as someone I could hold in high regard and maybe even like under different circumstances. How do I compete with that from here?"

"I know this isn't what you want to hear, Phen, but you really can't do much about it from here. You're going to have to trust in her. Be happy she's safe and has others there to help her."

He didn't have to say anything. His expression told her they both knew how hard that would be. "I'll try. No matter how I feel about it, we have our own problems to deal with right now. I need to focus on that."

He gave a nod toward the door, and she glanced over to see Alayne standing in the doorway with Jael behind her. Phendaril made a sweeping gesture to encompass the room with his uninjured arm. "Welcome to my office."

Alayne managed a tight smile, though the lack of any hint of good humor from Jael was what captured

Karsima's attention. She shifted her chair back to one side to make room for the other two. Then she met Jael's eyes. "What did you find out?"

"They're about 350 strong at a rough count right now. A little army of racist mercenary bastards," he growled. "They won't have a great deal of discipline or loyalty with the crew he's putting together, but that isn't going to make their weapons any less lethal. He knows something about Veylin as well, though he denied it. He knew the missing scout was female without my saying it, though he did state that none of our scouts were there. I got the impression he wasn't lying about that part, which begs the question, if she isn't there, where did they take her?"

"You already sent a missive to King Navaran?" Phendaril was looking at Alayne now.

"I did, but it will take a while for his troops to get here, assuming he even decides to send them. We need to delay Darrenton if we can. I could go and treat with him. I might be able to use my court influence to bribe him out of this course of action and maybe get him to drop some information about Veylin in the process." She met Karsima's eyes. "We have another problem, though. I'm hoping it doesn't turn out to be a big one."

Dread landed like a stone in her gut. "What is it?"

"A summons arrived just a few minutes ago. Father Wayland Mallebron has requested a meeting with us."

That name put a foul taste in her mouth. Phendaril's dark scowl told her that it did the same for him.

"Us who?" he asked.

Alayne held up a missive with a broken seal. "He's specifically requested me, you," she said, nodding to Karsima, "and Phendaril."

"Phendaril obviously can't go," Jael stated.

It was impossible to miss the frustration and anger on Phendaril's face, but they all knew Jael was right. His injuries were too severe. He needed to heal. Traveling now would only prolong that process.

Karsima took the missive, reading through it a few times before nodding to herself. They had several problems and only so many individuals capable of dealing with them. The one thing she was sure of was that she wasn't going to put anyone in Wayland's reach that she didn't have to. "Alayne, put together a group to go treat with Darrenton. I'll take some Stonebreakers and go to Pellanth to respond to Father Mallebron's summons. I can see about acquiring more materials for making weapons and armor while I'm there. We must ensure our people are well armed if discussions with Darrenton go badly."

"I don't like the idea of you going to the Brother-hood," Phendaril stated, his expression telling her he meant to argue the issue.

"I don't either," Alayne seconded.

Karsima glanced at Jael.

He shrugged. "It's up to you, milady. I can come with you if that helps. Phendaril will be here if the scouts need guidance. He may not be able to walk around, but he knows them, and he knows this place well enough to deal with most issues from here. Talis and Sameth can be his eyes in the field."

Phendaril nodded. "I would feel better if Jael went, not that I don't trust the Stonebreakers," he added, his gaze flickering to Alayne.

Alayne shrugged. "I understand, Phen. The Stone-breakers are excellent warriors, but it's comforting to have someone you know you can trust watching out for the people you care about." The look she gave Karsima over-flowed with affection. "I think a group of Stonebreakers and Jael would make for a reasonable accompaniment if you insist on going."

"I do. You make sure you have a reliable group with

you as well. I don't trust Darrenton." Karsima smirked at Phendaril then. "Looks like you're acting constable and scout leader for a few days. I'll tell Jenner to start calling you milady."

They all laughed at that, but the tension in the room remained almost palpable.

CHAPTER THIRTY

Raven refrained from reaching out to Phendaril for several nights following the first experience. What had happened with Synderis left her confused and adrift. He never returned after their encounter in the woods. She learned that night, after spending the day wandering outside the village alone, that he had volunteered to scout one of the posts near the edge of the forest.

With Synderis gone, Dellaura kept her occupied in the evenings and mornings. She told stories of Mellaine, taught Raven about life in Eyl'Thelandra, and asked endless questions about her childhood. They did more cooking and gardening together during those days. When Dellaura was at council meetings or away on some other business, Raven practiced moving through her fighting forms, careful not to aggravate her side in the process.

The fourth night, creeping guilt began to eat at her in earnest. Phendaril must be perplexed and wondering what was going on after the first dreamwalk. When Raven visited the healers to have her wound checked, it had closed thoroughly enough that they could remove the stitches. The Krivalen healer Sillara had done so and explained how to dreamwalk safely while she took the stitches out. Apparently, Synderis had asked the healer to talk to her, which further confused Raven's feelings for him. Sillara admitted she wasn't proficient in dreamwalking. Still, she knew enough to explain the process of anchoring to the waking world. The thought of going in without Synderis around if something went wrong left her a little uneasy still, but he was gone. He hadn't appeared in her dreams the last two nights, assuming she would notice if he did.

Tonight, she created the magic anchor, tying it to her bow since it was strongly connected to the individual she meant to dreamwalk. Then she did as she had the first time, weaving the magic through the talisman and back into herself. She slipped quickly into the dream.

•

Phendaril sat before the fire in the home they shared in Amberwood. She found it endearing that the version of the house in his dream had reverted to the rough state it had been in the first time she visited it. She stood silently behind him, her stomach twisted in knots. The kiss she had shared with Synderis played back in her mind, striking a chord of powerful longing in her. How was she supposed to speak to Phendaril with that in her head?

And what if she remained where she was now? What if she and Phendaril had no future? He would never have children if he stayed with her. How was he going to feel knowing that? She was safe in Eyl'Thelandra, and everyone she cared about in Amberwood was safer without her there. Maybe they were supposed to part like this.

He ran his hands through his dark hair in a gesture that reminded her of Synderis standing near the pool. Thoughts of the Krivalen elf weren't going away. She would just have to do her best to ignore them for now.

"Phen."

He stood fast enough to knock his chair back a few inches and hurried over to her. A moment of hesitation hung between them. Uncertainty where there had been none before. He searched her eyes as if seeking something. Whether he found it or not, she couldn't tell, but he closed the remaining distance and leaned in to kiss her while his hands slid around her waist.

Raven poured all the passion she felt for him and for Synderis into her response. She parted her lips, opening her mouth to him. Was it her memories that told her how he tasted and felt? They weren't actually here, after all, not physically. Perhaps it didn't matter. Real or not, his body was strong and solid when she pressed against him. He wrapped his arms around her, pulling her tighter still, eliminating any space between them. She slid her hands up into his hair.

After several seconds, he ended the kiss and shifted back a fraction. They stood there, arms around each other, foreheads touching, breath mingling.

"I miss you so much," he murmured.

Her chest ached at his words. The urge to run back to him and the simplicity of their life in Amberwood spread through her like panic. "I miss you too. I don't know what I'm doing here."

He drew back and squeezed his eyes closed for a moment as if something pained him. When he met her gaze again, he asked, "Are you safe?"

She nodded.

"Then you have to stay there, Raven. I don't know how long, but you can't come back here. Darrenton is preparing to attack Amberwood. Alayne sent a missive requesting help from her uncle. She's going to try meeting with Darrenton to see if we can avoid a fight, but this sinking feeling in my gut tells me it won't help. Veylin's gone missing as well. We're fairly certain he had some part in that. And..."

Her chest tightened with dread as he fell silent. Those she cared about were in danger even without her there. Hatred for Darrenton, for how he had killed Jaecar and now threatened others she loved, rose like a black tide in her.

"And what, Phen? What else?"

"Wayland sent a summons for Karsima, Alayne, and me. I can't go in my state, and Alayne is busy dealing with Darrenton, so Karsima is taking Jael and some of the Stonebreakers to Pellanth to find out what he wants."

"We know what he wants." She disengaged and stalked away from him, going to stare into the fireplace. The flames flared, reflecting the rage and despair swelling up in her.

"Yes." Phendaril wrapped his arms around her from behind, pulling her to him. He kissed her cheek and then whispered in her ear. "And he can't have you."

She clenched her teeth, struggling to keep from lashing out at him in frustration. The feeling of helplessness was almost worse than being afraid. She extracted herself from his embrace and turned to face him. "I thought breaking the connection and disappearing would get him to give up, but he's just going after all of you instead."

"He won't get anywhere. When he realizes you're really gone, and we don't know where to? He will give up."

Raven wished she could share his confidence, but she wasn't so sure. What happened in the dream would have made Wayland feel weak. She couldn't imagine him accepting that, not with his arrogance. A man of power and pride defeated twice by a female half-breed. No, he wouldn't let it go without trying every possible route to get to her. How many of them would he hurt or kill in the process?

"Raven?"

She looked at him, noting the suspicious narrowing of his eyes. He knew she would want to help them, and it worried him. He knew her in ways no one else did.

She stepped across the space between them and kissed him. A firm, demanding kiss. Her fingers began working at the laces of his shirt and he reciprocated instantly, sliding his hands up under her shirt and over her skin. She wanted to feel him in a way she couldn't right now, even if they were together, given his injuries. They could have that here, though. Maybe it wasn't real, but her body didn't seem to care.

They made quick work of discarding their clothes. Whether they actually removed them, or the items just disappeared in the way of dream things, she wasn't sure, but soon they were on the bed in their shared room. He moved over her, then into her, matching her desire and need with his passion. She wrapped her legs around him, moving with him until he found release. Then he turned his full attention on her until she reached climax.

Afterward, she lay in his arms, facing him, wishing she could share the peaceful satisfaction that eased the tension from around his eyes. But the instant he kissed her forehead, Synderis was in her mind again. She squeezed her eyes shut as if that would somehow chase the Krivalen elf away.

"I love you, Raven."

She opened her eyes, forcing herself to focus on Phendaril. "I love you too," she said softly. It wasn't a lie.

After a time, she drifted asleep in the dream and woke in her mother's old bed in Eyl'Thelandra. She stared at the ceiling, the ill-tidings Phendaril had shared racing through her mind.

Darrenton posed a considerable threat, but a measurable one. A threat that Amberwood might be able to handle, especially if King Navaran decided to send support to his niece. Some would die, though. That was certain. As much as she wanted to protect them and get revenge for Jaecar's death, Darrenton was also a threat she could do nothing about from here.

Wayland was something different. As a priest of the Brotherhood, he had too much power. He had his magic, the Silverblood warriors, and significant political influence. He could come at the folks of Amberwood in a variety of ways, and she doubted that anyone would stand in his way. If she still had her connection to him, she might be able to do something about him, but they had broken it.

How strange it was to regret being free of Wayland.

●

Morning found her still pondering the problem of Wayland. What would he say to Karsima? How would he try to convince her to divulge what little she knew of Raven's whereabouts? She didn't trust him not to hurt her or someone else. Amberwood had enough to worry about without Wayland adding to the issues. And what of Veylin? If she was missing, did Darrenton have her somewhere?

"I don't believe *mincing* the pepper was the original plan."

Raven glanced over at Dellaura, then down at the minuscule red nubs she had chopped the pepper into. "I'm sorry."

Dellaura let out a light laugh. "It's nothing. There's more where that came from. You do seem distracted, though. Anything you want to talk about?"

The list of things she wanted to talk through with someone was enormous. She just wasn't sure how many of them she should be discussing with the grandmother she had only just met. But who else did she have to talk to?

"If two Krivalen are connected by blood, can that connection be permanently broken?"

Dellaura's brow furrowed. She handed Raven another pepper. "Not unless one of them dies. Why?"

Wasn't sharing the same magic similar to sharing the same blood in a way? Or was it more like having an emotional connection, which she assumed could be broken if the emotions that triggered the connection waned. The Delegate had severed an emotional connection between her and Wayland, but didn't she still have the magic she had taken from him? What if there had been more than one connection to begin with?

"Can a connection be created through negative emotions? Like fear or hatred?"

Dellaura's usual bright demeanor faded now. "Aneiris, what's this about?"

Raven immediately missed that warm, welcoming joy that had dominated most of her moments with Dellaura. "It's nothing. I should probably ask the Delegate about it."

She started chopping the fresh pepper correctly this time. There was little chance that she would ask the Delegate. She couldn't imagine the Krivalen female supporting what she had in mind. That left Synderis, who had bolted off to the outer post for a reason. He might not appreciate it if that reason hunted him down. No one seemed to know when he would be back, and she wasn't sure what to say to him after their last encounter.

"Fear and hatred can both be powerful emotions, so, in theory, yes."

Raven paused her chopping to glance over at Dellaura. "We don't have to talk about this."

Her answer did provide the insight Raven was looking for. If the connection they broke was an emotional one born of the fear and hatred between her and Wayland, then perhaps another kind of connection remained.

Dellaura turned to the fruit she was cutting up. "Synderis would know more. Did something happen between you two?"

For no particular reason, Raven glanced at the back door then. It was standing open, as it often was during the day. Sitting just outside the doorway, watching her intently, was Koshika. She set down the knife and pepper.

"Dell?"

Dellaura looked up, then followed Raven's gaze to the door. Her hand went to her chest, and a look of surprise, but not alarm, swept across her face. "That's the lalyx Syn was talking about the other night, isn't it?"

Raven nodded.

"Then I suspect it's time for you to go talk to him. I'll pack you something to eat. It's almost a full day's walk out to the post." Dellaura began rummaging around the kitchen, collecting various foodstuffs and arranging them in a satchel.

Raven watched her, wondering absently if she had really woken up that morning or if this were some strange continuation of her dream. Dellaura's unquestioning acceptance that the cat's presence meant she should go find Synderis seemed peculiar to her. To be honest, many things about the elves here were odd to her. Maybe it was worth letting Dellaura's knowledge of this place guide her response this time.

She glanced at Koshika. The cat swished her tail and met her gaze. Something in her bearing gave Raven a sense of impatience. "I'll go get my things."

arsima stood at the entrance to the courtyard outside the Brotherhood Temple. It
hadn't been that long ago that she was there
watching Raven bleed to death in Phendaril's
arms. Loathing boiled up within her when
she lifted her gaze from the courtyard gate
to the temple entrance. She had personally never met
Father Wayland Mallebron, and she wasn't eager to do
so now. She already hated him.

At least Alayne had been with her the last time.

"Are you all right?" Jael's brows knitted together
with concern.

She glanced at the two Stonebreakers they had
brought with them, both of whom nodded in response
to her attention. Two others waited back at the ship
along with the crew and Talis, who had come to gather
healing supplies from the elven healers that had taken
care of Raven that night. There would not have been
enough room to get all of them into the coach. They
knew where she was, however, and would be paying
attention to how long her group was gone. Though
Karsima wasn't sure what they would do if something
did go wrong.

"I'm well enough." She turned a stony gaze to the
entrance of the towering structure. "Let's get this over
with so we can get our supplies and go home."

"Seconded," he said softly as they started toward the entrance.

The Silverblood acolyte standing beside the massive double doors moved into their path when they reached the steps.

"What business do you have here?"

"I'm Karsima, the Constable of Amberwood. Father Mallebron sent for me." And she came because refusing had the potential to end just as poorly as coming did, only for more people.

He nodded and opened the door. Before letting them pass, he leaned in to speak to another acolyte inside. "Constable of Amberwood, here to see Father Mallebron."

Karsima could see far enough in to catch the other acolyte's curt nod as the first one stepped back to let them pass. They entered a vast room, the arched ceiling lost in shadow despite numerous chandeliers, sconces, and candelabras. Muted light came in through the tall windows at the back. Not nearly enough to reach into the dark corners.

The acolyte inside narrowed his eyes at them. "Wait here. And don't touch anything."

He disappeared through a door to the left of the stone dais. After about five minutes, Karsima started wandering the room. By the time ten minutes had passed, she had concluded that, despite the room's impressive size, there really wasn't much of anything to touch in here.

About then, the door in the back of the room opened. The Silverblood priest's power stifled the air in the room as he glided in, creating a sense of pressure around her head and chest. The added elevation of the dais and his fine black and silver clothes exaggerated his height, maximizing his already-intimidating presence. He wore his impossibly silver hair bound back at the nape of his neck. The acolyte who had gone to notify him of their arrival positioned himself at the foot of the dais, facing them. Another followed him into the room, taking a similar stance near the door.

Wayland's silver eyes narrowed as he looked them over. "I believe I also summoned Lady Valassian and a different brooding elf." His lip lifted in a sneer when his gaze lit upon Jael. "Where are they?"

Even knowing that he had the upper hand in power and political influence, it was challenging to keep a civil tone. "Apologies, milord. Phendaril was in an accident and is recovering from his injuries. Alayne had other pressing duties to attend."

"Not the most promising start to our negotiations." He regarded her and her companions with open disgust. "But you can still be of use. I need to know where she is."

Her stomach twisted into a knot under his gaze. "Where who is?"

"Don't play stupid. The Silverblood half-elf." The silver in his eyes flashed brightly. "My Raven!"

His shout made her startle. She moved a step back. In her periphery, the Silverblood next to the dais dropped his gaze to the floor and shifted his feet. Perhaps he also found the possessive language disconcerting.

"Raven is—"

Wayland strode down the steps to loom over her. "Don't lie to me. Your scout did that, and it didn't go well for her."

Karsima stared at him, a weight of dread crushing her chest, making it hard to breathe.

"Yes. That little female elf. Veylin, I believe. She insisted that Raven was dead. I thought perhaps she was simply confused. So I had my men teach her a few things about the stages between life and death."

Red spread around the edges of her vision, but Karsima

fought it. Here, it would only get her killed. Jael took a stride forward, reaching for his blade, and she grabbed his arm. Father Mallebron offered a taunting smile. When Jael didn't move again, he went back up on the dais.

Karsima pounded down the rage, and grief swept in to fill the vacancy. She brushed away a tear, struggling against the spreading pain in her chest and throat. Was protecting Raven worth Veylin's life? Of course, it wasn't just Raven now. Phendaril's life also hung in the balance, hinging upon his love for the Silverblood female. With Wayland, she had a feeling no one was safe as long as he believed they stood between him and what he wanted.

"Let's try again. Where is Raven?"

This was a more precarious situation than she had realized. She would have to choose her words carefully to avoid following Veylin. "If she's alive, I don't know where she is now."

He came closer again, though he kept at least a sword's length between them this time. "Perhaps your companion knows. The elf, Phendaril. Adept Marek said he and Raven were close." She found it curious that he sneered when he mentioned Marek's name. Apparently, the adept really had fallen out of favor. "You say he's injured. I wonder how well he would stand up to questioning?"

"Stay away from him." Her hands curled into fists. "He doesn't know any more than I do."

Wayland took several step closer, using his superior height to force her to look up to meet his metallic eyes. "Your ignorance is much too convenient, constable. Perhaps if I were to sweeten the deal for you. I know Lord Darrenton is preparing to attack Amberwood. Should you help me find Raven, I can see to it that his efforts are halted."

She met his eyes, wishing for nothing more than an opportunity to stab the gloating out of them. She might have tried if not for her companions, but the four of them would never survive attacking him here. There had to be a way to earn Amberwood's freedom without putting Raven in more danger. Although, as long as she stayed away, Raven was probably safer now than the rest of them.

"Raven is alive, or was the last time I saw her," she finally said, a touch of relief sweeping in as his aggressive posture eased back. "She left some time ago to search for her family. That's all I know."

"She grew up near Andel, correct?"

A spike of panic swept through her. How did he know that? Unless . . . Marek again. It would win her nothing to deny something he already knew. "I think so."

"I might be able to work with that." He turned and strode toward the door he had entered through.

"Wait! Father Mallebron, what about Darrenton?"

He stopped and regarded her over one shoulder, his lip curling as if he'd tasted something foul. "You didn't give me what I asked for. But you told me more than the elf, so I will offer you something in return." He gestured to the acolyte near the dais before continuing on his way.

As he disappeared through the doorway, the young Silverblood opened a door on the opposite side of the room. Two more adepts, given the insignia on their armor, walked in, dragging Veylin between them. They dropped her at Karsima's feet and stepped back, hands on their sword hilts. Jael rushed to her side and helped Karsima turn the female elf over. They had beaten her severely. Her face was bloody and swollen. Blood covered much of her tattered armor. She was unresponsive but still alive, her breathing shallow.

"Bastard!" Karsima shouted at the door Father Mallebron had left through.

All four of the Silverbloods in the room drew their swords, making it clear they were no longer welcome.

"I suggest you take her and leave before he changes his mind," the nearest adept advised.

Karsima spat at his feet, then she and Jael helped one of the Stonebreakers lift Veylin. They hurried from the building. For the second time, she would leave this place, rushing to deliver someone she cared about to the elven healers. Somehow, she would make Wayland Mallebron pay for that. She just had to figure out how.

•

Synderis crouched on a high branch in one of the trees overlooking the monument, watching as the Silverblood adept knelt near the spot where Raven had fallen from the horse. The man lingered there on one knee for a time. They had done their best to obscure the traces of her passing, but it was hard to hide the horse's deep prints, especially from this particular visitor. He might be human, but he was a Silverblood.

The adept stood and scanned around, peering into the trees in the direction the horse had been heading. His shoulder-length dark blond hair and rough beard were in dire need of trimming as if he had been on the road a while.

Synderis wasn't worried about being seen. He'd used magic to muddle the man's perceptions. Once again, it was difficult because of what this man was, but Krivalen were all trained to work around that limitation.

Telandora climbed up to the branch below him. She refused to leave the post permanently, though she had gone to stay with Lindyl at the next outpost for the last few nights since he took over here. She was still unwilling to return to the village and deal with the family issues that waited there. She crouched in the tree with him, watching the adept wander around the area, staring intently at the ground.

"He came back again, I see."

Synderis nodded as he considered their options. They would have to find some way to get rid of him if he persisted in returning to the spot. "We're going to have to get more aggressive if he comes back again."

"I know. I hate that part of this post." The heaviness in her tone told him she'd dealt with such problems before. Most were easier to discourage than this one. His Silverblood nature made it harder to make a lasting impression on his mind. "You want me to drive him off?"

"No. I'm already working on it." Synderis focused, putting more magic into the work he had already started.

It didn't take too much extra effort to convince the Silverblood, for his own good, that he wanted to leave here. He stood in the monument for several seconds, staring into the woods. Then he gave himself a slight shake and walked back to his horse to mount up and ride away. They could only hope the man would give up this time.

He glanced down at Telandora. "How was Lindyl?"

She couldn't stop the flush from infusing her cheeks when she smiled. "Deliciously warm and welcoming."

Synderis chucked and started climbing down. "You can save the details for your own memories."

She laughed as she followed his example. "I did bring back something you might want to partake of."

"More wineskins?"

She dropped to the ground from a lower branch, and he landed next to her. "Of course. His nephew keeps him well-stocked."

Synderis picked up his sword from where he had left it at the foot of the tree. "Are you two just going to spend the rest of your lives visiting each other's posts?"

Telandora shrugged. "We have fun." She glanced around, her brows lifting a fraction. "Where's your guardian?"

Synderis peered into the woods, surprised at how the cat's absence left him feeling emptier. "I'm not sure. She was gone when I woke up."

They headed for the post in silence. When they arrived, they discarded their weapons, and Telandora pulled a wineskin out of her pouch. She offered it to him. Evening was creeping in. Dusk cast its obfuscating cloak over the forest, drawing out the insects along with bats and other nocturnal creatures.

He took the wineskin and sat in one of the seats next to the fire pit. Telandora had already gotten a cozy blaze going before she came to find him. After several sips of wine, he passed the skin back to her.

She claimed another seat and sat chewing at her lip for a few seconds before speaking, a sure sign that something troubled her. "Did Ilanya really say that to Raven, about it being better that she couldn't have children?"

Synderis worked to keep the fresh flash of anger from coming out in his tone. "She did."

She took a long drink of the wine, then capped it and tossed it to him. "I may go back tomorrow."

He raised one eyebrow in question. "To talk to Ilanya?"

"No. To talk to the council and the Delegate. That kind of behavior shows she isn't ready to be Krivalen. Whether they're willing to grant her wish or not, they should make her wait a few years." She clenched her jaw, the muscles tightening. Then she took a deep breath, the muscles relaxing, and glanced at him. "Are you going to drink that and give it back, or do I have to come take it?"

He exhaled a small laugh and took a drink. As he lowered the skin, he caught the sound of something moving in the brush. Even with the fast-falling dark, his Krivalen vision picked Koshika out of the bushes she was weaving through. She trotted over to him, looking quite pleased with herself. Then another figure emerged from the darkness.

He tensed, catching the motion out of the corner of his eye as Telandora shifted upright in her seat, both ready to bolt for their weapons. If it was a threat, however, the lalyx wouldn't be this calm. Then Raven stepped out of the deeper shadows.

He stood. A conflicting surge of happiness and painful longing blossomed in his chest. "How did you get here?"

"A pleasure to see you too," Raven answered, a nervous smile dancing briefly across her lips, belying the confidence of her tone. "Koshika came and got me this morning."

He glanced at the cat that had taken a seat next to him. The animal gazed at Raven as proudly as if she had given birth to her. "I see."

Telandora strode past him, offering a hand to Raven. "I'm Telandora. You can call me Tel if you like."

Raven's answering smile had a pleasing warmth in it when she regarded the Krivalen female. She accepted Telandora's hand in hers and held it for a moment, placing the other over it. "I vaguely remember your face from when I first got here. Thank you for helping me."

Telandora shrugged and took her hand away. She snatched the wineskin from him then and passed it to Raven. "Come sit by the fire and have a drink. I was just heading out."

"You don't have to go," Raven countered, a hint of something like panic in her hasty words.

Synderis watched with a faintly helpless feeling as Telandora gave them an impish grin, grabbed her things, and trotted off into the darkness.

"Enjoy the wine," she called back, offering a wave before disappearing from sight.

He considered Raven for a few seconds, at a loss for how to move forward. His plan had revolved around not seeing her for a week or so at the very least. Being forced to face her now only proved how unprepared he was to do so.

"Are you hungry?" he asked, hoping the offer didn't sound as lame to her as it did to him.

Her silver eyes flickered to the small structure, a hint of relief in the relaxing of her features. She nodded. "A little. I snacked along the way. Dellaura sent enough food with me to sustain five or six of us."

He chuckled. "Well, perhaps we can pull together a reasonable feast then."

Her answering smile was a balm to the ache within him.

For a time, they steered the conversation onto safer subjects. Synderis asked Raven how Dellaura was and how her hike out with Koshika had been. In turn, she pursued a line of questioning that stayed on less complicated topics like the council and the social structure of Eyl'Thelandra. It kept things from getting uncomfortable while they made a meal by pooling their provisions and ate, sharing from the wineskin Telandora had handed her. For the most part, she managed to relax with him as much as she had before the kiss. Still, she couldn't stop herself from noticing with a twist of longing how his lips touched the mouth of the same wineskin she drank from.

A perpetual knot in her gut reminded her that she would, at some point, have to address her reason for seeking him out.

Synderis eventually pressed the subject. "I'm guessing there was some reason for you coming all the way out here other than just Koshika's request."

The cat glanced up from where she lay curled next to the fire, surprisingly responsive to her name. Raven smiled at the animal, aware that she was delaying for a chance to compose herself. When she looked at him, she caught herself admiring the way the shadows from the firelight enhanced his distinct jawline and high cheekbones.

She refocused on a branch beyond his left shoulder. "If I understand correctly, the connection we broke between Wayland and I was an emotional connection." She waited for his hesitant nod before continuing. "But I took some of Wayland's magic when I fought him in the temple. I'm assuming that's still in me, in which case, wouldn't there still be a magic connection between us?"

Synderis sat up straight, taking his feet down from the piece of wood he had been resting them on. "Why? Has he come back?"

"No." She smiled, trying to assuage the concern that furrowed his brow.

He settled back again, though he didn't put his feet up this time. "I suppose having some of his magic in you could create a connection similar to that of sharing the same lineage. It's not a situation that comes up. Usually, when you draw someone's magic into yourself, it's because you're Accepting their spirit. In your case, the other party is still alive. I don't know if even the Delegate would know what to expect from that."

Raven drew in a deep breath and let it out again. He wouldn't like what she had to say, but he was the only one she trusted to help her. "Let's find out. I want to try to dreamwalk him."

His flat stare told her he hoped she was joking and didn't find it humorous. "After what you went through to break that connection. Are you serious?"

"I am." She met his eyes, holding her gaze steady to drive home how serious she was.

"You dreamwalked Phendaril again?" A hint of pain and jealousy shone brightly in his eyes, but he tamped it down quickly.

"I did. Sillara told me how to anchor myself. Thank you for asking her to do that." Seeing the resistance in his expression, she got up and went to sit on the log he'd been resting his feet on. "The thing is, Syn, I came here to find my mother's family – my family – but I've come to realize that I have family back in Amberwood too. They may not be blood, but they are family. Wayland and Lord Darrenton are both still a threat to them. Wayland hasn't given up on finding me, and Darrenton is trying to take Amberwood. I may not be able to stop them both, but I have to do something."

He met her eyes for several seconds before shaking his head. "It won't be the same as last time. Assuming you can follow that connection into the dreamscape, you won't be in your dreams. You'll be a visitor in his. He'll have more power there."

"But he may not realize that. Please. I have to try something." She cast a glance toward the edge of the deep forest. "I can go further away from the village if it presents a risk to Eyl'Thelandra."

He shook his head. "That's not as much of an issue now. There's more danger to us if he is the one entering your dreams, but I still don't want to get you hurt."

She took his hand in hers, doing her best to ignore how her pulse raced with the contact. "Please. Help me try. Just once."

He extracted his hand and stood, taking a longer than usual swallow of the wine. Stepping around her, he went to put another log on the fire, nudging it into place with the toe of one leather boot. Koshika came over to sit beside her while he paced next to the fire, back and forth, several times, his brows pinched together with worry. After a few passes, he stopped and handed her the wineskin. She got up at his beckons and followed him to the small building in the trees. Inside, he pulled the pillows and blankets from the hammock. Then he grabbed a bundle of extra blankets from a chest in one corner and made a makeshift bed on the floor. When he finished, he sat cross-legged on one side of the blankets and gestured for her to join him.

Raven walked over and sat in the center of the blankets. Koshika curled up in the doorway as if intending to keep watch.

"Do you have anything that reminds you of Father Mallebron? Something physical would be stronger."

Raven pulled at the laces of her shirt, opening it enough to reveal the top of the long scar that ran down her breastbone. "He gave me this. Will that do?"

The rage that swept across his features was startling but reassuring in that it showed his desire to protect her. He wouldn't let any harm come to her in this, not if he could help it. She closed the shirt front, and he met her eyes.

After several long seconds spent schooling the shock and anger from his expression, he nodded. "That should be more than adequate. Before we go any farther, I want you to anchor to me. That way, should anything go wrong, I can more easily feel your need and pull you out."

Raven focused on the anchoring process. To her surprise, it was easier to anchor to him than it had been to anchor to her bow. The connection between them served as something of a guideline.

"Nicely done." The flash of pride in his eyes boosted her courage. "Do you remember what it felt like when you took that magic from him?"

She shuddered. "I don't think I'll ever forget."

Sympathy softened his gaze as he gestured to the pillows. "If you're sure you want to do this."

Raven nodded and laid back. Synderis reached for her hand, then caught himself. When he started to take his hand away, she took hold of it, squeezing it tight in hers. The fear chilling her blood eased a fraction with the contact.

He let her keep his hand, though an edge of distress marred his attempt at a reassuring smile. "Reach out to me through the anchor if anything goes wrong."

"I will."

"You'd better." The warning in his tone brought a hint of a smile to her lips. "Now, search inside yourself for the feeling of that magic you took from him. When you find it, use it to put yourself to sleep, focusing into the scar as if it were the talisman."

Raven drew in a deep, trembling breath and closed her eyes. It took surprisingly little time to find that distinctive magic within herself that resonated with a sense of the Brotherhood priest. She seized hold of it and plunged down through the painful memory of the scar.

•

An old forest surrounded her. The brown of thirsty foliage and grasses suggested a dryer region than the forest around Eyl'Thelandra. A flicker of movement drew her attention to a figure standing amidst the trees not far from where she had appeared. The figure was tall, easily seven feet, and slender. They wore a skirt made of strips of dark material in varied lengths and black boots that tapered to a point above the knee. Over their back, shoulders, and along their triceps, external bone created an organic armor plating. Their face had a vaguely elven shape, though the bone structure was more sharply angled, the bones more prominent. The nose was barely more than two slits. Their eyes angled dramatically down toward the center beneath bony protrusions that swept up and out from their forehead like horns. Their skin was a pale, chalky blue, and their eyes solid silver, from edge to edge.

A wet breathing noise drew her gaze down to a second, similar figure that lay at the feet of the first.

"They're Acridan," she murmured.

"Yes."

Raven startled, moving a few feet to the side when Wayland stepped up alongside her.

He didn't look at her. His attention riveted instead upon the two Acridan. "This is the first time I saw Silverblood magic at work."

She shifted her stance to keep him within her line of vision as she glanced back at the two figures. The first knelt beside the one lying on the ground. They placed a hand—the long fingers bearing an extra joint—on the prone Acridan's chest and bowed their head. The one on the ground struggled through a few more wet breaths, then was still. A swirl of what looked like a silver mist twisted up around the arm of the kneeling one. It swept over their shoulder and vanished into their chest. Their eyes flashed a brighter silver for several seconds. She sensed that the Acceptance was through then, though they stayed knelt there with their head bowed, mourning the loss.

"It was much more peaceful and painless when they did it." Wayland turned to her then, his eyes narrowing. "Where are you?"

She met his gaze, his eyes almost as silver as the Acridan's, though the human whites and pupil were still slightly visible through the sheen of silver that coated them. She struggled to recall the fear she had seen in those eyes when the Delegate broke their connection. "I'm somewhere you won't find me. Even my old companions don't know where I am now, so you can stop bothering them. Let me disappear. I'm no threat to you or the integrity of the Brotherhood where I am now."

His smirk was cynical. "That may be true, but you still have something of mine."

"Do I?" She turned so that she was fully facing him. "Because I suspect what I took from you was merely something you had stolen from someone else."

His amused sneer made her confidence falter, sending

a flash of cold fear sweeping through her veins. "You know, I asked some of your companions where you went. The constable was good enough to tell me you went searching for your family. I was planning to follow up on that until now. Perhaps you'll save me the trouble."

Breathe in... and out. Focus. "Move on, Wayland. This is a waste of your time."

"I have nothing but time." He tilted his head to one side and smiled. "You know, that scout, Veylin, went so far as to lie to my face."

A sharper chill speared through Raven. If he had Veylin, he must be communicating with Darrenton at the very least. Could he have something to do with Darrenton's renewed interest in Amberwood? That would make her adoptive uncle a far more dangerous threat.

"You're thinking about that, aren't you? What it means. She assured me that you couldn't have survived your injuries." He chuckled. "I had my men recreate the injuries you sustained on her to show her she was wrong. Unfortunately, I failed to take into account that she isn't Silverblood like you. She's remarkably resilient, consider- ing. The last time I saw her, she was still breathing."

Blind rage burst through Raven. A sword appeared in her hand. She swung the weapon in a fast, upward slash, but a battle-ax appeared in his grasp in the same instant. He blocked her with it, catching her blade against the haft and twisting, using the blade and haft of the ax to break the sword.

Raven stumbled back, her rage faltering before an- other cold burst of fear. Still, she wasn't going to give up and reach out to Synderis. Not yet.

His lips curved up as he came forward, hefting the ax. "This is different, isn't it? This is my dream now."

He lunged at her with the weapon raised. She dodged out of the way, but a tree root appeared in her path, tripping her. Raven caught herself on her hands and sprang to her feet. She stepped back into the open space behind her only to come up against a tree that hadn't been there a second ago. The ax he carried morphed into a sword, and Wayland rested the point against her throat.

A maniacal gleam lit his eyes now. "As much fun as this is, I would rather have you here in person. I'm funding Darrenton's army. I was the one who encouraged him to try to take Amberwood. If you return to Pellanth, I will leave your companions in peace and stop him from attacking the town. If not..." He didn't need to say more.

The blade's tip pierced her skin, sending a trickle of blood running warm down her neck. If it was just a dream, why did it hurt so bad?

He had no interest in bargaining. The set of his jaw told her that much, but maybe she could buy her companions in Amberwood a little time. "No. Do those things now, or there's no deal."

A lock of liquid silver hair slid into his eyes. It added a certain wildness to his maniacal look. "I'm not an unreasonable man, my Raven. I'll grant you one week, during which there will be no hostilities toward your companions in Amberwood from myself or Lord Darrenton. Agreed."

She had to get back to the river and secure passage upstream to Amberwood. That would be challenging enough without the added difficulty of finding a vessel that wouldn't question her nature. "That's not enough time. I'm a long way from Pellanth."

His eyebrows lifted slightly. "Then I suggest you move quickly."

He thrust forward, and agony blinded her as the blade drove into her throat. She might have screamed aloud if not for the steel through her neck. Instead, she screamed for Synderis in her head.

•

Raven shot upright with a gasp, reaching for her throat. The memory of pain clung to her. Violent tremors shook her until Synderis wrapped his arms around her. He kissed her head and pulled her tight against him, his strength reassuring and welcoming.

"You're all right, Raven." He placed a kiss on her head again. "You're safe."

She clung to him for several seconds, catching her breath while the tremors slowly subsided. There was no avoiding it now. She had to go back to Pellanth. The dream only bought Phendaril and the others a week's reprieve. If Darrenton attacked, some of them would die, and Amberwood would be devastated. Once before, she had been ready to give her life up to protect Phendaril. By surviving, all she had gained was a brief time of freedom. It was worth it for the memories and experiences she got to have, but Wayland made it clear. She had to end him or die trying.

Raven drew back from Synderis enough to meet his eyes. Beautiful silver eyes, perhaps a fraction less bright than her own. Once she left here, she might not see him again. Right or wrong, she wanted to be with him. The thought of leaving him hurt as much as leaving Phendaril had.

His brow furrowed. "What happened?"

She brushed her fingers along his cheek, memorizing the color of his skin, the line of his jaw, the shape of his lips. Lips she desperately wanted to kiss again. She slid her hand around the back of his neck and gently pulled him toward her. He resisted for a second, searching her eyes, then he gave in to the pressure and met her kiss.

The kiss was light at first, almost tentative, as she savored the feel of his lips against hers. The careful way he held her, his hands trembling slightly with the effort of restraint, set her on fire. She wanted nothing at that moment more than she wanted him. Phendaril had shown her how to express love and passion in a physical way. She wanted to feel that. She needed to feel it.

Raven opened her mouth to him, kissing him deeper and with more desperation. He responded in kind, his hand sliding into her hair, holding her close. She started to unlace her shirt, then broke the kiss and leaned back from him. When she began to lift the shirt off, he caught one of her wrists, stopping her.

"Is this what you want?"

She swallowed against the tightness in her throat, determined not to let him see how close she was to tears. If this might be her last chance to spend time with him, she would hold nothing back. "Yes, Syn. I want you as close as I can get you."

It was enough. He let go of her wrist, watching as she drew her shirt off. When she sat partially naked before him, his gaze wandered over her exposed skin.

"So many scars," he murmured.

Self-consciousness raced in on the heels of his words, and she fought the urge to cover herself. "Do you find them ugly?"

"Not at all. You've suffered so much, and yet you still have such courage and heart. I am in awe of you."

The honesty and gentle affection in his gaze made relief crash over her in a giddy wave, washing away her doubts. "There are more on my legs. Do you want to see those too?"

He answered with a sly grin. "Are you offering?"

Raven smiled in response and leaned in to kiss him again. She slid her hands under his shirt, up along the ridges of strong, lean muscle, then lifted it off and touched her lips to his chest with several soft kisses. He let out a low groan, raised her chin with gentle pressure, and claimed her mouth again. His fingers moved down to undo the fastening of her pants. After he helped her out of them, he laid her back on the blankets, his hungry gaze promising pleasure.

Slowly, he kissed along the line of the scar on her breastbone, his hands brushing lightly over her skin. From there, he continued to make his way down until his tongue teased between her legs. Raven gasped, spreading herself to him. He teased and pleasured her until she could think of nothing more than the desperate longing to have him inside her. She grabbed one of his hands and pulled him up.

Synderis moved over her, poised on his hands so he could meet her eyes.

She stared back into his. "I want you inside me," she whispered.

He obliged in ways she hadn't expected. As he moved physically into her, she felt the magic between them growing stronger. He claimed her mouth again, his affection and desire moving through her, heightening every sensation. She tasted herself on his lips as she slid her hands over his back, feeling the muscles move as he thrust into her. The emotion swirling through their connection flooded her senses, driving her past the point of climax.

When the cascade of pleasure finished sweeping through her, she lay trembling beneath him. He had stopped moving in her. His eyes and smile overflowed with adoration when he leaned down to kiss her. Drawing back, he met her eyes.

"Do you want me to stop now?"

Raven shook her head. "Never."

She let her head fall back and moaned, shivering with pleasure when he began to move in her again.

CHAPTER THIRTY THREE

Raven woke with a muscular arm draped over her waist, holding her close. Though she was reminded briefly of someone else, the magic bond resonating between them was enough to erase any doubt about who she was with. She could never have that with Phendaril. Not that it mattered. It would have been better not to let it come to this. If she died confronting Wayland, would Synderis feel it because of that connection? Not that she meant to kneel before the priest's sword and let him end her without a fight, but she did have to face him. He was never going to let her live in peace. One of them had to die. She had a mere week to figure out how to make sure it was him.

Her mind wandered to the attack outside Lathwood. That had shown her, beyond a doubt, that the Brotherhood would not suffer her to live openly among them. If she survived, it made sense to return here. With Wayland's personal vendetta removed from the picture, the rest of the Brotherhood had no reason to keep actively hunting her once she disappeared. She couldn't go back to Amberwood. Staying there with Phendaril would put him and everyone else there in danger if the Silverbloods did come around. Eyl'Thelandra was the one place she could be safe and avoid endangering those she loved at the same time.

She looked over at Synderis, sleeping soundly beside her. Did she love him?

He opened his eyes when she rolled on her side to face him. Raven smiled and placed a light kiss on his lips.

He gazed at her with joy-filled wonder, reaching up to brush the hair away from her face. "I have never woken up happier."

"I'm glad I could give you that." And she was glad of it.

His expression turned more serious. "You don't regret it?"

She held his gaze for a few seconds, touched by his concern. Hurting Phendaril, she would regret. Being with Synderis? She shook her head. "I don't."

Soft snoring caught her attention. She looked down at their feet to see Koshika curled on the end of the blanket.

Synderis chuckled softly. "She decided to join us a little before dawn."

Raven glanced at the light shining in through the doorway. She needed to get on the road soon, so she had to devise a plan to slip away from him. He would try to stop her if she told him what she had in mind.

Synderis moved to get up, and the big cat made an irritable noise, curling into a tighter ball with one large paw draped over her eyes. Once he was up, he offered Raven a hand, lifting her to her feet with ease. She watched him stretch, admiring the shape of his body. When he caught her looking, he came and gave her a kiss that made her begin to forget that urgent need to get on the road. He left her breathless when he pulled away, the desire in his eyes telling her the kiss had the same effect on him.

He grabbed his shirt, slipping it on with some haste. "I need to do a patrol circuit, but perhaps we can finish that conversation later."

Raven said nothing. She hated the idea of outright lying to him. He deserved better.

"Do you want to join me?"

"I'd rather stay here, this time. I could use a little time alone to think things over."

His expression darkened a fraction, eyes tightening with worry. "We never did talk about your dreamwalk. Do you want to do that now? The patrol can wait a little while."

She picked up her pants and tugged them on. "Not now. Maybe when you get back."

When they were both dressed, he donned his bow and sword, then kissed her forehead. "Stay close. There was a Silverblood snooping around out near the monument. We drove him off, but it's harder to make the magic stick with them."

A jolt of alarm shot through her. "Do you think he was looking for me?"

"Perhaps. I wouldn't worry. He won't get near you. I shouldn't be gone more than a couple of hours. There's plenty of food in the packs if you're hungry."

Raven gave a quick nod, chewing at her lip as he started to walk away. Before he'd taken more than two strides, she rushed over and grabbed his arm, stopping him. When he turned, she threw her arms around his neck and kissed him to remember how he tasted. She pressed against him and breathed him in to remember how he felt and smelled. He responded to her passion in kind, sliding his hand to her waist and pulling her close. Guilt twisted in her gut, knowing he didn't realize he was kissing her goodbye.

He held her for several seconds after the kiss ended as if he feared she would disappear. If only he knew.

When he finally walked away, Koshika trotted out to take her place beside him. Raven managed a convincing enough smile and wave. The moment he was out of sight, the tears came. She cried quietly as she sorted enough food into her pack to last a few days without depleting his stores more than necessary. After that, she donned her armor and weapons and stood in the doorway of the hut, staring at the bedding on the floor. After several minutes, she drew the talisman out of her pocket. Dreamwalking Phendaril would be more complicated after this. She didn't want to lie to him about what had happened with Synderis or what she intended to do next. It was better not to see him at all. He would move on in time. She positioned the talisman on the pillow so Synderis would know she had left intentionally. Perhaps knowing she wasn't meeting Phendaril in his dreams would ease the hurt a little. Guilt dogged her steps as she hurried from the post.

It didn't take long at all to reach the monument. Raven found the footprints made by the Silverblood's distinctive boots quickly enough. She followed them away from the old stone structure, tracking them back to his camp. A horse would make her journey much faster, and he was sure to have one. However, what she found at the camp gave her pause.

She regarded the man cooking over his small fire for a couple of minutes, debating whether to knock him out or try a less hostile approach first. Finally, she stepped out into the open.

"Marek?"

He stood abruptly and spun to face her, an unsettling pleasure lighting his eyes. "Raven."

"What are you doing here?"

He lifted one foot as if to take a step toward her but stopped when she tensed. "I was at the Brotherhood in Chadhurst when they got word that you had been captured in Lathwood. I set out immediately, but when I reached the jail in Lathwood, you had already escaped. Quite spectacularly, according to the reports." A hint of pride lifted his tone that Raven found particularly disconcerting. "I spoke with Adept Edwin after that, the one whose horse you stole. I told him I would take over the hunt from there, and it was going well until I got here. I keep losing track of your trail at that monument. I was considering giving up. I never imagined you'd come to me."

She glanced around, spotting his horse tied in the trees. Her plan had simply been to steal the animal or fight the Silverblood for it if she had to. This complicated matters. "So you came to drag me back to the Brotherhood again?"

"No." He drew a deep breath and let it out. "I came to make sure you were all right."

Raven stared at him for several seconds, searching for the lie in the twitch of an eyelid or shift in his stance. When she found nothing, she rubbed at the sudden ache between her eyebrows. She had been out in the world for around a year, and a substantial portion of it still made no sense.

"I find our relationship very confusing."

He barked a laugh. "That makes two of us."

She met his eyes. "I need a horse."

"What happened to the last one?"

She considered that for a moment before shrugging. "I'm honestly not sure."

"You came here to steal another Silverblood's horse? I don't suggest making a habit out of that behavior."

Raven smirked. "I'll take that under advisement."

"If you're not against the idea of riding double, I could give you a lift to the nearest town and help you acquire a mount of your own."

"I can't go back to Lathwood."

"Obviously. There are other towns we can try, depending on your direction." He started kicking dirt over the fire. "I get the sense that you're in a hurry."

Raven nodded. She only had so much time to put on some distance before Synderis came looking for her. "I'm heading west, for the moment."

Marek took several hurried bites of his meal, then discarded the rest and began to pack up his things while still chewing. Raven strode past him and turned her attention to saddling his horse. Before long, they were riding out. It was awkward to be this close to him, and the warmth of his body in front of her in the saddle made her miss both Phendaril and Synderis. At one point, after they teamed up to take on the corpse eaters in the mine outside Amberwood, she had believed Marek could be a friend and ally. Since then, he had alternately betrayed and helped her. It was hard to trust him or even know what to expect. He didn't frighten her like he did before, however. Some of that she owed to Synderis for teaching her more about Krivalen magic. The rest came from something within her.

"Where are you going?"

"Back to Pellanth."

His back stiffened. "Why, of all places, would you go there?"

"I have to stop Wayland."

Marek was silent for a brief time, perhaps considering his position as a member of the Brotherhood and his own now tumultuous relationship with the Silverblood priest. "I do think his obsession with you has driven him a bit mad, but now I'm wondering if you aren't also losing your mind."

"Perhaps I am, but he's hurting people I care about and giving Darrenton funds to build up an army to attack Amberwood."

He twisted in the saddle as they moved onto the main road, looking back at her out of the corner of his eye. "How do you know all of this?"

"I..." She paused. He knew nothing of dreamwalking.

If she explained it to him, she would be exposing some of the magic the Eyl'Thelandran elves worked so hard to keep hidden from the Brotherhood. She didn't trust him enough to give him that. "It's a long story. All I know is that if I confront him, I can bring an end to all of this."

"At what cost?" When she didn't answer, he faced forward again. "This far out east, we could cut directly up north and come in on the eastern side of Pellanth faster than we could get there going the other way, especially if we get you a decent horse. And I might know just where to get one."

Marek took them to a point about a mile past the crossroad where he stopped and examined the tracks for a few minutes. He mounted back up and turned off the road heading northeast after the relatively fresh tracks of three horses. They crouched in the bushes a short time later, watching three Lathwood guards standing around a stump with a map spread over it. The men were arguing about which direction they should head next. One firmly stated they should turn back since they had lost her trail. Another suggested they go to Branwill and ask the locals if anyone had seen her. The third insisted that they continue northeast, as Adept Marek had advised.

Raven gave him a sideways glance. "You deliberately sent them the wrong way?"

He shrugged. "I didn't want them finding you."

"You really have gone rogue. I'm impressed."

He gave her a mock scowl. "Careful. I could still change my mind." He pointed to the horses tied in the trees not far from their hiding place. "I can draw them off if you can grab the horses."

Raven answered with a firm shake of her head. Her skill with horses was far better than it had been, but she wasn't ready to test it in a precarious scheme like this. "You don't want me getting the horses. I'll draw the men off and meet you back at that moss-covered log lying across the creek. The one you said looked like a sleeping water wyvern."

He started to shake his head now.

"Don't argue with me, Marek. I know how to do this. Our odds of success plummet the minute you put me in charge of horses."

The slow smile that crept across his lips reminded her of Jaecar when she had done particularly well hunting or sparring with him. Pride and respect shone through in it. "You've grown a lot since I helped drag you onto that ship in Manderly, sopping wet with an arrow in your leg. Confidence looks good on you."

She gave him a skeptical scowl, pretending the praise didn't fill her with giddy pleasure. "Just be ready to grab the horses."

Marek nodded.

Raven crept warily over to where the horses waited. The animals sniffed at her curiously but were unconcerned by her presence. She moved around in front of them, ready to sprint away from where Marek was hiding. The animals were far too calm, so she picked up a stick and swung it at the face of a pretty black as if intending to hit the beast. The horse tossed its head back but stood steady, apparently doubting her willingness to follow through. When she swept the stick at the next animal in line, it nickered and half-reared, startling the other two.

"Hey! Get away from those horses!"

Raven turned toward the men, her hood pushed back so they could clearly see her silver eyes and silvery-black hair.

"That's her! Get her!"

Raven bolted, dropping the stick as she sped away from Marek's hiding place. She was faster than mere human men like these, so she checked her pace, making sure not to get too far ahead too quickly. It would ruin the whole point if they decided to pursue her on horseback. They shouted after her, ordering her to stop, and a crossbow bolt sank into the tree she was dodging around. That made the chase more exciting than she had hoped for.

When they were far enough from the camp to give Marek time to collect the horses, she sped up, darting through a patch of high berry bushes. Sharp thorns grabbed at her armor, the few that found openings tearing at her flesh. She yanked free and ducked behind the root ball of a fallen tree, positioning herself so she could see the three men when they came staggering to a halt before the bushes. Drawing on magic, she reached into them with it, focusing on how they almost had her, how they merely needed to push a little deeper in the woods ahead to find her.

"Come on, we've almost got her," one of the men declared, plunging through the underbrush.

The other two followed confidently. A twinge of guilt twisted in her chest as they disappeared. Not for misleading the soldiers. That felt good. But she would not have known how to do that if it hadn't been for Synderis. He deserved better than to be abandoned with no explanation. It was too late to change how she had left him now, if she was going to reach Wayland within a week.

She gave it a few seconds, making sure the guards committed to their path, then sprinted back the other way, heading for the meeting point. Marek was waiting when she arrived, mounted on his horse with the other three animals in tow. A hint of relief relaxed his features when he spotted her.

"What are we going to do with the other two?" she asked, taking the reins of the black horse from him. The animal had already proven itself not to be skittish. She needed a mount she could rely on not to try to dump her at the first sign of danger.

"I thought we could release them a little farther north of here. The guards won't be able to chase us without their horses."

"Good idea."

Raven mounted up. Once she settled, she patted the horse's neck, determined to establish a positive relationship. They headed out at a trot, leading the other two animals behind. The black had a comfortable gait and was responsive to her commands. If he continued this way, she would have to give him a name.

CHAPTER THIRTY FOUR

The forest was stunning. Autumn colors – browns, reds, and golds – were beginning to show more prominently on the deciduous trees that mixed in heavily among the evergreens this close to the edge of the forest. Early morning light pierced the canopy, glinting on drops of dew and creating star-like sparkles of reflection amidst the undergrowth.

Koshika, apparently sharing Synderis's vibrant mood, loped about, chasing insects and small animals when she spotted them. She seemed more interested in merely playing than hunting, making him wonder if she was younger than he had initially suspected. Perhaps a grown cub who had little experience on her own before the injury to her foot. If they went too long between diversions, he would toss a stick into the bushes to give her something to chase. It wasn't long before she started watching him expectantly in the lulls.

They were out less than an hour when he caught a movement through the trees and tossed a stick in that direction. Koshika loped ahead, her intensity changing halfway there. Her body dropped low, and she bolted past the stick to snarl at something behind a towering evergreen.

"Easy." Telandora leaned out from behind the tree. "Care to call off your beast?"

"Well done, Koshika," he praised.

The big cat sprinted back to stand by his side, giving Telandora a warning growl when the elven female emerged from her hiding spot.

"Nice of you to praise her for threatening to eat me. This is the same cat that gave Raven a guided tour to the outer post. I see who the favorites are."

Synderis grinned at the thought of Raven. He worried about her encounter with the Silverblood priest in the dreamwalk, but the aftermath left him feeling certain they could manage those things together. That she chose to be with him . . . He could imagine nothing more fulfilling than being her partner and being the one beside her to face whatever challenges lay ahead. Once he was back, they could discuss the details of her dreamwalk and figure them out together. He could hardly wait to hold her in his arms again.

"That's the smile of someone who had an excellent night." Telandora winked at him.

His neck and face grew warm. "I, ahh... I thought you were heading back to town."

She laughed. "You're kind of cute when you're embarrassed. You seemed conflicted about her yesterday, so I wanted to ensure everything went all right. If it hadn't, I didn't want you to have to be out here alone. I'm happy to see it did, though." She glanced away and cleared her throat. "I also forgot my favorite cloak at the post," she added with a sheepish grin. "Come on. I covered the rest of the route on my way over. We can walk back together, so you don't have to be away from her any longer than necessary."

Synderis was more than happy to turn around and return to Raven a little sooner. When they started walking, he gave Telandora a nudge with his shoulder. "So, out of concern for me, you made yourself suffer through another night with Lindyl."

She colored. "I mean, don't let it ever be said that I'm not generous."

Synderis laughed and tossed another stick for Koshika.

It took them half an hour to reach the post. The Ialyx sprinted ahead, disappearing into the building. Seconds later, she trotted back out, peering about as if she'd lost something, her posture forward and tense. Sudden dread spread through Synderis, leaving him feeling nauseated.

"Raven?" He looked around the camp as he called her name, hoping for an answer that his gut told him wouldn't come. He stepped inside the building, noticing immediately that her weapons and pack were missing.

"What's this?"

He turned to Telandora, who had walked to the rear of the structure where the makeshift bed lay. She was holding up the raven-head talisman. He strode back and took it from her. For several seconds, he could only stare at the object resting in his palm. Raven had left him a message of sorts, one with multiple meanings since this was her only way of reaching out to Phendaril.

"This is goodbye." Rage and sorrow tightened his voice.

"How far could she have gotten? She's on foot."

"And that Silverblood might still be out there." He shoved the talisman in his belt pouch and stalked from the building.

They found Raven's tracks quickly. It didn't appear that she had made any effort to hide them. Despite his warning about the Silverblood, or perhaps because of it, she had gone directly to the monument, following the man's trail from there. They followed it as well, arriving quickly at a recently abandoned camp. Raven's footprints ended alongside a set of hoof prints.

"She got on the horse here, and so did he."

Telandora was searching the rest of the camp. "There's

no sign of a fight of any kind. Is there any reason she might have turned herself in to him?"

He clenched his teeth, trying to puzzle it out through the confusing vortex of hurt, anger, and fear that boiled over within him. "Maybe, if she thought she could protect the people she cares about that way. If she means to go after the Brotherhood priest, this Silverblood might take her right to him."

He kicked at the remains of the campfire, exposing the still smoldering coals beneath. He covered his face with his hands for a moment, stifling a cry of frustration, then swept them back through his hair. It couldn't end like this, but what was he supposed to do? He turned in the direction the horse had gone. How far could they have gotten? Was there any chance of catching them?

"You can't follow them, Syn."

He glanced over his shoulder at her. Couldn't he? Could she stop him? It was possible she could, actually. Telandora was more than capable of facing off against him.

She gave him a stern look, apparently reading the thoughts behind his expression. "I'm speaking as some-one who loves you like a brother. I hate to see you in pain, but Raven made a choice. No one forced her to hunt down the Silverblood, and from the looks of things, no one forced her to leave with him. Before you run off in a fit of passion and expose all of us to the out-side world, maybe you should dreamwalk her and find out why she left the way she did."

He pulled the talisman out of his pocket. What did it mean that she had left it? Had she been planning to leave last night? Was that her way of saying goodbye? Or had she made the decision after he told her about the Silverblood? Whatever the truth, she had made a con-scious choice not to divulge her plans to him.

He clenched his hand around the talisman. "I'm a fool."

"Why, for falling for her? I don't think that's true. You told me that you two formed a connection. That's proof that she cares for you too." Telandora came and set a hand on his shoulder, squeezing gently. "Go back to the village. Tell Dellaura and the Delegate that she's gone. Then, tonight, dreamwalk her and find out from her what happened before you make any judgments or choices."

Koshika butted her head against his thigh, making a series of soft chirping sounds that struck him as inquiries. He reached down to scratch behind her ears.

There was a sense of helplessness to the situation that he hated. It was just like when he was waiting for her to arrive in Eyl'Thelandra after she gave up the talismans twin, only worse now because he had dared to let himself love her.

"Come on." Telandora squeezed his shoulder again. "You know I'm right."

Synderis let her lead him away from the camp. Back at the post, he gathered his things and began the hike to town. He wasn't going to do what she recommended, not precisely. He intended to talk to Raven before speaking with the Delegate or Dellaura, so he took his time on the journey back. Koshika stayed close, her mood subdued in reflection of his own.

Everything in him wanted to go after Raven. Every step in the opposite direction was an internal battle. Even if she chose to go with the Silverblood of her own volition, he feared it would end badly for her. She had loved him in the night, letting him believe she wanted to be with him, then abandoned him to protect her family in Amberwood. At the same time, she'd left him the talisman, making it clear that she wasn't going to reach out to Phendaril again. She couldn't reach out to him now, at least not through dreams. Was there a message in that?

He stopped at several of his favorite places along the route, lingering in each so the night would fall before he arrived home. He alternated between being angry with her and wishing he could simply hold her close again. When dark fell, he made his camp in the shadow of two trees that had grown together, twining about one another like lovers. Koshika wandered off to hunt. He politely declined the rabbit she brought back for him twenty minutes later, though he was touched that she went to the effort.

About an hour after dark, he reclined on the soft layer of dirt at the foot of the trees and sought out the connection to Raven within him. Despite what had happened, it remained strong and vibrant. That told him his feelings had not changed, and neither had hers. There was comfort in that. Then he took hold of the connection and used his magic to drop himself to sleep.

•

Raven was waiting for him in the dreamscape, sitting beside a fire outside the post building. For a few seconds, the familiar setting left him too disconcerted to do anything. Then anger swept through him, and he took a few steps toward her, ready to tell her exactly how upset he was. Raven stood and faced him. A tear ran down one cheek, and his anger fractured upon a wave of grief and worry.

He strode to her and took her in his arms. A sob broke from her as she wrapped her arms around him, pulling herself tightly against him.

"I was so afraid you would hate me," she murmured.

"Don't think for a second that I'm not angry." He gave her a kiss on the forehead to soften the words. Then he pushed her away from him, hoping physical distance would help him keep a clear head long enough to get some answers. "What have you done? Did you turn yourself in to the Silverblood?"

"Not exactly." She looked into the fire that crackled nearby, the expectation of warmth giving it heat. "I was planning to steal his horse, but I recognized him when I got to his camp. His name's Marek. He's an... ally, I suppose. Unless he chooses to betray me again." She hugged herself, rubbing her arms as if she were cold.

"Not especially comforting. Why did you leave?" A dreadful aching tightened his chest as he asked.

She met his eyes. The torment in her expression made it impossible to hold onto his anger with her. Whatever she had done, it hadn't been an easy choice for her.

"Wayland isn't giving up, Syn. He can't find me, so he's going after people I care about. He's already hurt one of the elven scouts, maybe killed her. And now he's helping Lord Darrenton mount an offensive against Amberwood. Could you sit back safe and watch someone hurt the people you love?"

An edge of anger crept back in. "I don't know. It appears to be what you expect me to do."

She winced at that. "I wish I didn't have to do this to you, but I need to confront him. I have to try to stop him."

He moved closer and stared down at her. "And what do you think the chances are that you'll live through battling a Brotherhood priest in his temple a second time?"

"Not great," she answered softly, "but I mean to try."

He slid his fingers under her chin, putting gentle pressure there to encourage her to look up at him. When she did so, he kissed her, pouring his affection into the kiss and into their bond, letting it sweep through them both. Because that connection allowed him to enter her dream, the power of the bond swept the dreamscape as well, surging around them until it created a heady atmosphere of love and desire. Raven responded in kind, sliding her hands into his hair as she opened her mouth to him. The overwhelming intensity of her answering emotions surprised him as they merged with his.

For a few seconds, he forgot everything else. He wrapped her in his arms, tasting her and letting the power of their combined passion and love create a blissful storm within and around them.

The thought of losing her broke through the storm, and he ended the kiss. He gazed into her eyes, feeling a few tears as they ran warm down his cheeks. "How am I supposed to stand back and let this go? How am I supposed to let you go?"

She wiped away his tears with gentle fingers. "I don't know. I just know I have to do something. If I can figure out a way to survive this, I promise I'll come back to you."

That promise sent a thrill of pleasure through him. She would return to him... if she lived. The reality of the situation dampened the brief joy. "What am I supposed to do in the meantime? Just wait to see what happens?"

She swallowed hard, the fear and uncertainty in her eyes tearing him apart inside. "That's up to you. You can try to forget me and move on. That's probably the wiser choice. Or—"

"I can keep loving you in your dreams." He kissed her again, a kiss that he hoped told her exactly which of those options he would choose.

Raven slid her hands under his shirt, running her fingers along his skin. When she started to lift the shirt off, he simply made his clothing disappear. It was a dream, after all. He couldn't control everything unless she let him because it was her dream, but he could control himself. Raven grinned, a glint of mischief sparkling in her eyes. She kissed him again and, under his hands, her clothing vanished as well.

everal days of constant travel blurred together, broken only by dream visits with Synderis. Raven's body ached from long hours in the saddle. A few days of rest and relaxation would be welcome, but there simply wasn't time for such. She imagined the horses felt the same. Did their backs and legs ache too? She didn't see how they could not.

She eased the black gelding down from his fast trot and patted his neck. "Well done, Cyrleth."

Marek glanced over at her, arching one eyebrow. "Cyrleth. That means regret in the elven tongue, yes?"

She gave an absent nod.

With everything she had to regret, it seemed an appropriate name for the animal that would carry her to this potentially fatal confrontation. Her greatest regrets haunted her constantly with the visages of two entirely different elven males. With each day that passed, she missed Phendaril more. At the same time, she loved every moment she spent in her dreams with Synderis, though she could see how hard it was for him by the sorrow in his eyes. It didn't help that the Delegate and the council were upset that she had left and were pressuring him to get her to return. They feared her knowledge of Krivalen magic and Eyl'Thelandra could expose them.

Dellaura, he said, was heartbroken, though she suspected not as heartbroken as he was, despite the strong face he put on for her. When they were together in her dreams, she could see how much he despised being unable to help her. Phendaril would hate it just as much if she had maintained contact with him. That was part of why she hadn't. That, and Synderis.

The whole situation plagued her thoughts with questions. Did she choose to continue meeting with Synderis because she knew his devotion to his people would keep him from following her or had her heart truly chosen him? What did it mean that she left the talisman behind? Did she honestly believe Phendaril would try to interfere if he found out where she was going or had she taken the coward's way out to avoid telling him about her changed relationship with Synderis? Did it even matter under the circumstances?

Turning her focus back to her mission, she scanned the area, alert for any danger. They had unsaddled the other two guard horses and sent them running into the wilds the day after they stole them. From there, they had maintained a fast pace, wearing themselves and their mounts out each day with the hard riding. Now they were working their way north alongside a wide, shallow river. The riverbed and immediate bank were blanketed with round stone, making the footing nearly impossible for the horses. A little farther out, a blend of sand and dirt made for solid ground with few hazards that allowed them to keep a demanding pace through the morning. It was time now to give them all a brief rest.

Raven's mind needed a break as well. There had to be something she could think about other than the two elven males she'd fallen in love with or the hateful man waiting for her at the end of this journey. "Why are you helping me, Marek?"

He chuckled. "I'm surprised it took you so long to ask. You're extremely focused when you set your mind on something." He fell silent for several strides, his expression turning thoughtful. "I suppose there are three reasons. The most obvious is that, now that Wayland knows you're alive, he believes I betrayed him."

He did have a tendency to switch loyalties. It made it hard to be at ease around him, though several days riding through the wilderness together and sharing the duties of the camp had created a degree of comfortable familiarity.

She glanced at him. "Which you did?"

"Which I did," he agreed. "Needless to say, I'm not currently welcome at the temple in Pellanth, and many of my fellow Silverbloods are suspicious of me."

The rattle of rocks on the far bank caught her attention. She watched three river otters dart in and out of the water as they wrestled with one another. The sight lightened her mood a little.

"You could take credit for bringing me in. I imagine that would clear your name."

"Is that what you think I should do?"

She turned to look at him again. "Well, I wasn't planning to walk in the front door and offer my neck for the headsman's blade. So no. I think it's a terrible idea."

"Glad to hear it. I'll take your opinion on the matter under advisement." He offered a teasing wink, though it didn't put her any more at ease with the lack of a definitive negation. "The second reason is that I'm having a crisis of sorts. I have trouble trusting and respecting the Brotherhood like I once did, knowing that even their doctrine is full of lies."

She sat a little straighter in the saddle, managing a slight grin. "As a female, half-elven Silverblood made at the tender age of eight, I'll proudly take credit for your disillusionment."

He shook his head at her, though amusement shone in his eyes.

"What's the third thing?" she prompted.

He looked at her, his expression turning thoughtful. "I made the mistake of getting to know you in Amberwood. I don't think any of this is your fault, so punishing you for it seems wrong. And I've grown rather fond of you."

Unease tightened her shoulders. "Marek—"

"I'm aware you have a preference for males with pointed ears."

She snorted a laugh at that. If only he knew.

Her response earned a curious look from him, but he continued. "That doesn't mean I can't appreciate being around you, and it certainly doesn't mean I can't help you get yourself killed if you wish to do so."

Raven laughed again. "I'm not sure that puts our relationship in a better light."

He answered with a crooked smile and angled his mount up the bank toward where the main road ran beyond a buffer of trees. Curious, Raven turned Cyrleth to follow. When they emerged from the trees onto the road, she saw a crossroad ahead. Marek led them up to it at a trot and stopped. The weather-beaten wooden sign indicated that the road they were on led to Pellanth. Another established road from the east met up with it there, though the part of the sign marking had been broken off. A smaller, unmarked track continued west past that point.

"Where does that go?" She gestured down the side track.

"It comes out on the north side of Amberwood."

A charge of excitement swept through her. Cyrleth danced a little to one side in response. It pleased her that she'd gotten comfortable enough with the animal to gently correct such behavior without increased anxiety.

"To Darrenton's land?"

"I suppose it would be now."

Raven stared down the track. She owed Darrenton something for his brother's death. Maybe the time had come to see that through. Stopping Darrenton would also halt that threat to her companions in Amberwood, buying her more time to deal with Wayland.

"Marek."

"I don't like that tone. You sound like someone about to cause trouble."

A slow smile started to tug at her lips. "What if we don't bend to Wayland's demand by going to Pellanth? What if we send him a message instead?"

Marek stared at her for a moment before dawning lit his eyes. "By thwarting his efforts to hurt Amberwood, you mean?"

She gazed back down the track. "Yes. We stop Darrenton."

"By stop, you mean kill?"

She let the smile escape fully now and turned Cyrleth to face him. She had promised her parents at their grave that she would avenge Jaecar's death. This was a chance to make good on that promise before she risked her life trying to stop Wayland.

"I do." His skeptical look sparked an itch of irritation, but she waited, giving him time to speak his mind.

"We are Silverbloods, Raven, but the two of us can't take on an army. Even a small one."

She yearned to tell him she was Krivalen, not Silverblood, but that would send them down a path that led to the elves in Eyl'Thelandra, so she kept the correction to herself. "Maybe we won't have to. I only saw Darrenton once, but he didn't strike me as a man of the people. He won't be out with his mercenary troops bonding around the campfires any more than he has to be. He'll be holed up in his manor telling himself stories about the riches he's going to make when he takes over Amberwood."

Marek answered with a slow nod. "A fair conjecture. I've been on the land. Assuming he's built his manor where I would, it will be near the property's eastern edge. If we managed to get to him in his manor, we could cut the head off Wayland's pet nobleman, and the mercenaries might scatter."

She appreciated his choice of words. Darrenton was acting as Wayland's dog, and she was more than happy to put him down. "Yes."

"It could work."

She smirked at him. "I thought it sounded a little crazy."

He chuckled. "Maybe your crazy is wearing off on me. If we succeeded, Wayland would be furious." He untied a water skin from his saddle, the one she knew contained ale rather than water. He took a long swallow before holding it out to her. "West then?"

Raven accepted the skin and took a long swallow, grimacing at the burn as it went down. She still wasn't sure why anyone drank the stuff.

"West," she confirmed, handing it back to him.

●

At a knock on the door, Alayne hopped up, gesturing for Karsima to stay where she was with her feet up before the warm fire. A laugh from the other room caught her attention. Karsima sat up, turning to see Alayne lean over and give a careful hug to Phendaril. She stepped back from him and shook the water off her hands.

"You're soaked, Phen."

"You wouldn't believe how long and bumpy the trip from the healer's building is in this." He gestured to the clever wheeled chair Helar and one of the Stonebreaker smiths had come up with to make it possible for him to move around more freely. "When is someone going to fix the roads around here?"

"I believe you were in on the decision to postpone those repairs in favor of other projects." She pointed toward Karsima. "Roll your ass into the sitting room. I'll find you a towel."

Karsima watched him maneuver the chair. It was difficult, given that he only had one functional hand to do it with. Still, he stubbornly refused assistance more often than not. He could use the other hand a little, as long as he was careful, but it had a substantial amount of healing to do still. Between his elven blood and the extraordinary concoctions Talis had sent back from the elven healers in Pellanth, he was healing at a remarkable rate. That didn't do much to alleviate his frustration and boredom right now. They involved him in all the decisions about the town and had him managing the scouts again, with Jael standing by to perform any required physical tasks. It gave Phendaril something to do part of the time. Even with those things, she knew he still had too much time on his hands to think about Raven and wonder if he could have done something differently to avoid having to part ways with her.

Talis had stayed behind in Pellanth to help care for Veylin. The injuries she sustained were a reflection of the ones Raven had suffered in her encounter with Wayland. Unfortunately for Veylin, she wasn't magically enhanced. Those injuries had killed Raven, though the healers managed to pull her back. How was Veylin supposed to survive without that extra hardiness and healing ability? She might have died already, for all they knew. Whether she lived or not, they owed Wayland for his actions. There had to be a way to get at him.

"I hope I'm not the one you're thinking of with that expression," Phendaril stated, stopping next to her chair in front of the fire.

"Mm. No. Just thinking about Veylin."

He nodded, his jaw tightening.

Alayne entered the room, setting an extra mug of mead on the table. She helped Phendaril dry off a little, despite his protests that he could manage on his own. Karsima chuckled at the resulting struggle. After a few minutes of playful confrontation, he gained control of the towel. Alayne rolled her eyes at him before returning to her own chair. She picked up her mug and set her feet on the table next to Karsima's.

"Any word from Raven since that last dream?" Alayne asked.

As she was speaking, her attention on Phendaril, she reached out to run a few fingers lightly down Karsima's arm. Karsima shifted into the contact. How Alayne could still make her feel like she'd just fallen in love with a single touch was beyond her. She could only hope she did half as much for Alayne.

"Nothing." Phendaril exhaled heavily and stared into the fire. "I told her she couldn't come back here last time I saw her. Maybe she listened and decided to build a new life for herself with her mother's family."

"I can't imagine Raven giving up that easily, but if she did, at least she's safe there," Karsima offered, knowing how little it would help.

The muscles in his jaw jumped as he clenched his teeth against a deep pain she could do nothing for. "I'm trying to learn to be happy for her."

They turned their attention to their drinks then, each staring into the fire, lost their own thoughts.

After a time, Phendaril set his mug down and looked at each of them. "There haven't been any new units arriving on Darrenton's land in the last few days. If he's done growing his army, we might stand a chance against it."

Alayne curled her legs up into her chair. "Maybe he's reconsidering my offer."

Karsima nodded. "We can hope. I hate to give him anything, but rights to a few resources is better than risking the people here."

Alayne had gone to Aldrich Darrenton to offer limited logging and mining rights on Amberwood lands. According to her, he had acted underwhelmed with the proposal, but perhaps he realized how much it would save him given the cost and hassle of commanding an assault on the town.

A soft knock on the door drew their attention to the entryway. They all turned to see Talis walk in, not waiting for someone to answer. His eyes were bloodshot and rimmed in red. Alayne and Phendaril sat up, and Karsima stood. He shook his head.

"I'm sorry to barge in. I just got back." The muscles in his neck and jaw worked for a second as if he were trying hard to maintain control of himself. "I wanted you to know I brought Veylin's body back." His voice cracked, and he lowered his gaze. "We can return her to the forest where she belongs."

Liquid sorrow spilled from Karsima's eyes, and she sank to her knees. Phendaril buried his face in his hands, a tremble in his shoulders. Alayne knelt next to Karsima and wrapped her arms around her as they both wept. Karsima yearned to comfort Phendaril, knowing he had only just lost Raven, but she couldn't find the strength to move. Talis walked over and placed a hand on Phendaril's arm, and she offered him a look of gratitude through the blur of her tears.

Somehow, Wayland would pay.

ynderis watched the two females approaching his post. The Delegate, with her surreal Krivalen resplendence, and Dellaura, elegant and beautiful in a more traditional elven sense. He could pick out traces of Raven in her features now. Being reminded of her didn't help him feel better about how things were. No more than visiting Raven in her dreams made him happier about waiting for the night she might not show up.

He gazed out into the forest, letting them finish their approach along the elevated walkway. Koshika stood next to him and stared at the two females, a low growl rising in her throat. He found it odd that she insisted on following him even up here now, but he didn't mind it.

"Hush. We can't be rude to our elders," he said in a low voice, placing a calming hand on the big cat's head. The lalyx had taken to Raven so fast. He often wondered if that was because she sensed something good in Raven or because they were both a little feral.

He smiled at the thought.

The footsteps changed as the two females stepped onto the solid platform circling the tree. Both stopped far enough away to avoid distressing Koshika. He schooled his expression and turned to fully face them, greeting each with a respectful nod. The Delegate's metallic eyes were hard to read, so he focused his efforts on Dellaura, noting the sorrow as well as the faint gleam of determination in her gaze.

"Is it really a good idea to bring your companion up here?" Dellaura regarded the animal with genuine concern. "What if she panics and falls?"

He scratched behind the cat's ears. "I've tried to stop her. She won't listen."

The Delegate drew in a breath, and he turned his attention to her.

"You're still dreamwalking Raven."

Her tone made it less of a question, but he nodded.

"And she has not reached Pellanth yet?"

He shook his head. "They're getting close. And before you ask again, she isn't going to change her mind. I've tried."

"Perhaps if you guided Dellaura into the dreamwalk, she would listen to two where one has failed," the Delegate suggested gently.

Waste part of what could be his last night with her letting Dellaura try to convince her that her companions weren't worth her life? He knew how that conversation was going to go. He'd had it already. "No."

The Delegate narrowed her eyes.

Dellaura reached out to him. "Syn, I know you care for her, but this isn't helping her, and it's putting us at risk."

He shifted back from her touch, and Koshika growled. "I'm sorry, Dell. Raven may be your granddaughter, but I know her better than you do. I've dreamwalked her more times than you've spoken to her. She's made up her mind. She swears to take our secrets with her to her death—which could come any day now—and I believe she will. I'm not giving up my time with her. If you want to see her just to see her and perhaps say goodbye, then I'll take you in. You have to promise not to waste that time arguing over decisions that have already been made."

The Delegate tilted her head to one side, her brows pinching with anger. "Am I to understand that you're putting her above our people?"

"No. You can try to color it that way if you want to, but that's not what this is. I don't think Raven's a danger to anyone other than herself. Besides, our people are the ones who made this situation possible, aren't we? If we hadn't gone into hiding all those years ago, the Brotherhood might not have the power it has. Our people allowed three ordinary human men to own the Krivalen magic in the world outside of Eyl'Thelandra. Now any Krivalen not made by a Brotherhood priest is executed. You and I would be put to death out there. I can't even leave here to go help the woman I love. Raven has to put her life on the line so we can keep our secrets. I think we've asked enough of her." He was breathing hard when he finished, tears of pain and anger stinging his eyes. Next to him, Koshika was on her feet, her feathered hackles up. He noticed absently that the tips of the feathers over her shoulders acquired a reddish tint when she was angry.

Dellaura glanced away, tears streaming down her cheeks.

He took a step toward her. "I'm sorry, Dell."

"Don't be," the Delegate said, placing a hand on Dellaura's shoulder. Her gaze drifted down to the lalyx. "It's been a long time since one of us has had a predator companion in the town."

He glanced at her, confused by the sudden change of topic.

She reached out with her other hand, sliding cool fingers under his chin and looking him over with a thoughtful expression. "There is a fire in you, Synderis, that wasn't there before. I think Raven woke that in you. When humans found the Acridan people, we were already hiding in those woods, trying to avoid human-kind because of the destruction they had wrought upon our kind. We were used to hiding. It didn't occur to us to do anything else. If we'd had more like you then, perhaps we would have gone a different way."

She took her hand away and held it palm up before him. "She no longer has the twin to the talisman?"

His nerves crackled with the new unease between them. A tension he had created with his rebelliousness. He didn't know what to make of her words. "No, she gave it to someone else."

"May I see the one you have?"

For a few seconds, he considered refusing, but he had already cast a great deal of defiance at her. This was the Delegate. A figure he should be deferring to. He took off the talisman. Since Raven no longer had the twin, it was foolish to continue wearing it, but it had been the mechanism of their initial meeting. It was his one tangible keepsake of her. He had trouble letting it go, but he made himself set it in the Delegate's waiting palm.

She closed her fingers around it. The silver in her eyes flared brighter for a second. When she opened her hand, nothing but a small pile of shimmering dust remained. She turned her hand over, letting the dust fall away.

Dellaura's hand went to her chest. A sob escaped her.

The Delegate looked at her. "Go with him to dream-walk her if you wish to say goodbye. Do not try to bring her back." She met Synderis's eyes. "She's earned the right to die in peace if she has chosen that path."

With that, she turned and strode away. Synderis stepped up to Dellaura and put his arms around her, letting her cry against him. He glared after the Delegate. Perhaps there was some lesson in what she had done. From where he was standing, it was simply cruel. The talisman had been a link connecting Dellaura to her daughter and then to her granddaughter. The former was dead, and the latter might also be before long. Why destroy it? Was she punishing Dell for his defiance? Or perhaps she was trying to punish him, and Dellaura was an unfortunate victim of that.

"I'm sorry, Dell. That was my fault."

She stepped back from him, drawing a pale green silk kerchief from somewhere in her robes to delicately wipe her face. Koshika had settled beside him now. The feathers over her shoulders returned to their normal emerald color.

"Don't apologize, Syn. You aren't wrong. The Delegate knows it too. I think she wanted to make a point with the talisman. Its match is now in a stranger's hands, which means Raven risked our people's secrets to dreamwalk someone."

Anger flashed red in his vision, but he drew in a deep breath and took control of himself. "The talisman was out in the world for years before Raven got it."

"Not out in the world as you mean it. How do you think I knew when she got it? I was supposed to destroy it after Mellaine died, but I couldn't bring myself to do so. Instead, I kept it on me all these years to be certain that no one tried to use it. I'm not sure what I meant to do if someone did try to use it, but it was a memento of my daughter, so I kept it and promised myself I would destroy it if the need arose.

"For a time, right after Mellaine's death, I could sense a stranger through it, but it soon fell quiet. Whoever had it must have stowed it away and forgotten it. I felt nothing else until Aneiris took possession of it." Her sad smile held a gentleness and patience he wished he could match. "She is a victim of the path our people chose to take, but that choice was made a very long time ago."

He glanced down at the spray of silvery dust on the boards of the platform. A light breeze was already picking some up and swirling it away. Yes, their current path had been chosen a long time ago. Did that mean they could never change course? Was it too late to consider doing so?

Maybe the Delegate was right. Raven had changed him.

"Do you want to see her?"

A hopeful light sparked in Dellaura's eyes. "If you don't mind..."

He didn't want to share his time with Raven. He couldn't bring himself to be that selfish, either, however. Dellaura was Raven's blood family and had always been a parental figure to him.

He drew a deep breath and let it out, finding calm in the familiar smells of the forest. "I'll be by this evening."

"Thank you, Syn." She gave him a quick kiss on the cheek and left him there.

When night fell, he made his way to her home. Raven had only lived there a few days, but he felt her absence. Did Dellaura feel it as powerfully as he did?

They slid a chair up alongside Dellaura's bed like they had the times he guided her in dreamwalks with Mellaine. She lay back on the bed, and he sat in the chair, resting his hand over her forearm for the strong connection that physical contact would create.

"Are you ready?"

She nodded and closed her eyes.

Synderis closed his eyes as well, working the magic of his connection to Raven through both of them as he put them to sleep.

•

They appeared in a clearing near a cascading waterfall. At the base was a large crystalline pool. Ferns with violet blooms sprouting from their centers grew up between the stones around the pool. They were spring blooms, so this was probably something from memory. It wasn't one of the pools from around Eyl'Thelandra, though it was just as beautiful in many ways.

Raven stood gazing into the water, lost in whatever past experience brought her to this place. The tension in her shoulders and the way she fidgeted with the hilt of her sword told him something was different tonight. He regretted letting Dellaura come even more then, but there wasn't much for it now.

"I hope you don't mind," he said, catching her attention. "Someone wanted to see you."

She turned, her gaze sparking with a hint of pleasure when it lit upon Dellaura. She hurried and put her arms around her grandmother, wrapping her in a warm embrace that Dellaura returned just as enthusiastically.

"I'm sorry I didn't say goodbye," Raven said softly.

Dellaura pushed her back to hold her at arm's length. She smiled warmly. "I'm glad I could come to see you." A hint of gratitude brightened the glance she cast at Synderis. "I see so much of your mother in your features . . . and your personality. She couldn't stay put either." She breathed a laugh, though a tear rolled down one cheek. "I miss having you here, Aneiris. It seems like you barely arrived, then you were gone again."

Raven shifted out of her grasp and took hold of her hands. "I promise you, Dell, I will come back if I can."

"If you survive, you mean."

"Dell." Synderis put an edge of warning in his tone.

Dellaura cast him an irritated glance.

Raven also looked over at him, although he couldn't get a read on her expression before she faced Dellaura again. She smiled, though he could see the effort that went into the expression. "I've got a lot of motivation to do so. I can't imagine never having another of your glorious pastries."

Dellaura laughed again, though she sniffed as well, struggling with tears.

"Can I ask you something, Dell?"

Dellaura nodded. "Anything."

"Do you know why Mother made me Krivalen?"

Dellaura walked around her, staring into the forest that surrounded them. "You must remember that, for us, being Krivalen is an honorable and good thing. Your mother told me several times that she wanted you to choose that path, but she wanted you to have your childhood with your father first. She intended to bring you to Eyl'Thelandra when you were older so you could learn our ways and decide for yourself. I can't pretend to know what she was thinking at the moment of her death. It might be wrong of us to even assume clarity of thought at that moment. All I can say is that I'm certain she never meant to harm you." Her warm smile took on a hint of teasing. "She loved you so much that even I got jealous at times."

Synderis watched them talk for a while. Raven steered the conversation away from her current circumstances and other serious subjects, asking instead about Eyl'Thelandra, and the council, and drawing him in with questions about his nieces. He mostly paced when he wasn't directly involved. He loved Dellaura, but he was confident he would see her again tomorrow. Raven was a different matter. Did the unease in her manner mean she was in Pellanth now?

"Perhaps you can come again in a few nights," Raven said, glancing over at him.

Her words signaled an end to Dellaura's time there. They also kindled a spark of hope in him. If she meant to be here in a few nights, maybe she wasn't in danger yet. At least not in any more danger than she was always in as an unauthorized Silverblood.

Dellaura hugged her and gave her a kiss on both

cheeks. She took a deep, trembling breath as she turned to Synderis and nodded. "You two probably want some time. I'm ready now."

He returned the nod, squeezed her shoulder, and sent her out of the dream. The second she was gone, Raven was in his arms. He pulled her into a briefer-than-usual kiss before pushing her back to search her eyes.

"Something's different tonight. What's happened?"

She smiled, a sparkle of mischief gleaming in her eyes as she shook her head. "Not without a better greeting."

He relented willingly, letting his desire and love for her show in the kiss, appreciating how those emotions reverberated through the dreamscape. When he let her go this time, she nodded and took his hand, leading him to the edge of the pool.

"The first male I thought I could love showed me this place. This is also where he died." A hint of old sorrow tightened her voice. She gazed around at the ground as if looking at things that only existed in her memories. "I met Phendaril here as well. It seems tied to the males I have cared for and lost. Now I've brought you here. I'm not sure why, but I hope it isn't an ill omen."

It was strange to hear her speak of Phendaril and another male while standing there with him. Not that he expected her to never have loved before. He saw enough in the dreamscape with the other elven male to know she loved him. He disliked her train of thought because she was grouping him in with the ones she had lost.

He took her hand and squeezed it gently, bringing her attention back to him. "You'll never lose me, Raven."

Sorrow brought moisture to her eyes when she looked at him as if she didn't really believe his words. "I don't want to."

"Are you in Pellanth?" He heard the tightness of fear in his own voice.

"No. Marek and I changed our plans. We decided to

go after Lord Darrenton first. He bought the property on the north edge of Amberwood and is preparing to attack them. We're camped outside his property now, taking turns sleeping and keeping watch tonight. I'm not sure how much more time I have before he wakes me. Tomorrow, we'll scout out the manor and plan our attack. I might not get much sleep tomorrow night if we make our move once it gets dark."

She was warning him that she might not be there if he tried to dreamwalk her. He wouldn't know if she survived the assault on Darrenton. Unease skittered across his nerves. "I thought you said he was preparing an army to attack Amberwood. You can't fight an army."

She nodded, and something dark flashed in her eyes. Something he had never seen there before. "He is. We're going to end him before he gets the chance, hopefully without drawing the attention of his army. He owes me a life."

Synderis slid his hand across her neck and up into her hair, pleased that the gentle contact chased away the dark anger. Her gaze softened, and she stepped closer to him.

"Be careful, Raven. I'm not ready to lose you yet."

She slid her arms around him, stepped into his embrace. Her lips lightly brushing across his, she said, "You won't."

Then she disappeared.

He snapped awake.

Dellaura was sitting on the bed holding a cup of tea. She gestured to another steaming mug waiting on the nightstand. "I made you one too, in case you woke."

"Thank you." He lifted the cup, took a sip of warm tea, and thought about his earlier words to the Delegate. Maybe it was too late to change the course his people had chosen. Perhaps it wasn't. All he knew was that he wasn't sure how much longer he could sit back while the one he loved was in danger.

CHAPTER THIRTY SEVEN

Darrenton's manor was built on the eastern-most edge of the land, not far from the tree line. Several paddocks stood behind the two-story structure along with two large barns, one each on the north and south corners. Beyond the barns, stretching alongside the manor, were two outdoor arenas. The mercenary army had gathered in camps over the fields in front of the manor, far from where Raven and Marek were planning their approach.

Patrols rotated through the barns, though there was never more than one guard at a time inside them. There were fewer horses in the paddocks than she initially expected. Many of the mercenaries had assembled rough corrals of their own to keep the mounts they had, leaving the paddocks for horses that likely belonged to Darrenton and his guards.

There was a constant flow of activity around the manor. Mostly in and outside the south wing, which appeared to be the only part still undergoing significant construction. The upside was that few people working there were guards or mercenaries. In fact, the mercenaries didn't appear to be welcome in the manor. However, Darrenton's guards could be seen passing freely in and out of the structure.

They watched throughout the day from myriad

vantage points, getting a feel for the number of people going inside the manor. At one point, Darrenton appeared. He mounted a bay stallion that had been saddled for him and disappeared around front with three mounted guards. About an hour later, he returned, tossing his reins to the stablehand, and strode in through the manor's back door.

As night fell, they put on their armor and donned their weapons, then found a spot well-hidden in the brush where they could watch for the moment to make their move. The sword belt was still slightly uncomfortable over the wound on her side, though it was now little more than a long scar. It wasn't enough to distract her from her purpose. She'd made a promise to her parents to avenge Jaecar. Now she would follow through with that promise.

Marek gave her a nod when the house and grounds behind it seemed relatively quiet. She placed a kiss on the arrowhead pendant Phendaril had made her and took a few steps away from their hiding spot. Then she stopped and sank into the shadows again. Marek did the same, stalling mid-step and dropping back next to her.

They watched as a young man led the same bay stallion out of the northern barn. Darrenton emerged from the rear exit of the manor along with four guards this time. They mounted their horses and rode around front. If he was making the same circuit, they would have about an hour to clear as much of the manor as possible before he returned. She met Marek's eyes and gestured toward the building with a slight jerk of her head.

Marek nodded.

With the deepening shadows adding extra cover, they started to make their way from the edge of the woods to the barn on the south corner. That building appeared to get less use, making it a moderately safer route. They stopped on either side of the stable door to listen, Marek watching her intently as he drew his crossbow. He was willing to acknowledge that she had a sensory advantage as a Silverblood and a half-elf. She waited, catching the sounds of the guard inside yawning and shifting his feet.

She signaled Marek, indicating about how far in and on what side the guard was. He gave a decisive nod and loaded the crossbow. Then he leaned into the doorway and fired. The subsequent choking noise from inside told her he had struck his mark.

They both ducked into the building. There were no animals in this barn. It appeared to be serving as an armory for Darrenton's planned attack. Two stalls were crammed full of weapons and shields. Extra food and several barrels of mead were stored in the next three stalls. Three ballistae were lined up along the aisle in between the stalls.

Marek dragged the dead guard into one of the stalls, shoving his body alongside some crates. Then he yanked the bolt from the man's neck. After wiping the end of the bolt on the man's clothes, he started creeping down the aisle. Raven stopped next to the dead man, gazing at those lifeless eyes. They were the same shade of green as Eamon's eyes had been.

After several seconds, Marek came back to stand at her shoulder. "Remember what they mean to do to the people of Amberwood. These weapons aren't gentle."

Her stomach twisted.

"If that doesn't work, imagine they're corpse eaters."

A flash of anger burned through her at his words. She recalled how great a team they had made taking down the corpse eaters together, only to have him betray her soon after returning to town. She gave him a warning scowl. "If you ever try to betray me again like you did after we killed those corpse eaters, I'm going to imagine you're one."

"That's the spirit." He grinned and started down the aisle once more. "Come along. We've only got so much time."

Raven didn't allow herself to look at the dead man again. She killed many beasts to help make Amberwood safe before. This was no different. They were corpse eaters, threatening the safety of those she cared for. The corpse eaters endangering Amberwood just looked a little more like her this time.

She hurried after Marek. They both stopped at the same moment and turned toward a stall full of wood crates. The top of one sat slightly askew, revealing an opened bag of millet within. A canister lay on its side next to the crate, spilling more millet across the floor. Someone had been filling it when they entered, someone who was now hiding behind the crates trying to control their breathing.

Marek cocked an eyebrow at her.

She shrugged in response to the unspoken question. No, she didn't know how she had missed hearing this person when she listened outside. They must have been still at precisely the right time.

Something about the barely audible catch in the breathing struck her as feminine. She waved Marek back and stepped in, keeping her sword ready but not raised. The toe of a soft, worn shoe poked out at the bottom edge of the crate. The type of threadbare shoe a serving woman might wear. Raven sheathed her sword and stepped in front of the woman sitting there, her knees pulled tight to her chest. A lock of curly black hair that had pulled free of the headscarf she wore hung down between dark eyes, moist with terror.

Recalling how Eamon acted with her when they first met, making himself smaller and giving her extra space, Raven took a step back and crouched down to put herself at eye level with the woman.

"I don't know nothing," the woman declared, wincing as if she expected to be attacked for merely speaking.

"I won't hurt you," Raven assured her. "What's your name?"

The woman dared to look at her directly then. "Lily," she murmured.

"I'm only here for Aldrich Darrenton."

Lily met Raven's eyes, her own popping wide. "You're that half-breed Silverblood whelp Lord Darrenton was going on about. The one his brother adopted." She sat up a little, looking surprisingly relieved. "Goodness, I was afraid you were regular bandits. It ain't right what he did to his brother. All of us think so."

Raven sat back on her heels, taken aback by the sudden change in the woman. "Aldrich told you he had Jaecar killed?"

"Well, no. 'Course he didn't." She waved a hand dismissively. "There's a lot he doesn't tell us that we know. Can't help knowing. When that man gets on a tirade, I wouldn't be surprised if half the country could hear him. A master of secrets he ain't."

A smirk turned Raven's lips as she stood and held a hand down to Lily. The other woman accepted it tentatively, letting Raven help her up. "By us, you mean the servants?"

"Yes. We're a close group. Have to support each other when you work for a man like Lord Darrenton."

"Maybe you could help us, then."

"Darrenton's out riding through the camps."

Raven managed to hide her surprise. Aldrich certainly didn't inspire much loyalty in his staff. "We know. We were hoping to ambush him in the house. I'd rather none of the servants got caught in the fighting. Is there any way you could get them up in the north wing without alerting the guards?"

Lily looked down at her trembling hands for a few

seconds. Raven felt the itch of time creeping away from them. Marek was scowling and shaking his head, but he didn't try to intervene.

"Most of us are already in our quarters up there. Mostly just a few out in the kitchen at this hour. That's also in the north wing. I shouldn't have trouble keeping them there, but . . ." She wrung her hands and nibbled at her lower lip before continuing. "Not all the guards are so bad. Most of 'em are right bastards, but a few are decent enough."

Raven shook her head. "I'll let you go warn the servants, but the guards will try to stop us. It's their job. Leave them to us to deal with."

Lily nodded. "I understand, milady."

Raven reached out and gave the other woman's arm a gentle squeeze, trying to ignore how awkward the gesture felt. "Go then. Stay out of sight until this is over."

Lily nodded and hurried out of the barn.

Marek shook his head as he slipped up next to the barn door to peer after her. "I'll be amazed if she doesn't warn the guards."

Raven crept up next to him. "She won't."

They would have to cross an open area that stretched between them and the manor without being spotted. Lily went through the door immediately across from them, set there for easy access to the barn. They would wait a few minutes and follow the same way.

The south wing was still under construction, so they were less apt to run into as many guards on this end. The craftsmen doing the work had retired to their camp around the south side of the manor, far away from the mercenary camps set up on the northwest edge of the property.

They waited, watching and listening. Marek met her eyes after several minutes of silence, offering a nod. She returned it before she darted across, slipping quickly up against the building. No shrubs or other landscape decor were in place, so they had no cover next to the house. Raven took hold of the handle on the door, relieved when it gave to her pressure. If Lily had locked it, that would have been a sure sign that she meant to betray them. The new construction was high quality, and the door swung soundlessly. When she had it opened enough to duck in, she paused and listened one more time, then slipped inside.

She left it open a mere crack behind her in case anyone outside looked in that direction. When Marek determined it was safe to do so, he would follow.

This part of the manor was dark except for the moonlight coming in some windows. It was more than enough light for her to see by. Rooms to either side of the entry were empty of furniture. Lumber and an array of tools were piled within, construction materials that reminded her of her days helping rebuild Amberwood. It was strange to think how close she was to that place she had made her home. How close she was to Phendaril.

Marek ducked through the door. As soon as he clicked it shut behind him, she heard footsteps. A light came bobbing down the adjacent hallway. Raven stepped back into the room behind her. Marek met her eyes, then turned and entered the opposite room. He began rummaging around among the tools there. Hidden in the shadows, she watched the guard approach. He headed into the other room, drawn by the noises Marek was making.

"What are you doing in here this late?" The guard raised the candle holder he was carrying, trying to get a better look at Marek.

"Sorry, sir," Marek answered, changing his inflections and accent to make himself sound more common. "I left somethin' behind."

The man took a few steps closer, holding the candle toward Marek. Any second, he would recognize that the armor her companion was wearing was vastly different from a craftsman's attire. Raven padded silently up behind him and buried her dagger in the side of his throat. Marek turned, watching as she eased the dying man to the floor.

"Well done."

She swallowed a rush of bile, forcing herself not to look at the man's face as she crouched down to wipe the blood from her dagger and her hand on his green-and-black Darrenton guard livery.

If she weren't a Silverblood, perhaps Jaecar would have brought her back to Pellanth years ago and had her recognized as an adopted member of their noble family. Then she might be paying her Uncle Aldrich a social visit instead of preparing to take his life. It was a foolish fancy, though. She was, and always would be, unwelcome in his world.

Marek touched her shoulder. She shook herself and stood. They took turns checking rooms as they made their way along the main hallway. About halfway down, closer to the center of the manor, the sconces in the hall were lit, indicating an increased risk of encountering someone. A loud laugh sent them both ducking into one of the empty rooms. Raven walked to the wall adjacent to the next room and placed one ear against it.

More laughter and talking came from the neighboring room. She counted at least six distinct male voices as they made crude jokes about one of the mercenary groups' tiny horses.

Marek held up six fingers, and she nodded. He pointed to an almost invisible door in the back corner of the room that would lead to the servant's passages. Raven answered with a nod and headed that way. Marek stood watching her. The door opened to light pressure.

She gave another nod to him to indicate that the passage beyond was empty, waiting to watch as he returned to the main hallway.

She ducked into the nearly black passageway and crept along with her fingers feeling the wall in case her eyes missed the door. It took a few seconds for her eyes to adjust. In this complete, windowless darkness, even her enhanced eyesight was challenged to find the well-hidden wall section that would open into the occupied room.

"Do you think their dicks are that tiny too?" one of the men in the next room asked, receiving a round of uproarious laughter in response.

The voices were a fraction louder at one point. She stopped there and ran her fingers over the wall, feeling the crack that signified the door.

"Who the hell are you?"

The demand accompanied the sounds of furniture scraping the floor as the men stood abruptly. That was her cue. Raven pushed the door open. As soon as she stepped out of the passageway, Marek, standing in the doorway to the hall, lifted his arm and pulled the trigger, planting a bolt from his crossbow in one man's neck. She had her pick of targets with all of their attention on him. The nearest man had her sword through his back before they knew she was there.

Marek ducked a hasty, drunken swing from the man closest to the front. Then he brought his blade around, slicing into the man's chest at an angle. The next one Raven moved on still hadn't recognized the threat coming from behind him. He started to turn as she brought her blade around in front of him and dragged it across his neck, cutting deep into his throat. The man next to him was aware of her now. He caught her wrist. Raven ducked under his arm and spun, driving her dagger up in his armpit. Then she kicked him in the groin, slamming her knee into his face as he doubled over. Cartilage and bone crunched against her knee. When he hit the floor, she drove her knee into his back and grabbed his hair, slicing his neck with the dagger.

Marek was finishing his third opponent as well. They ducked back into the servant passages at his gesture, shutting themselves in the darkness. They both stood utterly still for several seconds, listening for sounds that might indicate their battle had drawn attention. Raven used the brief break to try to quell the sick feeling in her gut, a process made more difficult by the cloying stench of blood on her hands. When the room beyond the hidden door remained quiet, they started moving along the servant's passage, sneaking through the manor's walls.

The passage eventually ended in another concealed doorway. Again, they stood and listened. She could hear someone moving nearby. From another direction came the sound of someone clearing their throat. At least two people. Probably guards at the main rear entrance, judging by the direction and the distance they had covered. She held up two fingers and pointed in the direction of the sounds. Marek loaded his crossbow. He took the lead, opening the door and rushing out without hesitation.

Raven shook her head, hurrying after him.

Marek fired his bow and leaped to one side, leaving Raven barely enough time to try to dodge the small dagger that flew past him. It grazed her upper arm as she darted in the other direction, casting Marek a scathing glance before lunging at the nearest guard. The surprisingly large man who had thrown the dagger stood to the left of the rear doorway with a crossbow bolt in his left shoulder. Whether Marek had misjudged his shot or the guard had simply reacted that fast she didn't know, but she wasn't going to waste time worrying about it.

The closer guard opened his mouth, perhaps intending to call for help. Raven hurled her dagger at him. He dodged left but wasn't fast enough. The weapon cut a slice along his cheek and ear as Raven leaped into a roll and sprung up, swinging out with her sword to cut into his neck. She turned quickly then to see if Marek needed assistance. He was jerking his bolt from the other guard's shoulder where the man lay dead on the floor.

Their eyes met. They both stood silent, listening for the sounds of anyone else coming. When there were none, Raven gestured to the bloody cut on her arm, and he grimaced an apology as he walked over.

"Still used to working solo, I see," she grumbled under her breath, bending down to cut a piece of fabric from the guard's tunic.

"Yes. Sorry about that." He took the fabric from her and tied it firmly around the wound. "Are you hale enough?"

"This won't slow me down." It stung, but it wasn't deep enough to impair.

"I wouldn't expect it to." He glanced toward the door. "Darrenton seems to use this entrance when he goes out for his rides."

Raven nodded to a wide doorway behind him leading to a mostly furnished study.

"Good idea. Help me clean these two up. We don't want to put him on alert too quickly."

They made fast work of moving the two guards into an adjacent room. It was a little harder cleaning up the blood on the floor, but Raven snuck back to the room where they had killed the six guards and brought back a few tunics and some ale to wash up with. When that was done, Marek lit two wall sconces in the room from one of the lit ones in the entry, then sat behind Darrenton's desk. She positioned herself next to a window on the opposite side of the entryway. Then they waited.

There were occasional sounds from elsewhere in the manor. Distant laughter of more guards coming from the other wing. There were probably guards near the front door too, but they weren't going to have time to deal with that. She spotted Darrenton and his four men as they rode up to the stable and dismounted.

"They're here."

Marek set his crossbow on the desk, leaned his heavy sword against the side, and put his feet up on it. Raven took the crossbow and backed into the shadows of the room opposite that one.

CHAPTER THIRTY EIGHT

For all the guards he kept around him, Aldrich Darrenton wasn't the most cautious man. He stormed in through the back door with his four men following after.

"Those bastards actually think..." He trailed off, his attention drawn to the light flickering in the study.

Behind him, his guards drew their swords, following him to the study doorway. Aldrich stopped there, the tension in his posture easing a fraction.

"Adept Marek. Did Father Mallebron send you?"

Raven shifted her aim with the crossbow, leveling it at Marek's head. Why did Aldrich know him on sight?

"Ah, no." Marek put his feet on the floor and sat up, leaning onto his elbows on the desk. His gaze flickered to her for a fleeting instant. "Wayland and I aren't really on speaking terms."

"Then what are you doing in my house?"

His brows pinched, and he looked back at her again. "That's not really for me to say."

Raven adjusted the crossbow's aim and stepped forward to where the light would reflect off her eyes as Aldrich turned. "Hello, Uncle."

Aldrich opened his mouth to speak. Jaecar's body, lying dead over the back of a horse, flashed through her mind. She pulled the trigger. The bolt slammed home in

Aldrich's left eye. He stood there for a second, his body slowly catching on to the fact that he was dead. Then he fell. His men charged her. In the room behind them, Marek grabbed his sword and sprang over the desk. Raven tossed aside the crossbow. She ducked under the first man's swing, driving her blade up under his armor and into his gut and pulling to the side as she sprang in that direction, away from the next attacker. The first guard fell forward, his abdomen sliced open. She parried the next sword with her dagger, then brought her sword up into the crux of his thigh and groin. The man screamed in agony before she managed to finish him off with her dagger in his throat.

Another man went down with Marek's blade in his back before she could reach him. The fourth lay on the ground with his head cut almost off. The sound of footsteps racing down the hall caught their attention then, and they positioned themselves next to each other with enough space to fight.

Five men streamed into the room from the north wing, and two came from somewhere near the front of the building. They charged in fast. Raven's world narrowed down to their fighting. She felt blood spray across her face as she sliced into someone's neck at close range. There was a distant pain in her forearm above the leather gauntlet where someone grazed her with their blade. She blocked, dodged, and attacked until there were no more attackers, and she was standing back to back with Marek, staring at the bodies around them.

"This reminds me of our corpse eater adventure," Marek commented, breathing hard.

Raven spun. She cracked the pommel of her sword into his wrist, making him drop his own weapon, and swept his legs out from under him. He started to move to get back up the second he hit the floor, but she was a little faster. The point of her sword touched his throat, and he shrank back from it.

"How did Aldrich know you?" She was also breathing hard, someone's blood, possibly her own, trickling down her cheek.

"Raven—"

She pushed the tip into his skin. "How?"

He drew a shallow breath, wary of her blade. "Aldrich hired me to spy on Amberwood. That's why I was in Manderly when Phendaril and his scouts arrived. He wanted me to make sure they got their supplies so they could clean up Amberwood. Then he intended to claim ownership of the land since his brother was dead. I was also supposed to take stock of their resources and what fighters they had in case they tried to resist his claim."

Red closed in around the edges of her vision. She pushed on the blade. A trickle of red ran down the side of his neck and into his hair. Her rage begged for more, but she held herself back. "And Jaecar?"

"Jaecar was dead before I ever met Aldrich. I swear. I had nothing to do with his murder."

Raven held his gaze for several seconds, then moved her blade away. She wobbled on her feet, exhaustion hitting her like a powerful gust of wind. Marek was up in an instant, a hand on her arm to steady her.

"Are you all right?"

She looked at the carnage around them. Not corpse eaters. Just men. Her gaze lit upon Aldrich. Crushing sorrow threatened to knock her over. He had murdered his brother for a piece of land. Now he was dead too. Perhaps he deserved it, but she had difficulty feeling good about all the wasted lives lying at their feet.

Marek's arm came around her shoulders. "I think I may have found something you'll be interested in." He steered her into the study and sat her in the chair behind the desk.

He went to grab a dagger off one of the guards,

then he knelt next to the desk and used it to pry open a locked drawer. He nodded as if expecting what he found. Inside, several pages of parchment lay on top of a pile of fat pouches. Marek lifted one pouch, jingling it a little before returning it to the drawer. Raven picked up the parchments and unfolded them, skimming the list of names and numbers.

"What is this?"

"This, Lady Aneiris Darrenton, is the list of payments due to the mercenaries outside and the funds to cover them." He grinned. "Your mercenaries now, if you have a use for them. Assuming they're willing to work for a new employer."

Raven answered with a hesitant nod, doing her best to forget the bodies beyond the desk. She could think of a use for them. If they were willing, she knew a nearby town that might need some extra protection for a while. Then another thought occurred to her. "Did he have a wife or children?"

Marek shrugged. "I haven't a clue. If so, they aren't here." He took the parchment from her and set it back in the drawer before shutting it. "We should probably make sure no more guards are in the house."

Raven nodded. They retrieved his crossbow first, then thoroughly searched the house one room at a time. They found a few guards sleeping in a room near the end of the north wing. Marek dispatched them quietly. It nauseated Raven how easy it was to pick them off in their sleep. In a set of tiny rooms upstairs, they found several servants. Lily had already prepared the others for their arrival, informing them that Raven was Jaecar Darrenton's adopted daughter. Marek took advantage of this and introduced Raven more formally as Lady Aneiris Darrenton. Unsure how to feel about that, Raven simply told them Aldrich Darrenton and his guards were dead but that they were welcome to stay and no harm would come to them. More than that could be figured out in the morning.

When all was secure within the manor, Marek left her to bring their horses up into the north barn and let the servants there know the situation. Raven made her way to a sitting room she had noticed on their search. It was nicely appointed, with two deep, luxurious chairs and a matching couch before a large stone fireplace. She removed her armor, noting several new gouges in the leather, then sat in one of the chairs and took a few minutes to wrap the cut on her forearm.

Two of the servants entered the room, an older man with an armload of firewood and Lily carrying a platter on which rested two fine goblets and a wine jug. They hesitated in the doorway, the man bowing as low as he could without dropping the wood. Lily executed a graceful curtsy.

Raven stood.

"No need to get up, milady," Lily said. "Thought you might like a fire and some refreshment after your... exertions." She started to look back toward the hall, then stopped herself and offered a nervous half-smile

Raven exhaled softly. She couldn't blame them for being nervous. The number of bodies in the house were enough to make anyone uncomfortable. "You needn't call me my lady or wait on me." The two looked instantly worried as if they had offended her somehow, so she added, "Unless you really want to."

Lily nodded and came forward. When she did so, the man hurried into the room and began preparing the fire. Feeling more than a little awkward as the woman poured wine for her, Raven sat back down on the chair.

"I know it's late, milady, but I can bring you something to eat if you're hungry."

Raven considered her a moment. "Perhaps you could introduce me to your companion first."

Lily blushed. "Ah. Of course. This is Brek."

"Lily, I..." Raven trailed off, blushing furiously at a loud grumbling in her stomach.

Lily's smile came more easily this time. She pushed that same unruly lock of dark, curly hair back under her headscarf, her almond skin taking on a warm glow in the light of the new fire. "I'll bring something right away. Will your gentleman friend be joining you?"

Rather than openly question Marek's qualifications as a gentleman, Raven simply nodded. Lily rushed off and she leaned back in the chair, letting her head fall against the back. She listened as Brek finished up and left the room. Lily's footsteps entered again a few minutes later.

"Food's on its way. Anything else I can get for you, milady?"

Raven opened her eyes and lifted her head, surprised at how much effort it took.

Lily leaned in a little closer, peering at Raven's eyes. "You really are a Silverblood. I like those silver eyes better on you than on the others I've seen. Maybe because you're so lovely, and you have that extra bit of elven grace."

For a few seconds, Raven searched for something to say to that. She had learned a lot since leaving her home with Jaecar, but she still didn't quite know how to deal with compliments. Ultimately, she avoided it altogether, jumping to a different subject. "Did Aldrich have a wife or children?"

Lily settled on the arm of the other chair. "Had two wives. First one ran off with the captain of his guard. The new captain eventually caught them. She was pregnant and insisted the child was Lord Darrenton's. Given the timing and how far along she was, it was possible, but he didn't believe her. He had them put to death. Didn't marry again for many years after that. When he finally did, his second wife miscarried twice before she carried a child to term, but the child was stillborn. She was found dead in her room a few days later. They said it was complications from the childbirth, but one of the maids saw Lord Darrenton go into her room late that night."

It took her a second to realize what she was implying. "You think he killed her?"

"He blamed her for the miscarriages. Told her he'd kill her if it happened again. We all think he did it. There's plenty of reasons we stayed out of the way tonight. I'll tell you some more stories another time if you like." She hopped up from the chair arm when Marek entered the room, giving him a quick curtsy. "Should I have the master bedroom cleaned up for you?" She cast an appraising glance at Marek as he sank into the other chair, then met Raven's eyes.

Raven shook her head. "No. A couple of adjacent rooms somewhere else in the manor would be fine. I'd rather not sleep in the bed Aldrich slept in."

"As milady wishes." She filled the other goblet and handed it to Marek before leaving the room.

"Any trouble with the horses?"

Marek shook his head. Then he took a drink of the wine and smiled appreciatively. "They didn't shirk on the quality for your welcome." He met her expectant gaze. "I encountered guards in the barn who had to be dealt with, but the stable hands were amenable to a change in leadership."

"We should clean up the bodies," Raven remarked, taking a drink of the wine to try to calm the tremble in her hands.

His gaze lingered on the ripple in her wine glass, then he gave her a searching look. "Are you all right, Raven? I seem to recall a conversation we had in the mines in which you said you disliked killing even the wretched corpse eaters."

She swallowed against a wave of nausea. "I can't talk about it now. Please."

Marek turned toward her and placed a hand on her arm. When she met his eyes, he smiled fondly. "Raven, you stopped Aldrich Darrenton from killing a lot of people. You saw the siege weapons in the barn. He wasn't going to do this nicely. You avenged Jaecar, and you protected Amberwood. Give yourself a few minutes to forget the terrible things and appreciate the good you have done tonight."

"We. We did those things."

Marek chuckled. "I just came along for the adventure." He held the goblet up between them. "To adventure and protecting the people you love."

Something in his expression told her he might have been along more for the latter of those two things, but she wasn't going to question it now. He was right. They had saved Amberwood from Aldrich's attack. She had avenged Jaecar and kept her promise to her parent's memories. This would only escalate her conflict with Wayland, but that was something to figure out tomorrow. Maybe she did deserve a little time to sit and recover.

She lifted her goblet, trying to ignore how heavy it felt in her hand, and clicked it against his before taking a long sip of the wine. Then she put her feet up on the late Lord Darrenton's elegant table and rested her head back against the chair.

•

Karsima hurried to the house she shared with Alayne, arriving on Jael's heels. He was going to report to Phendaril, who spent much of his time at their home now. Usually, she trusted them to alert her if anything required her assistance, but the late hour and something in Jael's expression as he rode into the square compelled her to follow.

"Milady." Jael opened the door and stepped back, allowing her to proceed him in.

Karsima gave a nod of appreciation. "You have some news?"

"For the head of our scouts, yes."

She looked back, arching an eyebrow at his faint smirk. The tightness around his eyes and the set of his jaw told her something had him worried. She held in the jesting remarks she might have made at another time and led the way to the study.

Phendaril sat at her desk. An almost empty goblet of wine sat near his uninjured hand. He appeared to be staring at a map of the Amberwood territory, though the distance in his eyes said he was lost in thought. If this was like the rest of the time since his return, those thoughts were almost certainly of Raven.

He looked up when they entered, offering a nod to Jael before letting his gaze come to rest on her. "No wine?"

"No. I spotted Jael on my way to the tavern. I'm curious what lies behind his late visit and troubled gaze," she answered, casting Jael an inquisitive glance.

A light furrow lined Jael's brow as he looked from her to Phendaril. "One of the scouts keeping watch over our new northern neighbor saw something strange not long after dark. She said she spotted a couple of figures sneaking onto the property. They went through the southeast stable and in a back entrance. After they went inside, she snuck into the stable and found a dead guard. She could hear faint sounds of fighting coming from the manor around the time Darrenton returned from his evening circuit around the mercenary camps. She waited about twenty minutes to see if anyone else came in or out before hurrying back to report."

Phendaril glanced up at Karsima at the same time

she looked at him, their eyes meeting.

"I can lead a party up north in the morning," she stated.

Jael shook his head. "No point yet. I was planning to ride out and take the last watch over his land tonight. If it looks like it's worth following up on, I can be back here early tomorrow to let you know. I'll have Ehric bring a fresh horse to the midway post in case I need to return in a hurry."

"I wish I could come with you." Phendaril traced the borderline between Amberwood and the Darrenton estate on the map with one finger. "I doubt you'll see much. Those intruders are likely dead now, given the number of guards he has. It's a shame." He tapped the spot on the map where Darrenton's manor now stood, a ghost of a smile curving his lips. "I would have liked to meet anyone who hated him enough to face those odds."

THE END

ACKNOWLEDGEMENTS

After several years spent rebuilding my life—finding a new place to call home and finishing my degree, among other things—I am happy to have found inspiration again with Raven. Her story came to me as I was pondering the effects of pandemic isolation on our social skills (which I had only a bare minimum of to begin with). Those thoughts led me to wonder what it would be like to grow up isolated from other people. Throw in a dash of fantasy, and Raven was born.

As such, I must give a nod of acknowledgment to everyone for surviving in these challenging times. Whatever hardships you have faced over these last few years, I hope you find something in Raven's story to inspire you.

There are a few people I could never leave off this list. That includes my dearest friends and family to my heart, Rick and Ann, my most ardent supporter and loving mom, Linda, and my patient and all-around extraordinary partner, Kai.

As always, I want to acknowledge Robert Crescenzio, my amazing cover artist; M Evan MacGregor, my wonderful editor; and Brian Short, my fantastic formatter. I value everything you do and the people you are. Thank you for being such a pleasure to work with.

To my other friends and family, know that I value your place in my life even if I don't call you out specifically here. Supposedly you aren't supposed to turn your acknowledgements into a second book.

Lastly, I would like to take a quick moment to remember a few of those I have personally lost over the last few years. My beloved Huma, may you find a paradise of books waiting wherever you are now. My friend and fellow author, Jeffrey, who will be so deeply missed by the many lives he touched. My dear equine companion and friend, Cody, who is now running free in a place where his body can once again keep up with his spirit.

AUTHOR BIO

Nikki started writing her first novel at the age of 12, which she still has tucked in a briefcase in her home office. She lives in the magnificent Pacific Northwest with her wondrous cat-god. She feeds her imagination by sitting on the ocean in her kayak gazing out across the never-ending water or hanging from a rope in a cave, embraced by darkness and the sound of dripping water. She finds peace through practicing iaido or shooting her longbow.

•

Thank you for taking time to read this novel. Please leave a review if you enjoyed it.

•

For more about me and my work visit me at http://elysiumpalace.com.

OTHER NOVELS by NIKKI McCORMACK

CLOCKWORK ENTERPRISES
The Girl and the Clockwork Cat
The Girl and the Clockwork Conspiracy
The Girl and the Clockwork Crossfire

FORBIDDEN THINGS
Dissident
Exile
Apostate

ELYSIUM'S FALL
Dark Hope of the Dragons
Dark Savior of the Dragons

STANDALONE WORK
Golden Eyes
The Keeper

SILVERBLOOD RAVEN
A Path of Blood and Amber

Raven was never going to be able to fall asleep in a manor littered with dead bodies. Not even when the manor was Aldrich Darrenton's and the men his guards. Knowing how many of those lives she had taken only made it worse. She hadn't killed them for no reason. She did it to protect the ones she cared about in Amberwood from the attack Darrenton was planning and to avenge her adopted father and mentor, Jaecar's, murder. That second part was where the greatest conflict stemmed from. Revenge wouldn't erase the pain of his loss. She had understood that going in. But she hadn't expected to feel that loss more acutely when it was over.

After about twenty minutes of staring into the fire while sipping wine, the serving woman, Lily, returned to the sitting room to tell Raven and Marek their bedrooms for the night were ready.

"Go get some rest," Marek prompted when neither of them moved. "I'll keep watch and wake you in a few hours to trade off."

Raven looked over at him, her gaze going to a bit of dried blood in his jaw-length dark-blond hair. "I don't think I can—"

"Try," he interrupted, his silver eyes narrowing slightly with a stubbornness that mirrored her own.

"You need the sleep."

So did he, but she could tell by his look that arguing would be an exercise in futility, one she didn't have the energy for right now. Lying alone in the dark, fretting over the lives she had ended, would probably only make her feel worse than she already did. But Lily had gone to the trouble of preparing the rooms. It would be rude to snub the offer now.

Raven shoved herself out of the chair, her muscles heavy with fatigue. Lily led her to a room down the north wing, away from most of the bodies. The young woman was quiet, perhaps sensing that Raven wasn't in much of a mood to talk. Or perhaps too afraid to speak after seeing how effectively she and Marek had finished off the manor guards.

In the room, she slipped off her leather armor, trying not to think about how badly it needed cleaning and why. Then she lay down on top of the covers, prepared to stare at the ceiling for a few hours until Marek came around.

Sleep claimed her minutes after her head touched the pillow.

•

When she became aware within the dream, she was standing once more in the rear entry of the manor, slaughtered guards littering the floor around her feet. Every one of them looked at her. No. They *stared* at her. Each of them, blaming her for their deaths. Even those Marek had killed. And that was appropriate, because she had brought him here. Some of these men could have played a part in Jaecar's murder. All of them worked for Aldrich Darrenton, who had ordered the death of her adopted father. His own brother. Worse, he was gathering an army of mercenaries to attack Amberwood to lay claim to the town's natural resources. Aldrich lay there too, one of his eyes punched through with a crossbow bolt she had fired.

Why, even knowing all of that, did she feel so awful about ending their lives?

"Raven." Synderis's hands came to rest on her shoulders, drawing her back toward him. "You're alive."

She turned within the circle of his arms to face him, noting the distress that tightened his jaw and furrowed his brow when he looked around at the carnage.

He glanced down, his silver eyes reflecting the flickering light from a wall sconce. "Can I take us somewhere else?"

She nodded.

The dreamscape filled with Krivalen magic that carried the warm comfort of his presence. She willingly relinquished control, watching with a flood of relief as the bodies and the manor disappeared, replaced by lush forest. A shaded pond appeared next to them, teeming with life. Dragonflies and other insects danced around the water's surface. The intermittent deep croaking of frogs created an offset to the light twitter of songbirds. Two turtles rested on a log along the bank, basking in the sunshine. A family of ducks paddled through a spray of lily pads.

This was his counter, a bounty of life rather than death.

She looked at him again, admiring the silvery-white hair that hung long around his face. Distinct cheekbones. A strong jaw, softened slightly by elegant elven lines. Lips she would never tire of kissing. "It's almost morning. How many times have you tried to dreamwalk me tonight?"

He brushed his thumb lightly across her lips, then along her cheek. A faint tremble in his touch told her how worried he had been, waiting to see if she survived the assault on Darrenton's manor with no way to influence the outcome. Guilt twisted in her chest, not for the first time, at what she was putting him through. If only she could find a way to care for some of the people she loved without making others suffer.

A fond smile touched his lips, moving up to shine in his silver eyes. "More times than I can count."

The contrast between their dreamscapes pounded into the forefront of her mind. Her tableau of death against his beautiful forest bursting with life. She had killed. With minimal effort and almost as little thought, she had ended numerous lives that night. Somehow she had even managed to fall asleep in that manor full of corpses.

Where was he sleeping? In his hut up in the trees? At the outer post where he had made love to her, unaware that she meant to leave him in the morning? Some other place surrounded by the beauty and vibrancy of that magnificent forest?

She lowered her gaze, a heaviness pressing upon her chest. "I don't know that I deserve Eyl'Thelandra after what I've done tonight. I don't know that I deserve you."

"You do. We've all done things we're ashamed of." His voice was soft. That sense of safety and comfort radiated off him, inviting her to lay her burdens aside.

"What have you done?" She made herself look up at him, demanding his answer with her eyes.

He leaned down and pressed his lips to hers. She accepted that for the evasion it was, but only because of how it eased her sorrow, bringing a glimmer of joy into her heart at a time when very little about her felt good. Still, the hollow in her chest persisted, refusing to set her free that easily.

When he drew back, his brows pinched together as though he sensed the depth of her lingering distress.

"You defeated Darrenton?"

She nodded.

"Are you safe?"

She nodded again, almost casting a look around before remembering that she was asleep, unable to see her waking world surroundings. "I think so. For now."

"Are you all right?"

She shrugged. "A few small cuts—"

He cut her off with a gentle finger over her lips and looked deep into her eyes. "I wasn't asking for a physical assessment. This night hurt you in a different way. How can I help with that?"

Raven stepped into him, leaning her head against his chest, and he folded his arms around her the way she had known he would. His heartbeat was steady and reassuring. Such an odd detail to capture in a dreamscape. Was it her expectation or his that created that effect? In that instant, this place seemed more real than the blood-soaked reality she had made for herself.

"Hold me a moment. Tell me the things I've done tonight haven't ruined me in your eyes."

His arms tightened around her. "Heleath le'athana, anweyn."

Tears sprang to her eyes and sorrow tore through her as Phendaril's voice, saying those same elven words, echoed in her mind. What had she done? Why did she still love him? Even now, after giving so much of her heart to Synderis, she longed to see Phendaril again. Why now, when she was closer to Phendaril in the waking world than to him, did Synderis have to offer precisely those words of love?

"Raven?" He spoke her name in soft inquiry.

She realized she had started to pull away from him. The urge to flee swelled in her, but she wasn't going to do that. Running from him again, with no explanation, would be cruel.

She made herself look up at him, opening her mouth to tell him the thoughts that tormented her.

Suddenly, she couldn't breathe.

·

Raven snapped awake to hands cinching tight on her throat. A cloaked figure crouched over her, leaning all of his strength into the vice-like grip he had around her neck. The hood he wore shadowed his face, but her death lurked behind the pure loathing that burned in his eyes.

Realizing the desperateness of her situation, she grabbed one of his wrists. Her other hand went for the dagger she had stashed under the pillow. The instant her fingers closed around the hilt, she bucked her body. One mistake men often made was to assume she was weaker because she was female and slight of build. She was Krivalen, and those magic enhancements made her stronger than most men. The power of her movement flung him off to the side. She followed threw herself after him. They hit the floor with her straddling his body now, and she drove the dagger between his ribs.

His eyes widened with pain and the terror of realizing he had lost his last fight. He grabbed her hand on the hilt of the weapon, holding it there. Perhaps he knew as well as she did that he was going to bleed out much faster when she pulled the blade free.

"I don't want to die." His voice shook and tears spilled from the corners of his eyes.

Now that she got a better look at him with his hood thrown off by their struggles, she saw he was nothing more than a frightened youth. Her gut twisted. She yearned to take back the blade in his ribs and undo the damage, but it was much too late for that.

"Why?" She searched for any familiarity in his features.

"Why did you attack me?"

He squeezed his eyes shut as he coughed up blood. It trickled from the corner of his mouth through the stubble of his beard. When he opened his eyes again, she was struck by how blue they were.

"You killed... my brother." He groaned, his breath coming in shallow gasps. His hand shook over hers, his grip weakening.

The room shrank around them. A dropping sensation in her gut left her lost and confused. "Your brother?"

"Captain... Karth." He coughed again, harder this time.

Raven turned her cheek to him, wincing when a light spatter of blood hit the side of her face. Revenge was never simple. Everyone had family somewhere. In her quest for vengeance and to protect Amberwood, she had inspired that same hatred that drove her in someone else. She had become this man's Darrenton. Tears welled in her eyes, one spilling down her cheek.

His brow furrowed in response. "Why?"

She swallowed against the tightness in her throat. "He killed my father." She didn't know for certain that his brother, Captain Karth, was among the men who came for Jaecar that day, but it was as likely as not.

The youth squeezed his eyes shut. Fresh tears ran down the sides of the young man's face. A choking cough brought up more blood. "It hurts." His voice rose with fear.

"I know." The rest of her tears broke free. "I can stop the pain."

He met her eyes and nodded. Recalling how it felt when Wayland reached into her with his power, preparing to take her life from her, Raven guided the Krivalen magic into him. She sought out that dwindling vitality that made him more than an empty husk. While she did so, she held his gaze, and placed her free hand on his chest. Fear still shone bright amidst the pain in his eyes, but his face relaxed a little, and the hand over hers fell away.

Raven yanked the blade out as she drew on that faltering sense of warmth that was his life. He choked, his body jerking under her. After several agonizing seconds that seemed to draw on forever, the light left his eyes and he was still. A silvery mist swirled around her hand, snaking up along her arm and vanishing into her chest. She had expected pain, the way there had been when her mother first turned her Krivalen. This was more like a splash of warm water, except it sank inside her, spreading through her entire body before the sensation faded.

She shivered once, then shifted off him and sat back against the side of the bed, bringing her knees in to her chest. Mere seconds had passed when she startled at the sound of someone else moving in the room. Closing her hand around the knife hilt again, she looked up to see Marek take a few steps toward her from the direction of the open door.

"I heard a noise and came to check on you." His gaze flickered to the dead youth. "If it makes you feel any better, I know for a fact that Captain Karth was among the men who killed Jaecar."

She heaved a shaky breath. "Not really. And, right now, I'm not sure I want to know how you know that." With a quick glance around the room, she spotted the hidden door to the servant's passages standing open in the back corner. That explained how the young man had gotten in. Either he had been extremely quiet or she had been very tired. Perhaps both.

"I met up with Darrenton's men on my way north after killing that beast outside Andel." He stopped a few feet from her. She felt his gaze on her. "You took his life into you. How? In the Brotherhood, we're told that only the priests have that power."

Irritation prickled at her skin. She was tired and the hurt that Synderis had so sweetly offered to help with was worse now. "Why would that be true? Priests are made using the same magic that made you and I."

"They teach us that the magic remakes some people differently every now and then, blessing them with the ability to make others of our kind."

"And it never struck you as odd that no one has been remade in that particular way since the first three men who started the Brotherhood?" She wiped her dagger on the frayed bottoms of the young man's trousers – he wasn't going to care – and stood up. "Control, Marek. That's called control. It's just another lie they fed you."

His hands clenched into fists for a few seconds, then he deliberately unclenched them and took a deep breath. "How did you learn how to do it?"

"Wayland tried to do it to me. I paid attention." She looked down at the youth lying at their feet. "He's not a guard."

"No. He was one of the stable hands. I met him when I brought the horses in. I got no sense of threat off of him then. He hid it well."

Raven nodded. "The dead, they're all human?" She looked directly at Marek now.

He met her eyes, his narrowing slightly. "Yes."

"Then we'll bury the bodies, in individual graves, as their families would do."

"That will be a lot of work." There was caution in his voice and choice of words, as if he feared upsetting her.

She walked to a basin on the vanity. The blood on her face was a spray of black specs in the darkness. She picked up a hand towel and dampened it, using it to start cleaning the blood away. Was it more amusing or disturbing that neither of them thought to light a candle, relying instead on their enhanced vision to see? For herself, she didn't want a better look at the dead man laying behind her. It was bad enough simply knowing he was there.

"We've got fields full of mercenaries," she said, "I'm sure we can find some willing to help for a bit of coin."

"If that's how you want to handle it."

"It is." She glanced at him in the reflection, noting his wary regard. Part of her wanted to try to sleep again in the hopes that Synderis would dreamwalk her once more and help ease her mind, but that would have to wait. "Give me a few minutes to clean up, then I'll take watch so you can get a little rest before morning. We have a lot of work to do." A lot of bodies to bury.

He gave a nod and turned to leave.

"And Marek" – when he stopped, she said – "maybe put something in front of the servant's passage entrance into your room."

He glanced down at the body of the stable hand again. When he looked back up at her, some of the wariness had gone, but she couldn't quite read what had taken its place.

"I will. Thank you, Raven." He inclined his head to her before leaving the room.

Once she was alone, she stared at her eyes and hair in the reflection. Better light might reveal more silver in them now, but she didn't want to see it. Not ever. She walked over to the young man's body and bent down to brush his eyelids closed.

"I'm sorry," she murmured, fighting hard against the threat of fresh tears.

She had given him what she could. If the Krivalen in Eyl'Thelandra were to be believed, Accepting his spirit was an honorable act. She wasn't convinced, but it had felt like the right thing to do at the time.

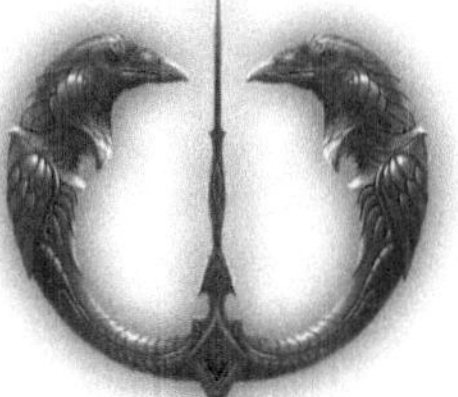